Noah's Boys in the City of Mother Earth

How do you keep a positive outlook when the whole world is going off a cliff? In this classic adventure story for readers of all ages, an aged patriarch relates his thrilling experiences in the Last Days of the Old World, a time of decline and impending catastrophe.

A budding young inventor, Japheth's peaceful plans are shattered when calamities strike, and his life becomes filled with perplexing moral questions, conflicting desires, and a seemingly endless series of dangerous challenges. Bolstered by his solid upbringing at the feet of the patriarchs, a healthy sense of humor, and the support of his faithful brothers Shem and Ham, Japheth survives sudden disasters, resists seductive beauties, and narrowly escapes death from monstrous behemoths. When corrupt politicians betray their homeland, the sturdy brothers fight, but are taken as hostages to the powerful but doomed City of Mother Earth. Determined to do what is right, the brothers turn the deceitful propaganda of their captors against them, save a beautiful Adamite girl from savage Cainites, and chase assassins through the fabled Zoo. Despite their successes, dangers mount, and the brothers must finally choose between embracing the illicit pleasures of an evil world system and trusting the faith of their father.

Join Noah's boys as they live confidently, purposefully, and even have fun, despite the utter destruction looming over them.

Noah's Boys in the City of Mother Earth

What Others Are Saying

"Noah's Boys – Because sometimes things end in catastrophe!" – S. Macbeth

"Finally! A Noah's story for adults!" --Enoch's Valley News

"A parable of modern times for Americans…really a personal testimony to the upcoming generation, clad in a believable story…a poignant juxtaposition of Eden or Shangri-la with the decadent culture sadly familiar to U.S. moderns." – Uncle Steve

"Excellent fast-paced action and suspense!" – Diane H.

"A Modern Classic; A Tour De Force!" --L. Clampett

"Realistic, yet hopeful; sheer fun!" --J. Springfield

"You finally finished your Dam Book!" –Uncle Don

"What if the Bible actually were true? These could really be the Last Days again! A marvelous book! –Anonymous

"The best adventure tale ever!" –Mrs. L. Horning

"I can't wait to see it on a theater screen!"--Karen S.

Noah's Boys in the City of Mother Earth

Or, Noah's Boys and the Dam Flood:

Adventures in the Last Days

Gregory Horning

Gregory Horning

Copyright © 2017 Gregory Horning

Paperback ISBN: 978-1-63492-289-0
Hardcover ISBN: 978-1-63492-290-6

All rights reserved. No part of this publication may be reproduced, stored in a retrieval system, or transmitted in any form or by any means, electronic, mechanical, recording or otherwise, without the prior written permission of the author.

Published by BookLocker.com, Inc., St. Petersburg, Florida, U.S.A.

Printed on acid-free paper.

The characters and events in this book are fictitious. Any similarity to real persons, living or dead, is coincidental and not intended by the author.

BookLocker.com, Inc.
2017

First Edition

Dedication

For all my boys: Mark, Joel, Bryce, and Jack. For the women in my life, too: my darling and ever patient Diane; Sara and Yehchun, my delightful daughters-in-law; Evie, my spunky granddaughter, and especially for my dear mother—my favorite writer.

With great appreciation for my collaborators and encouragers, brothers Steve, Don, and Andy, my nieces Hannah and Mary, and the many others who have supported me at every step, including Wayne, who shared the truth that creative work is done in the margins of life.

Acknowledgments

I have many to thank for opening my eyes to the accuracy of the biblical account, as well as to the overwhelming importance of worldviews, including Henry Morris, Duane Gish, Ken Ham, Francis Schaeffer, and David Noebel. And thanks to Rob and the many others who let me pick their brains and steal their ideas.

Foreword by the Author

It was only a brick. A decorative brick, to be sure: artistically inscribed with the ancient hieroglyphic writing of some long-extinct race—or so I thought. It had caught my eye while I poked through a dusty shop in the Old Souk of Damascus some forty years ago, during my junior year at the American University of Beirut. I used it first as a paperweight, then as a bookend. Somehow I found it intriguing, even fascinating, as though it had a story to tell. I kept it on my shelf through my four years of dental school, later through fifteen moves in a long Navy career; and finally through years of teaching and clinical practice.

One day it broke. It slipped through my fingers and fell with a crunch, making a grievous dent in the floor. Reaching down to pick up the pieces, I looked at it with astonishment. The top of the brick had cracked off—and thin, hard sheets had spilled out like a deck of cards! It had not been a brick at all, but a ceramic box! The sheets appeared to be metal, but glazed; and each sheet was densely inscribed with the same kind of hieroglyphs as the outside! I had never seen anything quite like it. What had I really had all those years? And how old was it--a hundred, a thousand years old? Questions began to haunt me. But we were in such a busy season of life. There were so many things to do, and so many things of higher priority than personal curiosity—especially about something that probably belonged in a museum. I wondered: should I donate it? Why should I? Simply to relegate it to a dusty corner, where it would sit for another forty years? No, I decided: this was mine. I would try to solve the puzzle myself.

I took one of the sheets, photocopied it, and began looking for someone who could read it—or at least tell me something about it. My search took a long time. I mostly discovered what it was not. The inscriptions were not, for example, ancient Egyptian hieroglyphs—hieratic or demotic. Language specialists told me the writing was not ancient Arabic, or Ge'ez, or Tifinagh, either; it was not Phoenician, Bamun, or ancient Greek; and it was not Sumerian, though it had some elements of early cuneiform. Even dating the metal sheets was a problem: they had a glazed ceramic coating that looked new, despite being encased in that ceramic brick for what must have been a very long time.

My search was frustrating and time-consuming. Finally I found help in the person of an old Armenian professor working in an obscure museum in the Middle East. He had some ideas about it, and was happy to take my money. He labored on it for quite a while. Early on, he tried to explain to me about logograms, syllabograms and determinatives, and how pictographs differed from consonantal alphabets; but I found that stuff bewildering. Ultimately the professor discovered a linguistic key for the language, and translated about a dozen pages. At that point he pronounced the manuscript a far-fetched, blasphemous forgery, though he still wanted the brick for his museum. Otherwise, he said he was quitting the project, and positively refused to have his name associated with it. But I had already invested so much! Finally, after much back and forth, he agreed to complete the translation of the first set of metal sheets. (Sorry, boys: the professor was shrewd at bargaining. My stubbornness cost a good part of your inheritance.)

Despite the expense, I enjoyed reading the adventures, and found myself pondering the issues and principles discussed, many of which were surprisingly contemporary. Living as we do in a declining, even dissolute period in America, I cannot help but fear we are living in our own Last Days, much like the author of the story. One note: the professor's grasp of English was not good, and his translation came out somewhat stilted. To improve the style and flow, I edited the stories for the modern reader, removing many obscure references, and adding chapter headings and a title. Why shouldn't I? It was my brick!

There are many questions I cannot answer. Was the writer actually the Japheth of the Bible? That would require a fantastic imagination. Our modern culture insists that any suggestion that an Almighty God has in the past destroyed the world, or will do so in the future, is ridiculous. There is no such time period, we are told, as "The Last Days"; there never has been, and there never will be: everything continues as it always has. My publisher, therefore, has recommended that I avoid controversy, and submit this story strictly as a work of fiction. Having said, then, that this is entirely fiction, I must confess I enjoyed the adventures, and found the ideas intriguing.

While I am as cynical as anyone, I suppose, I still wonder: what if our world really was hurtling towards a final catastrophe? What if the Bible were true, after all? Does that make life grim? After reading this story, I wonder: what if I adopted the adventurous attitude of this ancient patriarch? Would I take my troubles a little less seriously, and enjoy life a little more?

Gregory Horning

Chesapeake, Virginia 2017

LIST OF CHAPTERS

Book One: Noah's Boys in Enoch's Valley 13
    Chapter One: What Was It Like In The Old Days? 13
    Chapter Two: One Day At The Creek 20
    Chapter Three: A Dam Catastrophe 32
    Chapter Four: The Flaming Behemoth 43
    Chapter Five: Jared's Mill 56
    Chapter Six: Uncle Nebach's Workshop 69
    Chapter Seven: Something is Wrong In Enoch's Valley 82
    Chapter Eight: The Sabbath Day 95
    Chapter Nine: The Sabbath Feast 104
    Chapter Ten: Adam's Rest Park 113
    Chapter Eleven: The Big Race 123
    Chapter Twelve: A Ring of Vandals 135
    Chapter Thirteen: Ambushed 144
    Chapter Fourteen: The Patriarchs Overthrown 154
    Chapter Fifteen: Securing Assets, Preparing Defenses 166
    Chapter Sixteen: A Way of Escape 179
    Chapter Seventeen: Invaded 190
    Chapter Eighteen: Hostages 200

Book Two: Noah's Boys in the City of Mother Earth 212
    Chapter Nineteen: A March into Captivity 213
    Chapter Twenty: The City of Mother Earth 226
    Chapter Twenty-One: Willing to Serve 237
    Chapter Twenty-Two: Mother Earth Academy 244
    Chapter Twenty-Three: Choosing to Resist 256
    Chapter Twenty-Four: The School of Arms 267
    Chapter Twenty-Five: The Queen Mother 275
    Chapter Twenty-Six: A Religious Festival 287
    Chapter Twenty-Seven: A Rescue of Adamites 298
    Chapter Twenty-Eight: A Banquet 309
    Chapter Twenty-Nine: The Temple of Virility 321
    Chapter Thirty: Ham's Best Prank Ever 331
    Chapter Thirty-One: An Assassination Plot 337
    Chapter Thirty-Two: The Battle for the Zoo 347
    Chapter Thirty-Three: Heroes of Mother Earth 356
    Chapter Thirty-Four: A Duel 366
    Chapter Thirty-five: Father and the Queen Mother 376

Chapter Thirty-Six: Uncle Samlah 389
Chapter Thirty-Seven: The Great Dam Festival 402
Chapter Thirty-Eight: An Escape 413
Chapter Thirty-Nine: The Great Dam Catastrophe 424
Chapter Forty: A Happy Ending 428

About the Author **442**

Book One: Noah's Boys in Enoch's Valley

Chapter One: What Was It Like In The Old Days?

"What was it like in the Old World when you were growing up, Grandpa? Did you know that disaster was coming, or how much time was left? Were all the people then so very bad? Did they try to corrupt you? How did you meet Grandma? Was it love at first sight? Will you tell us your adventures?"

I have been asked these questions many times. For many years, I could sit my grandchildren around me to answer their questions, spin tales and give sage advice; but now, with my family scattered over the face of the earth, writing is the only answer. I put it off for years, but I think the time has come to do it. For one reason, I have grown old, and must soon join my fathers, but there is something else. Many of my own children have abandoned the faith of the patriarchs, and are making poor life choices. I feel a special urgency to tell them my story.

Frankly, I am a realist. If our children insist on holding onto a stubborn, godless attitude, the society they build will soon be no better than the one that was destroyed. I only wish that when our Creator washed off the world, he had thoroughly washed off the human heart, as well: something in it always wants to choose evil. Unless mankind is somehow given a new heart, I fear even our fresh, clean New World will one day end in catastrophe, just like the Old, and for the same reasons. At the same time, I am confident, as was the patriarch Enoch, that for those who walk with him, our Maker will ultimately provide our story with the Perfectly Happy Ending, and set everything absolutely right.

So, what was it like in the Old Days? Well, as I have often told you, it was completely different from today. There was no scorched wasteland of dust and sand to the south, and no frigid expanse of snow and ice to the north. There were no thunderstorms, tornados, or hurricanes. Exploding volcanoes, earthquakes, and lightning bolts occurred, but were very rare. Mountains were not jagged masses of naked rock erupting out of sandy sea-bottoms. Instead, gentle slopes arose into softly rounded hills and mountains. The entire surface of the earth[1] was covered with a thick blanket of rich black soil, and carpeted with dense vegetation and great forests. The whole world was lush and green, and filled with life.

The sky was deep blue then, and shimmering, as though it were all filled up. There was no ocean, of course; and it had never rained: but water was everywhere. Clean and clear, it bubbled up in springs and burst out of the ground every morning in heavy sprays and mists, nurturing rich woodlands and meadows. There were no harsh summers or winters. The seasons were always mild. We harvested two or three crops a year, and the fruits, vegetables, and grains were more delicious and satisfying than anything we can grow in today's thin, weak soil. I could weep when I remember the taste of my mother's cooked potatoes, so nutty and wholesome! But potatoes just don't grow like that anymore.

And animals? Why, every kind of creature, whether bird, fish, or reptile, whether plant eater or meat eater, teemed everywhere, and in far greater variety than today! The climate was altogether perfect. Plants and animals--and even some people--grew very, very big. The Old Days were the days of the Great Behemoths[2] and the Mighty Men of Renown. Even people came in wide variety: some were big, some were small, and some had spots or stripes. The earth was filled with people. Instead of the isolated little villages we have today, there were vast cities spreading out with millions of people: it was hard to find privacy! People grew more slowly then, and lived many times longer than they do today. Sometimes as many as five or six generations lived together. It was a wonderful thing to have the knowledge and guidance of the old patriarchs, and we treated them with great respect and honor.

Father was a preacher by calling, but a builder by trade, with a large construction business in town. We lived on a plantation in Patriarch's Plateau, above the Hiddekel River—the original Hiddekel River--in an agricultural district known as Enoch's Valley, right on the edge of the wilderness. Wilderness areas at that time were getting smaller and smaller as the population expanded, so we considered ourselves lucky to have wide areas to explore, and room to grow up.

We had vineyards, vegetable gardens, grain and bean fields, and pastures for milk cows and sheep. Beyond the pastures were groves of fruit trees, including orange, guava, breadfruit, apple, and papaya. And we had mangoes, too--my favorite--as well as stands of coconut and date palms, bananas, and walnut, pecan, macadamia, and other nut trees.

Our plantation was guarded by strong natural defenses. That suited father fine, especially after all he had gone through in his early life. Our stronghold stood on the edge of a great cliff overlooking the Hiddekel, and it was fortified with tall, thick walls and a tower. The tower, along with father's showcase barn, was easily seen from the river, which was good advertising for his business. The only way to or from our plantation was from the south, along a narrow road through a dangerous swampy jungle. The north and west sides of our plantation were protected by a dense forest of gopherwood that ascended into the vast wilderness of the Doubtful Mountains, an area notorious for gigantic, terrifying predators. They were called the Doubtful Mountains for good reason: if you ever found yourself in them, it was doubtful you would ever get out.

Now, the forest is worth telling you more about, because it was much of the reason we were protected for so long. The gopherwood trees had not always guarded the forest, we were told. In fact, they had only begun to take over a few decades before we were born, when father inherited the property. By the time we came along, however, the gopherwood forest formed an impassable hedge around the plantation, almost like it was planted just for that purpose.

Gopherwood may be rare today, but it was plentiful then, and father prized its tall, straight, strong lumber. As you know, the trunks are covered with long, stiff thorns; but the gashercut bushes that always grew around them were far worse. Their branches were thin, razor-sharp, and springy, like whips; and they dripped a poisonous sap that could turn a little scratch into hours of torment. We could not pay workers enough to clear out those bushes, and father finally stopped trying. Maybe that was just as well, because the gopherwood forest kept trespassers out, both human and beast. On occasion, though, a sabertooth, a bear, or perhaps a small behemoth would slip through and carry off a sheep, so we never left our compound unarmed. On quiet afternoons at the creek we could often hear deep roars and desperate shrieks in the distance. That gave us the shivers. We were very glad for our gopherwood hedge.

The three of us had a long, happy, and mostly carefree childhood. Time seemed to stretch on and on, and we saw no special rush to grow up. Each morning we awoke to a day that was fresh and clean, and filled with all kinds of possibilities. Enthusiasm pulsed through our veins: there was so much to see and do, and we were eager to do it! We had chores to do, of course; and we had schoolwork, for we were expected to learn reading, scribing, history, mathematics, geography, music, and lots of other things.

Our family had a special calling from the Creator, father told us: to save people. While he went on preaching trips, we made our own preparations for that calling. We learned about swimming rescues, fire safety, and first aid, and self-defense. It is very hard to save others, Uncle Krulak told us, if you are weak and defenseless. So he made sure we weren't. We had rigorous physical training, and diligently practiced at arms.

We grew up largely isolated from what our parents described as the hazards and temptations of the world of men. We could imagine the dangers of living among lawless people. Occasionally, we heard about the wild mobs that formed in cities, and our elders told us about Cainites, of course. Identified by their tiger stripes, Cainites were plunderers and looters. Just like packs of wolves, gatherings of Cainites were prone to slip into a wild rage. When that happened, they would kill and destroy until nothing was left. Temptations were a little harder to picture at our tender age. Our elders made sure, however, that we knew about the dangers of strong spirits, gambling, and idolatry. As we grew older, they hinted that "womanizing" was another ruinous temptation. We had no idea what that was.

While most of the week we stayed on the plantation, a day or two before each Sabbath we traveled down to Jared's Mill for worship meetings, lessons, and various events. Our elders tutored us, and offered us insights into the challenges of life. Sometimes we even asked for them, for as the patriarch cautioned, "Only a fool learns everything by personal experience." The years skipped by pleasantly as we acquired knowledge and developed skills, and we eventually entered the adolescent years, when we tackled the eternal question: what would we do when we grew up?

One day as I pondered that question, father gave me good advice. He said, "Do what you want to do!" What simple advice, yet how profound! Did I have any special gifts or useful skills? Of course! Then why wouldn't I want to employ them in a productive way? Perhaps a lazy or morally confused person might misunderstand; but for me, that simple bit of advice opened my eyes. Suddenly, I knew I wanted to be an inventor! A weight fell from my heart. I felt free and full of energy, and I saw the world in a fresh new way.

Outside of my own life, however, there was a big world, one filled with violence, crime, and continual evil. Things had gotten so bad, the patriarchs warned, that our Creator had found it intolerable. I believed them, but it was hard to picture that the Maker might actually step in to do something dramatic.

Anyway, time finally brought us to the threshold of adulthood. Powerful juices now flowed through our veins, bringing new desires and ambitions. We felt eager to accomplish great things and experience thrilling adventures. In fact, we even planned them all out. We had yet to learn the ancient proverb: "Man's heart may plan his way, but his Maker determines his steps[3]."

True adventures, we were about to find, often begin unexpectedly. And they are sometimes disguised as disasters. Oh, we had many exciting adventures in those Last Days; but I think they really all began one day at the creek, when the simple test of an invention turned into a dam catastrophe.

[1] *Editor's Note:* The text here indicates a round fruit like a pomegranate. The numerous apparent anachronisms, and the many seemingly modern concepts quite baffled the translator.

[2] *Editor's Note:* The term behemoth is apparently a transliteration of the original language, here very similar to ancient Hebrew.

[3] *Editor's Note:* The manuscript contains a number of such adages, which are reminiscent of the proverbs in the Bible. Man has apparently always struggled to acquire a perspective on life.

Chapter Two: One Day At The Creek

My invention was a pump powered by the flow of the stream itself, and I had great hopes for a successful test. Uncle Nebach and Uncle Lemuel had both liked the design, and had even promised to manufacture and sell it, if it actually worked. Having earnings was a happy thought; but I confess I had another motivation. How many students came to the renowned School of Tubal-Cain with an invention already in production?

Despite a full week of hard physical labor, when we got to the creek that day, our dam still measured less than the full six cubits[1] required: we needed more rocks. As it turned out, finishing the dam took more work than I had thought. By the end of the morning, we were drenched with sweat and nearly exhausted, but the dam was finished, except for attaching the sleeve pipe. Unfortunately, just when I needed his muscle the most, my youngest brother had to leave. The birds were not singing right, he said. That could mean a serious threat. Now to me, the birds were making their usual racket; but since Ham understood birds, I had to trust his judgment.

I sighed, but I was determined to finish the job alone if necessary. Mother had often said I was like a snapping turtle: I always got submerged in my work, and once I bit onto something, I never let go. Fortunately, my faithful brother Shem had a helpful, uncomplaining disposition, and he assured me the two of us could do it. After we carried the heavy piece of bronze over, we took a breath, braced our feet, and began to wrestle it into place. At just that moment, a loud voice startled us.

"Prepare to die, Adamites!"

I lost my grip on the sleeve pipe. It clanged onto the rock, nearly crushing my foot, and bounced off into the water.

"Judgment is here!" the voice shouted. "You were warned to flee from the wrath to come, and now you are too late!"

I looked up. A sturdy broad-shouldered soldier stood on top of our dam, dramatically silhouetted in the sun. He held a shield in one hand, and a spear in the other. I was alarmed. Shem and I were completely unarmed, and far away from help. And where was Ham? My heart pounded. The soldier's face lay in the shade of a wide turtle shell helmet. Metal rings on his stout armored breastplate held a sword and various pieces of gear, while a skirt of overlapping leather plates protected his upper legs. His feet, however, had strong leather moccasins much like our own.

"Why were you not prepared?" the soldier demanded harshly. "You were warned that these were the Last Days! And now destruction has come—by the hands of a cruel enemy! Doom! Doom! Doom!!"

As the soldier continued his rant, gesturing dramatically with his spear, my shock began to subside. Shem coughed, a sound he often made before laughing, and I looked more carefully. Dark hair curled out from around the soldier's helmet, which was emblazoned with a circled trillium. That symbol indicated devotion to the Creator God of the patriarchs, and it was just like the one on my own cap. Then I noticed a pair of monkeys chattering and jumping around the soldier. They gave the whole caper away. This was no enemy: it was our prankster brother!

While relieved, I was still annoyed that I had been so easily frightened. Ham liked to have fun, and pulling stunts like this was his greatest pleasure. Ordinarily he targeted vain, hypocritical people, but on rare occasions, he might decide to pick on gullible youths consumed by their work, though there were special risks in tricking brothers.

Ham's practical jokes often involved slimy worms, disgusting bugs, or animal droppings; sometimes they had a cruel edge. As a boy, he had always been cute enough to get away with his pranks. For a brief time, I had tried to imitate him, but I had quickly learned that what was darling for him only earned me scowls. In recent years, Ham had grown into a handsome young man with dark, romantic eyes and a winning smile; and he still got away with his pranks!

Having gained our attention, Ham continued his performance, affecting the serious manner of someone we knew very well.

"But, perhaps," he spoke gravely, but with twinkling eyes, "if you repent of your fornications, idolatries, and sins of every description, and ask for mercy, you may yet be saved. Otherwise, be sure that your sin has found you out! Behold! Even now, the ground opens its jaws to swallow you alive into the depths of hell! Turn back, or you will slip of your own weight, and…"

At that moment Ham lost his footing. Releasing his spear and shield, he flailed his arms wildly, but finally slipped and fell onto his rump. Shem and I grimaced, but Ham was uninjured, and soon offered us a humble smile. We could not help but laugh, but I had no intention of letting him off easily.

"Not a good time for a joke, Ham!" I said, as we helped him down. "Shem or I could have been seriously hurt."

"You needed a good fright, Japheth," Ham rebutted. "You have been driving us for days on this dam project. Anyway, I wanted to show you our new armor. With wars popping up everywhere, and now piracy on the Hiddekel, the council of elders finally agreed to fund new gear for Valley Vigilance. What do you think? It is stronger and lighter; and it makes me look big and tough! See?" Ham beat on his breastplate with his fists, grunting like a bull ape. The monkeys shrieked and beat their own chests, too, and we laughed again.

"The armor looks great," I agreed. "And it is time they did something! All this bad news is affecting everyone — even me. Maybe that was why I was so jumpy. The other night I dreamed we were suddenly attacked. I wanted to fight, but it was dark, and I could not even move. When I awoke, I found our dog Tar sleeping on my chest, which explained part. The rest of the dream must have been due to all the upsetting news. Maybe if we start preparing, we will worry less, and feel better."

"I agree," Shem said. "Things have been so grim lately that people have lost their sense of humor. Still, you may want to stick to animal impressions for a while, Ham. Father is hurt that so few take him seriously. Every time he returns from a preaching trip, he laments that he must be the poorest prophet ever. He risks his life to warn the heathen, but they only laugh at him. Father doubts they would listen even if he brought Enoch back from heaven, or raised Adam from the grave!"

"Father has a great sense of humor!" Ham retorted. "He often pokes fun at himself, and loves to pop inflated egos. Remember Cousin Sharezer finding his hat all covered with bird droppings? Or Auntie Pelosah pouring worms into her cup? I got those ideas from father!" Shem and I chuckled, remembering their faces.

"Well," I said, "maybe I have been pushing too hard. But once we fasten this bronze sleeve pipe, we are done! We can have lunch while the water rises. Remember: if this test is successful, we all win!"

My brothers finally consented. We fastened the pipe, closed the water gate, and climbed up the grassy knoll to enjoy mother's delicious lunch. I can still taste those cheese and potato-filled pastries, crunchy raw vegetables, and big, succulent fruits. Grapes then were the size of your fist, and strawberries were like apples! Once our bellies were happily filled, we stretched out to bask in the warm sun.

The three of us had spent countless days around that creek. It was the perfect place for swimming and playing, or simply catching frogs or turtles. Sometimes we pretended we were monkeys swinging from vines; other times we slid down the clay bank like otters, and splashed into the pond. We practiced fancy dives from the rock ledge, swam, shot with bow and arrow, and threw javelins and hammers. We daydreamed about glorious adventures, fantastic inventions, and hidden treasures of gold or precious jewels. Lately, we had imagined rescuing beautiful maidens of rare virtue.

"Hey!" Ham exclaimed. "See those black specks soaring above the ridge? I think those are death raptors[2]! There must be three or four of them, too! We may have to organize a hunt."

Shem and I looked. They were death raptors, all right. We had helped clean out a nest of the ugly winged behemoths the previous summer. It had been exciting, but very dangerous. The giant predators had been terrorizing herds on the other side of the valley, carrying off sheep and cows. Something had to be done. A hunting party was organized, and we got permission to join. While the hunt was successful, several men had been injured. Now we had a new family of death raptors. We watched them circle slowly in the distant updrafts. Living as we did on the very edge of the wilderness, we always had to be prepared to face snakes, leopards, or even carnivorous behemoths.

Our elders had taught us there were three types of evil in the world. The first was natural evil, like falling off a cliff or being gobbled by a behemoth. The second was moral evil, bad acts committed by wicked men. The third kind was supernatural evil, otherwise called "spiritual wickedness in high places." Whatever that was, it sounded scary. Now every time I looked up to the mountains, I thought about supernatural evil. Even today, watching the death raptors, I shivered.

"I don't need any more excitement, Ham," I answered. "I just want to test the pump, and enjoy being home. In just a few months, you know, I leave for Tubal." I took a deep breath. The air was filled with familiar scents: the fragrant flowers, the earthy smell of mud, and the fishy smell of water. A sweet, pungent smell of sour guavas wafted in from the old orchard, but the fresh breeze from the mountains soon blew it away. I heard the bright singing of nearby birds, and the busy droning of bees working the flowers. I lay back and sighed contentedly.

"We are lucky to live in Enoch's Valley!" I said. "We have a great plantation, healthy exercise, and plenty to eat. We have 'youth and vigor,' as the patriarch describes it, and even have leisure to think up inventions. I think I am happy!"

"Good for you!" Shem laughed. "Mother would approve. She says we should enjoy our blessings, and let the elders worry about the evil world system. Sure, there are wars and disasters far away; but we have our own jobs to attend to right here. When you go to school, Japheth, your job will be to pick the brains of your masters, and think up inventions. Before long, you will be rich, and can marry the girl of your dreams. I suppose Ham and I will have to seek out our own fortunes someday, too. Ham, what will you do? Become an entertainer?"

"Something like that," Ham said, watching a large groundhog retreat from the rising water. It was leaving very deep tracks up the hillside. That surprised me. Why would there be mud so high above the water? Had we disturbed a spring?

"I plan to build a zoo someday," Ham continued, "and train animals to perform tricks for my shows. I told Cousin Zillai that last week. I said I wanted everyone to come, so I planned to let people in for free. Do you know what he told me? He said he personally liked the idea of free admission; but he thought people might appreciate my show even more--if they paid for it! I realized he was right. Now I intend to charge a stiff fee!"

"Good thinking!" Shem said, laughing again. "A zoo will be perfect for you! The patriarch always says we should follow our gifts, so you have to work with animals! Do you think your zoo will be like the Menagerie in Hercules City, or the Great Zoo of Mother Earth?"

"Mine will be far better!" Ham declared.

"What about you, Shem?" I asked. "You are so gifted in dealing with people! You could be a fine preacher; but father says preachers are mostly paid with headaches, and one must eat. What about being a merchant or a politician?"

"I don't know," Shem replied. "With you two gone, father will need help with his business. But Ham's stunt made me think. What if these really are the Last Days? Will we even have time to become inventors or zookeepers?"

"Do you really think it might be, with God unleashing terrible earthquakes, wars, and catastrophes?" Ham asked eagerly. "That would be exciting! Maybe I shouldn't say this, but I think it might be kind of fun to see a disaster someday — as long as we could safely return home."

"Do you think so?" Shem laughed. "The elders tell us we have enjoyed supernatural protection; but father says we cannot count on it much longer. Despite having had the patriarchs to guide us, he thinks many people still have no heart for the things of God. He would not be surprised to see us get a little taste of divine judgment ourselves."

"Well, Uncle Krulak thinks our divine protection is going away," Ham said. "He says that the strangers all swarming in these days are bringing their crime with them, and now Valley Vigilance has to deal with it. At this rate, he says, Enoch's Valley will soon be no safer than the places those people came from!"

"It would be different if the newcomers embraced our faith," Shem said, sharing a glance with Ham. "Some have; but I wonder about others. For example, I know one family that worships with us sometimes, but I see no signs that their heart is in it. To me, their son acts more like a Cainite than a believer; and I even wonder about his pretty sister."

I was puzzled for a moment; but I finally realized that he meant Aziza, and unconsciously flushed. Why did he have to bring her up? That girl bothered me, though I kept thinking about her. While certain thoughts and urges were considered normal at my age, Aziza seemed to have some sort of spell over me. Yet how could I admit that to my brothers?

"She likes me, guys," I said, "so she cannot be all bad, despite her brother. If I rejected her without a good reason, it would hurt her feelings. And you have to admit, she is as pretty as a papaya!"

"And ripening nicely, too!" Ham said, whinnying like a horse. "Watch out, Japheth. She is laying out a trap when she flaunts her feminine equipment. Last week I saw her rub up against you like a cat! Remember the proverb: 'When a mare is in heat, the stallion is dead meat.'"

"That is so vulgar, Ham," I said, turning red. "People are not animals!"

What were my brothers thinking? That I was infatuated? Maybe I was. When Aziza had moved to Enoch's Valley, I was not the first one to notice her beauty. She had a gorgeous face with emerald green eyes; and her figure had all the swellings and curves that I had recently begun to notice. She was athletic, too, and her smooth, springy walk reminded me of a cheetah, though cheetahs did not wiggle like that. Aziza had instantly become popular. Her talk was smart and a little crude; but she was at the same time totally charming. Her accent fascinated me, and evoked images of exotic, faraway lands.

But there were warning bells. Sandal, her older brother, was strong and athletic. Annoyingly, pretty girls found him handsome. He had a short temper, was a bully, and seemed to hold a special resentment against our family. Someday, I expected we would have to settle things.

Aziza's mother was known as a great beauty, though she was somewhat of a mystery, and always veiled in public. Aziza's father Shahoot was a wealthy merchant, and so popular among the newcomers that he had promptly been elected an elder in the council. Still, father had reservations about him. For one thing, no one could figure out why

Shahoot had even moved to Enoch's Valley. It was not because of religious persecution, and certainly not because of economic distress. He was probably not fleeing the hand of justice, either, because he always liked to be seen.

Aziza had been amused at my interest. She began to tease me and ask me to fetch things while she joked and laughed with her girlfriends. She deliberately flirted with me, too, using coy smiles, flattery, and winks. I was drawn to her, though I sometimes wondered if her affection was real.

"Maybe you are right," I admitted. "She looks at me as though I were a spring sheep; but I have no wool! Why would she have an interest in me?"

"I wonder that myself," Shem said frankly. "Aziza is beautiful, talented and ambitious. Her family is very worldly, with both wealth and connections. I cannot imagine her marrying a quiet inventor like you, living on a sleepy plantation, and raising babies. She must have plans, but I cannot imagine how you fit in. On the other hand, maybe she is just dazzled by your good looks!"

I had not even thought about her motives. I had just been flattered to be noticed! Shem understood people, and he thought of such things. But this discussion was getting painful. I stood up, stretched, and looked around. No dangers that I could see. The water was rising pretty quickly: we could test the pump soon. Finally, I thought of something to change the subject.

"The race," I said eagerly. "Let's talk about the patriarch's race. I think we can win this year! We were so close last time!"

Ham was poking into the mud at the edge of the water with a stick, but now he turned around.

"Cush thinks we should win this year, if the race is honest," Ham said. "Both our teams have gotten better since we started training together. Sure: Sandal's team is good; but we could have beaten him last year, and maybe even the year before that, except for all those pesky accidents!"

"What are you getting at?" I asked, frowning.

Ham's eyes narrowed. "The broken steps to the climbing wall, the shredded ropes on the water swing, the loose wheels on both our carts: those are way too many accidents! Cush thinks Sandal has been cheating since his first race, and I agree. The more we know about him, the less we trust him."

"But do you have any evidence?" Shem asked. "That is a serious accusation. His father is an elder in the council, and the most prominent newcomer in the valley. If we accuse his son, there will be trouble. We need certain proof."

"We have no proof," Ham admitted, "but this time Cush and I are going to take a few precautions. Let's leave it at that."

We did leave it at that, because at that very moment the ground began to rumble and shake. The trees swayed, and entire flocks suddenly took wing. Leaves, sticks, and feathers began to rain down. With time, I began to feel dizzy, but the movement finally slowed and disappeared altogether.

A low whistling sound came from the mountainside. It became louder, and rose in pitch. A small puff of air rustled the leaves, and all became quiet. Suddenly, a powerful wind slammed into us, as cold as ice. The force knocked us right to the ground, and practically sucked out our breath. The trees around us were pushed way over, with their leaves shredding. With branches and debris flying everywhere, we pressed our faces to the ground, and protected our eyes with our hands.

An eerie cascade of foreign emotions swept through me. I felt guilt and fear, injured pride and uncontrollable anger. It seemed crazy, but I felt as though some terrible criminal had just escaped, and was rushing out to seek revenge. The whole thing was scary enough to make my skin tingle. Thankfully, as the wind subsided, the strange emotions passed away, too. All that remained was an unpleasant smell of sulfur. We lay on the ground for a good while, but when the leaves and twigs stopped falling, we sat up.

"What was all that?" I gasped.

"I don't know," Shem replied, "but it sure was spooky!"

Later, we learned that everyone in Enoch's Valley had experienced the earthquake and the eerie wind. Many speculated on what it meant, but at that moment I was convinced that some spiritual evil had occurred in a high place. I looked up at the sky. It was as blue as ever, and the death raptors were gone.

---

[1]*Editor's Note:* The cubit, an ancient standard of measure, is the length of a man's forearm, about 1.5 feet.

[2]*Editor's Note:* Death raptors were apparently very large flying creatures, and considered a type of behemoth, as indicated later in the manuscript. Their description seems reminiscent of the extinct *Quetzalcoatlus*, while their behavior appears similar to the legendary Sanskrit or Arabian Roc, as in the tales of Sinbad.

Chapter Three: A Dam Catastrophe

It took us a while to calm down. Eventually, three or four brightly plumaged parrots settled into the tree above us and eyed us suspiciously. Satisfied, they adjusted their wing feathers and began to preen, squawking in a friendly sort of way. It was a normal, pleasant occurrence, and helped restore my nerves.

"I think those parrots are the same breed as Enoch's old parrot," Ham said. "They have the same bright green heads and backs, and their breasts have those distinctive gold and silver stripes. I wonder if they could be trained to talk, too."

"They look smart enough," Shem said agreeably. "Why don't you catch one?"

I was astonished. "How can you think of birds at a time like this? We have a pump to test! That is all any of us have thought about for weeks!"

"Right," Ham said, looking down at the slope. "Just let me catch that salamander first." He leaped for it, and soon gleefully displayed the wriggling creature. However, as he stood up, his feet slipped, and he fell. Sliding rapidly towards the water, Ham flailed about for a handhold, and finally grabbed a root before plunging in. Shem and I laughed.

"That was your second fall today, Ham," I chuckled, "and the day is still young! But I am relieved you did not go in! There is more water in the reservoir than I thought: our dam looks almost fragile. If you caused a big wave, you could knock a hole in it. Actually, I am surprised the earthquake did not shake it down!"

"Don't worry, Japheth," Ham said, pulling himself up. "We made the dam with big, heavy rocks. I am more concerned that this slope is turning into mud!"

Shem and I looked down. Our feet had sunk in to our ankles. "I don't like this," I said. "We may have disturbed an underground spring, in which case this mud could turn into a landslide. Let's finish the test!"

We pulled our feet out of the mud and carefully climbed down the slope.

"You know, Japheth," Shem remarked, "this pump has been more work than your other projects, but it has been fun. I thought the best part was helping Uncle Nebach cast the pressure bell. Nothing is more exciting than pouring molten metal!"

"Brazing the pipes was fun," Ham added, "but finishing and polishing was a dirty job. Still, appearance is important to a buyer. I just hope this thing works!"

"It will work," I said confidently. "In fact, I think our success will make this a day we always remember! If my calculations are right, the pump should raise water as high as 30 cubits, which is high enough to fill a water tank on anyone's home. When they find it will give them running water, everyone will want to buy one! And this pump is only the beginning! I plan to invent a machine for every repetitive job we have. Someday, our long days of tedious chores will be history!"

"No more chores?" Shem and Ham asked doubtfully.

"Well," I said, "machines may need repairs, I suppose. But this stream pump is the beginning of a whole new world!"

"Friends," Ham intoned in a theatrical voice, "come see a pump powered by the flow of the stream itself! No more hand cranking or backbreaking step mills! No need for oxen to walk in circles all day! Irrigate your fields or bring spring water to the top of your home--without any work at all! For just a few pieces of silver, you can create your own Garden of Eden! Step right up and buy!"

"I like the idea," Shem added with a smile. "Okay, Japheth: show us how this pump is supposed to work."

"Give me a hand, and I will," I said.

We braced our feet on the rocks at the foot of the dam, picked up the heavy metal casing, and inserted it into the sleeve pipe so that the output hole faced up.

"This casing acts like a pressure chamber," I explained. "The moving water of a stream, or water pressurized by the weight of the reservoir, rushes in to fill the casing. When the casing fills up, the piston acts like a valve and shuts off the outlet at the end of the casing. That will probably make a clanking sound. After that, the water has nowhere to go but up into the pressure bell, so it squirts up there. The surge of water adds more pressure to the air already in the top half of the bell, compressing it like a spring. The pressure closes the intake valve here, and the extra water that entered the bell chamber is driven up this outlet pipe[1]."

"The invention is based on two principles: first, that air is springy, like air in a balloon, or a bellows. And secondly, that water cannot be compressed, but that it conducts force instead. These one-way valves, which Uncle Lemuel helped me design, are used to direct the surges of water. After figuring out the valves, the rest was simple."

Shem and Ham seemed pretty impressed. Next, we carefully hoisted the thick bronze bell, and seated it exactly onto the round opening on top of the casing. We were ready, so I opened the valve to the dam sleeve pipe. Water surged through the outlet, and soon began to spray out from the joints of the pump assembly.

"The fit between the pieces looks good," Shem exclaimed, wiping water from his face, "but it still seems to leak a little."

"Yes," I admitted. "I wish I had a good material to seal the joints and valves, but nothing has worked so far. Everything either leaks, or else gums things up. Bashak, Uncle Nebach's new forge master, helped me fit the pieces together. I noticed Bashak wore orange clothing, so I asked if he was from Tubal. It turned out that before he moved here last year, he worked at the school of Tubal-Cain! He knows all the masters that teach there!"

At that moment we heard a loud metallic clang. Our dogs Tar and Goon ran down to find the source of the noise, and began barking at it. Water appeared in the outlet basin. There was another clang, and water spurted out the top.

"According to my calculations," I continued, "we should get one measure of water coming up the narrow output pipe for every ten measures that flow in from the big sluice. We only brought twelve cubits of pipe today, but we can add more pipes next time."

"Wow!" exclaimed Ham, seeing the water flow up. "It's really pumping!"

"So far, so good!" I said calmly. "Help me put up this first pipe. The narrow end goes down." Shem pushed the pipe into place while Ham steadied the bell and the casing. The pump clanged again and again! The dogs barked at it a little more, but finally turned to race back up the hill.

"It's really working!" I said, no longer hiding my excitement. After a few more clangs, the water frothed over the top of the pipe. When we added another section, it soon overflowed with water, too. "That is six cubits," I shouted. "Let's add another pipe!"

Ham climbed on top of the dam. After inserting the third pipe, he had to stand to keep it in position. After a few more clangs, the water flowed over the top of that pipe, and became a fountain. The clanging sounds came faster, and the fountain turned into a geyser. Ham began to dance.

"Nine cubits!" I exclaimed. "We did it!" I could hardly believe it. I felt both relieved and deeply satisfied. This pump had taken so much effort! After my initial idea, the design alone had taken weeks, while the fabrication required months, between modeling, casting, brazing, and polishing. But it actually worked!

"Japheth," Shem shouted, "you finally got something right!"

As the water sprayed over us, I began to dance, too: it was the happiest moment of my life! The dogs returned to leap and bark furiously, no doubt sharing our excitement.

A few minutes later, Ham stopped cheering. Though water was still showering over him, he began to stare at the woods beyond the reservoir. I was curious about something, myself: the rocks of the dam were jiggling every moment or two. What was causing that? Another earthquake? It felt different somehow, more like shuddering than rocking. It was like a giant was walking along, or horse hooves were thudding on the dirt. I heard cracking and splintering sounds, and looked up at the forest. The trees were shaking! The dogs left us to race back up the slope, where the woods echoed with sharp, violent sounds.

"What in the…?" Ham began.

Two or three trees at the crest of the hill were suddenly pushed aside like reeds. A big green head appeared about 30 or 40 cubits off the ground, followed by a long, thick neck. The head slowly swayed from side to side as snake-like eyes examined us. Abruptly, thick mucous snorted from a dome on top of the head. The creature stepped forward, bending the trees aside and putting its entire figure on display. The front limbs were gigantic, supporting a massive torso, while the relatively short hind limbs held up a long, powerful tail. The creature opened its mouth, showing long rows of white teeth, and made a shrill, piercing sound.

I gaped. This was by far the largest behemoth[2] I had ever seen. It was at least 75 cubits long, seven or eight times as tall as a full-grown man, and its weight was at least that of a dozen elephants.

What had attracted this monster? How had it even gotten here? The behemoth lowered its head and began to slowly lumber down the slope. The rocks of the dam shuddered with each step. My mind raced ahead. If that huge body splashed into our pond, it would displace a vast amount of water, creating a huge wave. When it struck, it would shatter the six-cubit wall of rocks that stood above us. We would be buried! The pump continued to clang, but I stood frozen.

"Run!" Ham shouted above us. He turned to face the pond, crouched, and dove in headfirst.

Shem and I awoke from our stupor. Leaping to the side of the creek, we desperately began scrambling up. Behind us, the abandoned pump clanked one last time. The stack of pipes creaked, wavered, and slowly toppled over to clatter over the rocks. As we clambered up the slope, I caught glimpses of the behemoth ponderously descending to the edge of the reservoir. It placed its foot in the water delicately, as though to check the temperature. Satisfied, it smoothly advanced and flopped in like a big alligator. There was a great splash, and waves surged in all directions.

The dam bulged out, spurting jets of water, and then completely exploded. For a moment, the wall of water seemed to stand still; when it collapsed, a torrent of water swept over the valley, submerging bushes and saplings, and churning up the thick, rich soil. Everything was washed away, leaving behind only naked rock. We watched the wave violently surge through the valley with our mouths open. Uncle Lemuel had often told us that water held power; but I never dreamed that our own little reservoir could release such destruction!

"Where is Ham?" we shouted. Shem and I frantically looked around, fearing we would find his crushed, lifeless body. Finally, we heard a voice behind us. Spinning around in relief, we saw Ham kneeling beside a boulder in the now-empty reservoir, trying to catch his breath.

Shem and I had taken refuge on a shelf of rock, but as we looked for a way down, we discovered that the soil of the slope had turned into mud! As we puzzled over this, we heard slurping noises, and an earthy groan. To our horror, everything around us began to move! Trees and bushes on the slope tilted and slid down. Two or three big trees on the top of the slope wavered, and slowly began to topple directly over Ham!

"Ham!" we shouted together. "Watch out!"

When the tall trees crashed onto the creek bed, Ham disappeared. Muddy soil was already flowing down both sides of the valley, and now it all merged to form a thick river of gray-brown ooze. The mud made squishing, sucking sounds as it carried rocks and uprooted vegetation. There was nothing we could do but watch as the mud flowed around the fallen trees and down the creek bed. Eventually, however, the current began to slow, and subside. As soon as we dared, Shem and I tumbled and slopped down to find Ham.

When we got to the fallen trees, we heard rustling sounds, followed by coughing and spitting. An arm appeared to push aside a leafy branch, and a muddy figure painfully stood up. We hastily climbed over and helped Ham get out of the tree branches. He seemed to be all right, and in a few minutes he was able to tell us what happened.

"When I saw the behemoth heading for the water," Ham explained, "I knew it would blow out the dam. There was no time to climb down, so I went the other way, and dove to the bottom of the reservoir. Just as I got a good grip on a boulder, the water began to bubble and rush. Before long, the current was whipping me back and forth like a reed, with sharp rocks and gravel bouncing over me. I held on tight, knowing that if I let go, I would be swept over the rocks. It took forever for the reservoir to empty. My lungs were about ready to burst by the time I felt cool air on my back, and thought it was safe to come up for a breath. Suddenly a shadow came over me, and leafy branches crashed all around, knocking me down. Just as I started getting up, mud flooded in out of nowhere, and covered me over! I knew things were serious then, but I asked myself: what would a salamander do? Why, it would slither up! That's what I did. I crawled up onto a branch, and somehow managed to keep from being sucked back in!"

After wiping Ham off, we checked for damage. Amazingly, though each of us had bruises, cuts, and scrapes, none of us had been seriously injured!

We knelt down to thank our Maker. This had been a very close call: we could easily have been killed. It was time to call it a day. After rinsing off in a little stream, we climbed up the side of the valley, clambering over fallen trees and rocks. It was difficult, but by using roots as handholds, and helping each other, we finally made it to the top.

Our entire valley had been transformed. Steep walls of naked rock now stood where there had been lushly vegetated slopes, while the rich meadow of the valley floor had become a flat table of mud, except for sharp rocks and jagged protrusions of trees. Little streams trickled over the cliffs between the roots of trees, and fell into muddy pools. We looked on this scene in astonishment: the utter destruction was far out of proportion to anything I might have expected. And it had not taken long: the behemoth that caused it all was still nearby, placidly climbing up the hill.

"Well, you were right, Japheth," Shem finally said. "This was a day we will remember!"

"Well, it started out gloriously," I said, "though it turned into a dam catastrophe! But that reminds me. What did you think, Ham? Was this enough of a disaster to be fun?"

"It was!" Ham answered, grinning. "But don't forget that I warned you. I must be a prophet!"

We had a lot to think about on the way home. Certainly, we were thankful to be alive; even so, I was grieved to have lost my working model. If only that behemoth had not destroyed everything! If only I had time to make a new one before I left for school! Suddenly I remembered father's favorite riddle: "What are the two saddest words of all?" The answer: "If only!"

On further reflection, our experience made me realize how much all of us generally took for granted, like walking on solid ground, or having orchards and fields that were still intact. As we came up to our stronghold, we heard cheery squawking and clucking sounds from the trees, and saw that the green Enoch's parrots had followed us. They were odd birds, but I somehow liked having them around.

When we finally got home, mother took one look, and shook her head.

"Alas, Eden!" she exclaimed. "What in the world happened this time?"

"Just our usual day of testing inventions, Mother!" I assured her. "We'll be fine." Somehow I had acquired a silly habit of denying the obvious.

"Usual day, my eye!" she replied. "All muddy and scraped up like that? You look like you tangled with a whole troop of baboons!"

Mother clucked over us and applied medicines while we told her the story. She was relieved we had not suffered serious injuries, but was still very upset. Father took a more philosophical approach.

"You know that I believe in the cleansing effects of running water," he said, shaking his head, "but I liked that valley the way it was. I never dreamed you would completely destroy it!"

"Well, Noah," mother said sternly, "your boys have gone too far this time. When we get to town next week, I am having a talk with your brothers. My babies doing dangerous experiments? Indeed!"

[1] *Editor's Note:* Japheth's stream pump, by its description, is an early prototype of the modern hydraulic ram, still commonly used in rural areas today.

[2] *Editor's Note:* The size and description of this gigantic creature with a long, powerful tail appears surprisingly similar to an extinct dinosaur, the diplodocid sauropod *Supersaurus*, whose fossils were first discovered in Colorado in 1972.

Chapter Four: The Flaming Behemoth

The deep drone of a giant dragonfly awoke me a few days later. I reluctantly opened my eyes. Our weekly trip into town started early, but the rays of the rising sun had by now burned off the heavy night mist, and the glare was uncomfortable. I closed my eyes again, and let the creaking and joggling of our horse-drawn wagon lull me again to sleep. Nearly every Preparation Day we traveled into Enoch's Valley, a trip that usually took an hour or two. Once we got to Jared's Mill, my brothers and I met with our mentors, while father looked in on his construction business, and mother did shopping and other business.

As usual, my brothers and I were stretched out in the back between baskets of produce, which today was potatoes, beans, squashes, and apples. From the fresh smell of the breeze, I knew we were still on the cliff road overlooking the river. While still a distance from the swamp, we were already prepared for trouble. Over our usual light tunics, we had tough leather vests fastened with a long bush knife, a pair of gloves, a leather sling, and a variety of tools and implements. Bows and quivers of arrows were handy, along with long-handled axes, stones for our slings, and our walking staffs. Spears and javelins were stowed in a cradle behind the driver's bench, just in case. Mother and father were in quiet conversation up front.

"The City of Mother Earth? Now, that is a perfect example!"

I opened one eye. Father had been a warrior in his early life, and it still showed in his fearless manner, as well as his lean, powerful frame. Like many warriors, he cultivated simple tastes, had little use for luxuries, and tended to see things very clearly as either right or wrong. Although my brother Shem had the gift of framing words diplomatically, father was blunt. Called as a preacher, his job was to tell people the truth they needed for their own benefit. Though he tried to win his audiences over, his missionary trips rarely made him friends.

But father was not really as stern as he looked. Actually, he was very tender hearted, especially toward his family. His face was bony, with a generous nose, firm chin, eyes that crinkled with humor, and thick, closely cropped, mostly black hair. He deliberately cultivated an enthusiastic outlook, making him seem much younger than his actual age, which in that year of 1586 was 530 years[1]. Father had married much later than usual, and because he and mother were unable to have children for many years, we had some cousins old enough to be our parents, or even grandparents.

Mother sat up front next to father. She had been quite a beauty in her youth, and still was, in our eyes. While her figure was wiry, her face was very pretty, with steel blue eyes, full cheekbones and an aquiline nose. Mother was a hard worker, and she expected us to be that way, too, though she kept in mind our youthful limitations. A gentle, devout woman, she radiated kindness, compassion, and contentment, though she could be ferociously protective on occasion.

Mother had two favorite sayings: "Things happen for a reason", and "People make choices." Her household was orderly, and she practiced a loving, consistent discipline that was always related to the choices we had made. People made choices, and there were always consequences.

That day she wore her favorite blue dress underneath her leather vest, and a wide-brimmed white hat. As always, she had on her mother's heirloom necklace. The necklace had a pendant with three large orange diamonds arranged sideways to form the triune patriarchal symbol. The necklace was extremely valuable, and according to family legend, part of a prophecy. When we got a little older, she promised, she would tell us its story.

Mother glanced back to see if we were still asleep, and I closed my eyes just in time. Playing asleep was a skill we all cultivated, because the private conversations between parents were often the most interesting.

"Mother Earth, indeed," father continued. "The very name is an arrogant presumption! Everyone knows that Adam was made from the dust; but to call this created world our mother, or to worship some earth goddess named Mokosh? What rubbish—and how utterly foolish! Imagine it: people made in the glorious image of their Maker actually thumbing their nose at him, and groveling before dirt, water, and rock! Do they have any idea what they are asking for? And they even refuse to listen to those who would warn them!"

"Was it five years ago, Emma? My visit was right before we got our first big influx of refugees. Their king seemed interested at first. He was a little hard to read, and actually seemed a little reptilian. That should not have surprised me: after all, he is only half human. Anyway, he consulted with his queen mother, a veiled woman revered as the living embodiment of their goddess. In the end, he not only refused to repent, but even had the nerve to say that my own children would one day worship Mokosh!" He sighed.

"Sweetheart, this world is going off a cliff. All creation suffered when Adam sinned, but his descendants have learned nothing. Mankind today behaves worse than ever, despite our Maker's mercy and forbearance for fifteen centuries! Enoch warned that God's patience with the wicked would someday come to an end. But I wonder about those of us who still trust him. Will he provide a way for us to escape his awful judgment?"

"Sweetheart," mother said in a low, calm voice, "you think about the world too much! You should think on happy things instead—like our boys. Can you remember when they were little, and we dressed them all in blue? They were so fun to cuddle! Now they are sturdy young men ready to take on the world, and it is getting hard to put them on our laps. They have good minds, and good character. We have many reasons to be proud of them! They will never bow down to false gods. Look at those sweet, innocent faces. Noah, you have done a lot of things right. You have been a good father, and have provided them a secure, loving home."

Father reflected. "If there is any credit, it belongs to you, Emma. But I don't know how secure any of us are. This wilderness is dangerous, and plantation life has its own challenges. But even if it is not really safe, the dangers have made them alert, and have given them presence of mind. And there are other benefits. Our isolation has given us time to spend with our boys. Fortunately, they have embraced our faith. They have good hearts and strong, healthy bodies. And they are fast runners! I think they may win the patriarch's obstacle race this year!"

"They certainly have pluck," mother added. "Last week they chased off two sabertooth tigers that were stalking our cows! But I just want them safe."

"We have to trust them, Emma, and trust our Maker," father said. "The boys are going to flourish: they have unique talents, and are hard workers. Take Japheth, for example."

My ears perked up.

"Krulak is proud of his skill with the sword, and thinks he would make a fine military officer; but I think his gifts point more to engineering[2]. Nebach says he has rarely seen young men so gifted, and he spent fifty years with Tubal-Cain himself! My brother Lemuel, who was also a master at the school, agrees with him. They are both excited about his stream pump, and are eager to manufacture it, though the loss of the working model will set things back."

"Japheth has a sharp mind," mother said. "He loves to take things apart to see how they work, and mostly he can put them back together. But he still has things to learn, particularly about girls, who are starting to notice how handsome he is. One girl, I think, is testing his clay to see if it is moldable."

Girls again! I squirmed inside. Was this about Aziza? What did she mean by that?

"I will ask Aunt Naomi to talk to him," she continued. "People are marrying much younger these days, and she says most need help to make a wise choice. Your mother is on the job, too. She has three girls of good family visiting right now, and says one of them might be a suitable match."

"I will leave this matter in your hands, dear," father said, "but I think Japheth is far too young. If he is like me, he will need many more years to mature."

He brought the wagon to a halt. A warm breeze tickled my face, and brought the murky, peppery smell of rotting vegetation. That meant we were on the bluff overlooking the swamp, our usual place to rest the horses.

"Now, Shem," father said, "really loves people, and people instinctively trust him. Within minutes, perfect strangers are spilling their deepest secrets to him. Shem has a sound mind, a devout heart, and a good memory. We will not always have the patriarchs with us, and I could see him someday writing down the history of the world. He could be a great preacher. People would at least listen to him!"

"Oh, Noah," mother answered, "that is not your fault! Unbelievers are blind, and have no heart for the things of God. You must try to reason with them, I suppose; but unless their eyes are opened, they will never understand."

"Of course you are right, Emma," father answered soberly. Suddenly, he laughed. "And then there is Ham, our furry young ox. He always amuses me, but his fixation with animals is exasperating. To him, the whole world is nothing but a big zoo. And animals love him! Look at him right now, with a flying squirrel asleep on his shoulder! My nephew Zibach is famed as an animal healer, but even he says Ham is far more gifted! I just hope he someday finds a practical use for his gifts!"

"He will think of something, my dear," mother chuckled. "I just wish his humor were not so much in the barnyard! Nothing tickles him more than seeing a field hand step into a pile of cow droppings!"

"Oh, Emma," father said, "our boys are talented and capable, and they are turning out well. Unfortunately, all too soon they must face the dangers and temptations of our evil world. I hope they will be ready! If only things were not sliding downhill so fast! They could do such great things, especially now, when the world has so much potential for good as well as bad. We see such progress, with new inventions coming out practically every week. Our productivity is rising, and our standards of living are, too. Business is booming, even for my little construction company! I should be happy; but somehow I am convinced that doom is at our door. And whenever grandfather gets sick, I cannot help but feel that his father named him Methuselah[3] for a reason."

"Feelings cannot be trusted," mother said. "The patriarch is a tough old bird. I am sure he will be better this morning."

When we came to the finger of the swamp a short time later, father woke us up to keep watch. The deep pools of water that lay on either side of the road harbored uncounted numbers of giant snakes, crocodiles, and other formidable predators, as well as annoying insects that came in clouds. As we entered the swamp, a pair of giant blue mosquitoes zoomed over us, making a low metallic buzz, and paralleled our course for a few minutes. A gorgeous ivory-billed woodpecker with beautiful white and black feathers stood atop a nearby rotting tree trunk, hammering with slow, heavy blows, but it stopped to chatter at us. Further on, we came upon a meandering dodo with its small flock of chicks. They continued to rustle in the undergrowth, utterly careless of our creaking wagon. It became quiet as we drove into the deeper shade of the forest, and the noises of frogs and birds seemed louder. Rodents and lizards darted out of our path as the wagon rumbled along between the pools and streams of the swamp, and the road became narrow.

When we came to a small clearing, father stopped the horses. Just ahead of us, the lane was completely blocked by huge beast. At least 25 cubits long, it stood upright, with its heavy body balanced between two massive clawed hind legs and a thick, powerful tail. Its green scales were still wet, and glittered in the narrow sunbeams. The small front limbs of the beast held a tree fern. Despite our presence, it continued to eat the fronds in a very leisurely manner. In fact, if it planned to eat the entire clump at that pace, we would have to wait a long time. The creature had a long tube on its head[4], and showed no fear of being disturbed. Looking closely, we saw puffs of smoke curling out of its nostrils, and noticed a pungent sulfurous smell.

"Well, here is something to take our mind off the sins of the world," father reflected. "Boys," he said, looking back to us, "we seem to be blocked. Do you know what we have here?"

Ham looked carefully at the beast for a moment, and then eagerly raised his hand. "I know what it is, Father! A single-stalked flaming behemoth!"

"Okay, Ham: tell us about it."

Ham began to recite. "Popularly called a 'flamer,' this medium sized herbivorous behemoth keeps solitary habits, and is normally slow of gait. Considered quite dangerous, it is believed responsible for many deaths each year in the lands neighboring the swamps that form its habitat. It should be avoided, as it blows caustic flammable gases out of nostrils or mouth to a distance of thirty cubits or more. Fumes are generated from the long bony stalk on its head, which houses tubes continuous with its nostrils, and which are believed to comprise a combustion chamber. Its diet consists largely of swamp vegetation, as well as tree ferns, coniferous trees, and other plants. Violently attracted to certain pulpy fruits, it has been reported to react unpredictably to durian."

"Excellent! Any ideas in getting around it?"

"I don't know, but I have a durian!" Ham blurted. "Uncle Tobach asked me to bring one for him." He produced a tightly laced bag from the basket at his feet.

"I thought I smelled something unpleasant, Ham," mother said reprovingly. "You really should have asked me before bringing a durian[5]."

"Sorry, Mother. I wrapped it as tightly as I could."

"It's all right, Ham," mother said. "I should be used to such things by now, living with three young men. But remember this, boys: women like to be surrounded by pleasant smells. You will keep that in mind, won't you? After all, you may even marry one someday." We did not have a good response for that.

By that time I had an idea. "Ham," I asked, "did you say this type of creature is violently attracted to pulpy fruits?" Ham nodded. "Father," I said, "if you pull the wagon behind that tree, I have a plan to safely draw the behemoth away. Then, when the way is clear, you can drive the wagon on, and we will catch up to you."

Father liked my confidence, and looked at mother, who reluctantly agreed. "All right, my sons," he said. "But try not to get too close."

Grabbing javelins, and our bows and arrows, we jumped out. Ham took the durian. Crouching down, he quietly moved to some trees close to the water. I followed at a short distance, and hid behind a tree. Shem jogged ahead, keeping a wide distance from the animal, and climbed to the top of a little hill to stand watch. While we were busy, father quietly wheeled the wagon beneath the shade of a tree. Mother was shaking her head. I knew what she was thinking: her boys had again chosen to go into danger. But how could she doubt? My plan would work easily!

Ham found a tree at what he thought would be a safe distance. Taking the large spiked fruit from its bag, he propped it securely in a fork, and backed slowly away. The behemoth stopped munching, and looked directly at him. A large puff of white smoke blew out of its nostrils. Selecting an arrow with an iron tip, Ham drew back to fire. The beast, alarmed now, lifted its great tail, and it took a step forward. Ham fired. His arrow grazed the top, making it totter. I fired, too, and my arrow struck the fruit right in the middle, splitting it wide open.

A foul odor wafted to our noses, and we backed away to the edge of the water. The behemoth dilated its nostrils, snorted out a huge flame, and began lumbering towards the fruit. A patch of grass in front of the beast caught fire, but as the massive body passed over, it was snuffed out.

Ham and I ducked behind a clump of palm trees along the edge of the water to watch. The behemoth grasped the durian with its lips, tossed it up, and clenched it between its back teeth. Closing its eyes, it chewed up and down as happy puffs of smoke poured from its nostrils. The road was clear! We waved to father, who urged the horses on ahead. Ham and I slung the bows on our backs and raised our arms in triumph. Yet another success over the dangerous beasts of the swamp!

At that moment, we heard Shem yell, and saw him race down the hill toward us, waving his javelin excitedly. The behemoth made a strange sort of bellow and leaped completely into the air. Landing on one leg, it flopped onto its side and began to spin around in a crazy dance. I felt like laughing, but Shem was shouting as he raced toward us at full speed. When Shem passed the behemoth, it stumbled to its feet and followed him, blowing sheets of flame from its nostrils. As he approached us, Shem raised his javelin and threw it past us into the swamp.

There was a deafening roar! Whirling around, we saw the gaping mouth of a giant crocodile! The huge monster was at least twenty or thirty cubits in length, and water dripped from rows of razor-sharp teeth. Shem's javelin protruded from its back. Fixing us with an eye the size of a plate, the injured beast began to advance.

Stepping back instinctively, I raised my javelin and hurled it, and Ham followed my example. My missile struck the beast behind the foreleg, while Ham's went right into its open mouth. The crocodile snapped its jaw, shattering the javelin. We turned to run, expecting to feel the fetid breath of the reptile down our necks any moment. Instead, we heard an agonized wail. Looking back, we saw fire dripping down the monster's long snout!

Time seemed to slow down. I noticed that a large banana leaf by my shoulder was burning with an oily flame. It changed color from green to brown, and then curled up and turned to ash. At the same time, my shoulder began to feel hot. Suddenly I remembered the flaming behemoth!

"Run!" I cried.

Spinning about, the three of us sprinted for our lives, skirting along the edge of the swamp. We darted around trees, crashed through bushes, and probably ran faster than ever before. When we finally got up to the road, we felt it should be safe, and stopped to catch our breath.

Looking back, we found the creatures had not grappled together in combat, after all. Instead, each one had retreated. The broad silhouette of the behemoth stumbled erratically towards a stand of mangroves, while the crocodile smoothly moved through the reeds, heading deeper into the shades of the swamp. We watched silently until the monsters disappeared and the normal sounds of the swamp resumed. Monkeys chattered in the tall canopy above us, and we heard the distinctive squawk of parrots.

"Well," I said, trying to express modest satisfaction, "we got burned a little, and picked up some scratches and scrapes, but we had good success!"

"Success?" Shem marveled. "Japheth, we are lucky to be alive! Two monsters attacked us at the same time!"

"But they were beauties!" Ham declared. "Someday, my zoo will have a special exhibit of the most dangerous monsters in the swamp. It will feature giant crocodiles and flaming behemoths!"

I felt a little silly. "I guess I sometimes say stupid things. You saved our lives, Shem! If you had not been so alert, we would be half digested by now! The next time I get in a jam, I want you with me!"

Shem laughed. "Since we are brothers, and this kind of thing happens to you all the time, I most likely will be!"

I ignored the subtle slur, but Ham heartily echoed my thanks. Arm in arm, we walked back to our concerned parents. They had been alarmed to hear all the noises of the beasts. Mother noticed the burn on my vest as well as other evidence of our adventure, but our cheery outlook helped allay her fears. As Ham described the intoxicated behemoth, he had everyone laughing.

"So you see," Ham said, still chuckling, "study is never wasted. The fruit did attract the flamer, though eating it made it go crazy! But I have a question. Should I caution Uncle Tobach that eating durian may drive him insane?"

"Certainly, if you think Uncle Tobach is a behemoth!" Shem laughed. "But I have made a personal decision today. From now on I plan to follow the advice in Ham's guide, and avoid flamers!"

[1] *Editor's Note:* Some may find the age claimed here rather jarring. The translator, however, was certain that this specified year (1586 — Anno Mundi: since Creation) and age (530 years) was exactly what the writer intended. To him, these figures were unbelievable. However, I find it fascinating that the specified date and age corresponds exactly with the biblical account, as documented in Bishop Ussher's Annals of the World.

[2] *Editor's Note:* What I have called here "engineering" could also have been translated as "blacksmithing". It meant having to do with shaping metal, and designing new things, i.e., inventing.

[3] *Editor's Note:* I read somewhere that the name Methuselah means: "when he dies, judgment."

[4] *Editor's Note:* This behemoth would appear to be similar in appearance to the extinct dinosaur *Parasaurolophus*, whose skull has a bony crest with hollow chambers. The purpose of these chambers has long puzzled paleontologists, though Dr. Duane Gish made an interesting suggestion that is in striking accord with this manuscript. (Gish: Dinosaurs by Design)

[5] *Editor's Note:* Durian is a spiky, fleshy fruit from trees of the genus *Durio*. Commonly eaten in parts of Southeast Asia, it has a pleasant custardy taste, but its powerful, pungent, rotten onion smell has led airlines to restrict its transport.

Chapter Five: Jared's Mill

Our adventure had delayed us. By the time Jared's Mill came into view, the sun had already grown hot, and the shade from the eucalyptus trees lining the road was most welcome. The road gradually descended to the water's edge, where noisy seagulls glided in the drafts above or swooped down to catch fish. Along the great river, sailboats, freighters, and fishing boats moved along in a colorful parade. We inhaled deep drafts of the balmy breezes, snacked on olive pastries, and let our imagination fly to romantic adventures in faraway lands.

A flock of crows flew over us as we approached the wharf, which was normally a hive of activity. Streams of porters carried cargo between the ships and the large warehouses, four of which father had built for Uncle Shebach. Many of the ships had bright orange sails, indicating they were from Tubal, but others had white, brown, or blue sails, signifying other cities along the Hiddekel. Occasionally, ships came from Nephil or other places along the Euphrates, and on rare occasions we saw ships from distant Havilah or Cush. Today, we saw a sleek ship with unfamiliar black sails.

"That is a handsome ship," I said. "Where she is from, I wonder?" Father turned to look, and frowned.

"Take a good close look at the foresail, boys," father said. "Do you see the white patch with the green oak tree? That means the ship is from Mother Earth. Though their kingdom is geographically close to us, right over the Doubtful Range, the journey is a long one, as I found out five years ago. To begin with, you have to cruise down the Hiddekel well beyond Tubal before you reach the Gerga River, a meandering stream that finally connects with the Euphrates. Once on the

Euphrates, you must sail upstream for a week to reach the Mokosh River, which is still a couple of weeks from the City of Mother Earth. The journey is a long one; but in this case, I think it is just as well. Their king is a first-generation giant who means to conquer the world. This visit can only mean trouble."

"That sounds pretty bad, Father," Shem said. "But what do you mean by first generation giant?"

"Well, son, there are big people, and then there are giants. King Nezzar stands fully seven cubits tall—twice as large as a normal man. He would have to stoop to even enter one of our doorways. But his spiritual dimensions concern me more than his physical ones. He was born in Nephil, a vast city known for great wealth, but equally known for poverty, violence, and depravity. As a Cainite city, it is not surprising that there is open immorality; but some people there embrace the worst forms of demon worship!"

Father lowered his voice. "It is not proper to discuss such things with your mother around, boys. Let me simply say that the circumstances leading to the birth of a giant can only be described as sordid. What decent girl of her free will would ever entangle herself with a demon? How horrible! How tragic! At any rate, when a rebellious angel—a demon--takes a human wife, the hybrid result of that unnatural union is called a first-generation giant. The child is half human, half bad angel."

"But weren't the famous heroes Hercules and Dionysus[1] giants?" Ham asked.

"Yes, my son: they were half-human heroes--great men of renown. And in fact, this giant Nezzar is a hero to Mother Earth, for he and his mercenary army saved the city from an invading enemy. After that, the city made him king. Since then, he and his queen mother have totally transformed the culture. While it was once home to a thriving community of patriarchal believers, the people of the city have quite forgotten their Creator, and have eagerly thrown themselves into the serpent's evil world system. A friend visited the city only last year, and he said the zoo was great, but the people were angry, bitter, and rude. Merchants constantly tried to cheat him, and soldiers extorted bribes. He did not enjoy his trip."

As we talked, our wagon crossed the main bridge over Jared's River, a turbulent stream with dangerous cascades and waterfalls. Navigation had been impossible until the patriarch Jared had built a canal with locks. That had changed everything. The rich agricultural produce of the valley was now carried to the Hiddekel on barges, and large waterwheels produced power for the mills.

It was normally a pleasure to drive past Jared's mill and hear the cheerful songs of the workers, but today the waterwheel was stopped, and the workers were outside arguing. We saw Valley Vigilance officers running to break up a fight.

Father frowned. "What happened here? I have never seen the men act like that before!"

Passing through the gate, we entered the walled city and came to the marketplace. Cush, Seba and Dedan, our three cousins, saw us and shouted out, "Noah's boys!" Unfortunately, we were running too late to chat, and promised to visit later.

We passed the vegetable, fruit, and fabric sellers first, a crowded but entertaining bustle of familiar sights and smells.

Next we drove through the manufacturing area, where weavers, pottery makers, and forgers of iron and bronze produced their wares. Eventually we entered the merchant district, with all its warehouses and food shops. As our wagon creaked its way through the streets, friends and relatives continually greeted us. This was our patriarchal hometown, after all, and nearly everyone was a blood relation.

Driving by the shops, my eyes were drawn to an unusual sight. Some would say it was just two girls; but I had never seen girls walk like that! They practically demanded attention as they jutted their hips far to the left, and then far to the right. Their bodies had to wiggle to catch up! Something about them was even more provocative than Aziza. Their hair was long and tied with flowers. Their arms were bare, and their short green dresses were cut nearly to the hip, showing very shapely legs. The necklines of their dresses were cut very low in front, exposing quite a bit of female skin.

My eyes felt glued. The girls' necklaces seemed to caress their soft skin, while their ample bosoms, barely covered by the thin fabric, jiggled with every step. As the road narrowed, our wagon came close for a moment. Just then, the nearest girl turned and boldly looked me in the face! I was staring, of course, and blushed with embarrassment. Instead of a harsh rebuke, the girl gave me a big smile, and winked. Her eyelids were painted blue! I had to struggle to close my mouth.

Ham whispered: "I don't think those girls are from around here."

"They certainly got my attention," Shem added. "I think the tall one liked you, Japheth!"

By that time, of course, mother had turned completely around. She carefully studied the girls as the distance widened, and shook her head.

"Alas, Eden! I should give those girls a piece of my mind. And I would like to talk with their mothers, too! Indeed! Do you know them, boys? Have you ever seen them before?"

"I don't think so, Mother," I blurted. "I would have remembered that one!" Shem and Ham vigorously agreed.

"Well, their attire does not reflect well upon their character or upbringing," mother stated flatly. "The material in their dress is not cheap—it is not lack of money that determined the skimpiness of the fabric. No, those girls have deliberately chosen to dress and act that way. And they have a reason for it. Some girls, my sons, choose to arrange their attire so as to attract the male eye to their figure rather than to their face. They understand that an attractive female figure can seize command of undisciplined male thoughts."

"Did she take command of your thoughts, Japheth?" Ham asked mildly.

"You were staring just like me!" I retorted.

"Yes, yes," mother continued calmly, " but the danger for young men is that an attractive body can disguise a girl's true character. I will make some inquiries. You may think this a minor thing, but a person's dress and grooming often reveal their self-image, their goals, and their relationship with their Creator. It speaks of their respect for the people they expect to meet, and for their own family, especially her father. A girl's dress can sometimes scream out that she is making poor moral choices."

"I am very concerned about these young women," she continued. "If they go on this way, it will be the worse for them and for our community. If they become reconciled with their Maker, however, they will begin to reflect that in many ways, including by following the patriarchal principles for clothing--and by not winking at impressionable young men!"

"But, Mother," Shem asked. "What if they are visitors? Couldn't their dress be just a matter of fashion?"

"I certainly realize," she answered, "that people in other parts of the world have different styles. I was raised in Tubal, after all. And yes, I sometimes wore questionable clothes when I was their age, too. But the patriarch Jared thought carefully about these things, and decided that his children would dress in a modest manner. In my opinion, he was wise, and I think we should follow his principle."

"I agree with your mother, boys," father added over his shoulder. "You boys will soon be getting to the age where girls become powerfully attractive anyway, and some may even begin to flirt with you."

Shem and Ham raised their eyebrows and gestured at me.

"What? They are already?" father asked, looking at me. "Then listen to me, Japheth. I do not want you to be afraid of girls. In fact, at your stage in life you should look for safe opportunities to become acquainted with godly girls. After all, you must marry one someday. But in selecting and courting a wife, wisdom is critical. Marriage is one of the most important decisions of your life."

We looked at each other knowingly: more fatherly advice was coming.

"Be courteous—always—with the opposite sex," father began. "Be cordial and gracious. But do not get entangled with worldly girls, or trifle with godly ones. And when it is time to marry, get things in the proper order. The spiritual bond must come first! Make sure the girl holds to our patriarchal faith. Then you must see if your temperaments are compatible, as well as your goals and interests in life. And do not let physical intimacy charge up to the front. That should come only after marriage, or it can spoil things, and create lots of problems."

"Father," Ham snickered, "Uncle Zibach says that the biggest problem with young men is that, like young bulls, their bodies develop before their brains do!"

"A little vulgar, Ham," father answered, "but all too true. Use your brains, boys. Be wise in courting, and start your marriage on the right foot. If you find a good match, you will most likely be happy. As the proverb says: 'He who finds a wife finds great riches, and obtains the favor of his Maker.'"

Father smiled at mother, who patted his hand in turn. With three growing boys, their family conversations were rarely about crafts, fabrics, or the cultured things in life. Mother had learned to be tolerant.

"Okay, Father," I said. "I admit it: we were caught totally unguarded. Next time, we will be ready. Right, guys? Brains before romance!"

"Ha!" Ham said. "Japheth is the one who needs the advice! If we had not held him back, he would have leaped out and kissed her right on the lips! Instant marriage!"

After that, we had a brotherly tussle until our wagon passed beneath the carved stone archway of Grandpa Lamech's compound. As we along down the broad lane of crushed white shells, a large green parrot glided down from a palm tree to squawk at us.

"Awk! Praise the Maker! Glory! Awk!" The parrot repeated these phrases a few times, and then settled onto Ham's shoulder. Poking into the pockets of his vest, it found nuts, and grabbed them greedily. "Awk! Glory! Praise the Maker!" The bird was very old, with disheveled and missing feathers, a scarred beak, and a missing claw. Its feathers, however, were still bright green, and its distinctive silver and gold breast bands were shiny. The parrot walked around the wagon, inspecting the cargo and our clothing, all the time calling out: "Ungodly deeds! Ungodly way! Judgment on all!" Finally, the bird jumped up from Ham and flapped to the verandah of nearby three-story granite building, where the patriarch of our family was pacing back and forth.

The patriarch Methuselah had long been revered as one of the oldest and wisest men in the world. His appearance was striking enough to frighten a youngster of today, but in those days, extreme old age was not uncommon. We were accustomed to seeing thin wrinkled skin, deep-set eyes, and heavy silver eyebrows among the elderly. The patriarch's hands and fingers were big, while his nose was exceedingly long; his lower jaw and chin were massive enough to look exaggerated. His bone structure was remarkable, but only the natural result of almost nine hundred years of normal growth and maturation[3].

While stooped, the patriarch was still tall and broad in the shoulders, a reminder of the athlete he had been. That day, he was dressed in a white cotton tunic and an elegant snakeskin vest. As he hobbled carefully down the steps to greet us, his eyes twinkled with glee. He grabbed us affectionately as we climbed out of the wagon, making low clucking sounds much like his parrot. He had done that since we were children. He would hold us, rub our shoulders and bellies, and clop our heads with his knuckles. He did it today, while we tried not to giggle. And when father climbed down, he did the same thing to him! Father took it well, knowing how dearly the patriarch loved him.

"Noah—my most honorable grandson! Why are you so late? My father's old bird has been looking for you since the sun came up. He has been flitting from tree to tree, chattering like a young chick! That bird perks me up, you know: so much older than me, but still flapping with enthusiasm! And Emma, my dear," he said, embracing our mother, "you are just as beautiful as always! What a delight you are! And what fine sons you have! Welcome! Welcome!"

"Are you feeling better, then, Grandfather?" mother asked. "We were worried about you!"

"Much better now, thank you," the patriarch said. "Oddly, I began feeling stronger right after that evil wind blew through. I think it was the signal of something I have long feared. Perhaps it was inevitable, but choices have now been made, and consequences are inevitable. We must accept our circumstances, and trust our Maker to do what is right! Noah, my boy, remember this. No matter what happens, no matter how things seem in this life, our Maker will always watch over us, and finally bring us home. You just save people, Noah: that's your job! Now, come inside and eat! You all look hungry!"

The patriarch took my arm as I stepped up. "I feel good muscle, Japheth. A sturdy arm for a sturdy bow, that's what I say! But I see you burned your vest! Later I must hear the whole story."

Turning from me, he mussed Shem's hair. "What is the latest news, my boy? What have you learned from your friends? We must talk after we eat!"

Putting his arm around Ham next, the patriarch poked his stomach with his long bony finger. "And now, my honorable great-grandson, where is your newest pet? Is it a tiny one in a little basket? You must show me!"

"My newest one is far too big to bring here, Patriarch," Ham grinned. "It breathes out fire!"

"Ah! A fire-breather? Very good! I must come up to the plantation to see it!" He winked. "But I see your honorable grandfather! He has been poking around the kitchen for the last hour, and I think he is hungry."

Our grandfather, a sturdy gray-haired man with features similar to the patriarch's, but less extreme, strode out onto the porch. He greeted us fondly, but in the same business-like way he did everything. After embracing father and mother, he pushed us through the doors, chattering all the while.

"I am glad to see you, my boy," he said to father. "And what handsome, capable grandsons you have produced! The food is ready, and the womenfolk are starved, so let's get inside. I have much to tell you about our busy, fatiguing week! Later today our Council must meet this young prince. How shall we ever fit everything in? Your mother's cousin's granddaughters arrived from Cush this week—the land of Cush, not your nephew Cush--to spend time with us. They are very pretty girls, and they have been up since dawn, slaving away to prepare our meal. I fear they are exhausted! We should eat right away, for they refuse to rest until all is cleaned up."

We came to a great table heaped with fruits, vegetables, cheeses, and baked goods, as well as pitchers of water and juice. Our three new cousins stood at the end of the table, beaming with satisfaction. Despite Grandpa Lamech's comments, they did not appear tired at all. They were big, strong, healthy girls, and remarkably pretty and rosy-cheeked. I liked them instantly, but after overhearing mother, I was a little suspicious about their real purpose.

"Girls," Grandma Tirza said, "I would like you to meet my grandsons Japheth, Shem, and Ham. Boys, this is Adah, Pujah, and Shiphrah, three of the most accomplished young ladies in all of Cush. I hope you will make them feel comfortable during their visit."

Grandpa thanked them for the lovely meal, and the girls curtsied nicely. Adah, the oldest, nodded to the others and said, "Just wait until the Sabbath meal tomorrow! That will be a real feast!"

Grandpa Lamech stood to ask the blessing. "Creator, Lord God, we thank you for giving us these fruits of our endless toil and sweat. We ask for the strength to complete our difficult tasks and fulfill our heavy responsibilities. Thank you for the rest we enjoy in Noah and his family, and for the hope of real rest someday in heaven. We thank you, too, for these lovely girls, and for all their labor. Bless each of us, and give us wisdom to deal with all the terrible, terrible problems, threats, and anxiety we face every week! Thank you for this food to keep us going, and for the one you promised would finally rescue us from all the curses and drudgery we have had since our father Adam sinned. Amen."

With that, we dug into the meal. We were hungry, and it tasted delicious. I considered Adah and her sisters. Each one, I thought, had poise, intelligence, and excellent taste. Any one of them would be a fine choice for a wife, and would undoubtedly produce strong, healthy children for the family, something the elder women said was important. As I mused, I overheard the patriarch speak quietly to Grandpa Lamech.

"Thank you for your hospitality, my son, and for your prayer. But it grieves me to hear that your labor wearies you so! I always thought you enjoyed your work!"

Grandpa Lamech sighed. "I can see what you are getting at, Father. As the proverb says, 'Once a baby, once a lad, always a pupil.' Things are not really as hard as I say. I shall try to groan less, and be more content."

"Good boy!" the patriarch replied. "Honest work has many benefits, and it is a tangible way to serve the Lord. Even sweating itself is healthful: some say it is the best fertilizer for the soil. Working hands, as we know, are better than idle hands, which are usually busy with mischief! When food is too easily obtained, people waste days, even nights, in empty entertainments and amusements. Isn't that so? And none of it satisfies nearly as much as one wholesome potato—like this one--harvested, cooked, and mashed to perfection!" He winked at the blushing Pujah, and happily spooned a large dollop onto his plate.

The patriarch's interaction with his 700 year-old son[4] was typical. He conscientiously took time with all of his children, no matter how young or old, and always gave a word of exhortation or encouragement as needed.

"And now," the patriarch said, turning to me, "I would like to hear from my honorable great-grandson Japheth! I understand, Japheth, that you and your brothers have been conducting dangerous science experiments! Can it be that you destroyed an entire valley during the simple test of a pump? It must have been very powerful! And we must all hear of today's adventure, when the three of you fought off both a flaming behemoth and a crocodile!" He winked at the girls.

My brothers and I eventually gave a fairly lengthy account of both incidents, because the patriarch insisted on hearing every detail. He usually requested that stories start from the very beginning: "first, you got up."

"Life has unavoidable risks," the patriarch said afterward, "but broken inventions can be repaired, and bodies can heal. I am pleased that you lads did not allow your natural fear to paralyze you. Instead, you showed courage. Courage is like love: it is more what you do than what you feel. And I am glad you are learning from your experiences! Fools may endure countless experiences, but they gain nothing from them."

By the time we finished, we were late. Thanking Grandma Tirza and the girls, we dashed off to our respective tutorials. Mine was with Uncle Nebach, and I brought along a piece of broken pipe, the only part of the pump I was able to recover.

---

[1]*Editor's Note:* The professor translated the names phonetically, but they sounded so much like the well-known Greek demi-gods that I used those names instead. Hercules was believed the son of the god Zeus and the mortal woman Alcmene, while Dionysus was believed the son of Zeus and the mortal Semele.

[2]*Editor's Note:* Apparently, some adages have been around since man's earliest days. A form of this one is also found in the Bible, in Proverbs 18:22.

[3]*Editor's Note:* A clinical orthodontist (Jack Cuozzo, in Buried Alive) has detailed how normal skeletal growth, when projected over hundreds of years, can lead to a skull indistinguishable from the so-called Neanderthal skull. The description given here is amazingly similar. In the year 1586, 70 years before the Genesis Flood (1656 AM), Methuselah would have been 899 years old, according to Bishop Ussher's chronology.

[4]*Editor's Note:* It is fascinating to consider history in this fresh perspective. In the year 1586 AM, the patriarch Lamech would actually have been 712 years old, according to Bishop Ussher. The writer may here have only been estimating, and not intending to be exact.

Chapter Six: Uncle Nebach's Workshop

"Japheth," Uncle Nebach said, carefully examining the broken pipe, "there seems to be a law of nature that nothing stays the same. Sooner or later everything either decays, wears, breaks, or simply falls apart!" He looked up and grinned, showing a chipped front tooth. "Even tempered metal can break. The only remarkable thing here is that what always happens eventually, happened here suddenly!"

My uncle had devoted his life to the study of metals, and had spent many years at the school of Tubal-Cain with his brother Lemuel, who had made the flow of water his own life's study. The brothers had finally returned to Jared's Mill, where they formed a company to design and manufacture valves, gears, pipes, pumps, and even entire watermills, which they shipped in sections to customers around the world. Because of the high quality of their products, their factory had grown to become the largest one of its kind on the Hiddekel. After many decades, their factory now needed little supervision, and my uncles were free to do only those things that they found the most creative and enjoyable.

That day we were in Uncle Nebach's metal testing workshop, a place that had captured my imagination from my earliest childhood. The sparks and smells of working with metal had always fascinated me. The workshop had plenty of sunlight, and the breezes through the open shutters quickly wafted away fumes and smoke. At one end of the workshop, the open mouth of a brick furnace glowed red. A heavy anvil and a tank of water were next to the furnace, as well as a stone slab, where a red-hot mold was cooling. Shelves along the wall held gloves, protective eyewear, tongs and hammers, as well as clay molds and different sizes of crucibles. A variety of machines were on benches around the workshop, used to test metals for strength, fracture resistance, and resilience. The beams and rafters of the workshop were hung with assorted tools and metal objects. Although the stone floor was usually littered with grindings and bits of sharp metal, it was tidy now, because I had just swept it.

"It makes you pause to think," Uncle Nebach continued, looking at me with a penetrating gaze, "have you ever seen the opposite occur? No? Never once have I seen pieces of broken pottery spontaneously come together to form an intact bowl. Never have I seen corn arrange itself in neat rows, or weeds stay neatly in the corner. No: everything always decays, and goes to a lower state of organization. It never ascends spontaneously to a higher one. And this principle of decay is seen in every field of knowledge, from metals to agriculture to human society. There are no exceptions. It is a true law[1], one that predictably and consistently applies everywhere, and at all times. And that, of course, points to the rational Creator who made the heavens and the earth. Lately I have observed another law, one I do not yet understand. When something goes from a high state of organization to a low—such as when things fall down, or metal corrodes, or machines fall apart—energy seems to be released. That energy may be in the form of noise, or physical work, or perhaps heat. For example, when a stack of wood falls down, it produces noise, and ends up in a much lower state of organization, one that needs to be picked up. Or, when wood burns up and turns to ashes, it releases heat energy that was in some way stored within the wood itself."

"Well, Uncle," I replied, "there was a lot of noise when my pump fell down, but it was kind of drowned out by everything else. But since you mention it, I did find one thing very interesting. The next day, when we returned to the scene of the dam flood, the mud was hot, and it was becoming as hard as rock. In fact, I think if we had not pulled this pipe out just then, we would have been unable to retrieve it later. Could this be your law in action?"

"It could be, my son," Uncle Nebach mused, stroking his beard. "The mixture of minerals from the hillside may well have been crystallizing to form rock, and releasing heat from the reaction. Your father and I have a cousin in Tubal—Cousin Iddo—who has studied that phenomenon. He told me that the earth is filled with deposits of unstable minerals, which react when mixed with water, producing heat and eventually becoming what he calls sedimentary rock[2]. He has employed that principle to develop something he calls concrete[3], which he sells as a strong and durable building material. His company mixes and pours concrete to mold foundations for buildings, and it has been a profitable business. You must look him up when you get to Tubal. So you see, Japheth, metals and minerals are well worth studying. Since our Maker has given us the mandate to exercise dominion over nature[4], we must ask how we can most wisely do that. I believe that if we ask questions, keep our eyes open, and don't give up, we can find lots of answers!"

"That, Uncle, is exactly why I want to study at the School of Tubal-Cain," I said. "I would like to make inventions that make life better for everyone. But to do that, I need to know a lot more about metals."

Uncle Nebach smiled. "Japheth, for me it was wise to limit my study to metals. By narrowing my field I went deep. Over three hundred years of carefully focused study, I have learned a great deal that can help mankind. But I will not be on this earth forever, Japheth. It is my hope that the knowledge I have acquired with so much effort will not be lost. That is why I would like you to acquire what I know, and pass it on to future generations."

After his exposition, he picked up a silvery lozenge from the bench, and handed it to me. "Now, here is an interesting metal, Japheth. It is very light, as you can tell, but it is not particularly strong or hard. It hammers and shapes nicely, is resistant to corrosion, and heats and cools very quickly. Because of its silver color, some call it white copper[5]. I am told that the ore is quite common, but that it is exceedingly difficult to process. As a result, the pure metal is quite rare. I bought this piece at considerable cost from a trader who obtained it in Nephil, the only place where they know how to produce it. Someday I hope to learn their secret, because I think this light metal could have many uses. But I talk too much. Tell me, Japheth: which metals are your favorite so far?"

I thought about it. "Uncle, I think gold is the most fun. It melts at a low temperature, casts with little corrosion, and is the easiest to polish. And it even welds at room temperature, if you flame it. Nothing else does that! It hammers out into the thinnest of foils, so a tiny amount can be spread over a large surface; and it never tarnishes, but always stays shiny! Unfortunately, it is soft, and bends so easily that it cannot be used for the edges of knives, or for spearheads, or machines. I suppose it is good for kitchen utensils; but otherwise, it is only good for ornamentation, or as money."

Uncle Nebach laughed. "Yes, everyone loves it as money!"

I thought a little more. "Silver is a fine metal, too. It is easier to cast than gold, but it tarnishes so easily that any decorative object must be polished often. And then there is copper, a very useful metal, but one that casts more poorly than gold or silver. The castings have a rough surface that is hard to polish. But iron, I think, is the king of metals. Nothing else is as strong, or as hard, or as useful, especially when iron is fused with coal, or when you melt in other metals to make alloys. But there is so much I don't understand! Why does iron get harder when it cools slowly, but gold hardens best when suddenly plunged into water? I have a lot to learn about metals and machinery!"

Uncle Nebach glanced at his sundial. "Japheth, it is a delight for Lemuel and I to see you following our footsteps; but I see I have kept you late. You must go. Remember to take your new bronze pipes. Bezer, the young son of our forge master, can help you carry them. I shall see you at dinner tonight."

When I left the workshop, I carried one long section of pipe, while the boy, who dressed in the bright orange colors of Tubal, carried a few smaller pieces. The load was not heavy, and we enjoyed walking through the industrial district, past the makers of bronze and iron farm implements, cart and barrel makers, cabinetmakers, leather-curers, and jewelry-makers. I enjoyed chatting with my cheerful little companion. He was strong for his age, and would no doubt be one day as big and powerful as his father. Eager to be helpful, he often did errands for my uncle, whom he looked upon with great admiration. I paused outside a large textile store.

"Bezer," I said, "my brothers plan to meet me at that fountain across the street, but I am checking everywhere for something to seal my pump valves. If you keep an eye out for my brothers, I will meet you in a few minutes."

"Sure, Japheth!" Bezer said. "I will watch the fish in the fountain."

After entering the shop and looking around, I became discouraged. None of the fabrics were suitable. All of them were either too porous or too weak. As I left the shop, I pondered the problem. Suddenly, however, I heard a cry for help. There were other voices, too, both threatening and shouting derisively. Looking at the fountain where I had left Bezer, I saw three or four youths gathered around him, while another youth circled the fountain on horseback.

"Bezer!" I shouted, my heart racing. "I am coming!"

I called back for the shopkeeper to summon Valley Vigilance, and broke into a run. This was not right. In our patriarchal society, courtesy and brotherliness were our way of life. Any harsh or aggressive language was immediately reported to the parents of the offender, and correction was taken at the lowest level possible. Family relationships were clear, and our elders insisted that things be done in an orderly manner. Bullying of this kind simply never happened!

"Tubby little Tubalite," one shouted, as I came near. "How dare you? Your kind does not belong here!"

"Yeah!" cried one of the youths. "You filthy Tubalite monkeys think you own the place!" I recognized him as Ziph, a minor member of Sandal's gang.

"Yeah," yelled another. "Tubalite monkey!"

"Move back, comrades," the mounted youth directed, unfurling a whip. "Let me show you how to deal with Tubalites! Okay, monkey! We will teach you a good lesson. After that, your whole troop of monkeys will know to leave!" His speech sounded slurred.

"Leave the boy alone!" I shouted, surprising the bullies. I was not one to naturally assert myself, but this time I felt it was my duty. The youths stopped their monkey chatter, and looked at me before turning to their leader. He glanced at me, lifted a leather bottle from a bag, and took a long drink.

"Well, comrades," he said, smacking his lips, "it looks like the little Tubalite has a hero. Let's give him a good lesson, too!" Turning his mount to come close, he lifted his whip.

Things had gone too far: I had to deal with these bullies. The horse's hindquarters were right beside me, so I grabbed the tail and gave it a sharp wrench, jumping clear at the same time. The horse reared up in pain, and the rider was not well seated. He fell backwards onto the ground and lay stunned, while the contents of his bag fell all over him.

"Japheth!" Bezer cried in relief. He stood on the edge of the fountain, holding up a bronze pipe in defense.

With their leader incapacitated, the others were unsure what to do. Finally, someone shouted, "Let's get him!"

As they charged, my years of training with Uncle Krulak kicked in. Ducking under the first bully's wild punch, I drove my fist into his belly, which took away his breath. I turned to the second one. Brushing aside his fist, I delivered sharp blows to his midsection and chin, and knocked him down before spinning to the third bully. He was already backing away.

The fourth one had not charged with the others, but had lingered by the fountain. He suddenly yelped and staggered away, holding his hand to his head. Bezer, I saw, had a satisfied expression on his face, and held the pipe ready to strike again. Smiling, I turned back to the formerly mounted bully. He had finally caught his breath, and was ready to get up.

"Explain yourself!" I demanded. "Who are you, and what do you think you are doing? I don't know what you have against Tubalites, but you cannot bully children here! I suggest you apologize: Valley Vigilance is on its way."

"Apologize?" he exclaimed, slowly rising to his feet. "That punk kid insulted us, and needed a lesson." As he stood up, I realized that the bully was a full head taller than me. He was fat, but he also looked strong. Sneering at me with contempt, he puffed out his chest.

"And who do you think you are, boy? And why would you try to protect a Tubalite? They are no friends of yours—they are not even human! You should have stayed out of this!"

The other bullies began edging closer. I marveled: I had never encountered such a violent, hateful attitude before. This young man was obviously a godless foreigner. Could he even be reasoned with?

"You must treat others as you would like to be treated," I told him firmly. "Would you like to be bullied like that? Apologize, and clear your conscience!"

"You stupid religious fanatic!" he screamed. "Are you preaching to me?" He lunged, swinging his meaty fist at my head. I ducked. He tried to kick me next, but I caught his foot and spun it further along, unbalancing him. When I kicked away his ankle, he fell heavily onto his face. Grunting in pain, he rolled back to face me. His nose was bleeding.

"You are not allowed to bully people!" I shouted angrily.

Suddenly, I realized Uncle Krulak would not be pleased. He constantly warned us against losing self-control in the heat of passion. Self-discipline and cool composure were to be maintained at all times, particularly when provoked. Succumbing to anger leads to wild actions, and opens you to attack. Remembering his admonition, I decided to cool down. I took a step back and smiled. Unfortunately, that seemed to enrage him.

"I'll kill you for that," he roared. Charging like a gorilla, he swung wildly at me, but I was able to sidestep his fist. Striking him hard in the belly, I doubled him over, and then followed it with an uppercut to his jaw. That one knocked him to the ground. Blood oozed from his mouth, but he still struggled to rise. I thought about it. This bully was probably the biggest and strongest opponent I had ever fought, and he was pretty tough. This fight was not over. If he even connected with one of his punches, I could easily be done for. It was just like Uncle Krulak often said: battles are never safe, but once you begin, you must fight with everything you have. If you perish, you perish.

The other bullies stood back, astonished that their leader had not easily crushed me. When he stood up again, his eyes looked crazed. Bellowing like a beast, he stumbled towards me, reaching for my hands. I surprised him with a kick that knocked him sideways, and followed it with a staggering left jab. Finally, putting my whole weight into it, I punched him with my right. That lifted him right off his feet, and he fell backwards. On the way down he struck a water trough, and bounced off into a deep pile of horse droppings. Groaning, he rolled over in the droppings, and lay still. Was I done, I wondered? My fist felt numb.

"Japheth!" Bezer called, pointing down the street. "Your brothers are coming!"

Looking down the street, I saw that Shem and Ham were on the run, carrying their long staffs. A few shopkeepers were also starting to walk in our direction. Seeing reinforcements on the way, the four bullies took off running.

I heard hoof beats, and turned to see a very large horse coming to a halt just a short distance away. The rider dismounted. I judged that he was pretty young, perhaps only a few years older than me; but he stood at least five cubits tall: nearly as tall as a giant! His white tunic was elegantly edged in green, and covered with a black military breastplate. He seemed to possess wealth, for he wore a heavy gold chain around his neck with an emerald as big as an egg, and his sword handle was crusted with jewels. The young giant looked down at the groaning bully.

"Groveling before the locals, Rogar?" he asked in a deep, resonant voice. "Here less than a day, but already disgraced and covered in filth! You are not worth this trouble. I suggest you apologize for whatever you did, get back on your horse, and return to the ship. Don't worry: I will protect you from this unarmed youth, and this child holding a dangerous metal pipe."

The defeated bully grunted and pushed himself up. Giving me a look of raw hatred, he muttered, "This is not over, preacher-boy! I will get you for this."

"I said apologize, you drunken sot," the young giant said forcefully.

The bully looked away from me, and said, "I apologize." Shaking off mud and filth, he wiped his bloody mouth and stood up. Awkwardly remounting his horse, he roughly urged it into motion.

The tall horseman laughed derisively as the bully departed. When he was gone, he turned to me with a smile that imparted sincerity, openness, and dignity.

"I am very impressed with you, young man!" he said. "That took courage and considerable skill. Well done! And your little friend showed grit, too: he was not about to let them escape without striking a blow! Good for him. Please allow me to apologize for his boorish behavior. I assure you he will not go unpunished. May I have the honor of knowing whom I address?"

"My name is Japheth," I answered, not quite knowing what to think. "I am the son of Noah, the son of Lamech, the son of Methuselah, the patriarch of Enoch's Valley."

"The son of the notorious preacher Noah?" The tall young man laughed with real pleasure: his manner disarmed me. "It is a pleasure to meet you! I am Malek, prince of Mother Earth. Your father speaks very bluntly, and I think you will be worthy of him. Our visit here was meant for good, so I hope this little incident will be kept in its proper proportion. I am glad you taught my man some manners, and I assure you he will not bother you again. When we return next month, I trust that our visit will be entirely pleasant. Your little community is strategic to us, and we would like good relations. Please accept this as a small token of my apology."

Mounting his horse, the prince tossed me a heavy gold coin. As I closed my fist around it, I realized that my knuckles were raw and bruised. Fighting bullies comes with a price, I thought, even when you win.

When he left, Bezer ran up. "I said nothing to them, Japheth!" he cried, holding back tears. "They just began screaming at me!"

"What was this all about?" Shem asked breathlessly, having just come. "Who were those thugs, anyway?"

"They seemed to have something against Tubalites," I said. "I recognized one of them from Sandal's gang, but not the others. Fortunately, none of them were well trained. The big one was tough, but when he lost his composure, I got lucky. The prince of Mother Earth rode up afterward, and made him apologize."

"Let's look at what he left," Ham said, looking at some objects on the ground, including trinkets, a heavy bag, and a leather bottle. He picked up the bottle first and sniffed, wrinkling his nose. "Strong spirits!"

"Alas, Eden!" Shem exclaimed. "That bully may be young, but he has adult vices!"

Ham untied the cloth bag and brought out something that looked greasy. His face became pale, and he abruptly dropped it and backed away.

The tradesmen looked down in grim recognition. "Animal flesh!" one said, shaking his head. "The hind leg of a boar, if I am not mistaken. It smells as though it has been smoked!"

"Revolting," said another. "I have heard that such things are practiced in heathen lands — but never in Enoch's Valley!"

"Barbaric!" Shem added. "The patriarchs will be shocked!"

Two Valley Vigilance officers arrived a short time later, and we reported the incident. Later, we walked Bezer back to Uncle Nebach's workshop. Bezer's father turned red with anger.

"We come here to worship God freely, and now face this? There is nowhere else for us to go! If Valley Vigilance does not find those boys, I will. I will give them one chance to repent. Otherwise...!" He grasped a stick in his powerful hands, and broke it in two.

"Do not fear, Bashak," I said. "Valley Vigilance will track them down, and Uncle Krulak will make sure they receive justice! Those bullies are going to be very sorry they picked on your son."

---

¹Editor's Note: Uncle Nebach seems to be discussing aspects of the second law of thermodynamics: the principle of entropy. This kind of discussion, plus the presence of specialized testing machines, suggests an advanced understanding of metallurgy, and science generally.

²Editor's Note: Sedimentary rock is today considered one of the three main types of rock: sedimentary, igneous, and metamorphic. Modern geologists speculate that "dissolved minerals" served as the cement that glued the sediment into rock. Uncle Nebach's discussion suggests that antediluvian geology may have been quite different from today.

³Editor's Note: Concrete is a building material that was extensively employed in the Roman Empire, but forgotten from the fall of Rome (400 AD) until about 1756, when John Smeaton, a British engineer, discovered how to make cement.

⁴Editor's Note: This reference to "dominion over nature" seems to parallel the biblical mandate in Genesis 1:26.

⁵Editor's Note: Could this metal called "white copper" possibly be aluminum?

Chapter Seven: Something is Wrong In Enoch's Valley

Preparation Day evenings were normally reserved for quiet, pleasant conversation, but that day had been too exciting not to discuss. The patriarch insisted I tell the story of my fight. After finishing, I had just taken a bite of a mango-mushroom pastry when we heard the familiar voice of Uncle Krulak in the atrium. Taking off his sword and plumed helmet, he washed his hands in a basin and walked in to join us at the table.

Everyone waited for him to speak. As a born leader, he naturally commanded attention. Although he had first been famous as a swordsman, Uncle Krulak had later become famed as a general. His calm, determined spirit inspired confidence, and his ability to bring order to the confusion of battle had often produced decisive victories, many of which were still studied as examples of superior military leadership. When he had finally retired to Enoch's Valley, no one was surprised that he was asked to take command of Valley Vigilance.

Uncle Krulak was a big man, and his powerful body carried a wide assortment of scars from battle. While his meaty hands were surprisingly gentle with those he loved, they were quite capable of dishing out violence when necessary. Violence, he taught us, while sometimes necessary to stop evil, should only be used when all other means fail. When employed, however, it was to be used skillfully and decisively.

"Something is wrong in Enoch's Valley, Patriarch," he announced. "For a week now, ever since that cold wind blew through, people have been irritable and disrespectful, and filled with the spirit of Cain. But today was the worst day Valley Vigilance has had in fifty years! My men had to break up two month's worth of fights! Several otherwise upstanding citizens were found abandoned to strong spirits, and stumbling around in broad daylight. We even had to lock up a member of the council!"

Uncle Krulak took a potato dumpling, gave thanks, and began to eat, while shaking his head. "There were several reports of foreign women dressing scandalously, but even some of our own women behaved improperly. One of them addressed an officer in words so vulgar they cannot be repeated! There were several incidents of gang activity, too, including the bullying that Japheth confronted. Three involved Tubalite baiting, something that puzzles me. We will investigate everything when we can, but today was overwhelming. By the way, Japheth, I was pleased that you taught those young punks a lesson. Well done! It did not surprise me to learn that Sandal's gang was involved. We have treated them too lightly for too long. I have never understood why the elders insist we be so gentle with foreign hoodlums. It is a mistake that needs to be corrected."

Grandpa Lamech nodded. "I agree with you, my son. Too many hands among these strangers are available for mischief. But that is a subject for after dinner."

On such evenings, it was a custom for the men folk to retire to the central hall after dinner to discuss community problems. Since my brothers and I were now old enough to serve in Valley Vigilance, we were included in those discussions. We found them illuminating, though sobering.

The remainder of our meal was devoted to lighter subjects. At the end, Grandma Tirza's pretty grandnieces brought out deliciously crusty raspberry treats, slices of fresh cucumber, and cups of soothing herbal tea. Several had brought musical instruments, and Cousin Asaph, our most gifted musician, led us in singing hymns and songs. Afterward, the patriarch thanked everyone, and the men retired to the central hall, each taking a steaming mug of tea. As soon as we settled in, the patriarch opened our discussion.

"My sons," he began, "Krulak is right: something is wrong in Enoch's Valley. When we see bubbles rise to the surface of a pond, it is not wise to swim without checking for the reason. In the same way, when problems pop up in our community, it is wise to look carefully for root causes. Zillai, my honorable great-grandson, will you please tell us what happened at the mill today?"

Cousin Zillai was the money manager of our family, and our mentor in accounting. Tall and somewhat stooped, he had a slow, careful manner that reminded people of a stork. We all liked Cousin Zillai, but found his manner amusing.

"I am sorry to tell you, Patriarch," Cousin Zillai replied, "but the mill disturbance was rooted in moral corruption. The mill foreman told me he had come to work early, but soon discovered that Uncle Shebach's trusted accountant, a Lamechite--that is, a man from the city of Lamech, no relation to Uncle Lamech--had vanished with the money chest. The workers needed to be paid today, but with Uncle Shebach away on a holiday, the foreman had nothing with which to pay them. Something had to be done. After reporting the crime to Valley Vigilance, I calculated what funds were needed, and lent them to the foreman. That solved the immediate problem, and calmed the men; but Uncle Shebach's loss was considerable."

Cousin Zillai's report sparked anger, and reports of similar robberies.

"I hear, my sons!" the patriarch said, raising his hands. "A spirit of envy, bitterness, and greed has been at work all around us. But calm yourself! Lamech, my son: let us turn from crime. Tell us about this prince from Mother Earth. While I found him quite personable, I would like your perspectives as the chairman of the council."

"While what we hear about Mother Earth is uniformly bad," Grandpa Lamech replied, "the council actually liked this young prince. He is a handsome young man, for one thing, and courteous. Although big, I understand he is not pure giant himself. His mother, who died in childbirth, was fully human. Anyway, he pleasantly surprised us with his wide knowledge about Enoch's Valley. He knew quite a bit about Noah, perhaps because of his preaching visit to Mother Earth; but he knew me, too, and even the names of my other children. He made a special point to honor you, Patriarch, as a renowned source of wisdom, and assured us that Mother Earth had no designs on Enoch's Valley. He did mention how wealthy our community was compared to all our neighbors, however. His purpose, he said, was simply to spread goodwill, and to open trading along the Hiddekel River. While Mother Earth is in dispute with Tubal about certain territories, he said they are negotiating a peaceful solution. At the end, he said he regretted that the Doubtful Mountains separated us. Otherwise, he said, Mother Earth would long ago have joined us in a close partnership."

Uncle Nebach scowled. "Father, I do not trust this prince. Several towns near Mother Earth have simply disappeared. Recently, one of my colleagues sold some equipment to Mother Earth. He was paid in gold, and every piece was minted in Parnach, one of the vanished cities!"

Grandpa Lamech frowned as he poured juice, and took a long swallow before answering. "I know your reasons for doubt, Nebach. But the prince was very charming, and one elder even endorsed the idea of uniting with them, though that troubled me deeply. How could a community of believers even consider partnering with a godless, violent kingdom like Mother Earth? Has something changed in us?"

My brother Shem raised his hand. "Grandpa, may I ask a question? Why do we always hear that Enoch's Valley is so rich? Why isn't every nation as wealthy as we are? All people have to do is follow Cousin Zillai's law of money sowing and reaping[1]! By saving no less than one tenth of their earnings, and investing it wisely—sowing the money--their savings would produce a harvest every year. Then, by sowing that harvest together with the ongoing savings from their regular earnings, their wealth will soon begin to multiply. By repeating that process year after year for a century or two, no one could fail to become rich, even if a few individual investments go bad!"

There was silence for a moment, and then laughter erupted. Cousin Zillai stood to speak.

"Perhaps, Shem," he suggested, in his wry manner, "I have not emphasized that rocks can sometimes fall into the gears of that law. A major rock for our envious neighbors is that the investor must reside in a land where the people are honest, with absolute moral standards. Also, the authorities must respect private property, and not simply take it away."

"I think we all agree," Grandpa Lamech added, "that Zillai's law is a wise one for everyone to employ. It is undoubtedly the main reason why the oldest of us can afford big plantations, grand houses, and a lifestyle that is frankly luxurious. But we were not always rich, Shem. When the patriarch Jared first settled here, his family had little, and gaining wealth was never his main goal, anyway. He simply wanted to find a place where he could worship the Creator as he saw fit, without fear of persecution. But after being protected for many years, and following Zillai's commonsense law, prosperity has naturally followed. Unfortunately, the serpent's evil world system still stretches out against us, and it will continue to, until…"

"Judgment! Judgment on all!" A voice shrieked from the corner of the room.

We had forgotten about Enoch's old green parrot. Somehow it had been activated. Squawking and flapping, it repeated: "Judgment on all! Ungodly deeds! Ungodly way!" After a few more painful shrieks, the parrot blinked, dropped to the ground, and began to peck at seeds. Grandpa Lamech took another sip of juice.

"Where was I?" Grandpa Lamech asked. "Oh, yes. Wealth. It took a tremendous effort to tame the wilderness, Shem, but there was hope that we would conquer it by the time I was born—which is why I was named 'conquerer'. I often wish, though, that I had not been given the same name as the godless Lamech that founded the city of Lamech."

The patriarch cleared his throat.

"I am sorry, Father," Grandpa Lamech said, seeing his expression, "but I think we recycle names far too often. Recently I heard of a distant land where a small stream was named the 'Euphrates'. Now, I like that name as much as anyone, and if I had the opportunity, I might even name a brand new river the 'Euphrates'. But this gets ridiculous!" He paused again.

"I have again lost my train of thought! Oh, yes. Some fancy that Enoch's Valley became rich because our people were smarter and shrewder than others; but we are not. We have only one real advantage, Shem: an accurate view of the world, one that both includes our Maker, and takes man's sin into account. With that realistic view, we can see the importance of protecting man's natural right to own personal property, including the right to buy and sell. These may be intangible things, but they are essential in creating a culture in which everyone can reap financial success[2]. These intangibles are what allow Zillai's principle of sowing and reaping to actually work."

"Our worldview also produces virtues that promote prosperity, my son," the patriarch added, "including industry, patience, and thrift. And our Maker has given us two hundred years of peace and stability, as you said. Unfortunately, many of our neighbors lack these virtues, and choose instead to cry out like the beggar, 'Something for nothing!'"

Great Uncle Seth raised his hand. "Patriarch, I hesitate to tell you this, but I fear some of our own elders are becoming worse than beggars. One of them has even adopted the worldview of a thief! Lamech, tell Father what Cousin Achbor said."

"Very well, my brother," Grandpa Lamech said, frowning. "But he will not like it. A few days ago, Achbor announced a grand proposal to cure poverty. Enoch's Valley could become a paradise again, he said, just like the Garden of Eden, if each of us simply gave up all the property we had accumulated—all the gold, land, food, that kind of thing—and then redistributed the property to give everyone exactly the same amount[3]. He graciously volunteered to undertake the redistribution himself! Instantly, he said, our society would achieve equity, harmony, and contentment. And we could keep it that way, he said, by simply not allowing anyone to sell things for more than they actually cost. That was his plan! He was serious, too, although even a donkey could see that his plan would remove any incentive to work and produce things of value in the first place!"

"But the most ironic thing," Great Uncle Seth added, "is that we all know Cousin Achbor! He is lazy, selfish, and covetous, and he never personally gives to the poor. Oh, he enjoys his role as an elder in the council! He blithely votes to spend the hard earned money taxed from other people, and then claims credit as though he were spending money from his own purse!"

"And wait until you hear this, Brother!" Grandpa Lamech said. "He informed me, that while I was made to enjoy the sweat and effort of work, he was not gifted in that way. Instead, his gift was to enjoy leisure activities. Therefore, he said, I should do what I enjoy, and he should do what he enjoys. 'Everything is relative,' he explained. 'What is right for you may not be right for me.'"

"Everything is relative?" Great Uncle Seth asked. "He told me that, too, so I asked him what he meant. Did he mean it as an absolutely true statement, or was his statement only relatively true? I tried to clarify, but I could never make him understand that his assertion was an absolute statement, one that made his whole statement nonsense!"

"Thank you, my sons," the patriarch said, stroking his chin. "It seems that some of our own elders have truly strayed from the accurate worldview of our patriarchs. That commonly happens to many who seek their fortunes abroad. They adopt the local worldview, and their souls are lost." He stopped. "I am sorry I brought that up, Lamech. I know that is a painful truth for you."

"It is, Father," Grandpa Lamech said sadly. "We all know of my eldest daughter, the most beautiful girl in Enoch's

Valley. She rejected our ways, and ran off to the wicked city of Nephil. She took her brother, too, who was just as stubborn and reckless. They wanted excitement, fame, and luxury, and were bored with the simple country life! They are long gone, of course; but I have never forgotten them. Even today I imagined that she was still alive, but trapped in sin. She had gotten everything she wanted, but still was angry and bitter. I will always mourn for her!"

"Well, my sons," the patriarch said soberly, "we all have heartaches. But our homeland must fight against the continuing encroachment of the serpent's evil world system. Many foreigners are fleeing to our peaceful valley. That is understandable, for who among us would not run from violence and oppression? Unfortunately, these newcomers are mostly unbelievers with a faulty view of the world, and they bring problems that spring from their wrong worldview."

"As a principle, our elders have always believed that every stakeholder should be represented in the council, and that the majority should rule. I agree with that, and that is why we give proportional representation even to newcomers. Recently, however, I have realized that fully one third of our council members are newcomers, ones that have never embraced either our Creator or our view of the world. Can we trust them to act in the best interest of everyone?"

"Grandfather," Uncle Krulak said, "the serpent works at every level, and uses every hand he can control. Cousin Zillai's story of the employee who betrayed his trust reminds me of the relative who was in charge of our borders. His immoral affair with that pretty Cushite girl quickly escalated to bribery, corruption, and treason. He was as old as I am, but he chose to value his pleasure over duty and honor. Because of his betrayal, we have lost any control over those who come here.

Not only has crime in Enoch's Valley greatly increased as a result, but our entire future is in jeopardy."

"Many of our newcomers are as blind in heart as Cainites," Krulak continued. "Their main fault is that they simply do not see the world as we do. They have no desire to worship our Creator, and see no need to follow his authority. Their incentive to sojourn here has been to share our wealth and freedoms, and they behave just as carelessly as we let them. Should we ever be attacked, I fear they would prove treasonous."

Uncle Krulak raised his hands. "But there is more. In looking at the most recent wave of refugees supposedly fleeing persecution, it is obvious to me that most are young men of military age, and few have wives or children. Patriarch, I do not believe they are refugees at all. Instead, I am convinced they are a foreign army in our midst, just waiting for orders."

Uncle Krulak's comments provoked others to talk about foreign threats, traitors, and the recent surge in public drunkenness and debauchery. The parrot became agitated, and began shrieking about judgment.

"My sons," the patriarch said, when the noise subsided, "as you know, I often ponder the sin of the world, though it makes me sick. That sin is so bad that our Maker has determined to send judgment, as my father's parrot often reminds us!" He took a sip of tea. "But it is not my job to tell the wicked to repent: I leave that to Noah or others who are called to it. As your patriarch, I have one main job: to help my children see the world clearly and accurately."

"Recently, Noah's boys narrowly escaped disaster when a great behemoth destroyed a dam across their creek. But how did such a huge creature get through the gopherwood barrier?

There must have been a big opening in the barrier! In the same way, when I look at the troubles we have in Enoch's Valley, it is evident that the protective fences we rely on are no longer doing their jobs. And without the protection of those fences, we invite in a different kind of behemoth, one that will destroy our community. Let me just point out three of these fences."

"The first fence is the one around our children. Did you know that only two out of every five of our young people ever return home once they leave to seek their fortune? All too often, they choose to adopt a foreign worldview and culture. Somehow, they are deceived into thinking that faith in our Creator is only a preference. It is not: it is the only proper response to the truth! But unless young people learn to taste and handle the truth at home, they grow up lacking discernment. If so, when tempted by money or pleasure, they will naturally make the wrong choice, and fall into the world's evil system."

Pausing while many agreed with him, the patriarch took a sip of tea before continuing. "The second fence involves the worldview that our community holds in common. That common worldview determines the rules, and what we accept as right or wrong. Oh, my sons! An accurate worldview is the most important thing in life! It affects every one of our decisions, both individually and as a people. If our community is not strongly united by a common view of the world, we are ripe for the harvest. The influx of foreigners attracted by our prosperity would be no problem, except that they see the world so differently! Unless we see the important things in common, our conflicts will become increasingly violent, until one side dominates and suppresses the other. Frankly, unless we can successfully win over unbelievers to our worldview, we ought to expel them for our own protection."

I heard a few gasps. The patriarch was not usually so assertive.

"A third fence," he continued, "is civic virtue. By that, I mean proper behavior by our citizens in public, including the enforcement of our rules. This, of course, requires personal integrity and courage, character traits that only come from good homes. When people think only of personal peace and affluence, moral failures become common, such as the public drunkenness and immorality we had today. Noah's son Japheth showed admirable civic virtue in confronting those bullies."

The patriarch lifted his hands to indicate he was done. "My sons, I have said enough. I do not know if Enoch's Valley has enough time left, but I pray that these fences are quickly restored. Unless they are, moral decay and political turmoil will only worsen, until..."

A loud screech echoed through the room. "Ten thousands of saints!" Enoch's parrot squawked. "The Lord comes! Judgment on all!"

The patriarch half smiled. "Well, yes. But let us not end this day on a gloomy note! Asaph, my son, before we retire, let us have a cheery song!'"

Asaph began singing 'The Sun Shall Rise Tomorrow," and we all joined in. The music lightened our hearts considerably. When we finally got to bed, I felt mostly at peace. My body was tired, my burn throbbed, and my knuckles were raw; but I instantly fell asleep.

---

[1]*Editor's Note:* This seems to be an ancient description of the principle of compounding interest. It reminds me of the laws of personal prosperity advocated by George Clason in his classic book The Richest Man in Babylon.

[2]***Editor's Note:*** These principles are reminiscent of Adam Smith's classic work The Wealth of Nations, and bring nostalgic thoughts to at least one American who grew up in the economic freedom of the 1950s and 1960s.

[3]***Editor's Note:*** It is interesting that the utopian myth of socialism mentioned here (and in Proverbs 1:14) is still being promoted today, even though it has brought the modern world a century of misery and death.

Chapter Eight: The Sabbath Day

I was flying like a bird when I awoke the next morning. With my wings outstretched, I was zooming down an immense wave at an exhilarating speed, and then soaring up to the mountains. I took in a deep draft of the brisk sea breeze, but found it smelled like freshly baked bread! Putting my dream aside, I opened my eyes.

After quickly dressing in our white Sabbath day tunics, my brothers and I raced down to enjoy a hearty breakfast of fresh bread, cheese, raw vegetables, and fruit. Soon afterward, our family took our walk along the quiet streets to the park, and then pushed through the dew-drenched foliage of the gardens to the meetinghouse. The thick, white mist of the early morning was cleansing: I came in feeling refreshed and awake. Shaking off the dew, we found seats and began quietly chatting with nearby cousins. When the patriarch came in, a hush fell upon the large assembly. It was time to prepare our hearts, and leave the busy thoughts that ruled every other day. The Sabbath was supposed to be different!

Cousin Asaph opened the worship service with soft instrumental music. When the women's quartet began the sweet melody of a familiar tune, the entire congregation stood to sing. The title was a long one: "Let the heaven and earth praise Him, the seas, and everything that moves in it." Rhythmic hand motions and swaying accompanied the "through the seas" sections. Our bodies and voices warmed to the work, and the walls of the meetinghouse began to reverberate. After all the bad tempers of the previous week, the wholesome music was restorative. Asaph took requests, and we sang one favorite hymn after another. I got a little hoarse, but I loved to sing like that!

Cousin Jazer made announcements, and as usual, his droll manner made us laugh. When he finished, we had prayer and another hymn, and came to the central part of our worship: the teaching of the Creator's Word[1] as given to Adam and the patriarchs. Several elders served as teachers, occasionally including Methuselah. That morning, however, father was speaking. As usual, he jumped right in.

"Beloved, these are the last days! Awful, awful judgment is being prepared for wicked mankind, and it will come soon very soon!"

My brothers and I sat in the front row of the men's side of the congregation. We knew we had to be an example to the others, especially when father was preaching, but after the first sentence, Ham winked at me. Father had begun preaching just like Ham! He continued along the same line for a while. My seat was very comfortable, and I began to feel warm and sleepy, almost nodding off, though I still listened.

"Beloved, ever since Adam, ever since Cain, the human heart has naturally inclined to evil. Sin has continued its deadly march across the world, filling it with bloodshed and wickedness. Believers in the God of Creation are now being persecuted, and some of you have had to flee for your lives. Here in Enoch's Valley, we usually take peace and safety for granted, but this week we had our own little taste of the serpent's venom, haven't we?"

Two or three people shouted "Amen!" I opened my eyes.

"Our Creator," father went on, "is far too holy to keep tolerating such flagrant sin! His righteous fury is building, and it shall soon erupt! The wicked people that disobey God, and follow the serpent of Eden[2]—that bad angel, that deceiver and accuser--shall soon receive exactly what they deserve. They shall be removed from the face of the earth! And when their bodies die, their eternal souls[3] shall immediately enter a nightmare of fiery torments, an end too horrible to contemplate! But it does not have to end that way for us, beloved, sinners though we are! Our Creator is merciful, and wishes to forgive all those who ask Him! Oh, trust in our Creator, beloved! Though your sins are worse than Cain's, if you truly repent, he will forgive, and welcome you into his New Eden!"

Father looked over the congregation. "Now let us go to the words of Enoch's prophecy: 'The Lord comes with ten thousands of his saints, to execute judgment upon all[4].' These words are very familiar to some of us," father said smiling, "because Enoch's parrot will not let us forget!"

Many laughed, but father continued. "Now, if our Maker were only coming with one saint, it would be enough. But with ten thousand, it will be overwhelming! The wicked will have nothing to say, and judgment will be executed. Now let me ask you, brothers and sisters, so that we are clear: exactly why is God sending judgment? It is an important question, because our Maker is completely fair. If we commit the sin that the wicked are being judged for, why, we will be, too!" There were frowns, for some people did not like pointed messages.

"Answer me, brothers, and let us finish! The sun climbs high, and we need recreation to work up an appetite. Man has been sinning since the beginning; but why should our Creator decide now to send such awful judgment? What sin made him give up? Was it murder, like Cain committed? Or blasphemy? Could it be adultery, or lying? Those are all terrible sins; but which one has really led God to send judgment?" Father stood back, waiting for the answer.

"Drunkenness?" said Great-Uncle Tobach, our horticulture instructor. He had always warned us against strong spirits.

"No, Uncle, but that is a bad vice!" father said with a smile.

"Breaking the Sabbath?" We heard tittering around us. The cousin who asked this was considered somewhat lazy.

"No," father answered patiently. "Yet the Sabbath is set aside for our good, and we should enjoy it—once a week."

"Dishonoring parents?" An old widowed aunt had spoken. Her story was a sad one, of abandonment by all her children.

"Again, no." father answered.

Many guesses were now shouted, including gambling, cursing, taking potions, and persecuting the people of God.

"Those are all terrible sins," father answered.

"We give up!" someone shouted. "Tell us!"

"Beloved, God is not sending judgment," father declared, "because of any of the bad things that we have done! So why? Let's go back to the very beginning. Cain would have been accepted, the Creator told him, 'if he did well'. The 'if' means a choice! My dear wife often says, 'people make choices,' and 'choices have consequences.' So, which choice leads to 'doing well?' Two principles are important. First, our Maker loves us, and want the best for us. Second, people cannot walk together unless they are agreed. The good choice the patriarch Enoch made was to honestly agree with God about his sin, and to repent of it. As a result of that, his loving Creator did not judge him, but took him for a long walk to heaven. Cain, on the other hand, had the same opportunity, but refused. The reason judgment is coming, beloved, is simply this: God has given people the opportunity to repent, but they have chosen not to!"

Father took a drink of water. "If we choose to be honest with our Maker, and walk with him, he reserves a home in heaven for our souls[3]. Of course, he wants to purify us while we walk on earth. That is why he sends tests and troubles, and even lets us die. Except for Enoch, every child of Adam has passed through the gates of death. But we should not fear death, because it brings us home to heaven."

"As you know, beloved, God has sent me many places to tell people to repent. They rarely do, because most sinners are blind fools. But even fools can respond to a warning. Of course, how they respond is not our responsibility, but I always pray that at least one will repent and be saved from God's terrible judgment. Brothers, be honest about your sin, and trust your Maker! Come clean, and set things as right as you can! And do not be intimidated by wicked men! Question their reasoning, and patiently insert the truth when you can. We are on the winning side! Live before you die, and die like men. And may God help us!"

With that, father sat down. Cousin Asaph led the congregation in singing, and we were dismissed. On our way out, a few elders headed for father, as usual.

"But, Noah," Cousin Nergal objected, "people are not that bad. If they just keep the rules our Creator has given, they will be accepted!"

"Not that bad?" father asked. "How well are you keeping the rules, Cousin?"

After thinking a moment, Nergal scowled and walked away. Great Uncle Taanach, the youngest brother of Grandpa Lamech, came up next. He and his twin brother Raamach loved to talk about theology, and soon got father cornered.

"Noah, my boy, you are right, as far as you go," Great Uncle Taanach began. "But don't forget about national sin. The Creator will judge entire cities by the way they treat our fellow believers. If they are good to them, and favor them, then the Creator will be merciful. Otherwise..."

These discussions were interesting, but they could go on for hours. We had a weekly training engagement with our cousins Cush, Seba, and Dedan, and had to leave. With only two months until Sports Day, our training had gotten pretty intense, and we were eager to get to it. Just as we got to the playing field, however, Shem tugged at me.

"Someone is coming for you, Japheth."

I saw a girl approaching from the archery range. She carried a bow and quiver of arrows, but from her swaying hips and subtle wiggle, I knew even from a distance that it was Aziza. When she came close, I could not help but sigh: her beauty was perfect! She grabbed me close, and held me tightly enough to take my breath. Her perfume did not help.

"Japheth," she said, loosening her hold, "did you know that everyone is talking about you?"

"What do you mean?" I stammered. As usual around her, I was not thinking clearly. She had that kind of effect.

"That big, handsome prince told my father about you. He was impressed, Japheth! Do you know what that could mean? It is a big opportunity! It means you could make something of yourself!"

"Um, look," I said. "We did not exactly meet under the best of circumstances. One of his people was bullying a young boy."

"Yes, yes," Aziza replied impatiently. "I heard all about it! You stood up for some little Tubalite brat. It was not the wisest thing, but it worked: you impressed the prince! Unfortunately, the young man you knocked down was Rogar, the son of Mother Earth's prime minister! Even so, think of where the favor of a prince could lead you—and those with you!"

"What are you getting at, Aziza?" She did have ambitions, just as Shem had said! "How could some foreign prince possibly help me? And as far as the bully is concerned, the prince is not bringing him back, and I am not looking for him!"

Aziza looked at me with pity. "Oh, Japheth! You know so little! Opportunities like this must be seized! You don't have to spend your life tinkering around with stupid machines! With the favor of a prince—and someone like me to help—you could achieve status, wealth, and real power in the City of Mother Earth!"

"Mother Earth!" I exclaimed. "How do you even know these people?"

"My father has business with a great many people," Aziza replied, somewhat evasively. "The prince dined with us, you know, and he intends to return for Sports Day. Japheth, you must follow my advice. It is for your own good!"

Aziza and her family moved in important circles, I thought. Aziza looked at me intensely for a moment, but then relaxed, becoming coy.

"Oh, Japheth!" she said. "You did not ask about my bow and quiver. I plan to compete in girl's archery on Sports Day, but my mother fears the string may injure me. What do you think? Does my figure swell out too much?"

She turned her body left, and then right, watching my eyes. The string of her bow and the strap of her quiver certainly emphasized her curves. I opened my mouth, but no words came out.

"I have to go, Japheth," she smiled, "but remember what I said. The world is changing. Let me help you open doors! And be a friend to my half-brother. It is very important that he impress the prince, too."

"Half-brother?" That surprised me.

"We share the same mother. Sandal's real father made life very hard for him. But now, if he can win the race a third time, this time in front of the prince, it would change everything. Sandal never had your advantages, Japheth. Let's help him out. His team is going to win anyway; but if you just slowed down a little, or maybe stumbled, then when Sandal pulled farther ahead, the prince would take notice. It would mean a lot to me, Japheth. I can be very appreciative, and very affectionate!"

She reached out to touch my stomach, but I pulled back. Teasing, she reached out again. "Are you ticklish, Japheth?" She grabbed me for another hug, and ran away laughing.

I was dumfounded. I remembered the relative who thought pleasure was more important than honor or duty. Was this what happened to him? I had always thought myself a brilliant young inventor and a fine athlete; but today I felt like soft clay in Aziza's hands. I had not sinned yet, but I still felt stupid and weak, and wondered about it. Would I end up betraying my brothers and my self-respect, just to please a pretty girl?

---

[1]*Editor's Note:* The order of worship indicated here appears remarkably similar to the pattern of Christian worship advocated by Henry Halley of Halley's Handbook, including

congregational singing and expositional Bible preaching. There seem to be strong parallels between the patriarchal society of Enoch's Valley and the Protestant Christian culture formerly seen in Europe and America, as well as in traditional Jewish culture.

[2]*Editor's Note:* The term "serpent of Eden" seems to refer to the reptile mentioned in the third chapter of Genesis, and presumably to the devil. The manuscript gives other references we can only guess as, such as the "New Eden."

[3]*Editor's Note:* This concept that people have an eternal soul (as distinct from a mortal body) is reminiscent of the Old Testament book of Job, considered one of the oldest books in the Bible.

[4]*Editor's Note:* I was astonished when my brother, a pastor, pointed out that this ancient prophecy is actually included in the Bible (Jude, verses 14 and 15), and in almost exactly these words!

Chapter Nine: The Sabbath Feast

After a vigorous hour of running, swimming, and climbing, we were tired, relaxed, and hungry. We joked and laughed on our way down to the crowded pavilion, where we smelled delicious flavors, and hundreds of our closest relatives. We quickly found our places, for the patriarch had already stood to pray.

"And now, our Maker, we thank you for this marvelous bounty! Let all creation praise your name!"

After praying, the patriarch sat down next to Grandpa Lamech and Grandma Tirza. Great Uncle Seth and his wife were nearby, next to Great Uncles Taanach and Raamach, the twins, and all their wives. Father and mother were seated with Uncles Lemuel, Nebach, Krulak, Tobach, and Shebach, who had finally returned from his trip. The great pavilion was pleasantly shaded from the hot sun, and the breezes wafting in from the Hiddekel were delightful.

We helped ourselves from long tables loaded down with food, and happily chatted with various cousins. As usual, each family had brought their favorite dishes. Mother had made apple pies, while Grandma Tirza had not only made potato cakes garnished with cucumber, but sago palm jubilee, a favorite dessert. Pitchers on the tables were filled with orange and tomato juice, as well as plenty of clear spring water.

The Sabbath meal had certain customs. One of them was to place a large piece of fruit at the head table to remind us of the forbidden fruit, as well as the tree of eternal life we would enjoy in the New Eden. Another custom was to change our seats each time the bell rang. That gave everyone an opportunity to talk with different relatives each week, something otherwise difficult in such a large family. In one of these rotations I joined Cousin Zibach, who was already talking with Ham.

"Ham, I have to agree with you," Cousin Zibach said. "Giant sloths have no attention span except for eating; and harnessing them up would be a challenge, though it might be fun to try. I am sure the beasts must be good for something, though in the big scheme of things, I suppose they at least provide food for large carnivorous behemoths."

Cousin Zibach noticed me, and clapped me on the shoulder. "Good job, Japheth," he said, grunting. "You must always be firm with wild beasts!"

"And speaking of wild beasts," Ham said, "did you know what that bully was eating? The hind leg of a boar! It had been sweetened and smoked brown. The smell nearly made me sick! How could any human being eat the flesh of an animal?"

"Well, Ham," Cousin Zibach said, "the way you put it, that does sound pretty terrible. But meat eating is fairly common among the savages."

Zibach took a bite of a juicy peach as he considered the subject. He was not a particularly quiet eater; in fact, the squishing, grunting sounds he made while eating often made him the target of unkind jokes. "It takes an animal to know one," some said. Cousin Zibach, however, was really a kind, thoughtful person, and we overlooked his idiosyncrasies.

"Unggh, unggh; that was good!" he snorted in satisfaction. "Now, let's talk about eating meat[1]. You have to remember, Ham, that all carnivores eat meat, and they grow strong and healthy, don't they? For them, meat is nutritious. Do you think dietary purity earns us any special favor with our Maker? I think not! Still, I can think of a few good reasons for us not to eat meat."

"First of all," he said, wiping his lips with a cloth, "up to now the Creator has not endorsed it. It is not just a matter of taking an animal's life. We sacrifice animals today as Abel did, and burn the meat as a sweet-smelling offering to the Maker; but the life of the animal is not taken lightly. Sin is a serious business, and it requires blood to atone for it. We try to maximize the sacrifice, but we do not eat the blood, for the life is in the blood. Remember how the blood of Abel cried out from the ground? And what did God tell the patriarch Adam? He was to eat the produce of the earth: the herbs, and the fruit of trees."

"Interestingly enough, all baby mammals[2] require milk, which is perfect for them to digest. But cows and goats were designed to produce more milk than their own calves can drink! Why would that be? Obviously, God intended us to drink milk, and make cheese! In a similar way, we use animals as beasts of burden, or raise them for wool. If we sacrifice them, we waste nothing, but use the skin for making leather, and so on."

"Boys, we have a responsibility to exercise proper dominion over nature, but that is not always easy. When I am called upon to treat sick animals, I cannot always cure them. Sometimes all I can do is put them out of their misery, one aspect of my work I do not enjoy. But animals under our care ought not to suffer. But as far as eating them, this is my own opinion: while our Maker has not yet endorsed eating of animal flesh, I can imagine that if a time ever came when plants were no longer as nutritious, and if the animal's blood were thoroughly drained, he might permit it. But for believers living at this point in history, this is probably another example of the maxim: 'Others may, you cannot.'"

"But what about fish?" Ham asked persistently. I smiled. Ham was sometimes like a badger, much like me. "Or eggs? Many believers eat them."

"Ham, I don't have all the answers," Zibach replied. "I like fishing, and eat fish myself. I was raised that way, and do not condemn myself in it. But as far as eating eggs, I think we may, if we candle them first to make sure there is no life developing inside." He paused to pop a fat grape into his mouth, and grunted with pleasure. "These dietary matters can be difficult. While we respect the life of our animals, we must recognize that animals do not have the same breath from our Creator that people have. Animals are here for our service, not the other way around."

"But what about the similarities between animals and people?" I asked. "Our bodies have hair, blood, skin, and internal organs just like theirs."

"And some people even act like animals!" Zibach laughed. "I have been accused of that! No, boys: despite our physical similarities, only fools think that people are animals. But that brings up a point. Perhaps one more reason not to eat animals is precisely because we are somewhat similar! That is why civil manners are so important, such as using utensils to eat rather than fingers. And it is another reason why traditions like marriage are so important. Animals do not marry, because they are, well, animals! Animals do not give thanks before eating, either, but people should. We must make it clear to everyone that people are not animals at all, and that we do not share their behavior or destiny. Unlike animals, people are made in the image of their Creator, and are meant to have special fellowship with him!"

The bell sounded. "Ahhrrrrh," Zibach said. "Ham, you would soon have me preaching like your father. But we shall talk again."

During the Sabbath feast I also talked with Uncle Lemuel and Cousin Abdi, the patriarch's chief steward. When Mother Earth came up, I asked them what they knew of that kingdom, and how advanced they might be scientifically.

"I know very little about Mother Earth, Japheth," Uncle Lemuel replied, "though I have an old hydraulics[3] friend from the School of Tubal-Cain who is building a dam power system for them. Personally, I would like to know why they went to such trouble to visit us. I suspect we must have something they want."

"Well, I can think of one thing," Cousin Abdi said. When he spoke, the people around us suddenly became quiet—so quiet that I almost laughed. Abdi was considered a very shrewd businessman, with an uncanny ability to make profits. Though Cousin Abdi had long been the patriarch's chief steward, he was extremely wealthy in his own right. When Cousin Abdi spoke, people listened[4].

"It may mean nothing, Lemuel," Abdi continued, "but as you may know, the patriarch has a small mine that produces exceptionally pure sulfur, which is mainly used for medicine or for tanning leather. The market for sulfur has been quite steady for a century, but in the last year, the demand has surged. When I inquired, I discovered that the source of this new demand was Mother Earth. No one knows what it is used for. Somehow, I cannot imagine that they have more skin rashes than other places, or that they tan more leather. Their purchasing agent insists upon the purest sulfur, and he will buy all we can produce. That is good business, and we are increasing our production, but it still puzzles me."

Uncle Lemuel frowned. "Interesting. Ah, there is the bell. Japheth, tell your father I will stop by next week to inspect your destroyed valley. I am always fascinated by the power of water."

Our final rotation brought me next to Great Aunt Naomi, Great Uncle Raamach's wife. She was known as the matchmaker of Enoch's Valley, so you can imagine I was a little reluctant to begin the conversation.

"I am glad to talk with you, Japheth!" she said. "You are certainly growing big and strong! Your character, by reputation, is very good: you remind me much of your Grandpa Lamech at your age. He was one of my first matches, you know. It made our whole family happy, because I found for him, not exactly what he wanted, but exactly what he needed. Theirs has been a happy match, and it has produced generations of godly children and grandchildren. I remember the day Lamech finally admitted I had been right all along: that cute little girl Tirza was everything his heart had ever desired."

I smiled at the description of my grandmother as a "cute little girl." I did not know how to respond, which I feared was becoming my normal condition. Great Aunt Naomi smiled. She was a sweet, patient lady, and easy to trust: she really wanted the best for me.

"So, what about you, Japheth?" she said. "Early marriages are very popular these days. Though you are still very young, well under thirty years old, I think, your grandmother tells me you are already thinking of marriage!"

I stammered a bit. I admitted she was right, though I doubted that my parents would approve of the girl. Anyway, I was leaving for school in a few months. Great Aunt Naomi asked what I found so attractive about her, and what I knew of her family. In answer, I gushed a bit about her eyes and her alluring manner, but tried to avoid mentioning her wiggling figure, though I imagine she guessed. She pursed her lips, making me wonder if she knew Aziza's family by reputation.

"But what about your pretty cousins from Cush, Japheth?" she asked. "Are they not just as attractive, with healthy, feminine figures? Could you not be happy with one of them? They are solid believers, you know, and come from a good family."

"They are sweet girls, Auntie; and I like them a lot. But they are not like Aziza, somehow." I blathered on a bit, but she was not one to waste time.

"Japheth, you are a handsome, talented, hardworking boy," she said, "and your family is a noble one. Those are wonderful gifts! If you do not squander them by a momentary impulse, they make you eligible for an excellent match, one that will bless your descendants for generations!"

"Auntie, I have to confess that I have not given that much thought. I don't know that I am ready to start raising children."

"But, Japheth," she said, "children must be considered before selecting a wife! You must not submit to any sudden urge to marry, even if it is strong. Marriage is not an urgent thing, nor is it something to put off when the time is right. But when the time does come, I can help. Working together, we will find a lovely girl with physical charms and compatible interests, one who will be loyal to you and provide emotional support. Those things are important for a lasting marriage. But for now, I think a season elsewhere will be good for you. Go to a new city, learn your craft well, and begin your life's work."

That was what I expected to hear: career first, and then marriage. Suddenly, Auntie Naomi started, and looked up. Two or three green parrots had flown in to perch on the beams of the pavilion, and were pecking at things. Naomi looked at me again, and patted my knee.

"A little bird tells me not to dismiss you too quickly, Japheth. Let me do something. You may not understand this, but trust me." Standing up, she put a hand on my head, another over my heart, and gripped me firmly. It felt strange. I was unable to move or even blink as Auntie Naomi searched my eyes as though she were watching ships on the Hiddekel. After a while, she relaxed, let me go, and laughed merrily. I was so relieved that I laughed with her.

"Japheth, I have good news," she said. "An extraordinary wife is being prepared for you, and a remarkable heritage! But I am puzzled. I saw two or three possibilities, not just one! Which wife shall it be? You must use wise judgment, Japheth, as well as discernment and self-discipline. If you do, the Creator will provide you with a gentle match. If not, I am afraid he will let you have an abrasive match, one that will shape and polish your character. With that kind of wife, you may have some miserable years ahead."

Aunt Naomi took both of my hands in hers. "Japheth, listen to your parents, and to advisors who love you. Choose a girl with spunk, but one that is pleasant and gentle, with a godly character. If you do, yours will be a very happy marriage, and your children will be a blessing on the earth until the very end! I will keep an eye on you! Use your head, be patient, and trust your Maker to provide. Who knows? The perfect bride may fall right into your arms!"

Just then, the bell rang twice, indicating the conclusion of the meal. The guests rapped their cups on the tables to offer their appreciation, and we stood up. No one seemed to have noticed my unusual interaction with Auntie Naomi. Around us, our relatives and friends said their normal goodbyes, and everyone gathered their things to head home.

Before long our family was in the wagon, creaking our way up the hillside. Shem, Ham, and I were stretched out on pillows, contentedly munching on pastries.

"Hasn't this been great?" Shem sighed contentedly. "We had terrific music, preaching, exercise, and fellowship; and now I have my favorite dessert: persimmon rolls! There is only one thing left to do: enjoy a good nap!" He closed his eyes, folded his hands, and pretended to fall asleep, smiling broadly.

I agreed with him. It had been a very good Sabbath day, especially after such an upsetting week. But I now had a lot to think about. What if I did marry the beautiful Aziza? She might be very affectionate, as she suggested, when it suited her; but I did not think of her as being particularly gentle.

---

[1]*Editor's Note:* It is interesting that the topic of vegetarianism has become important in the West in recent years, perhaps ever since the late 1960's, when the Beatles popularized the Hindu/ cosmic humanist worldview.

[2]*Editor's Note:* The word translated "mammal" was a collective grouping of living creatures with certain traits in common, including growth of hair and secretion of milk.

[3]*Editor's Note:* This word apparently refers to the study of flowing water, according to the professor, so I used the word "hydraulics." The manuscript contains other surprisingly contemporary references to what we today might call "technology" or "science", meaning sophisticated advances in machinery or labor saving devices.

[4]*Editor's Note:* Many of the insights on human nature in the manuscript seem timeless. This reference is so similar to a recent financial service advertisement that I found it amusing.

Chapter Ten: Adam's Rest Park

The next two months passed quickly, but every time we came to Jared's Mill we noticed unpleasant changes. Some were subtle. The marketplace was a little subdued, without its usual cheerful banter. People did not smile easily, but seemed distrustful, and avoided eye contact. Strangers were everywhere. Valley Vigilance was kept busy, as we learned from Uncle Krulak. One evening as I came in, he was venting his frustration on father.

"Noah, my officers encounter public cursing, drunkenness, and fighting every day now. Young men loiter aimlessly in the streets, without employment or even respect for authority. By their dress and manner, they lack self-discipline and even self-respect. Actual crimes like assault and robbery have become common enough that I have had to assign full-time investigating officers. We even had a murder, Noah! While most crimes still take place among the newcomers, they are spilling out into other areas. My men are starting to feel surrounded."

This was upsetting to hear. Frankly, it made me even more ready to leave, and I was already counting down what was keeping me. While I would have liked to rebuild my stream pump, there just was not enough time left. I had designed a water-powered conveyor to lift hay into the barn, and that had a high priority. But really, the only thing I absolutely had to do was to run the patriarch's race with my brothers. After months of anticipation, the day of the race finally arrived.

Sports Day was always held at Adam's Rest Park, a large scenic park on the escarpment overlooking the river. Originally a pasture, it had been given its name during a visit by the first patriarch. According to the story, when the patriarch climbed up to the escarpment, he found the view so peaceful that he fell asleep. After that, the patriarch Jared turned the pasture and surrounding land into a park.

Over the centuries, beautiful gardens, fountains, and graveled walkways had been added to enhance the natural beauty. The climb from the town was delightful, and meandered past immense shade trees, gurgling brooks, and quiet meadows before finally emerging onto the playing fields. A magnificent panorama greeted the visitor, stretching from the northern mountains past plains, forests, and farmlands, and ending in the shimmering buildings of distant Tubal. The Hiddekel River lay below the escarpment, providing an exciting parade of colorful sails as well as the romance of shipping from faraway lands. Above the escarpment rose the deep green forests and mountains of the Doubtful Range. Great waterfalls and exciting rapids cascaded down the slopes to feed Jared's River, which could be seen flowing through the town to join the Hiddekel. The spectacular views, pleasant river breezes, and soaring birds attracted many sightseers each year. The park had become a popular site for weddings, with couples coming from distant lands to have their marriage "blessed by the patriarchs."

One field of the park was devoted to riding events, and long bridle paths led from it to the nearby peaks. The small lakes fed by the cold waterfalls were perfect for swimming, since they were free of alligators or other dangerous wildlife. Agricultural fairs were held in Adam's Rest Park seasonally, with Jabal-tents[1] being erected for livestock, and Jubal-tents[1] for traveling troupes of entertainers. Several fields were devoted to team sports, while various ranges were reserved for archery, stone slinging[2], javelin, discus, and hammer. Boat races and swimming events were held on the lakes and streams, while footraces were held on a number of different tracks.

All the events of Sports Day were well attended, but Patriarch Methuselah's obstacle relay race[3] had long been the most popular. An excellent athlete in his day, the patriarch had designed the course to include elements requiring strength, speed, skill, and endurance. In recent years, a cart race had been added just for fun. It was a grueling and exciting contest, and the members of the winning team were universally acclaimed as the finest athletes in Enoch's Valley.

My brothers and I had had excellent success in the preliminary races, and had advanced to the final race held on Sports Day. Our cousins' team had advanced as well, which made us happy. As everyone expected, the team that had won both of the two previous contests had also advanced. This team consisted of Sandal, Rekem and Zur.

The course consisted of four major elements and four minor ones. The first element was the "barrel-pull." For that, we put on sturdy gloves, climbed into a barrel that left only our head and shoulders free, and hooked our feet into loops at the bottom. There were three lanes, and the race simply involved pulling our barrels through the sand pit using only our hands. After that came the boulder toss, in which we threw a heavy rock into a bucket six cubits away. If we missed the bucket the first time, we could grab another rock, but that took extra time and energy. The cart race came next. After jumping in and pushing off, we steered our carts down the hill along a curved path, using sticks fastened to the sides of the cart to steer or brake. The cart race had dangers: scrapes and bruises were common, and broken bones had sometimes occurred when carts flipped over or ran into trees or rocks.

Once we got to the bottom, we ran to a wall that was seven cubits high. There was a short ladder at the base, but considerable skill and strength were still required to climb over it. Once over the wall, we sprinted to the next obstacle, the mud pit. We used a rope to swing over the pit. Falling in, of course, meant humiliation, and having to slog through the thick mud. After the mud pit came the swim, a thousand cubits of cold water. When we emerged from the river, we had to cast a javelin at a wood target twenty paces away. Again, in case of initial failure, extra javelins were available. After successfully hitting the target, the final leg of the course was a grueling uphill sprint past the viewing stands, either to tag our teammate at the barrel pull, or to finish the race. During the race, volunteers repositioned the barrels, carts, and targets as needed.

The crowd that day was large, but everyone was in a festive, light-hearted mood. That was a relief, because for months, irritation had hovered over our town like a cloud. Almost every citizen of Enoch's Valley had come, along with many visitors from Tubal and other cities along the Hiddekel. The warship from Mother Earth had returned, and I eventually spotted the black and green uniforms of her sailors. The prince of Mother Earth was easy to find, because he stood head and shoulders above anyone else.

With so many events, it was impossible to see everything, but we took in as much as we could. The children's competitions were especially fun, and it was obvious that the patriarch enjoyed giving out the prizes, which included toys, hats, musical instruments, or story-tablets. I was delighted to see Bezer win the second prize in the children's barrel-pull. He waved his brightly decorated hat to me from atop his father's shoulders. As we walked between the events, friends continually came up to congratulate us for making the final race, and promising to cheer for us. The women's archery contest was particularly interesting. To my amazement, Aziza took the first prize!

The day passed quickly, and it was finally time to prepare for our own race. My brothers left for the warm-up area, and I was just about to follow, when soft arms suddenly encircled me in a close embrace.

"Japheth," Aziza purred, pressing her warm cheek against mine. I turned carefully, but her lips nearly brushed mine. This was embarrassing, especially when I saw some nearby aunts raise their eyebrows. I would hear about this later.

"Aziza!" I protested. "Not in front of everyone!"

"I don't care, Japheth. I felt like it," Aziza pouted. She slowly released me to arm's length, and jiggled her body teasingly. Her leather archery vest was unfastened, revealing a tantalizing cleavage.

"Don't you want to congratulate me, Japheth?" she asked. "I won the women's archery contest! 'Foreign beauty outshoots the local girls!' That's what the news-criers will say. The girls will all be jealous of me for a while, but when you and I marry, we will all be related, and they will get over it."

"Congratulations, Aziza!" I replied. "But you are way ahead of me! You know I have to leave for school soon, and I may not return for years. Even after that, I will have to build a business. It may be a long time before we could marry!"

"Rejecting me after all my strenuous efforts, Japheth?" Aziza cried dramatically. "I feel faint! In fact, I think I may swoon!" Raising her hand to her forehead, she slowly toppled against me. I caught her, but she was heavy enough that we both fell down. In a moment, Aziza opened her eyes. "You saved me, Japheth! You are my hero! Now you will have to run away with me!"

We lay on the ground together for a few seconds, laughing, but Aziza soon became serious, and looked me in the eye. "Actually, Japheth, this is our moment. The prince is here. If Sandal can impress him today, his career is made, and ours can be, too. Listen to me! The prince already likes you, so you have nothing to lose. Just make a small mistake. Slow down a little, just for me. No one else will know. Let Sandal have his triumph! He needs it!"

I was immediately angered by her suggestion, but as she continued, my anger gave way to compassion, even pity. Aziza was so sweet and pretty; but she was so very innocent, and so terribly gullible. This was not her speaking: it was her brother! He had obviously taken advantage of her admirable brotherly affection!

"Listen to me, Aziza," I said, not wanting to hurt her, "I admire your loyalty to Sandal, but he does not need your help to win, or mine, either. And this prince of Mother Earth has nothing to offer us!"

I tried to get up, but she gripped me firmly, with wide-eyed intensity.

"Japheth, everything you know is about to change. Your future is with this prince, with me, and with Mother Earth. Take hold of it, Japheth! This is your chance, and now is the time! Today could be your key to wealth, luxury, and power! Join me now, Japheth! Do this little thing! Do not let your pride get in the way."

"I have to go, Aziza." She was making me upset.

She fluttered her eyelids and pressed her curves against me. "Give me your heart, Japheth, and you will have my affection. Think of me, Japheth. Think of me!"

I detached myself and stood, flushed with emotion. She still had a spell over me, but it was weakening. This was only a race. Did she really think I could be so easily persuaded to cheat? Could she imagine that I wanted power and wealth so badly that I would betray my brothers and family? And why would anyone want to gain the approval of a wicked city like Mother Earth, anyway? I decided not to think of Aziza again-- at least until the race was over.

I turned and ran to the warm up area. Shem was stretching, but Ham was not there, and he did not arrive for a few minutes. When he did, he was red with anger, and being practically dragged along by Cush, Dedan, and Seba.

"What is going on?" I asked with alarm.

"Ham had an argument with Sandal," Cush explained, as Ham shook himself off. "We pulled him away, but just barely. This boy is a gorilla! Valley Vigilance was watching. If Ham had gotten into a fight, we would all have been ejected from the playing field."

"He insulted our mother!" Ham said angrily. "First, he tried to butter me up by inviting me to join his gang! Can you believe it? He said I was the only one of Noah's boys who knew how to have fun. He said I might enjoy pulling some pranks, and earn silver at the same time. That is, he said, unless I was some kind of Tubalite lover! I asked what he had against Tubalites. He laughed, saying he couldn't help it that they were monkeys! If Cush and Dedan had not grabbed me right then, I would have knocked him down. Then he said that he had forgotten that our mother was a Tubalite! Japheth, I don't care if Aziza is your girlfriend: I'm going to smash him!"

"She may not be my girlfriend anymore," I said. "Sandal tried to use her to get me to cheat."

"Guys, we have no time for this," Shem said. "You know what Uncle Krulak says about losing our composure! Right now, we have to focus on good technique, and on running this course as fast as we can."

"I agree," Cush said. "We cannot go in angry. If we are cool, and avoid mistakes, we can beat Sandal. That would be the best revenge of all! Ah! Here comes Cousin Nimrim."

Nimrim was small for his age, but shrewd and canny. In the past, when Ham and Cush had used him to set up pranks, he had always been discreet. Today he spoke quietly, as though he were simply wishing us well.

"My boys have been keeping an eye on Sandal's buddies," he said. "As we expected, they are pulling tricks. They fiddled with your ladders, and did something to the ropes, too. Do not trust them. I have little Bezer keeping an eye on the cart track, and I plan to join him there, because it is a perfect place for mischief. I hope the race is fair today; but if not, we are ready." He winked broadly. "As they say, what is good for the goat is good for the ram[4]."

We walked up to the barrel track, which was close to the edge of the escarpment, and directly in front of the viewing stands. The stands provided an excellent view of most of the course, including the cart track, the swim, and the final uphill run. The seating was already full, with hundreds of excited, noisy spectators. Mother and father were seated halfway up, next to Grandpa Lamech and Grandma Tirza. Aziza was above the finish line next to her parents, and the tall prince and his officers. Aziza's father stood up to shout loudly to the crowd.

"Ten gold pieces on my son Sandal! Does anyone dare to bet?"

"What are your odds?" a spectator cried back.

"Odds?" Shahoot asked, surprised. "Why, three to one!"

I did not hear if anyone took his offer. We put on our helmets and gloves, and looked over the course below us. A cool gust came from the river, and I took a deep breath. Personally, I would have preferred to go first, but we had decided that Shem would take the first circuit to compete against Seba and Zur. Ham would be next, against Cush and Rekem, while I would go last against Dedan and Sandal, who were their strongest competitors. My heart was already beating fast: I just hoped I would not be exhausted before I even began. We helped Shem into the barrel, making sure his feet were firmly hooked into the loops.

The patriarch walked to the starter's block carrying a pair of cymbals. Our moment had arrived, and we were determined to do our best.

---

[1]*Editor's Note:* It is fascinating to see the names listed. They are apparently the same as those listed in the Bible, where Jabal was recorded as the father of those who dwell in tents and have livestock, and Jubal was the father of those who play the harp and flute (Gen 4:20, 21).

[2]*Editor's Note:* The use of slings in hunting and warfare is ancient, but artifacts are rare because of the fragile materials used. The oldest known extant slings from the Old World were found in the tomb of Tutankhamen (1325 BC).

[3]*Editor's Note:* The obstacle course described here might suggest that organized athletic events existed well before the Greek Olympic Games, which were held as early as the 8th Century B.C. Military training, of course, has always included practice in breeching walls, and crossing moats and rivers. Obstacle courses remain important in training today, as I have learned from personal experience.

[4] *Editor's Note:* This seems somewhat akin to the modern English expression: "what is good for the goose is good for the gander."

Chapter Eleven: The Big Race

We looked over the competition. In the center lane, Seba was in his barrel, stretching his shoulders as Cush and Dedan gave him final instructions. He winked at us. In the right lane, Zur flexed his well-muscled arms while Sandal and Rekem stood behind him, looking pretty cocky. Sandal saw my glance, and sneered.

The patriarch gave a few words of encouragement, and glanced at the judges. When they nodded, everything got quiet. We took a deep breath. The cymbals clashed, and the race began.

When the initial cheers of the crowd faded, we could hear the grunts of the racers, and the grinding of wood against sand. Taking advantage of his long arms, Zur took the early lead. As they warmed to the work, however, Shem and Seba increased their speed, and they began to catch up. Zur started slowing, but he was still in the lead when the three of them hit the planks. Cheers exploded from the crowd as the racers squirmed out and ran to the boulder toss.

Although arms are always tired after the barrel pull, I was surprised to see Shem have difficulty even picking up his rock. And once it was in his hands, he took precious seconds to carefully throw it. Seba started out quicker, but his rock slipped from his hands as he threw. It fell short, forcing him to pick up another one. Zur had no such problem, and was well ahead when he turned to run to the cart track.

By the time Shem and Seba finished the boulder toss and entered their carts, Zur was already coasting down the hill. Shem had less momentum than Zur, but showed good technique by leaning into corners and avoiding unnecessary braking, while Seba was particularly skillful in cornering. They began to catch up. Zur was careless around a turn, and ran off the track. By braking vigorously, he was able to return to the course, but he had lost considerable speed. Shem and Seba accelerated nicely down the steep track through the woods, and overtook him at the bottom. All three climbed out of their carts at the same time, and sprinted to the wall together.

Our technique for scaling the wall was to spring onto the second rung of the short ladder, and jump up to grab the top of the wall. With that handhold, we could swing our leg up, and then roll over the top. Since our teams practiced together, we used the same technique. When Shem and Seba sprang onto the ladder, however, the second rung broke on both of their ladders! Shem stumbled a little, but got back up quickly. Trying this time for the top rung, he was able to spring up and clamber over successfully. Seba, however, had sprawled out, and took more time to get back up. He used the top rung as Shem had, and also succeeded in scrambling over; but they were both clearly behind.

By the time Shem got to the mud pit, Zur had already swung over, and was on his way to the water. Shem jumped onto the platform, brought his rope back and began his swing over the mud. He lost his grip, and slid right down the rope to flop into the deep mud! Once there, he wasted no time, but immediately began to crawl his way to the edge. Time raced by. Seba had seen Shem's misfortune, of course, and felt sorry; but this was a race, after all. Seizing his own rope, he swung out over the pit. Surprisingly, he lost his grip, too! The spectators groaned in sympathy. Such bad luck!

By the time Shem and Seba finally climbed out of the pit, Zur was already well along on his swim. The cousins were fast swimmers, however, and over the long distance they closed the gap a bit, though Zur still emerged from the water far ahead of his competition. When he came to the javelin station, he easily struck his target, and he was well up the hill by the time Shem and Seba even completed their swim.

Shem cast his javelin right in the center of his target, but the shaft shattered! Astonished, Shem picked up another one, and stuck it deep. Seba finished his swim behind Shem, but completed his javelin throw without incident. They began their run up the hill together.

Zur was tired, and slowed considerably as he approached the top. That allowed Shem and Seba, who were lighter and in better condition, to gain a little. Nevertheless, by the time they finally ran past the cheering crowd, Rekem had already been tagged, and was pulling his barrel down the track. Ham and I, of course, were frustrated: both Shem and Seba had experienced far too much "bad luck!"

When their barrels were slapped, Ham and Cush took off like lizards. They had exceptionally strong arms and shoulders, and considered this their favorite part of the race. Before long, they slammed their barrels into the finish plank and squirmed out efficiently, having lessened Rekem's lead. Nevertheless, before they even came to the boulder toss, Rekem had already tossed his in, and was pushing his cart onto the track. Ham and Cush popped their rocks in satisfactorily, and sprinted to the crest of the hill.

Hopping into their carts smoothly, they tried to avoid unnecessary braking, and quickly built up speed. As they entered the lower half of the course, they were quickly gaining on Rekem. They came to a section where the track steepened and passed through a thick stand of trees. Rekem emerged from the trees at a fast pace, and sped down the smooth curve of track to complete the run at the water's edge. Ham and Cush were accelerating nicely as they passed from view, but as time went by, their carts never emerged from the woods! The crowd stood up in alarm, while Shem and I held our breath.

Ham and Cush later described what happened. As their carts entered the woods, they saw Cousin Nimrim step out onto the track, waving frantically. A large tree limb had fallen across the track! Although they braked immediately, it was too late. Ham's cart slammed into the limb, careened up the slope, and crashed into a clump of bushes. After Ham struck it, the limb spun around and crunched into the right side of Cush's cart, which began skidding sideways. By leaning into the hill and grabbing for dirt, Cush was able to slow his cart enough to keep from flipping; but it slid quite a distance before coming to a stop.

Ham got himself untangled from the bush and ran over to check on Cush. Although battered and scraped, Cush was otherwise unhurt. Both their carts, however, had lost wheels.

"Let's run!" Ham urged. "We can still catch up!"

At long last, Ham and Cush finally reappeared—on foot! The crowd roared. Ham and Cush ran down the final section of the cart track, and continued running to the wall. Rekem was far ahead, having already climbed the wall, swung across the mud pit, and entered the water. Knowing that the middle rungs of the ladder were broken, Ham and Cush promptly sprang to the top rung and safely scrambled over. When they got to the mud pit where their teammates had slipped, each took a moment to tie a knot on their rope. With that to keep them from slipping, they successfully swung across and ran for the water.

Ham and Cush were fast swimmers. Although Rekem was far ahead, they noticeably ate into his lead. When they completed their swim, they came to the javelin throw. Both of their missiles struck dead center, but Cush's javelin, like Shem's earlier, snapped in two! Fortunately, the head of his javelin remained in the target, and the astonished judge motioned for Cush to run on. Ham and Cush further narrowed Rekem's lead on the run, but it was not nearly enough: by the time they reached the top of the hill, Sandal was already dragging his barrel through the sand.

Sandal laughed loudly as their paths crossed, even though it slowed him down. Ham and Cush, however, received vigorous applause they ran past the stands. Though their teams no longer had any reasonable hope of winning, the audience still appreciated that they put their whole hearts into it, and held nothing back.

Meanwhile, I lay in my barrel, reflecting that this was the final circuit of the race. Sandal was far ahead, steadily pulling his barrel along the course. Although my heart raced, there was nothing I could do until Ham slapped my barrel. The crowd quieted for a moment.

"Ten to one odds on my son!" Shahoot shouted. "Any takers?"

Sandal's lead looked insurmountable, and the crowd began to chant his name: "Sandal! Sandal!" Everyone loves a winner, I suppose. After winning the race three years in a row, Sandal would have good reason to brag. But I refused to think like that. I had one thing in mind: to drag my barrel down the track as fast as I could, and complete the race.

Though it felt exhausting to wait, when Ham slapped my barrel, strength surged through my body, and I took off fast. I heard a loud groan from the audience. At the end of the track, I saw Sandal crawling over the pieces of his barrel, which had fallen apart! For once, he was having bad luck!

The incident did not really slow him down, and he still had a huge lead. Strutting up to the boulder toss like a silverback gorilla, he picked up his rock easily, and heaved it with a grunt. If he intended to show everyone how strong he was, he succeeded: his boulder sailed right over the bucket! He was forced to pick up another rock, and he cursed, drawing a frown from the judge. He put the second one in squarely. After glancing to assure himself that we were still far behind, he leisurely rambled ahead to the cart track.

Dedan and I used good technique on the barrel pull. Exiting my barrel smoothly, I got to the boulder toss a few steps ahead of Dedan. However, when I tried to pick up my rock, it completely slipped through my fingers! It seemed greasy! Quickly grabbing another rock, I succeeded in tossing it into the bucket. Dedan was quicker in his toss, and was ahead of me as we ran to the carts.

Sandal's cart was far down the slope, but he was having trouble staying on course. After carelessly approaching the first turn, he overcorrected, and nearly drove off the track. His skid made a big cloud of dust, and the crowd screamed with excitement. The mishap reduced his speed, and he drove a little more cautiously after that, allowing us to cut further into his lead. Dedan and I braked very little, turned carefully, and approached the long, straight stretch at a good clip. Sandal accelerated, and was going very fast as he turned onto the steep section of track hidden by the trees.

The crowd was silent for a long time. When Sandal's cart still did not reappear after a reasonable time, the audience stood in alarm. I was busy steering, but as my cart approached the woods, I saw Sandal finally emerge from the trees. He was running on foot like Ham and Cush! Dedan and I both applied our brakes as we made the turn into the woods. Sandal's cart was in the middle of the track, having made a long skid before finally coming to a stop. Its back wheels were nowhere in sight!

Carefully steering around the disabled cart, we accelerated nicely and soon emerged from the woods. As we coasted down the final stretch, I looked ahead. Sandal was at the base of the climbing wall, trying to brace the pieces of his ladder together! After a few attempts, he finally succeeded in jumping up and grabbing the top. He pulled himself over, but the two incidents had cost him much time. As we brought our carts to a stop, Dedan smiled at me: our chances were improving. With rising hope, we ran to the wall, jumped onto the top rung of the ladder, and bounded up and over. In a moment we were on our way to the mud pit.

Sandal still had a big lead, but bad luck was pursuing him now. When he jumped upon the platform and grabbed his rope, his hands slipped off just like Shem and Seba! His high-pitched shriek sounded like a hyena. Cursing loudly and repetitively, he slowly waded through the mud to the edge, and eventually climbed out and stumbled for the water. He must have been frustrated to resort to that kind of language, but I felt very little sympathy. As we ran up to the pit, the crowd at the top of the hill roared with excitement: this was turning into a real race!

Both Dedan and I made use of the knots our teammates had tied. Swinging over easily, we ran without delay for the water.

"We can do it, Dedan!" I cried. Sandal was a good swimmer, but I was confident we were faster.

Sandal was a hundred cubits in the lead as we approached the water's edge, but Bezer and Nimrim encouraged us.

"You can catch him!" they cried.

Dedan plunged in first, but I was right behind him. After kicking off my footwear and throwing down my gloves, I made a running dive. As my swimming mentor had advised, I stroked vigorously underwater before coming up for air. Swimming was my favorite part, and as soon as I surfaced, I got into a smooth rhythm of strokes and kicks, and began to catch up. When Sandal climbed out of the water, I was only a body length behind him.

He never suspected I was that close, but he saw me when he picked up his javelin. Enraged, he instinctively raised his javelin to throw at me! The judge that was standing by cried out, and Sandal realized he was being watched. Cursing, he turned back to throw at his target, but his aim was too high. By the time he picked up another javelin, I was casting mine, and Dedan had come, too. Our own throws were quick and accurate. As the three of us turned to begin running up the hill, we were exactly even.

Nothing is more painful or difficult than an uphill run. You either run so fast that you exhaust yourself, or you slow down too much and get passed. My initial burst of energy was long gone by this time, of course; and before I was even halfway up the hill, my lungs and legs felt like they were on fire. Only one thing kept me going: my determination to beat Sandal.

As I approached the crest, my leg muscles were quivering and cramping. I figured Sandal was probably breathing right down my neck, so I ignored it, and kept my legs moving. I just wanted the agony to be over. Finally cresting the hill, I drove myself along the final stretch. I think I heard roaring, but the crowd sounded very far away. Shem and Ham were standing by the finish line, and I tried to speed up for the finish. As I ran past the stands, my lungs wheezed and my heart seemed to pound out of my chest, but I kept going.

All alone, I dashed across the finish line and raised my arms in triumph. We had won! My brothers came over to put their arms around me, and we laughed from joy and relief. The crowd's applause was enormous, and we drank it all in. What a satisfying, happy moment!

Dedan crossed the line just a few moments after me, and Cush and Seba happily encircled him, too. Our teams headed for each other, for this was a victory for all of us. After suffering all those accidents, and overcoming such a huge deficit, winning was sweet, and we gave ourselves the freedom to enjoy it.

Sandal staggered up a minute or two later, the very picture of frustration, fury, and exhaustion. He had apparently stumbled and fallen before reaching the crest, and found it difficult to run after that. Zur and Rekem approached him cautiously, suspecting he might not be a gracious loser. They were right. As soon as he caught his breath, he began striking the air angrily, and shouting the same string of vulgar oaths over and over. The crowd that had cheered so loudly for him now turned away in disgust.

For us, though, the crowd went wild. As spectators milled around, friends shared their delight with us, and declared it the most thrilling race they had ever seen. Children actually danced in excitement, giving us an image we would long treasure. Even Prince Malek came over to congratulate us, and I introduced him to Shem, Ham, and our cousins. He was very complimentary.

"I am glad to meet each of you! The gods certainly favor your family with surprising victories; and today I shared in your luck. Your win turned my single gold piece into three, and ten gold pieces into a hundred! My faith in the sons of Noah, and my dislike of arrogance, paid off handsomely today! You are certainly sturdy lads: just the kind we need in Mother Earth!"

Aziza made an appearance later. Her vest was closed up this time, and her eyes flashed furiously. "I am very angry with you, Japheth," she pouted. "When you dropped your rock, I thought you had chosen to join us. But later, when Sandal was having bad luck, you did not slow down at all! You caught up with him in the swim, and ran up the hill as fast as you could! You never gave him a chance!"

I took a breath, and remembered that she was still under the influence of her brother! How could I be angry with someone for simply trusting her brother too much? In fact, with her heightened color, she looked very desirable. I felt like embracing her just as she had embraced me only an hour before, but something held me back.

"Why did you have so little faith in your brother?" I asked. "His team had won the race twice before, and he was everyone's favorite! I could not cheat, Aziza. The rock really slipped. It was only a race, but I had to do my best!"

"Only a race to you!" she replied.

She was seriously angry now, and deeply flushed. Suddenly I noticed something I had never seen before. Her cheeks had diagonal stripes, just like a tiger! They were faint, but at that moment very clear. That could not be, I thought! Those people only lived in lands far away! I started feeling dizzy.

"We knew you and your brothers were fast," she continued, not seeing that I had turned pale, "but if you had slowed down even a little, he would have won the race for the third time, and the prince would have been impressed! Instead, you made him look like a stupid loser! Now what is he supposed to do?"

I was still shocked by my discovery. The flush in her cheeks gradually began to lessen, and her stripes faded.

"Still," Aziza said pensively, working up a smile, "the prince was even more impressed with you, wasn't he? That may still be useful. And I suppose you did show a little...what is the word? Integrity? Perhaps I will keep an eye on you, after all. But do not presume on my affection. I am still very angry with you!" She shook her head in disapproval. But before she ran away, she winked.

I marveled. She was a master at toying with my emotions! But who and what was she really? I was tired: could I have been mistaken about her stripes? I was still wondering when Nimrim and Bezer ran up with my brothers.

"Japheth!" Bezer exclaimed. "I saw him do it!"

"Saw who do what, Bezer?" I asked, still thinking about Aziza.

"One of the bullies that attacked me!" Bezer declared. "I saw him throw the limb onto the track!"

"I saw it too," Nimrim added with a grim smile. "After that, I figured it was time to even things out. Fair is fair, I always say."

The patriarch awarded the prizes a short time later. After welcoming the visitors, he thanked all those who had helped, and praised the contestants for their strength, speed, skill, and vigor. "Can anything be better," he asked, "than wholesome exercise and friendly competition in a beautiful, healthy setting? Hasn't our Maker been good to us? On such a day as this, we have every reason to be thankful and content!"

Three of the contestants, I learned later, left the field with a different opinion. Frustrated, humiliated, and furious, their only consolation was the hope of revenge.

Chapter Twelve: A Ring of Vandals

We were heroes for a time, and enjoyed our moment of glory. Adolescent girls giggled at us, relatives showed their pride, and even strangers came up to congratulate us. That lasted about two or three weeks. After that, we gradually reverted to being simply Noah's boys.

From a personal standpoint, however, the victory remained deeply satisfying. It had not been just a race: it had been a milestone, the product of years of training. And that training had molded our characters, as the patriarch often said.

But now that the race was over, it was time to focus on other challenges. I was ready to leave my childhood behind, and maybe let Aziza go, too. Since the race, a loud voice inside was shouting for me to run from her. And Jared's Mill was no longer fun, either: its atmosphere had become foreign. People were rude, vulgar, and even reckless. More than once, I had to jump out of the way when youngsters raced their horses down the streets. And Valley Vigilance was now dealing with a wide variety of offenses every day, from willful overgrazing of common lands to robbery and assault. One evening Uncle Krulak was particularly upset as he talked with father.

"Noah, I keep talking to the council members about the increase in crime, but except for father and a few others, I get little support. It makes me angry, especially because I am becoming convinced some of the elders are actually working against us. Shahoot even had the nerve to say Valley Vigilance was to blame for the crime! My officers are 'too heavy handed!' Why, I nearly lost my composure!"

Uncle Krulak nearly lost his composure? Astonishing!

"If it were only me, Noah," Uncle Krulak continued, "I would round up all the newcomers, including Shahoot, and ship them back to wherever they came from. That would practically eliminate our crime. Mother says I am getting tired of being compassionate for the less fortunate[1], and she is right. But my men are not heavy handed. They only respond as they must in the face of unrepentant criminal attitudes and criminal actions."

"When people refuse to discipline themselves," father added, "someone else must do it for them. But I am concerned. Any of us may occasionally have a foolish impulse, but if our conscience is healthy, it restrains us. But this organ is not working now in many people: they have become morally confused. I tell you, there is supernatural evil afoot, Krulak!"

Father's use of that term reminded me of the cold wind that had swept through our valley. Since then things had gone crazy—how else could you explain it? I wondered if our supernatural protection been taken away.

"I agree!" exclaimed Uncle Krulak. "The punks[2] we arrest have very hard hearts. They justify themselves before they even commit their crimes! They say our patriarchal society has robbed them somehow, and that their tender little feelings have been assaulted. When they steal, they are only getting back what is rightfully theirs. Their victims deserve it! Once a person thinks like that, Noah, all he has left are two calculations: first, what is the chance he will be caught and punished, and second, is it worth it?"[3]

"So, what can we do about it?" father asked.

"For one thing, Valley Vigilance can begin strictly enforcing even the smallest crimes," Uncle Krulak answered. "Have you heard about something called 'mudding'? It is a type of vandalism practiced against Tubalites. When they return from a trip, families find their home spread with animal droppings and mud. Often, the walls are scrawled with vulgar curses or obscene threats. So far, we do not know who is behind it, but the Tubalites are getting anxious, and some of them have even left. I would love to catch some mudders in the act, and punish them severely. That, I think, would begin to put the fear of God into these criminals."

It was upsetting to hear all this. Tubal would have problems too; but they would at least be different. The new king of Tubal despised patriarchal believers, I heard. Even so, Tubal was still better than some far-off lands that had wars, epidemics, and earthquakes. At least I thought so. Later that week, we had our own earthquake. It shook me out of bed, and it was followed by a flurry of smaller quakes.

Things got worse. One day I returned from the fields to find mother weeping. A ship had arrived that day with terrible news. Tubalsik, a prosperous, growing port on the Hiddekel, had been found utterly destroyed, with the walls broken down, the buildings burned, and the streets filled with bodies. Outside the ruins, an army from Mother Earth had pitched a camp. Father's company had been constructing a warehouse there, and Uncle Jimna, mother's brother, had managed the project. Although he normally reported his progress every week, we had heard nothing from him for a month.

The destruction of Tubalisk was clearly an act of war. With its conquest, Mother Earth had seized a port from which it could blockade Tubal's trading partners, or even stage attacks against other settlements on the river. Suddenly, we saw the visits of Mother Earth in a sinister new light.

Uncle Krulak immediately brought to the council a plan to activate the militia and build up shore defenses. To our surprise, the council refused to consider it! There was a lively family discussion in Jared's Mill that night. Father and Uncle

Krulak were sure that war would soon come to Enoch's Valley, but Grandpa Lamech and Great Uncle Seth, among others, thought we would not be affected: we were too small, and far away. The patriarch, who had for most purposes retired from the council, was not pleased.

"It concerns me, my sons," he said, "that our council is more interested in providing entertainment for a summer festival than in taking steps to defend our valley, which is its primary duty. While there may be no immediate danger, and watching and waiting is sometimes reasonable, the risks of being caught unprepared surely outweigh any expense. While our representative government has in the past been appropriate, if we have come to the point where sensible, responsible elders are no longer the ruling majority[4], we are in trouble."

"Father," Grandpa Lamech answered, "as chairman of the council, I had to consider all points of view. Shahoot pointed out that Mother Earth's dispute is with Tubal, not with us. Furthermore, Tubalsik is farther from us than Tubal, so Mother Earth would have to attack them before they got to us. While Mother Earth is geographically close, we have the Doubtful Mountains to protect us, with its impenetrable gopherwood barrier."

It occurred to me that if a huge behemoth had been able to slip through the gopherwood barrier to destroy our dam, it was not so impenetrable. While silence is generally wisest when elders are in a heated discussion, I wondered later if I should have spoken up.

Very early in the morning some weeks later, Shem, Ham, and I left Jared's Mill to bring supplies back to the plantation. Ham drove our largest wagon, which was drawn by two great aurochs[5]. The two beasts, by the way, were well known in town because of one of Ham's pranks.

Ham told our plantation foreman one day that he was testing two young calves with a new kind of tonic, one that was supposed to cause very fast growth. Every morning for weeks afterward, Ham asked the foreman if the calves were growing any faster than normal. The foreman always answered no. One morning the foreman ran up to father, breathless with excitement! Overnight, Ham's two calves had become twice as large as the previous day! Ham's tonic had worked a miracle! Coming over to inspect the calves, father saw us behind the barn, rolling with laughter, and knew something was up. Ham had switched the normal calves with the huge aurochs calves. The astonished look on the foreman's face had been priceless, and we laughed about it for months.

Anyway, the thick fog and spray of mist that morning made visibility poor, so Ham drove very cautiously, listening for oncoming horses or other traffic. Just as our wagon turned a corner, we heard the sound of pots breaking. Ham halted the great beasts, and we all listened.

"That's odd," he said. "It is far too early for people to be at work. Do you hear those pots breaking? And what is that slopping noise?"

"It's coming from Bashak's place!" Shem whispered. "Let's get closer and find out."

We knew the home well. Since the bullying incident, Bezer's family had often invited us for evenings of spicy food and lively Tubalite music. Alighting from the wagon, we quietly sneaked through the mist. The crashing and slopping continued. We came to Bashak's high wall, which was fortified with jagged pieces of broken pottery. The large double gate to the courtyard was wide open. Though it was dark, we could make out four figures. Two of them held buckets, from which they were swabbing the walls. The mist swirled for a moment, and the moonlight revealed a face we knew well.

"Zur!" whispered Ham. "Let's get him!"

"Wait!" I said. "I have a better idea." Drawing them back, I explained my plan. A few moments later, Ham stealthily returned to the wagon, while Shem quietly took off running in the opposite direction. I remained at the gate, discreetly observing the vandals as they continued their mischief.

A few moments later, the wagon slowly emerged from the mist, plodding straight for the gate. The oxen were pretty quiet, but as the wagon approached the gate, I heard Zur shout to the others. It was time for us to move. Taking the gates, I slammed them shut, and Ham jammed the wagon tightly against it. That made noise, of course.

"Somebody's here!" Zur shouted. "Let's run for it!"

We heard the sound of padding feet, and hands slammed against the gate, trying to open it. There was cursing. A hand suddenly appeared at the top of the wall. It must have caught a sharp edge of the broken pottery, for we heard a scream, and the hand disappeared. Ham and I climbed onto the wagon and looked over the wall. Zur and his gang were desperately looking for a way out, and they saw us watching. I am afraid we smiled. They had been caught red-handed, and now they were trapped. They bellowed violent threats, but in a few moments there was a rapid clopping of horses, and a half dozen mounted Valley Vigilance officers rode up through the mist. It was too late for the vandals to escape. In a matter of minutes, Valley Vigilance had them secured, and led them away. As he passed us, Zur spat.

"You brats of Noah are going to be sorry."

We said nothing. Entering the courtyard with the inspecting officer, we looked over their work. The stonework of the terrace had been painted with mud, and the walls of the house were defaced with vulgar threats. Rotten fruit and animal droppings were scattered around, and broken vases had been knocked over, along with their flowers. The officer observed that a pile of combustibles had been put against the front door, and a pot of burning coals hastily abandoned on the walkway.

"That makes it attempted arson," he remarked, "something more serious than a typical mudding. You sons of Noah have done us a real service this morning. We have been looking for this gang for a long time, but we had no leads. Now, we will learn everything. With Zur here, we know that Sandal is involved. He is a shrewd one, and gets others to do his work. This time, though, he will not get off completely, even if his father is a council member."

We kept quiet about our adventure, but the report came out anyway, and once again we were lauded as heroes. Bashak and his family draped us with garlands, and other Tubalites invited us to dinners and receptions. When we walked through the marketplace, people ran up to thank us. At first, I tried to say it was nothing; but I learned it was better to quietly accept thanks. The vandalism had been a big concern for many people.

Under questioning, the members of Sandal's gang admitted to a whole series of crimes. As punishment, they were humiliated by being locked in a cage at the marketplace, and then they were required to work off damages while dressed in orange, the color of Tubal. Shahoot angrily objected to his son's punishment. Ironically, by claiming to be a victim of what he called "harsh patriarchal rule," Shahoot became even more popular! This was outrageous, father declared. It gave him little optimism for the future of Enoch's Valley.

After that incident, my remaining time passed quickly. I worked hard with my brothers to prepare for the harvest, and in my spare time finished making the hydraulic hay conveyor. Uncle Nebach cast the gears in iron, and had them ground and polished. He and Uncle Lemuel took over the task of rebuilding my stream pump, and promised to have it in production by the first time I returned home. I had done everything I could. Jared's Mill seemed to calm down after the breakup of Sandal's gang. Despite some objections, Valley Vigilance cracked down hard on petty crimes, and the town felt relief. Things seemed to be returning to normal.

The day of my departure finally arrived. I suppose I had some anxiety about leaving home, but otherwise I was eager. Mine had been a long, happy childhood, and I had learned all I could from my mentors: it was time to stretch my wings and fly. When our wagon lumbered into town that morning, I saw a freighter at the dock with a bright orange, blue, and white sail: it was my ship! We would push off within hours, and arrive the next day. I planned to stay with Aunt Zema and Uncle Zuriel, and since I would arrive weeks before classes began, I would have plenty of time to explore the city.

It was a gorgeous morning, with a very blue sky. The cool river breezes were exhilarating, and I had everything ready to board the ship. Unconsciously, I began to hum.

"Happy to leave your family, Japheth?" mother asked, with a tear in her eye.

I stopped. I had never considered how she might feel to have her first child leave. The fact was, I really was happy.

As our wagon entered Jared's Mill, I saw that the marketplace was crowded, but something was not right. People were running too much, and talking too loudly. They looked scared. Cousin Cush saw us, and ran up.

"Have you heard about the treaty, Uncle Noah?" he asked excitedly.

"Treaty?" father asked, puzzled. "Who made a treaty?"

"Tubal!" Cush sputtered. "Tubal made a treaty with Mother Earth! They sold us out!"

Father thanked Cush for the news, and gave our mother a look that was hard to interpret. He urged the horses along quickly. My stomach began to feel queasy. Today was supposed to be the beginning of a grand new adventure, and for once, everything had been going exactly according to plan! But now, after just a few words, I was no longer sure. In my mind I pictured a great behemoth, lumbering downhill to splash in my pond.

---

[1]*Editor's Note:* "Compassion fatigue" has lately become a popular term in America.

[2]*Editor's Note:* The original word indicated a small animal, perhaps a skunk or weasel; I thought the colloquial term "punk" seemed to fit better.

[3]*Editor's Note:* I was surprised to find similar thoughts recently expressed in book by Theodore Dalrymple: Life at the Bottom.

[4]*Editor's Note:* The idea of a representative government deciding by majority rule is ancient, from at least 500 BC in the Roman Republic and the Athenian Democracy.

[5]*Editor's Note:* Aurochs (*Bos primigenius*) is an extinct type of cattle known for its great size. It is estimated to have weighed as much as 3300 pounds.

Chapter Thirteen: Ambushed

Enoch's old green parrot swooped over our wagon as we drove through Grandpa Lamech's gate. This time he was accompanied by a small flock of green parrots with silver and gold stripes. I had always assumed Enoch's parrot was one of a rare breed, but now they were everywhere. The ancient parrot found a perch on Ham's shoulder, while the other parrots settled along either side of the gate, almost like an honor guard.

"Ungodly deeds!" Enoch's parrot screeched. "Ungodly way! Judgment on all!" It began climbing over Ham, poking through his clothing for nuts.

"Thanks for the reminder, parrot," father said dryly.

Grandpa Lamech, Grandma Tirza, and the patriarch were sitting on the shaded verandah when we arrived. After their usual warm greetings, Grandpa Lamech soberly reported what he had learned. After Tubalisk, it seemed, the new king of Tubal had no stomach for war, and had quickly sued for peace. The king of Mother Earth responded that he would be content if Tubal simply gave up any claim over the west bank of the Hiddekel. Unfortunately, that included Enoch's Valley.

"But we have always been Tubal's best ally!" Grandpa Lamech said angrily. "In betraying us, this foolish young king buys only temporary peace. Appeasement does not work. Tyrants, like fire, are never satisfied: any sensible counselor could have told him that! In fact, after such easy success, King Nezzar would be a fool himself not to push for more. I wish now we had never relied on Tubal's navy. Although the council balked before, now they must surely agree to activate our militia, and approve funds to build our port defenses. Sweat from labor saves blood in battle, as they say."

A few minutes later, mother came in holding a message tablet[1]. She looked grieved.

"It is from my sister Zema," mother said. "She writes that Jimna was killed in the defense of Tubalisk. His wife and daughter, however, escaped and made their way to Tubal. For the time being they are staying with Zema. They would like to return to Enoch's Valley; but Zema has advised against it. She has learned, she writes, about a new treaty that their new king is making with Mother Earth, one that will put us at great peril." She looked up. "The treaty must not have been public news when she wrote. Anyway, she calls their new king a cowardly schemer. He blames all his troubles on the Adamites, which is what they call patriarchal believers. He has incited the rabble against them, and there have been murderous riots, with shops destroyed, and Adamites dragged out and murdered." Mother shook her head, and looked at me. "Tubal is dangerous for believers now, she says. She recommends that you delay your trip until things settle down."

Delay my trip? I had planned everything around that trip! My heart sank. Suddenly, I felt an urge to go for a vigorous run. Physical exercise always helped put things into perspective. On my run, I chewed over all the possibilities, and came up with some ideas. When I returned, I convinced mother and father to simply delay my trip for two weeks. That would give plenty of time for troubles to die down, and still get me to school before classes began. I was sure that once I was there, it would be reasonably safe, if I used discretion.

The two weeks passed slowly. There was no more troubling news from Tubal, and my hopes began to rise. On the appointed day, we again drove into Jared's Mill. This time, however, instead of seeing a passenger ship with orange sails, we saw a warship with the black sails of Mother Earth! Father urged the horses along faster. Grandpa Lamech was not at home when we arrived, but returned a short time later, looking troubled.

"Their king is a bold one," he announced. "He wasted no time. His envoy today brought a long list of accusations and demands. Our patriarchs, the king claimed, have 'oppressed and exploited' newcomers, taught our children the 'enslaving idea of a single Almighty God,' and even harbored 'criminal Tubalites, the cockroaches of the world!' He demands tribute in the form of grain, cattle, and sulfur, and demands that the leading patriarchal families in Enoch's Valley provide sons as hostages. In return, he promises to protect us from our enemies, build new roads, provide education for our children, and allow our current officials to stay in leadership. If not, he threatens to utterly destroy us. At the end of his letter, he asked a question: "And who is the God that can stop me?"

"This king sounds pretty sure of himself," father said wryly.

"Our full council must meet tonight to consider this," Grandpa Lamech said. "I am having copies of the letter sent to every council member. Obviously, this is a declaration of war! There can be only one honorable response: we must activate our militia and prepare to defend ourselves! Yet I feel very uneasy about our council lately. It has been sluggish in dealing with important trade issues, and even voted to cut the budget for Valley Vigilance--on the same day it voted to increase benefits for its members! And just today I learned that our treasurer has secretly been borrowing money to pay for the council's frivolous spending. Enoch's Valley is now heavily in debt!"

"What?" the patriarch exclaimed. "This is not acceptable, my son! It has been years since I took an active role, but tonight I will attend this council meeting."

"Do you really think so, Father?" Grandpa Lamech asked.

"I do," the patriarch replied firmly. "I am still the patriarch of Enoch's Valley, and tonight I intend to show myself."

A short time later, my brothers and I left for the marketplace: father wanted us to scout the sentiment in town. I was happy to get out: after having all my plans overturned, I would have been happy to go anywhere. It did not take us long to hear the rumors and fears. Even our cousins seemed on the edge of hysteria.

"My father said," Cousin Lael asserted, sticking his nose in my face, "that this is all your father's fault. He kept our army from slaughtering their defeated enemy as God intended when we won our war against Nephil. The survivors later colonized the City of Mother Earth, and now their children want revenge!"

"Yeah!" his brother Pagiel said. "So this is all your fault!"

"What? Our father showed mercy to an enemy two hundred years ago, and now they want to punish us for it?" Shem asked calmly. He was always so diplomatic! Ham and I were ready to beat them up! "That makes no sense at all! Anyway, isn't that a long time to hold a grudge?"

"Well, I hear that when Mother Earth conquers a city," Cousin Mushi interjected, "they brand the captives as slaves. The male captives are sent to the copper mines, but the pretty girls are sold to the highest bidder!"

"Yeah!" added another cousin. "And they murder all the Tubalites, and anyone that looks too weak to work!"

"Well, I heard," Pagiel said, "that they make their captives bow down to Mokosh. If they refuse, they kill them!"

"That all sounds pretty gloomy, cousins," Shem said. "What do you suggest we do about it?"

"I say we fight to the death!" Lael declared. "Pagiel and I know how to shoot. Sharp arrows in tender places: that's what I say!"

"And I will toss rocks from the wall," Mushi said. "I will crush their heads like eggshells!"

"Yeah!" Pagiel said, raising his fist. "We will show them!"

"But aren't we a little ahead of ourselves, cousins?" Shem asked. "Mother Earth may make threats, but their prince seems reasonable. This is a bluff! Anyway, what would they gain by destroying our rich economy? Don't you think our council will come to some sort of compromise?"

I hoped Shem was right, but I thought their demand for hostages was outrageous, and our elders would never stomach the worship of false gods. Unless Mother Earth backed down, it sure looked like war to me.

When we returned home, father said he wanted us to attend the council meeting. He, too, had heard disturbing rumors. He even thought it would be prudent for us to come armed. That surprised me. Usually, our greatest fear in attending a council meeting was falling asleep!

Before we left, we sat down to a nourishing meal prepared by our three distant cousins. They were returning home soon, and they knew we would miss them. Lovely, talented girls, they were always full of lighthearted banter, and were fun to tease. Ham liked to remark that the better their cooking got, they prettier they looked! We agreed the girls would have no problem in winning husbands of their choice. I might even have been interested in pursuing one myself, if my mind had not been occupied elsewhere.

As we finished our meal, a servant brought in a message for me. That was a rare occurrence, and my brothers made me read it out loud.

"It's from Aziza," I said. "She says, 'I am leaving Enoch's Valley on the next ship. Meet me at my home tonight before the council meeting. Affectionately, Aziza.'"

Shem and Ham whooped in laughter, but I was puzzled. She had not sought me out since the race: why would she want to meet me now?

"What do you think?" I said. "Can we make a quick stop?"

"It says 'affectionately,'" Ham said, "but I trust her like I trust a cobra. I bet she is spying for Mother Earth, like the rest of her family! I say ignore it."

"I hate to agree with Ham, but it sounds fishy to me," Shem said. "Why tonight? Why not say goodbye at the dock tomorrow?"

Unfortunately, the thought of seeing her had already removed my ability to think clearly. I promised to be quick, and they finally agreed to come. Father had already left, but mother simply shook her head, cautioning us to not be late: the meeting was at dusk.

As we rode for Shahoot's secluded neighborhood, Shem remarked that we were dressed rather roughly. With our breastplates and swords, we were more prepared to meet wild beasts than elegant members of society.

A servant in green, black, and white livery opened the tall portal. Looking at us with obvious disdain, he asked our business. When I explained I had received a message from Aziza, his sour expression quickly became an oily smile. He opened the door and admitted us into a spacious pillared atrium.

The room had much to admire. Gorgeous carpets of yak[2] hair covered the polished floor, which was inlaid with colorful mosaic tiles. Detailed paintings on the walls depicted a zoo with various mammals, birds, and behemoths. Ham was delighted to see a flaming behemoth, which the painter had given fire shooting out from its nostrils. Shem lingered over the beautiful statues of famous heroes, while I was absorbed with a scale model collection of pumps and waterwheels.

The sun grew low as we waited. Finally, the servant returned to inform us that neither Miss Aziza nor Master Sandal was at home: they had gone to the council meeting. I felt both infuriated and foolish. The servant must have known of their absence all along! Shem and Ham gave me wordless looks: "we told you so; now we will be late!" The servant indicated that the fastest way to get to Council Hall was through a large wooded park.

"Take the path to the left," he said. "It leads directly to the hall, and is a short ride."

We urged our horses into a quick trot, for we had no time to lose. The first part of the trail was along a straight, easy incline. When we topped the rise, we saw that the path descended through a dense patch of woods, and then emerged to climb the slope to Council Hall. I frowned. This was just the kind of area that would be very dangerous close to the wilderness. Sabertooth tigers loved to wait in shadows like that, while giant snakes often slithered up to an overhanging branch to fall on their unsuspecting prey.

We came to the patch of woods where the branches had grown into the narrow path, and slowed our horses. The air was still and quiet. Pushing the branches aside, we urged our horses ahead.

Suddenly, there was a loud "Awk!" followed by a series of chirps and clicks. We stopped. On a branch directly over us were perched three large Enoch's parrots. Clucking and squawking, they rotated their heads to look down at us. Ham opened his mouth in surprise. In a moment, he hopped off his horse, and gestured for us to do the same.

"Those birds are alarmed," he whispered. "Something is wrong. Let's leave the horses here and walk ahead through the brush."

Grabbing our bows and arrows, we quietly moved into the shadows and advanced, paralleling the path. As our eyes adjusted to the darkness, we saw the light from Council Hall through the trees. From that faint illumination, we saw movement next to the trees lining the path. As we crept further ahead, we could discern men crouched behind the trees facing the path. I gestured to Shem and Ham, and whispered my plan. We quietly moved closer, selected sheltering trees, and notched our arrows. When Shem and Ham nodded, I stood up.

"Who goes there?" I shouted.

The dark figures turned our way and immediately released a flight of arrows. I ducked behind my tree just in time. The missiles whirred past, only narrowly missing. A horse whinnied. It was our turn. Since we had a good idea where the figures had been, we quickly leaned around our trees and fired. There was an agonized grunt, indicating that at least one arrow had found its mark.

The men took to their heels. We fired again, and heard another cry of pain. Four men passed in front of the light. One seemed to be hobbled, but it was too dark to see. We heard footfalls and snapping branches, but the sounds soon faded. All became quiet, except for our racing hearts. I hated seeing them escape, but blindly running through the woods in pursuit would have been foolhardy.

"Are you okay?" I asked.

Once assured we were all fine, we sighed in relief, and thanked our Maker for safety. Ours had been a narrow escape! Our assailants had chosen a dark spot for their ambush, and we would have been easy targets.

"Those parrots gave us a timely warning," Ham said. "I begin to like that breed more and more!"

When we got back to the horses, Ham found an arrow in his horse's hindquarters. He removed it gently and held a cloth on the wound to stop the bleeding. As we stood, a cool breeze sprang up. I was sweating, and felt the chill.

"That ambush was carefully planned," Shem said. "Do you suppose we were really their targets?"

"I don't know." I said. "I cannot believe that Aziza would have set us up. She is really a sweet person, though perhaps a little too trusting."

"Japheth, I admire that you think the best of people," Ham said, "but I don't trust Sandal at all. I bet he was behind this!"

"We don't know that," I cautioned.

"Let's just get to the council meeting, guys," Shem said. "It must be pretty important if the serpent of Eden is trying so hard to keep us away!"

¹***Editor's Note:*** The word translated "message tablet," indicates a thin tablet or sheet of copper with inscriptions, probably like the metal sheets of the original manuscript.

²***Editor's Note:*** Even today, the hair of yaks (*Bos grunniens*, a relative of cattle found throughout the Himalaya region of south Central Asia, the Tibetan Plateau and as far north as Mongolia and Russia) is valued for making rugs, tents, rope, and even wigs.

Chapter Fourteen: The Patriarchs Overthrown

There was a big crowd outside the front of Council Hall. We went to the side entrance, where a guard that knew us slipped us in quietly. Climbing the stairs to the visitor's gallery, we barely found enough room to stand, but somehow were able to push through to the railing. Grandpa Lamech was seated in the chairman's seat below us, next to the patriarch, while father was seated with the rest of the elders in the ascending rows facing the speaker's dais. Mother and Grandma Tirza were with other wives in the opposite gallery, directly above the chairman. Aziza, I saw, was not far away, along with her mother and brother. When our eyes met, her mouth opened in surprise. Her brother followed her gaze, and scowled.

We began to work our way through the gallery to mother, apologizing frequently for having to push through. With so many visitors, the gallery was warm. The air was thick with the smell of unwashed bodies and garlic, and men talked loudly, making it difficult to hear. Shem shouted in my ear.

"I doubt these men had any interest in politics before today."

I agreed. These were not the public-spirited citizens that normally attended council meetings. Instead, they were rough looking young men dressed in the attire of farm workers or common laborers. Their mutterings were coarse and vulgar, and many appeared to be looking for trouble.

"Our stable smells fresher," Ham added. "This gallery needs shoveling."

As we slowly moved through the packed crowd, one of the elders stood and began speaking. I was not really paying attention, being more interested in reaching our family. The gallery, however, was totally absorbed.

"Mother Earth is telling the truth!" the speaker shouted. "The patriarchs have played on our fears to rob and enslave us! As workers, we must unite to seize power! We must be freed from patriarchal corruption and oppression! Once we are liberated, we can make our own peace with Mother Earth!"

The crowd around us roared their agreement. I had assumed I was hearing incorrectly, and that the speaker was actually warning of the dangers of Mother Earth. What he said made no sense at all! A few elders stood to object, but the huge numbers in the visitor's gallery shouted them down. I peered between heads, and finally recognized the angry speaker. It was Shahoot, Aziza's father! Before, his manner towards the patriarchal elders had always been oily and flattering. Tonight, he projected hate and violence.

"No wonder the City of Mother Earth feels betrayed," Shahoot continued, pacing back and forth. "No wonder they threaten to invade! The patriarchs of Enoch's Valley and their greedy Tubalite accomplices have cheated all of us! While we sweat and labor, they pile up gold and recline in luxury. And they use their oppressive religion to keep us in bondage! I say thank the gods for Mother Earth! Without them taking a stand, the patriarchs would continue to persecute us, extort us, and rob us. Workers! We have been helpless cowards too long! We must demand justice, and put an end to patriarchal tyranny!"

My first instinct has always been to believe my elders. If I had not known who these "patriarchs" actually were, I might have been inclined to join in against this terrible enemy that enslaved everyone. But these patriarchs were my parents, my grandparents, and everyone who loved me! In real life, the patriarchs never treated their workers harshly, let alone cheated or extorted them. Shahoot was completely making these things up! But why would he do that? I looked at the faces in the crowd. They looked bewitched. When Shahoot talked of robbery and suffering, their faces sank in anguish. When he cried for justice, they scowled vengefully, and raised their fists.

"Shahoot is no simple merchant," Shem shouted in my ear. "He has been preparing for this a long time."

Like a professional actor on a stage, Shahoot waved his arms broadly to emphasize his points, and jabbed his fists as though he were fighting. The elders were shocked, and sat meekly in their seats. My brothers and I decided we had been polite long enough, and began aggressively pushing through the crowd. Shahoot held up an inscribed tablet to the audience, and leered with contempt at the elders. He had whipped the crowd up to a fury: they were ready for their orders.

"Elders, the workers are prepared to violently take back their rights," Shahoot said. "If you wish to avoid that, then pass this proposal. It simply restores justice to the workers and makes peace between us. Of course, the patriarchs must return what they have robbed from Mother Earth, but our workers must have their fair share, too. The arrogant, greedy, fanatical patriarchs must be removed, and the government returned to the people. Vote yes if you want to live! You can read it later, but you must vote now! We demand justice[1]!"

The assembly roared its approval. Shahoot smiled triumphantly at the elders, who had shrunk into their seats. For a long moment no one moved.

Finally, Grandpa Lamech stood up. His face was white with anger, something I had never seen. Father stood, too, along with Uncle Krulak, Uncle Shebach, and a dozen others.

Last of all, the patriarch himself arose. Disappointingly, many of the elders raised in Enoch's Valley, from whom we might have expected loyalty, remained seated. This group of elders included Cousins Achbor and Sharezer. Grandpa Lamech attempted to speak, but the angry crowd shouted him down with curses, jeers and threats. A chant arose.

"Vote yes! Vote yes! Vote yes!"

With our hands on our swords, we pushed hard, and finally reached our mother and grandmother, together with the other wives. Emotions in the chamber were high: a fight could have broken out any moment. Abruptly, the majority of the elders wilted, and agreed to vote. The crowd in the gallery was disappointed at winning so easily, but grew quiet.

"I am glad you finally came, boys," mother said. "This mob is awful. It has shouted down our elders, and intimidated the rest into voting on a proposal that no one has read!"

Grandma Tirza shook her head in stern disapproval. Although I knew her as the kindest, most elegant lady imaginable, she had a strong sense of propriety, and could not abide deceit or injustice.

"We should have suspected that a plot was afoot," she said indignantly, "but your grandfather could not believe that so many of our elders could be this corrupt. Tonight's barbaric disruption was not spontaneous, but carefully planned. Shahoot probably knew the demands of Mother Earth weeks ago. He whipped up the rabble very skillfully, and successfully intimidated the elders. Remember this evening, boys. Tonight marks the end of honest government in Enoch's Valley, and the beginning of tyranny."

The foreign elders crowded around Shahoot with barely disguised glee. Some elders glanced about furtively, showing pale, timid faces. The patriarch and his leading elders were angry, but looked determined. Unfortunately, they were outnumbered.

"Emma, girls," Grandma Tirza said, standing up, "it is time that we left. Boys, open a way through this beastly crowd. I will not abide this treasonous disgrace any further. When you have finished escorting us, return to provide backup for your father and grandfather. They are surrounded by degenerates and weaklings, and a mob like this is apt to become violent."

Forming a spearhead for the half dozen ladies, we firmly pushed our way through the distracted crowd, and reached the side door in moments. Very few people even noticed us, being fascinated by what transpired on the council floor. Grandma's carriage was waiting near the exit, guarded by the driver and several sturdy servants, and the ladies departed uneventfully. My brothers and I returned to the hall just in time to hear the result of the vote.

"The vote is 27 to 23 in favor! The workers have spoken!"

Loud, gleeful whoops burst out. Many in the gallery began to dance, while others whinnied like horses, or sang out their newfound hopes.

"Hurray! Someone else can do the hard work now!"

"Now I can eat and drink as much as I like!"

"I'm getting new clothes, and a donkey!"

Shahoot stood quietly for a long moment, enjoying his triumph. Finally, he raised his hand to silence the crowd. "Tonight we have voted for real change," he said. "Tomorrow will mark the beginning of justice for us as workers. Now, as your new chairman, unless there is any objection, I shall adjourn this historic meeting."

One of Shahoot's lieutenants prepared to swing the mallet against the great brass gong. At that moment, however, a voice rang out. Shahoot's mouth fell open in astonishment.

"Oh? Does the patriarch Methuselah wish to speak?" Shahoot laughed. "Is he even capable of it? Comrades, be quiet! Our victory tonight has been overwhelming. Let us hear what this ancient patriarch has to say! Will the doddering old fool even be able to assemble a few stray thoughts? This should be fun." He chuckled derisively, and waved for the patriarch to speak.

"Before the Creator and his angels," the patriarch declared loudly, "some things must be said." The crowd became quiet, though still sneering. The patriarch took time to look over the faces in the council, and shook his head in disappointment.

"Nine hundred years ago, my grandfather, the patriarch Jared, settled along this isolated stretch on the Hiddekel River and built a mill. His purpose was to raise his family far away from the malignant sin that was even then spreading over the earth. He and his son, the patriarch Enoch, welcomed those who believed in our Creator, and in time their community of believers developed this entire fertile valley. Since then, our people have faced troubles ranging from monstrous behemoths to marauding bands of Cainites, but we survived every test because we had one great advantage. What advantage is that, you ask? Our advantage was our accurate view of the world! And where did we get that? We got it from Adam, the first patriarch, who got it from the Creator himself."

"Adam, whom I knew myself for more than two hundred years[2], passed his accurate view of the world on to his faithful descendants, the patriarchs Seth, Enosh, Cainan, and Mahalalel, my great grandfather. Because these patriarchs knew the sin in man's heart, they designed a system of human government that curbed these evil tendencies, but still protected man's God-given rights[3]. These rights include life, liberty, and property. Have you noticed that we have no slaves in Enoch's Valley? We do not think people are property. We have a rule of law here, a free market, and a representative council of elders. Our patriarchal system has given rise to a very happy community, and a prosperous one, in which personal creativity and hard work produce true wealth, something that is created, not taken."

"But our system of government," he continued, "can only work in a community where the large majority believe in our Creator, and share our worldview. Otherwise, when people see the material blessings we enjoy, but do not understand their true source, they are easily deceived, as you have been tonight." The patriarch became stern.

"Tonight, like Cain, you have chosen to believe lies. The first lie was that the Creator is like you. Well, he is not. He is holy. The second lie was that man was not all that bad. Well, you are that bad. 'We can keep our own rules,' you say. No, you cannot even keep your own rules. You say, 'If we change our government, or change our circumstances, we can have paradise again.' You are wrong. The basic problem of man is man, not man's circumstance. None of you can curb your basic tendency toward evil, and you have not even tried tonight! You have invited disaster from our righteous Judge!"

The patriarch glanced coldly into the eyes of Achbor, Sharezer, and the other treasonous elders. They lowered their eyes and shrank into their seats. "Tonight you have agreed to obvious lies, and have given in to envy and greed. You have voted to seize riches instead of earning them, and you have become traitors to both your Creator and his people. Instead of obeying the Creator who loves and preserves us, you have chosen to serve the wicked kingdom of Mother Earth with all its false gods. As a result, the thing you greatly fear will come upon you, and our Creator will judge each of you by your works. Elders Achbor and Sharezer, you should know better, and you will be judged especially harshly. Though deaf now, I wish you could hear, for even now, if you repented, our Creator might relent. My conscience is clear tonight, for I have now warned you. And while you elders refused to begin this meeting with prayer, I will end it with one: Lord God, Creator of the heavens, have mercy on us all!" The patriarch looked over the elders a final time, before waving his hand disdainfully. "Now, you are dismissed."

The gong was struck, and the rich, musical tone reverberated throughout the hall. One or two people shook their heads, as though trying to wake up; but most seemed to bitterly resent what the patriarch had said. The frustrated crowd had been promised loot and vengeance; but so far, they had gotten nothing. Faces around us grew ugly, and we heard low muttering and growling. As the patriarch's party prepared to leave, the mutter grew louder. Violence was bubbling to the surface right before our eyes!

Shahoot nodded to someone in the gallery opposite us. We heard a shout: "Death to the patriarchs!" A dozen rough-looking thugs began to push down the stairs toward the council floor, violently shoving people aside. At least twenty thugs followed them, waving their fists and repeating, "Death to the patriarchs!"

It was time for us to act. The three of us formed again into a wedge and descended the stairs, forcing others out of our way. Unfortunately, it looked as though the violent thugs would reach the patriarch first. While we were still on the stairs, the first thugs gained the council floor and headed for the elders.

Suddenly, I saw something that made me sigh in relief. Out of nowhere, three or four fully armed Valley Vigilance officers appeared in front of the patriarchs! Each was an exceptionally big, powerful man. Even from a distance, I could tell they were tough, seasoned warriors with the skill, discipline, and determination needed in battle. I just knew they would do their duty fearlessly. They were the kind of men I would have prayed for, had I thought about it. I had never met these particular officers, though I thought I knew most of Valley Vigilance. Their helmets and armor seemed to be of a new design, with green breastplates decorated with strips of silver and gold. The shields in their left arms had fine steel plates overlapping like feathers, while their swords were the shiniest I had ever seen. Although I had polished many steel forgings for Uncle Nebach, I had never been able to achieve that kind of finish: their blades were like mirrors, and actually glittered in the light. I instantly determined to ask them later how they did it.

It was a pleasure to see those men in action. When the leaders of the mob, driven by the weight of so many others behind them, came face to face with the Valley Vigilance officers, their courage evaporated. Gasping in terror, they desperately tried to escape, and pushed back violently. Their followers stumbled and fell over them, while the thugs above them on the stairs tripped and tumbled into the crowd. In just moments, a large part of the ugly mob had collapsed into a jumble. Unaware of the chaos they had caused, the leading thugs still kept frantically crawling backwards, whining like chastened dogs. I found it very gratifying, even hilarious! I could have cheered!

I don't think the Vigilance officers actually even had to touch the thugs. The mob simply melted away before them, and a broad path opened up. The patriarch and his elders smoothly proceeded in a calm, dignified manner, scarcely deigning to notice the jumble of ruffians groaning on the floor. But I laughed. My brothers and I stood respectfully until the elders passed, and then wheeled about, joining their party as a sort of rear guard. It was a proper military exit, but the angry crowd was left feeling puzzled and frustrated.

As we marched down the steps outside, I was so relieved that my knees practically trembled. At least, that was what I thought. Shem touched my arm.

"Do you feel that?"

It was not my knees, after all! The ground itself was moving! I heard a clanging in the hall behind us. Curious, I hopped back up a few steps to look inside. The great brass gong used to close the meeting was swinging back and forth from the rafters like a pendulum. The mallet had been placed carelessly on the stand beside it; now, instead of the mallet striking the gong, the gong was striking the mallet! The disorganized crowd swarmed around the council floor like angry bees, oblivious to both the earthquake and the gong. Men shouted, pushed, and fought, producing a drone of hateful noises. That was enough for me. I skipped back down the stairs to join my family.

Father put his arms around our shoulders.

"I thank the Maker we are out of that! And thank you, boys, for escorting the women to safety! Things had gotten dangerous. It somehow reminded me of my first visit to Nephil, when Krulak and I went to look for our lost sister. The demons could almost be felt. It was like that here tonight: everything was dark. I felt confused, and it was difficult to think. It took me a long time to figure out what Shahoot was up to. Later, when the mob shouted for blood, it occurred to me that he had no intention of letting us leave peaceably. I prayed for the Maker's protection then, but I still think it was a miracle we got out alive!"

"I think so, too!" I agreed. "I was so relieved when those new Valley Vigilance officers showed up to clear a path for you!"

"Clear a path for us?" father asked, surprised. My brothers looked at me doubtfully--as though they had not seen them in action, too! Father studied their faces, and glanced up for a moment. "New officers, Japheth? What did they look like? Were they unusually big, powerful men, with swords polished so brightly they gleamed?"

"Those were the ones, Father," I said. "I would like Uncle Krulak to introduce me to them. They are my kind of warriors — strong and fearless!"

"Hmm, yes," father said. "They are my kind, too. These are uncertain times, and we certainly need their help."

Our return to Grandpa Lamech's compound was uneventful. Along the way, we told father about our ambush. He was outraged to hear of it, but relieved we had escaped without injury. He charged us to make a full report to Valley Vigilance the next day. When we got home, the patriarchal elders of the council went into conference. After the disastrous council meeting, they had much to discuss. My brothers and I, however, retreated to our loft. We were exhausted, and immediately fell asleep.

---

[1]***Editor's Note:*** Shahoot's harangue reminded me of the big lies and propaganda used by the Communists in the previous century, and even more recently, to gain power. The lures of greed, envy, self-justification, and hate are apparently timeless.

²***Editor's Note:*** It had never occurred to me that the lives of the Genesis patriarchs could have overlapped so much, and that they might have actually talked with each other!

³***Editor's Note:*** The astonishing parallels with the American Declaration of Independence and the U.S. Constitution are really too obvious to point out, but I do it, anyway.

Chapter Fifteen: Securing Assets, Preparing Defenses

When I awoke the next morning, the sun was already peeking through the trees. I felt refreshed and as hungry as a wolf. Shem and Ham were still sleeping, so I got up by myself to find breakfast. Only when I was halfway to the kitchen did I remember what happened the previous night. Stifling a groan, I filled a platter with fruit and potato pastries, and brought it outside. When the night mist evaporated, the air in the courtyard was always fresh and cool, and a certain bench had become my favorite spot. It was quiet, and today I had a lot to mull over.

In the space of a single day, our entire government had been overthrown, our homeland threatened, and all my plans for the future had fallen apart. For the time being, or at least until things clarified, I would have to relinquish my seat at the School of Tubal-Cain. And I was displeased with myself on a more personal level. Aziza was a beautiful girl, with highly tempting physical charms and manners; but was my attraction to her real love? How could I know? I was so young! I just wanted to be an inventor and live happily ever after. I gazed at the clear morning sky and sipped hot orange tea, but it was still too early to think.

A while later, father, accompanied by Grandpa Lamech and the patriarch, walked into the courtyard carrying a tray with tea and a basket of pastries. They saw me sitting on the bench, smiled, and came in my direction. I heard noisy squawks high above. The patriarch's old green parrot, accompanied by a half dozen others, glided down to perch in the great mangrove tree above me. I smiled. Those birds always cheered me up.

"May we join you, my son?" father asked, putting down the tray. He pulled up chairs for Grandpa and the patriarch, and they all sat down. "I hope you slept well. That might not have been easy after our exciting day yesterday. It is not often that a foreign power threatens war, or that a government system that has worked for hundreds of years is suddenly voted out."

"I suppose not," I replied.

"And it is not every day that a young man's plans for school are changed at the last minute, either," father said. "We need you at home now, my son."

"I know, Father," I said, nodding. "I have already decided to write to the school. I will ask if they can hold a place for me until things here resolve."

"I am sure they will!" father said. "But speaking of that, I must write a letter as well. When I met King Nezzar five years ago, I told him he needed to repent personally. But now, I must warn him for the sake of his nation. Great Uncle Taanach was right, you know: our Creator will judge nations by how they treat his people. This foolish king has defied our Maker, lied about him, and threatened his people. Unless King Nezzar repents as its leader, an awful disaster may fall upon him and his entire kingdom."

"Noah, my son," Grandpa Lamech interjected, "you are good to be concerned with the eternal destiny of the lost. But how can one think of the fate of the wicked when childhood dreams have been shattered, like poor Japheth's, or when we suddenly find ourselves out of a job! We have so little control over life! We rise up early to work, and stay up late, day after day, year after year, confident we are building a pleasant, secure place in life; but suddenly a covetous schemer like Shahoot comes along and takes it all. I have finally realized something, my boy, though it has taken me seven hundred years. It is vain to think we can guarantee a pleasant, secure life, no matter how hard we work. From now on, I will continue to do the best work I can; but I will not set my heart on seeing the results. Instead, I will trust them into the hands of our Maker[1]!"

The patriarch looked at Grandpa, and laughed.

"I am still trying to learn that lesson myself," he said, "after nearly nine hundred years! Adam often told me that the heart of man may plan his way, but the Lord determines his steps. I often think of that. Lamech, my boy, our Creator really does love us more than he loves the works we do. When I forget that, I become like a jellyfish, working ever so hard to bob up and down, but still only getting where the current takes me."

The patriarch poured some tea and reached into the basket for a freshly baked potato-pomegranate muffin. He smiled at me.

"Japheth, my son, you look glum. Do not despair about your school. You are still young enough to attend many schools, and have lots of careers. And do not fret over Enoch's Valley, either. God's people have always had enemies. We must be aware of them, of course: it would be foolish not to be. But we must trust God's chain of command. When we do, we are happier, have less stress, and are freed to perform our own responsibilities. Enoch's Valley has faithful elders whose main responsibility is to understand the times. They are the ones who should know what to do, even though we now are only a minority in our civil government. Your job, Japheth, is to strengthen yourself in mind and body. Let the elders provide the leadership they must, and you do your own part. We will soon enough need all your ingenuity, strength and courage. Do not weaken yourself by fretting."

"I shall try not to, Patriarch," I said. "On the other hand, it does help to know the big picture, and see how my little role fits in."

"Then perhaps we should bounce some thoughts against your head," the patriarch replied, chuckling. "After that disgraceful council meeting last night, we talked a long time about what had brought us to this crisis. We have much to blame ourselves for. We chose immoral, dishonest officials, failed to enforce our own laws, failed to insure safeguards against corruption, and failed to pass our accurate worldview and faith to our newcomers. It is always important to be honest about your sins, Japheth; otherwise, you will never turn things around. After our painful self-examination, we were ready last night to consider our new challenges. Shahoot's mob intended to slaughter us: we see that now. On their part, that would have been shrewd, for they could then rob our people at their leisure. But our Creator stepped in to protect us."

The patriarch sipped his tea, and took a bite of a pastry. "So now, Enoch's Valley, the home of God's faithful patriarchs, has become exactly like the other nations. Some of our people believe in God, some are heathen; some are productive citizens, some are looters. But the patriarchal believers here are stronger than Shahoot's new council may think. He may begin to regret acting so hastily. We still control most of the land and the industry, and our households have faithful armed retainers to defend us. We can negotiate from a position of strength. Ultimately, however, we must either drive out these parasites, or they will consume us. They made that clear last night. That brings us to Mother Earth. Will she give us enough time to solve our civil problems? Lamech, my son, would you explain more to our young grandson? My tongue is dry from all this talk."

"Certainly, Father." Grandpa Lamech turned to me, while the patriarch sipped more of his hot tea.

"Japheth, Mother Earth has a powerful military force, we know that; but any army must organize a supply train. We think we probably have at least three months before they could arrive in force. So, what shall we do? Shall we submit, or run away, or stand and fight? We shall not submit: our elders agreed that we were not ready for cultural suicide. Should we flee from Enoch's Valley? We did not feel it had come to that. Where would we go? Tubal? They have already abandoned us to Mother Earth, and their new king is hostile to our Creator. On the other hand, we have many faithful relatives there who would take us in. Tubal may have to be our place of refuge, if things here become intolerable. But Enoch's Valley has strong natural defenses in the Hiddekel River, and in the thorns and beasts of the Doubtful Mountains. We think the only way our enemy could attack is from the river, and we still have time to strengthen our shore defenses."

"In short, we have decided to fight. We shall see how Shahoot's new council responds. If they resist building defenses now, we can be sure that they are actually traitors working secretly for Mother Earth. That, of course, would precipitate an immediate civil war. In that case, your Uncle Krulak plans to take vigorous measures to drive the traitors back and establish a defensible position. That, Japheth, is the big picture you requested. And now my own mouth is dry! Noah, would you please tell your son how he and his brothers fit in with our strategy?"

"Certainly, Father. Japheth, our family has two immediate tasks. The first is to secure our assets, and the second is to prepare defenses. With all the violence on the Hiddekel, our construction business has already been drawing down. We will draw it down further, and transfer our financial assets to Tubal or elsewhere: it must be kept from the hands of looters like Shahoot. Your uncles will take on the work of strengthening the walls and port facilities of Jared's Mill, but we have been tasked to strengthen our own plantation as a fallback position. For a few weeks, I must remain here in town to arrange things. I would like you and your brothers to return to the plantation and think of ways to strengthen our defenses."

"That will be fun, Father!" I said, already thinking of some ideas. "And from now on I will try to concentrate on my duties, and let the elders do theirs. I will not fret, but work, and leave the results in the Maker's hands. Is that what you mean?"

"Exactly!" All three spoke together.

"You listened, Japheth!" the patriarch added approvingly. "None of us is personally responsible for the entire world, but only for our very small part of it. In that area, however, we should do all we can do, with what we have, where we are[2]."

Somehow, I felt better after this discussion, although my circumstances were still the same. I would not be able to attend school in Tubal, and our homeland was just as likely to face a civil war or an invasion. But at least now I knew where I stood, and what I had to do. It was not my job to worry about my homeland's success or failure: others had that responsibility. My own job was to do all I could, with what I had, where I was. And right now, our family's mission was to secure assets and prepare defenses.

When we returned to the plantation, my brothers and I made a careful inspection of the stronghold. Much had changed in the centuries since the patriarch Enoch had first cleared land on the edge of the plateau.

In the beginning, he had surrounded his home and livestock yard with a rough wooden fence. Before long, however, he discovered that giant carnivorous behemoths ranged throughout the area, so he decided to rebuild the simple livestock fence into a tall stockade of sharpened timbers. Some years later, when plundering bands of Cainites came into the area, he further reinforced the timber stockade with rock.

By the time we were born, our stronghold had a thick wall of granite more than twenty-five cubits high, tall enough to look down on a death-behemoth, something that actually happened more than once. A parapet at the top of the wall had cutouts to protect those shooting arrows or throwing rocks, while our protected walkway[3] ran completely around the stronghold. The walkway was wide enough for all three of us to walk abreast, and we often raced around it, though a more leisurely walk provided restful views of our plantation and the entire Hiddekel River valley. Turrets on the wall had loopholes, as well as vents in the floors, suitable for pouring boiling water over the attackers.

The top two stories of the stronghold had openings to provide light and fresh air, but the casements were barred, with strong shutters. Finally, a lofty central tower had been built on the cliff side of the stronghold, with an observation deck that commanded the entire plantation. Spacious apartments, kitchens, shops, and storage rooms had been built along the interior wall of the stronghold, housing both our family and the fifty or so members of our plantation staff. If necessary, many times that number could be comfortably housed within the walls.

The original livestock yard of the stronghold had been turned into a lovely courtyard, with shade trees, fountains, and gardens, but it could easily be converted into additional housing, or again shelter livestock. A natural spring bubbled up in the middle of the courtyard, providing delicious drinking water, but we had plenty of running water for washing and bathing from the old stone aqueduct, which brought water from a clear mountain stream. Unused water poured out over the cliff to form a picturesque waterfall that dropped hundreds of cubits to the Hiddekel.

As children, we had often playfully considered building a drawbridge, as well as digging a deep fosse, or moat, to defend against ladders being raised. These were not bad ideas. We could block up the second gate with timbers, we thought, and reinforce it with packed earth to defend against battering rams. Cutting down trees and bushes would provide a clear view of the approaching enemy. Unfortunately, one big obstacle could not be easily removed: father's prized barn. Fully three hundred cubits in length and several stories tall, it was made of solid gopherwood. The great structure housed milking stalls, a cheese kitchen, great storage lofts, and a parade ring for horses, elephants, or cattle. Its walls were too open to be defended, so we decided to build an observation platform on top, but abandon it in case of serious attack.

When father returned home a few days later, he brought Uncle Krulak with him, and we presented our ideas. They liked them all, and commissioned us to get started right away. The loyal members of our patriarchal clan had come together in this emergency, and they told us we would have plenty of help.

The very next week we began to dig the fosse, and before long we were cutting trees, blocking up the second gate, and working on the other projects. All of it required physical labor. Father brought in a crew of trained construction workers from his building firm, but our primary laborers were our relatives. The work was strenuous, and the days were long; but the men drove up wagons of supplies, the women brought in food and drink, and we found great camaraderie among our cousins. We labored steadily, and had a lot of laughing and joking. We took breaks as needed, and slept well at night.

Shem was put in charge of labor, and he showed a real knack for leadership. Cheery working songs rang out everywhere, even from the trenches, where the digging required a backbreaking effort. Animal strength was needed, too, and Ham skillfully handled the elephants and aurochs hauling the heavy rocks and timbers. As an experiment, he tried using a giant sloth and a glyptodon[4], but they proved more entertaining than productive.

Father gave me the job of designing the drawbridge, with its hoist, pulleys, and counterweight system. Uncle Nebach cast the gears right away, and the entire project was completed surprisingly quickly. We had a special party to celebrate, and everyone had a chance to raise and lower it. After completing the drawbridge, it occurred to me that the hydraulic conveyor I had made for the barn could also be used to transport dirt. With the help of Ham's elephants, we moved it from the barn to the wall of the stronghold, where the water from the aqueduct provided power. The conveyer could be spun around an axis to direct the flow, and we soon had a stream of dirt pouring out of the trench to create an escarpment[5] around the moat. I might not be able to attend the famed School of

Tubal-Cain, but it pleased me that I was designing and building machines anyway!

Weeks raced by. Food and forage were brought in, heavy stones were carried to the top of the wall, and large numbers of javelins and arrows were made and stored. Uncle Krulak organized a unit of militia from our plantation staff, and gave us training in basic military maneuvers. My brothers and I practiced with sword, bow, and spear every day.

We felt a crisis would come soon. Practically every week, Shahoot's revolutionary council passed new taxes and intrusive new laws; they continually attempted to confiscate property. Grandpa Lamech and the patriarchal elders, though in the minority, stood firmly together, and stopped the worst of their actions. Hostilities grew between the patriarchal believers and those we called "looters." Many patriarchal families had to close their businesses on the south shore of Jared's river, where the looters dominated. Valley Vigilance, which patrolled the south bank, received no support from the revolutionary council, and the patrols were sometimes showered with rocks. This, of course, led to fewer patrols on the south bank, more crime, and diminishing business. With jobs disappearing, the newcomers living in these areas became desperate. That polarized Enoch's Valley even more. Civil war approached.

One day I turned around in the marketplace, and found myself face to face with Aziza. She had not left town, after all! She looked as beautiful as ever, and her green dress accentuated her curves in a breathtaking way. Watching my eyes, she jiggled her body, and smiled at my reaction. I had often reflected on the questions I would ask if I ever saw her; but now I found it hard to think.

"I heard that you visited my home that night, Japheth," she began, speaking carefully. "But I never sent you a note. I would never have asked you to see me, especially knowing what my father had to do. Actually, I was surprised that your patriarchs even allowed you to visit me. They must feel terribly guilty about the horrible things they do to our people."

What was she talking about? Her father had made accusations like that, but Aziza could not possibly believe them: she had known us for years! Was she that deceived? If so, could we salvage anything from our relationship?

"Look, Aziza," I said. "I am sorry that our families are at odds, but must we share in the quarrel? Yes, my brothers and I beat your brother's team in the race, and we caught his gang in the very act of mudding innocent Tubalites. I am sorry, but those things were not our fault. And you know how good the patriarchs have always been to the newcomers, giving them jobs and all kinds of help! Your father is wrong to tell such lies, and to try to loot us. Can't you see that?"

Aziza's tiger stripes reappeared almost instantly.

"And are you sorry for humiliating my brother in front of the prince, Japheth, or for betraying him to Valley Vigilance? Do you think treating newcomers like dirt does them any good? I really am leaving soon, Japheth, and your whole stinking patriarchal society is going to be wiped out. You could have done something with your life, Japheth! You could have been somebody big, if you had only listened to me! But you refused. Just remember, if we ever meet again, that I told you so!"

"Aziza, let's not hold grudges," I said. "Perhaps when we meet next time, it will be under better circumstances! But where are you going, anyway?"

"What?" she asked suspiciously. "Where do you think I am going?" Her stripes began to fade.

"Isn't your family from Nephil?" I asked. "Are you going there?"

"Yes," she said after a moment, faintly smiling. "I am going to Nephil. If we ever meet again, it will be in Nephil. But you will not be happy to see me, Japheth. You will be very sorry, and filled with regrets. If only you had been wise enough to follow my instructions during the race! If only you had done as I said, and kept your nose out of a little harmless vandalism!"

Her tiger stripes soon disappeared entirely, leaving only perfect beauty. Shaking her head regretfully, she reached out to touch my cheek. "Just imagine what might have been, Japheth!"

It was sad that such a beautiful girl had been so deceived. At some deeper level, she had to realize that her one hope for happiness was to find someone like me, and run away from her family. Even today, she probably wished to say that she would always have wistful regrets about me, imagining how happy her life might have been.

I took a deep breath, and shook my head. Her charms were certainly powerful! Still, I was responsible for the choices I made. I was no animal! Great Aunt Naomi had spoken about my descendants. Should I continue to daydream about winning the affections of this sleek beauty? Would she be the happy match that would bless my entire family, or should I wait for another?

[1]*Editor's Note:* Lamech's conclusion reminds me of Dr. Charles Stanley, the noted American Bible teacher, who often said: "Obey God, and leave all the results to him." Wisdom seems to have recurring themes in all of human history.

[2]*Editor's Note:* This appears much like a statement attributed to Theodore Roosevelt during the Spanish American war.

[3]*Editor's Note:* Battlements, crenellated parapets with protected walkways or platforms for defenders, have been used for thousands of years, and are even pictured in bas reliefs in the ruins of Nimrud, ancient Greece, and Egypt. The stronghold described here, although ancient, is somewhat reminiscent of a medieval castle, built against a similar enemy.

[4]*Editor's Note:* The animals named in the text seem to suggest two extinct mammals. The giant sloth, or Megatherium, was an elephant-sized mammal, while the glyptodon was a huge relative of the armadillo, with tessellated scales and fluted teeth.

[5]*Editor's Note:* While an escarpment can be a natural cliff-like formation separating two plateaus, it can also be a steep slope in front of a fortification that attackers must climb while exposed to the fire of the defenders.

Chapter Sixteen: A Way of Escape

Although we felt safe on the plateau, the troubles in Jared's Mill kept getting worse. Vandalism and violence occurred almost every day, and the rift between the patriarchal families and the looters grew openly hostile. Civil troubles cropped up in other cities along the Hiddekel as well, and business in the entire region began to slow. Imported goods became expensive, and our marketplace gradually became deserted. When vandalism against Tubalites was no longer prosecuted, many of them left, but they were more than replaced by a new influx of refugees. Many of the new ones were patriarchal believers fleeing persecution. Our family in town helped as much as they could, but the sheer number of refugees was overwhelming.

Meanwhile on the plantation, we continued to work long hours building defenses. Early one morning, father came to breakfast with an announcement.

"Boys," he said, "your mother and I have invited the patriarch to stay with us. His health has gotten fragile, and we think the fresh breezes up here might help. Also, the elders in town worry he is a target. They believe our plantation would be safer." Father suddenly looked old. "Grandpa Lamech said things are feeling just like they did before the last war, and I agree with him." He lapsed into silence.

"The patriarch will not be coming alone," mother continued cheerily. "His sisters, your great-great aunts Libusha and Haddassa, are coming, too, as well as his youngest daughter, Auntie Zora. The three of them had a narrow escape from Havilah, where believers are being savagely persecuted, as we have heard. They just arrived this week. Aunties Libusha and Haddassa have long been widowed, and they thought this might be a good opportunity to revisit their childhood home."

We were happy to hear of their visit. Our constant labor was getting boring. Fresh company would liven things up, and add stories, games, and laughter. The family always seemed more complete with another generation or two, anyway. We already knew and loved Auntie Zora as the classic maiden aunt. She had a wry sense of humor, and many colorful anecdotes from the faraway lands she had visited. She had always talked to us as adults, even when we were little, and she never failed to have curious toys or exotic souvenirs to share with us. We had not met the great-great aunties, because they had lived so far away; but we had heard stories about them from the patriarch, and were eager to meet them.

"Terrific!" we exclaimed. "Shall we get them today?"

"The sooner, the better," father said. "You will need to take our large carriage and a wagon, for the patriarch is bringing his valet Abidan, and your aunties have servants, as well. There will be quite a bit of luggage."

"We shall open up the cliffside wing," mother said happily. "The patriarch has always loved the view, and I think it will suit him best. I will have Anah and Zibiah clean out the rooms and put in fresh linens. But that reminds me. Boys, be sure to bring the patriarch's favorite swinging chair[1]. We can put it on the back verandah, where he will have a lovely view of the Hiddekel."

It was fun to meet our great-great aunties, who were very perky and talkative. Except for being female, they looked remarkably like the patriarch himself. The aunties were in high spirits: this was their first visit to their childhood home in centuries, since well before our father had inherited it. As we drove through the swamp and onto the plateau, they reminisced about the once-familiar sights, and Auntie Zora related her experiences while touring through Havilah. She was a marvelous storyteller, and the trip passed quickly.

"Havilah is an incredibly wealthy land!" she said, her eyes sparkling with excitement. "The rocks are marbled with onyx, bdellium, and every kind of gemstone. Rubies, emeralds, sapphires, and diamonds are mined in large quantities for export[2], and gold is so common that it has surprisingly little value. One day I found a heavy nugget the size of my fist, and my host laughed. 'Keep it,' he said. 'Iron is more precious here!' Boys, silver is so abundant they use it to make pipes to conduct water! Oh, it is a rich land, a land for young men to make their fortune! Someday, when the troubles subside, you must see it! Let me show you something from Havilah that has an unusual property." Taking out a polished black disk, she held it in the sunlight to give us a good look.

"What does it do, Auntie?" I asked.

"If you have an iron or steel blade, I will show you!"

Shem offered her his bush knife. She held the disk a thumb width away from the blade, and let go. We gasped in surprise as the disk flew out of her hand and snapped onto the blade, making a loud clang.

"Now," she said, smiling at our astonished faces, "try to pull it off."

Shem and I both tried, but the disk seemed glued in place. Finally, we slid the mineral along to the edge of the blade, and using another knife blade, pried it off, barely keeping it from sticking to the second knife. We handed it back carefully.

"Fascinating, is it not?" Auntie Zora asked. "I have no idea if it has any practical use, but perhaps you boys, as smart as you are, can think of one."

"Hmm," I said. "A mineral that is violently attracted to iron[3]? There must be some use for it!"

The patriarch and his party were quickly at home on the plantation. They entertained us for hours with exciting stories from the days when their father Enoch carved the plantation out of the wilderness, and fought off ferocious behemoths and savage Cainites. Even father had never heard many of their tales.

A few weeks later, we met after breakfast to discuss our progress.

"Boys," father said, "I think I have secured our assets as well as I can. I have sold our inventory, and sent our gold and silver to Tubal. All our construction projects have either been completed or contracted out, and I have no plans to take on new ones until things here are settled, one way or another. Our elders have done everything to encourage the new council to build defenses, but it has refused their suggestions. Thankfully, you boys have strengthened our walls up here on the plateau, built a moat and a drawbridge, and have otherwise prepared our stronghold. It is now the most secure position we have in Enoch's Valley."

"But considering everything, I am afraid we must do one more thing. Krulak thinks that if Mother Earth does invade, our weak defenses will make the conquest of Jared's Mill easy, especially if the looters prove as traitorous as we think. Unfortunately, once the town was taken, the rest of Enoch's Valley would soon be gobbled up. By falling back to the plateau, we could resist for a while; but unless we have strong military help from Tubal, which we cannot expect, it would ultimately be futile. We must have a way of escape. Neither Krulak nor I can think of a good way to do that, but perhaps you boys can come up with something."

We had a new project! That morning, we poked around our plantation, checking our defenses. We tried to imagine how we might escape, if the enemy came up through the swamp to attack.

"It seems to me," I said, "That from our stronghold, we really have only two choices. One is to escape by way of the river. If we could climb down the cliff, and had rafts, we could float downstream to Tubal on a dark night. The other choice is to hike over the Doubtful Mountains. But could our party even survive the wilderness?"

"Very doubtful," Ham sighed.

"So the river," Shem said, "is really our only way of escape. But how can we safely climb down the cliff? It is at least three hundred cubits!"

We peered over the edge. In all our years of exploring, we had never found a path down: it was a sheer drop. Ham threw a stone, and we watched it fall a long time before it struck the rocky shore.

What could we do? Lowering a basket would be cumbersome and dangerous, while sliding down a rope, or climbing down a rope ladder, would be too difficult for women or older folks. Floating down on a big parasol was a silly thought, and constructing a long wooden walkway was not really practical. Days passed as we pondered the problem. The probability of either invasion or civil war crept closer, but we could not think of any good way to escape. Our frustration finally came out one day when we were having lunch with our great-great aunties.

"But my dear nephews," Auntie Libusha exclaimed. "Why don't you use the secret passageway? Haddassa and I often played in it as girls, though father thought it dangerous. Isn't that right, Haddassa?"

"Of course," our auntie agreed. "Father made us promise to keep it a secret. After all, what good is a secret passageway if others know about it?"

The sisters winked at each other, and laughed. It was delightful to see them take such pleasure in each other's company after nearly eight hundred years[4]. But we had never heard of any secret passageway!

"Surely," Auntie Libusha asked incredulously, "you must know of it! I thought you had lived here your whole lives! Such secrets are the very stuff of little boys—I mean, sturdy young men!"

"Show us!" we cried out together.

Lunch was immediately concluded. Our aunties guided us over to the main tower, where they stopped at the foot of the large stone staircase. Auntie Libusha reached out her bony hand, and began feeling over the rough surface of the wall.

"It was right around here, I think, but this wall has been plastered over. Yes, it was right here, I am sure of it! We would press on a small stone to release the latch. Then, by pushing hard here, the wall would slide back to reveal the secret chamber. I am afraid, boys, that you will have to scrape off all that plaster to find it. But once you open the door to the chamber, you will find the secret passageway. It leads all the way down to the river!"

We looked at each other with wide eyes, and ran out for tools. Within an hour we had found the special stone, but it took another hour of careful scraping to free it up. Finally, we heard the latch click; but the wall still stubbornly resisted our efforts. We returned to scraping. Suddenly, we heard a screech. The wall moved, and a thick cloud of fine dust billowed out. Coughing, we ran out for fresh air.

When we returned, we tied cloths over our noses and mouths, and cautiously descended the short staircase. As we went, we swept the stairs and removed cobwebs. At the bottom was a large chamber illuminated by dusty sunbeams that streamed in from small openings in the wall. Another cloud of dust erupted as we stepped onto the floor. When it subsided, we saw shelves along the walls, holding earthenware jars, blankets, and bundles of arrows. One shelf was stacked with inscribed sheets of copper foil, which we assumed were receipts or other business records. Furniture in the chamber consisted of a small table with a stack of blank copper sheets and scribing instruments, as well as an oil lamp and two chairs. Several heavy chests stood in the corner. Behind us, we heard Auntie Libusha cough. She and her sister had followed us in.

"Look at this, Haddassa," she said, waving away dust. "I wonder if anyone has even entered this room since we left home! The grain in this jar is as hard as rock: I would hate to try to make bread from that! And the water jars are dry."

Auntie Haddassa walked to the shelf and picked up a copper sheet. It was green with corrosion, but the inscriptions were still legible.

"This document dates from 977, Libusha[5]! That was the year father walked home with God! By then, of course, both you and I were married, and Methuselah had his own plantation farther down in the valley. I remember now. Grandpa Jared moved into the plantation while they were searching for father. He may not have known about this secret chamber to enter it. If not, it has been sealed for more than five hundred years!"

Auntie Libusha walked to the far wall of the chamber, where a wide opening was chiseled in the rock. "Here, boys! This is what you are looking for." We raced over to see. A solid wood door with bronze straps was set in a casement, and heavily barred.

She raised her hand to caution us. "Let me suggest that before you open it, we sweep and mop this room. A draft may blow when you open the door, and the dust could choke you!"

An hour or two later, after we finished cleaning, we brought our parents, aunties, and the patriarch into the chamber. As they looked on, we raised the heavy bar. When the door did not budge, we put crowbars into the casement. After a few heaves, the door slowly creaked open. Cold, musty air began to blow in, bringing more dust. With cloths to our faces, we felt the rush of air gradually become steady, and much warmer.

Holding up a lamp, we looked down the steeply descending tunnel. Broad steps had been chiseled on one side of the tunnel, while on the other side there was a smooth ramp with a clay surface. A nearby stack of dry leather mats and wooden tubs suggested the method by which goods had been brought down to the river. We cautiously descended a few steps, and saw that the tunnel was dimly lit from a series of holes chiseled into the cliff wall. Laughter erupted above us. We hastily retraced our steps. The patriarch had stepped down, and was nearly jumping with glee.

"I completely forgot about this tunnel! My brothers and I used to spend days sliding down on these skins! When you wet the clay, boys, you can pick up quite a bit of speed! The mined part of this passageway leads in another fifty cubits or so to the natural cave. After that, the track gets rough, but it winds all the way down to the river, where it spits you right out into the water. You boys are going to love this!"

When we returned to the chamber, we saw that our mother, hearing the patriarch's glee, had a very doubtful expression. The patriarch sobered.

"Of course, boys," he said, "you must use the stairs first, to familiarize yourself with the passageway; and it must be completely cleaned out. Who knows what bugs, bats, or other creatures may be living in the caves by now? You should wear helmets and heavy protective footwear, of course, and have your parents' permission!"

"Perhaps I should explain the history," Auntie Haddassa said, smiling at her brother's discomfiture. "A family of aquatic behemoths were terrorizing some nearby settlements, so father joined a party to hunt them down. They discovered that the behemoths were nesting in a large cavern along the cliffs of the Hiddekel—actually right beneath us. After the beasts were routed, father explored the cavern and found that one passageway led all the way to the top, though it got very narrow. Later, when the plantation became productive, father had the narrow sections tunneled out, and put a small boat slip at the bottom to ship out his goods. Unfortunately, it was exhausting to carry cargo up to the top using the stairs: it was easier to have an ox pull the wagon back and forth from Jared's Mill. Thinking it might someday be useful in case of Cainite attack, father disguised the shore entrance to the cavern, and turned the tunnel into a secret passageway."

"Amazing!" father exclaimed. "When I inherited this plantation from the patriarch Jared a century and a half ago, I never dreamed this was here! Boys, would you like to fix this secret passageway up?"

"Yes, sir!" we said. "Leave it to us!"

Two weeks later, our family gathered at the staircase of the tower. Instead of plaster, the wall was now trimmed stones and heavy wooden beams, exactly like the rest of the tower.

"Auntie Zora gave me this mineral disk when she came," I said. "We have found an interesting use for it." Holding the black disk up to a wooden beam, I let it go. While a few gasped in surprise, the disk flew out of my hand and snapped onto the beam. There was a loud click, and a three-cubit section of wall swung noiselessly inward. Shem, Ham, and I took a bow while everyone applauded.

"Thank you!" I said modestly. "After Aunties Libusha and Haddassa showed us the secret door, we took Auntie Zora's disk and built a spring-loaded magnetic lock. Uncle Nebach helped me design it, and Shem, Ham, and I built it. It has a steel lever in the wooden beam that the disk attracts and moves, unlocking the mechanism. If you will come inside, you will see how easily it can be opened and locked from the inside, too. Shem will explain what else we have done."

"As you can see," Shem continued, as our party entered, "we have brought down fresh food and water, and have stocked the chamber with everything we may need for a quick escape. The staircase has been cleaned, and the ramp has been given a fresh layer of clay. Ham quietly brought up rafts and boats from Jared's Mill, and stowed them just inside the cavern for an easy exit to the river. The entrance is well hidden with bushes. Once out, we can paddle or drift down to safety in Tubal."

After we had finished demonstrating the secret chamber and tunnel, everyone in the chamber joined hands. Father offered a dedication prayer.

"It is our prayer, Sovereign Creator, that a peaceful resolution may be found to the wicked demands of Mother Earth, and with the treasonous people who are attempting to loot us. But if not, we are grateful that you have given us time and resources to prepare these defenses, and have even provided a way of escape. We remember your promises to bless our descendants long into the future, and cling to them. We do not presume to know the outcome of this particular conflict, but our eyes are on you."

When father finished, we knew that we had done all we could to prepare for either civil war or foreign invasion. All that was left was to watch and wait.

---

[1]*Editor's Note:* As someone who appreciates La-Z-Boy recliners, I find it interesting that luxuries such as rocking chairs were also known in this ancient but civilized culture.

[2]*Editor's Note:* The Bible also mentions Havilah in Genesis 2 as a rich land of gold and minerals.

[3]*Editor's Note:* This mineral may have been magnetite, a naturally occurring iron oxide in the spinel group of minerals.

[4]*Editor's Note:* Though I have noted this before, modern readers may find the life spans indicated here almost unbelievable. Is it possible that people, as the Bible indicates, previously had life spans of nearly a thousand years?

[5]*Editor's Note:* The year 977 is apparently from Creation, or Anno Mundi (AM), as Bishop Ussher put it.

Chapter Seventeen: Invaded

Two months passed without civil war or foreign invasion. An uneasy truce seemed to form between the patriarchal party and the looters, and the marketplace became a little busier.

Once or twice I saw Sandal, and wondered about Aziza. Was she enjoying Nephil? Had she had found another foolish boy to tease? She came to mind almost every day, making me feel guilt that she still had such control over me. Why wasn't I stronger and tougher than that? Aziza might be alluring and desirable, but would she be a steady, faithful wife? Would she respect my family, and raise godly children with loving discipline? One Sabbath afternoon I retreated to my quiet corner in Grandpa Lamech's courtyard to think. Suddenly, I felt someone pat my knee. Startled, I looked up. Great Aunt Naomi sat beside me, smiling.

"Sorry to disturb your thoughts, Japheth!" she said. "I had promised to keep an eye on you, but with all this trouble, it has been months since we talked. Tell me: are you still fond of that foreign girl, or have you found someone else?"

I hemmed about, but finally answered that the girl had returned to Nephil. Since then, I had found no one else that tempted me as much.

"Tempted! Like Adam was tempted? That is an odd word to use, Japheth! I sense you feel some guilt about her. Should you? Is temptation a sin?"

"Well, I suppose not, Auntie."

"Temptation is not a sin, Japheth. Falling into fornication is, of course. It spoils something, even if you escape disease or death, and it is an unwise choice. Thankfully, many who fall into it are able to make amends, cleanse their conscience, and return to build a happy, godly life. No one is without sin, as your father says: we all must deal with it. But illicit pleasure is hard to resist after once giving in. It often becomes a habit, one that leads to shame, poverty, slavery, and even death. And trust me on this: it is a major hindrance to finding a happy match. Japheth, let me ask something: did you kiss that girl on the lips? Sorry to be old-fashioned, but it is a significant thing, and it can easily lead to fornication."

I gasped: Auntie Naomi was certainly blunt! In a way, her talk was just as earthy as Uncle Zibach discussing cattle breeding.

"No, Auntie," I said humbly. "Something always held me back. Maybe I knew that she was only playing with me, or maybe our Maker just protected me! Do you think I am still okay for a good match?"

"Yes, Japheth," she said, smiling. "You are still okay. I am relieved that your conscience is clear, but you must in the future guard your affections, and not let yourself become infatuated[1] with a pretty face and figure. The devil would love to cheat you. Wait for the right match."

"Auntie, can I ask you a question—strictly hypothetical?" I was not quite sure I should, but I asked anyway. "What if the girl were a Cainite?"

"Oh, my!" she replied, her eyes wide. "What a question! Let me think about that. Would this hypothetical Cainite girl walk with our Creator? Would she view the world as we do? I suppose such a match might work; but as far as I know, no one in our family has ever married one. I imagine that a Cainite girl could be very seductive and passionate, but Cainites are not known for gentleness or selfless love. Instead, they are known for implacable hatred, cruelty and barbarism. They are a race of human tigers, Japheth. I would be very cautious!"

In retrospect, it was a relief to talk with Auntie Naomi, for it helped me see things more clearly. Though I might have been infatuated with her, I had not really become entangled, which was a good thing. If she really were part Cainite, she might well be using me for some selfish purpose.

I decided that my head should rule my heart. Marriage is at least partly a matter of business, after all. It is best if you like the girl you marry; but true love is more what you do than what you feel; and feelings of love grow with time. Those thoughts comforted me. Marriage was not just about me, after all; it was about our whole family, and generations to come. As the weeks passed, I had fewer pangs about Aziza, and turned my attention to other things. If conditions in town continued to muddle along, I thought, I might write to the School of Tubal-Cain, and ask about a seat in their next class.

Early one morning my brothers and I were riding elephants as we led a caravan of wagons loaded with produce along the road into town. When we emerged from the swamp onto the bluff that overlooked Enoch's Valley, we rested our mounts. Exhaling the thick, dank air of the swamp, we took in deep drafts of the fresh breeze from the river, and gazed at the beautiful panorama spread out before us. Broad, rolling pastures covered the slopes, which were dotted with dairy cattle and sheep. Along the floor of the valley, the wide fields of oats, corn, amaranth, and barley were interspersed with carefully pruned vineyards, orchards, and lush vegetable gardens. At our right shoulder were the tall mountains and peaks of the Doubtful Range, while to the left along the Hiddekel lay the town of Jared's Mill. It was a peaceful, soul-refreshing sight--at least for a moment.

"Alas, Eden!" Ham exclaimed. "That looks like smoke!"

It was common during the workweek to see a light haze from the fumes of cooking stoves and baking ovens, or to see thin dark plumes from the blacksmith shops. But this was heavy black smoke, and it billowed up over a big section of the town near the back gate.

"Look at the road, guys!" Shem cried out, pointing below us. "People are coming this way!"

I looked. Hundreds of people had left the city from the gate nearest us, and they were heading in our direction. Some pulled small carts, but most were on foot, and the predominant color of their clothing was orange. I wanted to think they were fleeing an accidental fire; but invasion had been on our minds for months.

"We have to help them, Japheth," Shem urged. "They are fleeing for their lives."

I waved for Kedar, our plantation foreman. He and a dozen farmhands had accompanied the four big horse wagons filled with corn, squash, other vegetables, and grain. He galloped up.

"Kedar," I said, "we have trouble. Jared's Mill is on fire, and people are fleeing the city in our direction. I think we need to unload our wagons, and help bring them to safety. They may be pursued."

He instantly grasped the situation, and turned back to get his men started. My brothers and I urged our elephants down the hill, and finally got to the closest group. It consisted mainly of women and children, though there were a few old men. Some of the people were wounded, while many of the women had torn their clothes in grief, and wept. As we climbed down from our mounts, I heard my name, and saw Bezer running up to us.

"Mother Earth invaded, Japheth!" Bezer said. "Father stayed behind to fight. He told me to bring my mother and sisters to your plantation, but I want to go back and help him fight!"

Bezer's mother stepped up to put her arm around her son.

"Has the town been completely taken?" I asked her.

"We don't know, Japheth," she answered. "The enemy came in the west gate and marched straight to the Tubalite district, where they immediately began the slaughter[2]. We heard no alarm, but a friend came to warn us. Bashak told us to flee to your father's plantation, but said he had to join Valley Vigilance. He promised to give us as much time as he could. We grabbed an armful of valuables and ran out the north gate." She put her face in her hands and sobbed. "Oh, Japheth! We will never see him again!"

A short time later, Kedar and his men clattered down the slopes with the empty wagons. While most of the fugitives could still walk, many of the frail or injured ones had reached their limit. We loaded as many as possible into the wagons, and Kedar led them back up the slope. Our farmhands grabbed spears and formed a rearguard, while we hastened the stragglers along. Our progress was quick and orderly. It took a while to retrace our steps, but our big party finally crested the hill and began to enter the dense jungle. I looked back. Fumes were now pouring from a wide area of the town. The great mill, the landmark of the town, was on fire, with tall red and orange flames flickering through the billowing smoke.

"Japheth," Ham called, "about a hundred horsemen just galloped out of the north gate. Do you think they mean to pursue the fugitives?"

Shem and I looked carefully. A half dozen people had just run out the gate. Horsemen peeled off from the main party and struck them down.

"I am afraid so," Shem said.

Looking up, I offered a quick prayer. "Lord God! Help us!"

Kedar, our grizzled old foreman, heard me.

"Remember the words of Methuselah, young master," he said. "Courage is not what you feel. Courage is what you do."

"Thanks, Kedar," I replied. "I needed that." I glanced at the dense woods behind us. "We have to stop those horsemen. I have an idea that just might work, if we have enough time."

In just a few minutes, the rear guard of our party entered the jungle. The leading edge had already passed the bridge onto the narrow causeway winding through the most dangerous part of the swamp. As soon as our rearguard got to the bridge, my brothers and I, along with Kedar and his men, took axes and weapons from the wagons, and sent them on ahead with the women and children. I had already put Bezer on a fast horse to warn the plantation.

"Men," I said, "we are all familiar with the dangers of the swamp, and know that this bridge is the only way through. If we can stop the enemy here, or even slow them for an hour or two, it may give these Tubalites a chance to reach safety. Are you with me?"

Their response was a hearty cheer. All of us had been anxious for months about invasion. Now, after seeing our town on fire, and hearing tales of slaughter from the refugees, we were eager to fight. Taking axes, we began cutting down trees. Ham used the elephants to haul the trees onto the road, and we made a blockade. Some men sharpened stakes and dug them into the road, while others cut brush to use for cover. When we finished the first blockade, Ham took the elephants further up the causeway to begin another barricade for a fall back. The rest of us selected places and waited.

"The way I see it," I said, "we have our bows ready, but stay out of sight. When they stop at our line of stakes, we fire, and keep shooting as long as we dare. When we have to, we retreat to the next blockade and take another stand. If they still keep coming, we separate in the woods, and pick off as many as we can."

"God steady our aim!" Shem prayed, "and give us strength to fight like men! Honor and courage, friends!"

"And may our Maker bring bloody vengeance on the head of these wicked men," Kedar added grimly.

Shortly after Ham and his men returned, we heard horses gallop into the jungle. The horsemen slowed a little to adjust their eyes to the deep shade of the forest, but they were not expecting any resistance, and rode confidently. Their mission, after all, was to slaughter defenseless women and children. As they approached, we notched our arrows.

Still galloping, they turned the bend approaching the bridge. Suddenly, the commander saw the sharpened stakes, and cried, "Halt!" He was too late. His own horse, along with two others, rode directly into the stakes. Those behind them stopped so suddenly that their riders were thrown over their heads. Others that pressed closely collided with the fallen horses and tumbled over. With the surrounding woods so dense, there was no place for the horsemen to spread out: the column came to a confused halt directly in front of our barricade.

"Now!" I shouted. Hidden behind the trees of the barricade, we fired volley after volley. It was hard to miss at that range, and we killed at least twenty before the rest even realized they were under attack. Wheeling about in terror, they hastily retreated, but we kept firing as long as we had targets.

A short time later, we heard the breaking of branches beside the road: men were creeping up through the underbrush. This was not surprising: these were seasoned soldiers, and not men to give up easily. They approached as close as they dared. We heard a command, and the soldiers rose from their cover to shoot at a high trajectory. They apparently thought that their arrows would come down upon us. They paid a price for the attempt. The dense canopy of the jungle simply absorbed their arrows, and we had a good view of the archers. We shot another half dozen.

"Only about thirty men attacked us," I whispered to Shem. "Where are the others?"

The remaining archers dropped to the ground after their failed attack. They resumed their advance, carefully taking advantage of every bit of cover. We fired at every opportunity, but the soldiers kept getting closer. I got ready to call for a retreat.

Shrieks erupted from the swamp around us, and long, horrible screams. Splashing sounds and the bellow of horses was mixed with deep reptilian gurgles and trills. I suddenly realized what had happened, and shuddered. The enemy had attempted to outflank us. Not knowing that the murky waters of the swamp harbored a vast number and variety of savage predators, they had waded their horses through the waist-deep water. While some of the deadly creatures were small, others were huge, including giant crocodiles, giant snakes, and meat-eating behemoths. To them, the horses were soft, chewy treats, while their riders were tender, succulent prey. The sound and vibration of forty or fifty humans and their horses was all the invitation they needed. Once the frenzy began, hungry monsters poured in from every part of the swamp.

There was nothing we could do. We put our hands to our ears, but the awful screams and shrieks went on and on, and were echoed in the trees. It took a long time for their cries to subside. When they did, they were replaced by something equally horrifying: the crunching and slopping sounds of eating.

The enemy archers stood transfixed in horror: this was no way for men to die. Kedar nudged me. Our battle was not yet over. Aiming carefully, we shot again. The survivors, seeing and hearing nothing but nightmarish death, lost heart. Dropping their weapons, they ran down the trail screaming in terror.

We stood to cheer, and thanked our Maker for the victory! Out of a hundred enemy soldiers that entered the swamp, less than a dozen escaped, while only three of our men had been injured.

Kedar turned to me. "Japheth, let my men see what we have done." He paused. "It might be better for you and your brothers to stay here." I was feeling queasy, and nodded in agreement.

A short time later, Kedar returned. His men were laden with weapons and valuables.

"We counted thirty seven bodies, Japheth," he said. "I took this from their leader."

He handed me a green helmet, a leather purse, and a heavy gold chain. The symbol on the helmet was the oak tree of Mother Earth. I held up the chain, which had a large emerald pendant.

"Were any still alive, Kedar?" I asked.

He did not answer right away. "Young master, many of my young men are from Tubal, and all have relatives in town. I think we should go. The jackals and hyenas are coming, and the ants are already at work."

I had never killed anyone before, but now I could smell blood. I turned away and was sick.

---

[1]*Editor's Note:* The translator said this was the same root word as the magnetic mineral in the previous chapter, combined with sickness, to make an "unhealthy/sick attraction." I thought that infatuation, which the Merriam-Webster dictionary defines as a foolish or extravagant love or admiration, might be the right word here. Several other words and concepts similarly required a little imagination to bring into the 21st Century.

[2]*Editor's Note:* Massacre, "the indiscriminate and brutal slaughter of people" (Oxford English Dictionary) has apparently been an ugly part of man's story since the beginning. The Bible describes several incidents of wholesale slaughter as part of warfare. Infamous massacres in the modern era include the St. Bartholomew's Day massacre of Huguenots (1572), the Adana Massacre of Armenians (1909), and the Nanking Massacre by the Imperial Japanese (1937-1938).

Chapter Eighteen: Hostages

We were halfway home when we saw a band of horsemen approaching at full speed on the plantation road. They saw us almost at the last minute, and reined in. Father was in the lead, and quickly jumped off his horse.

"I was afraid we would be too late!" he said. "When Bezer brought the news that Mother Earth had invaded, and that Tubalites were fleeing to our plantation, we hastened to make preparations. I did not realize you had stayed behind to fight the enemy! Once I did, we immediately took horse! But I can see you had a fight! Tell me what happened!"

We briefly sketched out our defense of the bridge, and explained that the enemy had tried to outflank us by wading through the swamp. When he heard of their horrible fate, father shook his head grimly.

"Oh, my sons! War is a grievous, hellish thing, but it only exists because of sin! Oh, how our Maker hates sin! Until sin is finally dealt with, I fear that every generation of men will face war. Yet, by God's mercy, you have survived your first battle. For that, we give thanks!"

"It was a bloody business, Noah," Kedar added, "but your sons did not shrink from it. They kept cool, used their heads, and did their duty like men. You should be very proud of them!"

"Thank you, Kedar," father said. "I am proud; and I am thankful for you and your brave men, too! I only wish our work were done. When they learn what you have done, our enemy will be furious. Once they have secured Jared's Mill, we can expect them to march here in overwhelming force. We must not face them blindly. I shall have my men ride on to learn all they can."

Because father had brought extra horses, our return to the plantation was quick. As we approached the stronghold, I was pleased to see that the lookouts were posted, the drawbridge was up, and the walls were manned: our months of labor were paying off. Inside the gate, there was a beehive of activity, with mother directing the preparation of rooms, food and bedding for the exhausted refugees. The patriarch was busy too, in directing the preparations for defense. This was something, he explained, he had done more than a few times before. The plantation workers and their families had been called in. Some were putting on armor to man the walls, while others brought out arms, drove in livestock, or prepared foods.

Mother saw us arrive, and embraced us with tears of relief. After exchanging news with her, father left, while mother brought us to a table loaded with food. We were ravenous. With father now back on duty, the patriarch hobbled over, accompanied by his sisters and daughter. We found a quiet corner, and though sparing our aunties some of the bloody details, we told them our story. Before long, we were nodding with fatigue, and the patriarch sent us off for a nap.

When we awoke, we came downstairs to find that father's scouts had returned. With them were two more refugees from the city: our cousins Lael and Pagiel.

"We were betrayed!" Lael declared. "There was no alarm! The back gate, which was supposed to be guarded by the looters, was wide open. The enemy marched right in, and half the city was taken before the gongs were even struck. Valley Vigilance never had time to fully assemble. We heard that Uncle Krulak still held the harbor gate, so Pagiel and I ran in that direction; but before we got there we were cut off. We turned a corner and almost fell into the arms of the enemy. Fortunately, they were busy shackling prisoners, and we ducked back out of sight. Slipping around the soldiers, we ran up a deserted alley, climbed over fences, and finally got to the north wall. We were nearly captured a few more times, but finally managed to climb over the wall. We dropped into a cornfield, crawled to the river, and swam across. When we ran up the hill we found your men."

"Uncle Noah," Pagiel said, "Lael and I wanted to fight, but we never had a chance. Let us fight with you: we want our share of revenge!"

"Well, my zealous young nephews," father said, "we can use your help. We have bows for you, and lots of arrows. But you must remember that real vengeance belongs only to God. It is a rare thing on the earth to see the wicked recompensed, but someday, our eyes will behold God's perfect justice. When we do, I fear it will be more awful than we can bear."

After taking our cousins to our quarters to rest, we returned to hear the scouts' report. The fighting in Jared's Mill appeared to be over, they said, and the fires were being controlled. Two Mother Earth warships were moored at the dock, but our fleet of trading boats was entirely gone, hopefully taking many to safety. Thousands of enemy soldiers were bivouacked outside the city, together with hundreds of wagons and herds of horses, oxen, camels, and elephants. There were a number of large wooden machines[2] in the camp that the scouts could not identify. A broad muddy trail proceeded from the western slope of the Doubtful Mountains to the camp.

That evening we were invited to a council of war.

"Men," father said, "we never anticipated that Mother Earth would cut a road through the mountains. The planning, cost, and effort must have been enormous. But here is our situation. Except for this plateau, Enoch's Valley has been conquered. The enemy's army is powerful, well prepared, and well led. After our successful rescue of the Tubalites, they will think we have a strong force up here, and almost certainly come after us. While our stronghold is well suited to guard against behemoths or bands of Cainites, and it might hold out for a few days, it cannot resist a real army for long, especially if they have siege machines. What shall we do? Patriarch, what are your thoughts?"

The patriarch stood up. "My sons, my first impulse was to take my family and flee to safety. But the Creator spoke to me. He still would like to save all of Adam's children, though their hearts continually dwell on evil. Because he commands me to stay here as his ambassador, I cannot leave. However, I think we should send our women and children to safety. We all know how Mother Earth treats such captives: death is preferable. But once they are safe, you must escape while you can. If you stay behind with me, you will either be killed or enslaved."

There was discussion, but in the end, the men refused to leave their patriarch. They insisted on fighting until all hope was lost. Only then would they try to escape. All agreed, however, that we must evacuate the women and children, as well as the injured or infirm. The biggest problem was that Mother Earth knew we had received hundreds of Tubalites. If they did not find them, they would know they had escaped by water, and would block the Hiddekel to search.

Many ideas were proposed, but when Shem suggested a clever diversion, his plan was immediately adopted. The women and children were organized into groups of twenty, the number that would fill a boat or raft, and everyone got to work. After building frameworks from sticks of wood, the

Tubalites removed their distinctive orange clothing and arranged it on the framework. Cloth was sewn together to resemble heads, headgear was arranged, and the whole was stuffed with straw. After a few artistic touches, the dummies appeared as remarkably lifelike representations of Tubalite men, women and children.

When all our preparations were complete, and the moonless sky was dark, the women and children entered the secret chamber to descend the long passageway. Arriving in the cave at the water's edge, they began to enter the rafts and boats. The leader of each boat was instructed to paddle their craft to the opposite side of the Hiddekel, staying clear of the ships of Mother Earth. After father offered a prayer for protection, the crafts were shoved off one by one. The downstream current was strong, giving us hope they would reach Tubal by dawn.

Our mother and aunties were in the last group. Mother had strongly resisted leaving, but in the end she realized that for us, her absence would be a comfort. She commended us to our Maker, kissed us, and pushed off. It was a heart wrenching moment, but we felt some relief. Mother had taken her jewels and a heavy purse, and we knew she would be well taken care of by our relatives in Tubal.

After the women and children were gone, we began our heart-pounding ascent up the long stairway. By the time we climbed through the chamber and closed the secret door behind us, we were exhausted. We collapsed onto our beds, and did not stir until the sun was well up. The Creator gives his beloved children sleep, the patriarchs say, and this time we were glad for it. We would soon need all the wit and energy we could muster.

The enemy did not appear until late that afternoon. Our pickets ran in with the news, and we raised the drawbridge. The army of Mother Earth, they told us, thousands in number, was coming up by the swamp road. We rang the gong, donned our helmets and armor, checked our weapons and missiles, and set the water to boil. Our moat was already full of water, and we had fifty or sixty men to put on the walls, enough to make a brave show. Two advance companies of enemy horsemen rode up, each similar to the one we had fought the previous day. The infantry came next, company after company of black-armored soldiers. Each man carried a shield and a long spear, and they formed into fighting squares in the field opposite our stronghold. To our surprise, we saw yet more companies of soldiers marching in from the northern edge of our plantation!

"They are coming from the creek, Japheth!" Ham exclaimed.

"Mother Earth must have cut their road through the gopherwood forest near us," Shem said. "That explains how the behemoth got through!"

A small party of enemy officers rode up to inspect our walls. After circling our now-abandoned barn, they examined the steep cliff in back of our wall, and galloped back to the formation. A short time later, the squares dispersed, and soldiers scattered to the woods at the edge of our plantation. Father joined us to watch them.

"Their commander is following standard procedure," he said. "He will have some men gather sticks into faggots[1], while others cut trees to make scaling ladders. Once they fill in our moat with their faggots, they can raise their ladders against our walls. Depending on how many ladders they raise at any one time, we may be able to beat them off. But we will also have to watch the aqueduct. I expect they will divert the water, and send men up along it. All these preparations take time. We should eat now, and rest while we can."

A few hours later, horns sounded, and the army formed into squares. After another signal, the squares began to advance. When they got close, we heard another signal, and archers began to rain arrows over our walls. At the same moment, with bloodcurdling cries, the mass of the soldiers charged, dragging faggots with one arm, and holding their shields aloft with the other. We were ready for this, and our keen archers were able to hit many. Most, however, got to the moat and threw in their load before retiring. Their progress was steady, though at considerable cost.

On our part, while we were somewhat protected by our parapet, and wore good armor, we still had to expose ourselves when firing. Several of our defenders were killed, and others were seriously wounded. Our numbers began to thin. Unlike the enemy, we had no reserves. In a short time, the moat was filled in enough places to permit a regular attack. The squares were reformed, and after a new signal, another cloud of arrows was launched. Howling savagely, the enemy ran up to our walls. Some carried tall ladders, while others raised their shields, which could be locked together. A squad of soldiers with axes ran to the drawbridge, and began hewing away at the wooden beams.

Shouting our defiance, we threw rocks and boiling water onto the ladders, breaking some, knocking men off, and producing shrieks of pain. With their men exposed, our archers seldom missed. Ladder after ladder was overthrown with our long pikes. A few soldiers managed to climb onto our wall, but each was successfully thrown back. Eventually, a horn sounded, and the enemy retreated, carrying back their wounded and dead.

A dozen of our men were killed in the attack. We used the pause to carry them out, bandage wounds, and replenish our supplies. Father made rounds on the wall to encourage the men, and we all took the opportunity to eat and quench our thirst. As dusk approached, my brothers and I stood on the wall above the drawbridge, and watched a train of elephants come along the swamp road. They were pulling big wooden machines.

"Have you seen such machines[2] before, boys?" father asked. "The two big ones nearest us are called hurlers. Their rocks may be heavy enough to crunch in our walls, though they might have a harder time with those of a real fortress. The machine on the end is a battering ram on wheels, and it has a shield on top. This army is well equipped and trained, boys. Our game will soon draw to an end. The patriarch says he cannot personally leave, but he is pleased that we have fought with honor. We must escape tonight. Mother Earth will probably let the patriarch live, for he would be useful leverage over our people, but for us, there is no point in staying. It is better to live to fight another day. Boys, spread the word. As soon as it is dark, we light the torches and execute our plan. I do not want another man killed if we can help it."

After setting our plan into motion, we returned to watch from the wall. The enemy was assembling their machines, which had been transported in sections. Elephants and oxen were hauling boulders to the machines to serve as ammunition. We wondered when they would start. If they employed the machines that night, the walls would be crumbled in time for an easy morning assault. We were getting anxious. The sun had set, but it was not yet dark enough to carry out our plan.

Suddenly, our lookouts gave a shout. A small party was approaching our wall. Behind a burly senior officer, several soldiers pulled along an old man and a woman. Father and the patriarch were already climbing the steps, and joined us on the wall. The senior officer got right to the point.

"We have your whole family, Patriarch, including your son Lamech and his wife. While we have orders to be merciful, you have caused us considerable loss, and my patience is over. You must surrender with your son Noah, and give us Noah's sons as hostages. We want all the fugitive Tubalites: we know you have them. If you surrender, the rest of your people will be free to serve as subjects of Mother Earth. But if you resist any further, we will slaughter Lamech and his wife before your eyes, batter down your walls, and throw any survivors over the cliff. That is my offer. Make your choice."

This kind of pressure was hard for the patriarch to take. He nodded to father, and turned away, tears flowing down his cheeks.

"Give us an hour!" father shouted to the officer. "We must clear the drawbridge." He nodded to Kedar, who left with a torch.

"Boys," father said quietly, "are you willing to serve as hostages? They have offered us hope. We have no choice, really; but I believe our Creator permits things for a reason. By surrendering, I can stay with the patriarch. Otherwise, he would be all alone except for his servant Abidan, who refuses to leave his side."

Shem, Ham, and I looked at each other, and nodded. "We are not afraid to die," Shem said, speaking for all three of us.

"We trust that our Maker has a plan to bring us home in his own good time."

"Very well," father said. "We are in our Maker's hands. We will surrender. But first, we will save as many as we can." He glanced at the sky. "It is dark enough." He gestured to Kedar.

Moments later, the flickering light of torches revealed a dozen white and orange figures along the back wall of the stronghold, above the cliff. The enemy shouted in surprise. Most of the figures, by their size and dress, were girls or women, though there were a few boys and old men. Their orange clothing fluttered in the breeze for just a moment. Then, to the astonished gasps of the soldiers, they dropped over the cliff! There was no hesitation, and no cry. As soon as one figure jumped, another took its place, and made its own leap. As the enemy soldiers watched and cursed, the numbers of suicides grew to dozens, scores, and finally perhaps two hundred. The soldiers shrieked in frustration: their prey was getting away! The soldiers ran to look over the edge of the steep cliff at the dark rocks far below. We heard loud, bitter complaints. They had been cheated! They could not even search the bodies for coins!

A few minutes later, father gave us the nod. We lowered the drawbridge, and immediately ran back to join him, the patriarch, and faithful Abidan in the center of the courtyard. As enemy flooded in, a young officer ran up to us with his detail.

"Bind those six," he ordered. "Do not harm them! Kill everyone else!"

We were quickly bound, and hustled over the drawbridge. Our guards shoved us roughly, expressing frustration that they were missing the sack. No women, and no loot! We soon approached the light of a fire, and were brought before a grizzled but powerful looking officer. He sat on a stool examining a map, but turned to inspect us. His face looked brutal and hardened: killing six more would mean nothing to him. After gazing at us for a few moments, he turned to address someone hidden in the shadows.

"Well?" he asked. "Are these the ones?"

The person he addressed moved into the light, and leered an ugly smile.

"General, you are favored by the gods!" Sandal said, speaking with obvious satisfaction. "The ancient one is Methuselah, the patriarch of Enoch's Valley. The one to his left is his manservant, whose name I do not know. The old one on his right is Noah, the son of Lamech. The three dirty boys are his sons Japheth, Shem, and Ham. May I suggest you kill at least one of the boys right now, as an example? The oldest would be my choice. You only need one hostage to control these religious fanatics!"

The general grunted. "I did not ask for your suggestion," he said flatly. "You may go. Search their stronghold for souvenirs, if you like; but I think you would do better to return to your father. He is quite adept at looting. And yes, I know all about your important relations. Just keep your distance from me. While I find traitors useful, I do not like their smell."

Sandal glowered in anger, but bowed deeply, and backed away into the darkness. The general turned to the patriarch. When he spoke now, it was in a surprisingly respectful manner.

"Patriarch Methuselah," he said, "I am General Zabadanah, commander of the forces of Mother Earth. I have been given instructions that you are to be treated with respect. The king thinks you may be useful to us, and he intends to keep you as a leader, if you are willing to cooperate. If you do, your great grandsons will be kept safe as hostages. Though they will be slaves, if they embrace our culture and work hard, their lives will be useful ones. I shall give you a moment to say farewell."

There was little to say. We embraced, committing each other to our Creator, and the patriarch, father, and Abidan were led away. When they were gone, the general turned to us with a puzzled, irritated expression.

"I do not know why I was ordered to spare lives in Enoch's Valley. I have never been told that before, and it has cost me many good men. But perhaps you three will be of some value to us: we shall see."

He nodded to our guards, and we were marched away. We heard a crackling, whooshing sound, and felt heat on our backs. I glanced back to find father's treasured show barn on fire. Orange flames sprang out of its casements, raced up its sides, and licked all around the patriarchal weathervane, which slowly began to topple. Although being pulled forward, we could still occasionally glance back as the barn was consumed in flames. The great beams were the last to go. Right before it collapsed, the framework took on the appearance of a fiery skeleton, as though some devilish monster had just emerged from the depths of hell.

Our childhood had just ended, and rather abruptly, with our homeland betrayed and conquered, and our dreams up in smoke. As branded slaves, any future looked pretty miserable. This was not my idea of an adventure. In fact, if this was not a catastrophe, I did not know what was.

[1]*Editor's Note:* "Faggot" is the traditional term for a tied bundle of sticks.

[2]*Editor's Note:* Siege machines were used earlier than 150 BC by the Roman armies, who in turn had adopted the technology of the Greeks. Several types were used, including ballistae, which looked like large crossbows and hurled stones or large spears, and various kinds of catapults that propelled large stones or incendiaries.

Book Two: Noah's Boys in the City of Mother Earth

Chapter Nineteen: A March into Captivity

The next morning I awoke feeling disoriented. My clothes were soaked from the night mist, and the pungent smell of cattle dung filled my nostrils. And no wonder: we had slept in a cattle pen! The memories of the previous day swept over me. I knew I should feel grateful to be alive; but there was no virtue in it, and no honor. I felt a wave of misery and shame. It was not my fault, of course; but somehow I still felt guilty, and sick at heart[1].

We were kept prisoner along with a few hundred others, and for the time being, we had nothing to do. Soldiers dumped grain mush into a trough for our breakfast. I did not know if they deliberately meant to treat us like animals, but I found I had no appetite. My thoughts were more than enough to digest.

I had never liked the idea of national sin. Individual people do not usually commit all of the sins of a nation, but we all still somehow share in its corporate guilt, and in the inevitable consequences. The patriarchs had assured us that those who walk with God would not face the awful judgment predicted by the patriarch Enoch[2]. Nevertheless, while only some — well, perhaps most--in Enoch's Valley had risen in defiance against our Creator, we had all shared in its humiliating defeat. Father had long warned us that sin was eating through our community's timbers. If only we as a people had been more alert, and zealous! If only we had weeded out the corruption as it sprang up! If only we had implanted our clear patriarchal worldview in the foreigners that flooded in!

I found one aspect of our disaster bitterly ironic. Father had been completely convinced that God's judgment was about to fall on the wicked city of Mother Earth. He had even sent their king a letter warning him to repent. Yet, he had been wrong. Mother Earth had not been destroyed. Instead, we had been destroyed—and at their hands! And now we, the faithful children of the patriarchs, were at their mercy, not the other way around. How could this have happened? Had our Maker somehow misunderstood who the bad people were?

Finally, I got tired of moping, and became disgusted with my bitter thoughts. Returning to the water trough, I filled a gourd and poured it right over my head. The cold water woke me up in more than one way. Father had always believed in the cleansing effects of running water, and that was just what my mind needed. Noah's boys were in trouble, and I had no right to indulge in self-pity: I needed to toughen up and be strong, if only for my brothers' sake.

I rejoined them in a much better frame of mind, and we talked. Mother had always said that things happen for a reason, and that people make choices. What choices should we make in our new situation?

"What would the patriarchs say?" Shem asked.

We already knew. They would tell us to guard our attitude, and be alert. Things may not be as bad as they seem. Another useful bit of advice, of course, was to do all we could do, with what we had, where we were. But the patriarchal advice that appealed to me most was this: live before you die, and die like men. That was the attitude I wanted!

Unfortunately, being a prisoner did not make keeping a positive attitude easy. Our situation was degrading. We were stripped, our hair was shaved off, and we were lined up naked to be scrubbed down with harsh soap. After that, we were examined and sorted like animals before being given our final humiliations. Like shorn sheep, we were pushed along a narrow chute to a screened area, from which we saw captives emerge holding their shoulders. I thought about that. If something painful was about to happen, I did not wish to give them any satisfaction. However, when the red-hot iron was pressed against my skin, my resolve disappeared. There was a wisp of smoke, and searing pain. A wild shriek forced its way through my clenched teeth. The soldier holding the iron gave a brief, cruel smile, and turned to the next captive. At the end, we received our slave collars. The officer checked our names against the inscriptions on his copper sheet, and looked up.

"So you are sons of the ruling patriarchs!" he sneered. "The cliff dwellers! Let me tell you, we were sorely disappointed that your women jumped to their deaths. What a waste! Our men felt lonely, and had looked forward to becoming acquainted with them. But at least your town provided loot. In return, we shall give you silver collars! I trust this new jewelry meets your noble standards."

Riveting the slave collars proved painful. Cush, Seba, and Dedan had been taken captive, too; but they wore copper collars. What was worse, they were separated from each other, while we had been kept together. I decided not to think too much: it was painful. Another question kept popping up. There were no females in our camp. What had happened to them? I did not want to speculate.

When the last captives were brought in, they roped us all together and marched us out. Bands of soldiers joined us along the way, bringing wagons of loot. Just before we entered the wilderness, a small party of well-dressed civilians galloped up, laughing and joking as though on a lark. A nearby prisoner muttered, "traitors!" I looked up and recognized the newcomers as our old adversaries: Sandal, Rekem, and Zur.

After a lifetime of hearing about its dangers, it felt eerie to pass through the gopherwood barrier and actually enter the Doubtful Wilderness. Gashercut branches were strewn on the ground in places, and a few unfortunates stumbled onto them with bare feet. Their screams of pain, and later moans, cautioned the rest of us to watch our step. I pondered the tremendous effort Mother Earth had made to construct the road. It must have required many months, with thousands of slaves working under the whip. Why had they done it? Was the loot from our homeland enough to pay for their trouble? Or was our port on the Hiddekel so valuable?

As our column marched steadily higher into the mountains, the sights were interesting, and my spirits began to improve. The upland brush was thinner in areas because of heavy grazing, and we occasionally felt cool mountain breezes. We hiked up through cool forests of immense trees, and came down through dank thickets of vine-covered jungles. We never directly encountered monstrous predators, but we saw evidence of them, for one time we had to step around the half-devoured carcass of an immense herbivorous behemoth. On more than one occasion, we felt the pounding of giant behemoths running through the forest. There was lots of wildlife, including countless varieties of birds, as well as flying mammals and reptiles. Large snakes and lizards slithered through the underbrush. One time we all had to halt as a great herd of bison rumbled across our path. Another time, as I bent to drink from a stream, I saw a sleek black panther studying me from the nearby shadows.

Late in the afternoon, we halted before a large stand of bamboo. General Zabadanah came over and addressed the captives in his gravelly, yet penetrating voice.

"Prisoners, your old life is dead. For your own benefit, I suggest you have your funeral, and put it behind you. You belong to Mother Earth now. If you serve her well, you will live. If you serve her poorly, you will die. Now that we are in the Doubtful Mountains, I shall permit you to be untied so that we can march faster. Your bonds slow us down. If you wish to escape, do so, but bear in mind that behemoths abound here. Your only hope is to keep up with the rest of us."

The soldiers moved down the column, unfastening the prisoners. It was a relief to have our hands free. About that time, a foolish young man—a distant cousin—decided to speak out. After loudly cursing Mother Earth, he offered the general an obscene gesture.

"I know my rights as a prisoner of war," he said defiantly. "We are not really slaves, and you can't threaten us like that."

"Young man, are you not pleased to serve Mother Earth?" the general asked, smiling humorlessly. "Then I release you. Go ahead, run away!"

The youth hesitated, perhaps having second thoughts. The general frowned and nodded to a nearby soldier, who prodded the prisoner with his spear.

"Run away!" the soldier ordered, drawing back for a second prod.

The youth backed up, looked at the long line of prisoners, and repeated his obscene gesture. The soldier laughed and shook his spear, while the youth ran to the edge of the bamboo thicket. Pushing the bamboo aside, he began making his way straight towards home. The reeds swayed back and forth, marking his progress, but the soldiers did nothing but watch.

Moments passed quietly. We heard a high-pitched bellow in the distance. Another bellow sounded from a different direction. A few moments later, we heard more bellows of the same kind, and more yet. With horror, we realized that the creatures were communicating. The youth crashed hurriedly through the forest now, and the bamboos clattered. The bellowing sounds finally converged. There was a long scream, a flurry of bellows and growls, and a faint gurgling cry. After that came a terrible chorus of bellows, grunts, and shrieks. They lasted a long time. We felt sick.

The general finally spoke. "Would anyone else like to escape? No? Then if you wish to serve Mother Earth, obey orders!"

After that, we marched steadily for days, drinking from streams, and occasionally halting to eat a thin porridge of grain or a stew of vegetables. Sometimes we plucked small fruits or nuts as we marched: the soldiers allowed that, as long as we kept marching. Our time on the trail passed quickly, and our various wounds, including our painful brands, began to heal. I looked at my brand one day. It was a very simple mark—just two intersecting lines[3]--but it was irreversible and humbling. It would always reveal me as a slave.

As we climbed ever higher into the mountains, the path became more difficult. One day we found ourselves making a series of switchbacks up a steep hill. For the first time, we came side by side with the traitors. I had often wondered if it might happen; but Sandal saw me, and reined in his horse. Rekem and Zur were right next to him.

"Stand by for trouble," I told my brothers. They followed my glance.

Sandal and his companions abruptly forced their mounts down the slope. It was dangerously steep, and although their horses sank their rear hooves deeply into the earth, they were only barely able to control their descent. As soon as Sandal and his friends came to us, they struck out with their long staffs. I jumped away, but still received enough of a blow to be knocked down. Scrambling to find something with which to defend myself, I came up with a good-sized stick. My brothers found other weapons. We faced our assailants as they returned.

"I see you found us, Sandal," I said, "and you have your friends with you! Cheaters, bullies, and traitors always flock together, don't they?"

Sandal cursed, but paused his mount, apparently having something to say. I clearly saw the tiger stripes on his red, angry face.

"I have always hated you, Japheth," he said. "You religious fanatics think your perfect family pedigree makes you better than anybody else. But I am just as good as you. And we won! It is time for you to get the beating you deserve."

"Well, Rekem," Ham interjected, hefting a big rock. "Is that scar on your leg from an arrow? What a coincidence! I shot a coward in the same place when he was hiding behind a tree to kill us."

"I almost didn't recognize you, Zur," Shem added, holding a big stick, "in such elegant dress. The last time I saw you, you were covered with mud from vandalizing Tubalites!"

Our words seemed to provoke them. Moving in, they began to rain blows on us with their heavy staffs. We protected ourselves as well as we could, but their mounts gave them a strong advantage. Sandal's solid blows to my head and shoulders dazed me, and I felt ready to collapse.

Suddenly, the attack ceased. Soldiers had come to our defense! Galloping down with drawn swords, they forced our attackers to drop their weapons, and then drove them back up the hill. The column halted for a time as order was restored. We washed our wounds in a little stream, and a short time later returned to the march, nursing a painful assortment of bruises and cuts. General Zabadanah, we learned, had observed the attack, and had ordered soldiers to our aid. We began to feel more kindly towards him.

A week or so later we were high in the mountains, where the air was fresh and cool. We halted in a grassy clearing on the edge of a steep slope, and enjoyed the splendid view. The general, along with some of his officers, climbed to the top of a nearby rock to see the full panorama. A rich green forest blanketed the gentle slopes and peaks of the range below us, while great waterfalls splashed down the neighboring slopes, and streams gurgled through meadows and valleys. In the distance we saw the rich pastures of Enoch's Valley extending to the Hiddekel River, which curled away as a silver ribbon between the hills. The city of Tubal could be discerned on the horizon, too, though its great buildings were hazy.

Although the vista was delightful, my attention was suddenly drawn to Ham, who was poking around a bare patch of ground on the edge of a precipice. Large broken shells lay in the middle of the patch, while dark droppings, and white bones, were scattered all around. Shem and I joined him.

"See these droppings, guys?" Ham whispered urgently. "They are fresh. And look at these shells! They are as big as watermelons, and thick! Only one thing hatches out of shells like these."

"There are dozens of shells!" Shem exclaimed.

I was already searching the sky. I soon found them, circling almost directly overhead! I had seen that kind of circling before, and did not like it. Standing in any open space left us vulnerable. I glanced at the officers, who were still enjoying their view from the tall rock.

"Alas, Eden!" I blurted. "Look where the general is standing!"

We shared a horrified look, and immediately took off. The two guards saw us coming, and raised their spears to stop us, but we had no time to discuss. I sidestepped the first guard, seized his spear, and began scrambling up the rock after the officers. Similarly, Shem took the spear of the second guard, while Ham pulled his sword right from its sheath and followed me up. When I got to the top, Shem and Ham were right behind me.

"Get down!" I shouted, running towards the general. "Death raptors!"

The officers were startled, but did not understand. Thinking I was attacking them, they immediately reached for their swords.

A great shadow fell over us. I jumped, thrusting up with my spear. The point sank deep in flesh, but was wrenched from my arms. A loud gurgling screech almost deafened us. Giant claws closed around the nearby officer, and yanked him into the sky with his arms and legs flailing. The shadow glided away, and we could see the monster in the sunshine. It looked like a scaly black bat, but it was immense, with wings spanning at least 20 cubits. Its great reptilian head was pointy, with round eyes and a long sharp beak. My spear had impaled its throat, from which it was still dangling. As we watched, the monster flapped its wings a few more times and rose higher, but it was severely injured. Dropping its prey, it began an awkward spiral into the valley, as we watched in horror.

"Here comes another one!" Shem shouted, and cast his spear.

A second shadow darkened us. This time the great claws grabbed General Zabadanah. Because I was right beside him, I grabbed his leg, and the monster lifted us both. Ham jumped up at the same time, and managed with his sword to slash through an entire section of the monster's wing. In return, he was showered with blood. The monster carried us up another ten or twenty cubits, but the air spilled through its slashed wing, making it lurch sideways. I held tight onto the general's leg as the creature began tumbling and spinning, but soon lost consciousness.

I awoke a short time later, and groaned. Opening my eyes, I found the death raptor on the slope just a short distance away, thrashing about furiously. One wing looked crippled, and Shem's spear protruded from its body. Long, sharp claws on the bony edge of the wings opened and closed frantically as the great beast flopped about. I closed my eyes again. I did not think I had broken anything, but I felt numb all over. A few minutes later, I heard my brothers call. Opening my eyes again, I slowly sat up. Shem and Ham scrambled down the earthy slope, followed by soldiers. They looked very concerned.

"Japheth!" they asked, "are you okay?"

"I think so," I said, "but if those bushes had not cushioned me, I would have broken every bone in my body!"

My brothers helped me up. The soldiers fanned out, and found the younger officer barely in time. He had broken his leg in the fall, and two small carnivorous behemoths were already circling him. The general was found bruised and shaken, but otherwise uninjured. He insisted on administering the final blow to the injured death raptor, and then ordered the head taken off as a trophy.

That night there was a special ceremony. With a big bonfire illuminating the severed head of the death raptor, the general made us stand up, and praised us as examples of alertness, courage and skill.

"I begin to think," he said, "that believers in the Creator God are not entirely the spineless cowards most call them. The men of Enoch's Valley, though surprised and betrayed, were well led by the famous General Krulak, and proved themselves to be worthy adversaries. They fought with honor and skill, and gave us some surprises. One band of their warriors ambushed and killed nearly an entire mounted company before escaping into the jungle. After all that, I am not entirely surprised to see these three youngsters show such initiative and courage. They have brought great credit on themselves and their people. If any of the rest of you demonstrate such ability and zeal in serving Mother Earth, I can promise you that your service will be richly rewarded."

Taking wreaths of olive branches[4], the general held them up for the audience to see, and placed them on our heads.

"Lads," he said quietly, "you saved my life today, and you will not find me slack in returning the favor. If the king had not already spoken for you, I would buy you myself and set you free. As it is, I will certainly speak to him on your behalf. But take heart. If you continue like this, you may well earn a place of honor. I know: I was once a slave like you."

"The mission of our family, General, is to save people." I answered. "We are glad that our Creator gave us success, and that lives were saved."

"Your mission is a good one, lad," he said, turning us to face the audience.

A great cheer was raised from both soldiers and prisoners, and for a brief moment we almost forgot we were slaves. For the rest of the journey, the soldiers acted more kindly toward the captives. The general placed us at the head of the column of prisoners, and often engaged us in conversation. We felt our confidence improve. Before long, I saw that Ham's sense of humor had returned, too.

A few days later, our caravan halted to rest in a meadow of wildflowers, and we again found ourselves near Sandal and his friends. While we ate our meager porridge of corn and barley, the privileged traitors grazed their horses in the tender grass along a stream, and enjoyed a luxurious spread of cooked meats, vegetables, fruits, cakes, and fermented wine.

Ham strolled over to a nearby hollow tree where there was a big swarm of industrious honeybees. When he began to examine it, Shem and I knew something was up. It was amazing, Shem whispered, that Ham could put his stick right into the hive without disturbing the bees. A little later, I noticed that Ham, completely unnoticed by the guards, was petting and conversing with the horses grazing by the stream, and adjusting their saddles. He loved all kinds of animals, we remarked, and they certainly loved him. Sometime later, Ham quietly returned, but said nothing. His face, however, had that certain smile that we knew well: the prank was set.

A moment or two after the order to mount up, we heard wild shrieks of terror. Sandal, Zur, and Rekem were frantically running away from their horses, screaming and slapping themselves. An angry cloud of bees hovered around their heads! Ham chuckled openly, and Shem and I could not help but find satisfaction. We were not the only ones to enjoy their suffering. Their fellow traitors were delighted, and cheered on the bees, while a group of soldiers gathered around them, laughing heartlessly, and shouting their advice to run faster.

Eventually, Sandal and his friends dove into the stream, but the bees hovered around for a long time. When Sandal finally emerged, cursing from the pain and humiliation, he and his comrades received no compassion. Instead, they were made the butt of jokes for the rest of the journey. The incident delayed our departure from the meadow, but we resumed our march with a lighter heart.

---

[1]*Editor's Note:* This description reminds me of my father's experience as a prisoner of war in Germany. Though he rarely discussed it, shame and degradation were some of the worst parts, though the physical hardships, including lack of food and medical care, were considerable.

[2]*Editor's Note:* The writer, though seemingly frustrated, still seems to express a doctrine that is central to Christianity: believers in the God of the Bible need never fear condemnation with the lost, but are justified by faith in the perfect atoning sacrifice of Jesus Christ (Romans 5:1, Hebrews 10:12). Unrepentant sinners, however, will face the eternal condemnation that the patriarch Enoch warned about (Jude 14-15). The historical consequence of national sin is a more difficult question, but I think it may include war, pestilence, or even national suicide, something we have seen recently.

[3]*Editor's Note:* It is intriguing that Japheth's slave mark was a cross, which has such meaning to Christians. It might be best not to read too much into this, however, for the cross was also a common symbol in ancient Egypt, Greece, and India.

[4]*Editor's Note:* Olive wreaths were considered tokens of victory even before their use in ancient Greece, and were used to honor athletic achievements or wartime victory.

Chapter Twenty: The City of Mother Earth

Early one morning a few weeks later, we halted along the crest of a mountain ridge. A stunning view of a magnificent valley was spread out before us. Long, steep slopes descended to the valley floor, with cascading streams and waterfalls that glittered in the sunlight. Three rushing rivers tumbled out of steep, narrow gorges to flow into a great city on the valley floor. The narrow rivers merged to form a wide river that flowed on to nurture a rich agricultural plain. A whisper raced through the column of prisoners: "The City of Mother Earth!"

Fascinated by the sight of so much rushing water, my mind jumped to the potential for hydraulic power. As I looked, however, I realized others had thought of that before me: the city had dozens of slowly revolving watermills! But what did they use the power for? Was it to saw lumber, or hammer metal, or power textile machines[1]? I saw smoke billowing in tall columns from one part of the city. Was this from smelters purifying copper or iron? As I studied the city, I found myself becoming excited at the thought of so much manufacturing. I noticed a great construction site across the narrow head of the great valley. Uncle Lemuel had mentioned something about his colleague building a hydraulic power station. If this was a dam under construction, it was big!

It took us two days to wind down the slopes, and we had many opportunities to see the city from different perspectives. There was a large palace just inside the wall, while huge temples sprawled beside the river in the center of town. One temple had a particularly large park, with animals so huge they could only be behemoths: this had to be the famed Mother Earth Zoo! Many stone bridges crossed the rivers, which were paralleled by broad tree-shaded boulevards. As we got closer, we could distinguish wealthy residences, marketplaces, parade grounds, theaters, and lush gardens. Crowded outside the walls of the city were bleak rows of slave quarters, while large warehouses stood by the docks. Farther downstream lay a large military reservation with barracks and parade grounds, and beyond that were farmlands, grain fields, and vast pastures with cattle and sheep. Above the pastures, the steep slopes were terraced with vegetable gardens, orchards, and vineyards.

It was late in the afternoon when we entered the military reservation, and the next morning we were prepared for the parade of triumph. Our sandals and meager shreds of clothing were stripped off, and we were roped together into long lines. Our column was marched to the wall of the city, and made to stand before a massive gate with columns resembling oak trees. We were instructed to be silent, so we observed our surroundings quietly. Two words in large characters were written on the lintel: Mother Earth. We watched the progress of a flock of noisy pigeons flying into the city. Behind them came a trio of brightly colored birds.

"Enoch's parrots!" Ham whispered with a smile.

The great parade was assembled in front of the gate. When all was ready, General Zabadanah rode up on a black stallion. As he approached, I felt the ground tremble beneath our bare feet. Alarmed, I looked at the massive stone block directly above us—the one that proclaimed "Mother Earth." It was moving, but only slightly. No one else seemed to notice the tremor, which soon subsided. To me, however, it was a disquieting sign. Riding behind the general were his senior officers, immaculately attired, with burnished armor, and capes of black and green. Even their armored horses were gaily decorated[2]. The general raised his sword, and the gate opened. A gigantic roar swelled from a vast crowd. It seemed that the entire city had come to celebrate.

Our column of captives remained at the gate as the head of the parade passed into the city. After the senior officers, a loud military band marched through, playing a bright martial tune with trumpets and drums. Prancing warhorses and stately camels of the mounted troops came next, followed by brightly decorated elephants and oxen pulling engines of war. The proud battalions of foot soldiers marched in, with spearmen first, carrying their great shields, followed by the squares of broad shouldered bowmen, and row after row of swordsmen. Despite their large numbers, their steps were perfectly synchronized, and thousands of studded sandals struck the pavement all together. The warlike spectacle thrilled the crowd, and they thundered in applause.

After the soldiers, the small group of traitors rode in, dressed in expensive garments of yellow and gold. They received very little applause, even though their role had been critical to quick success. When they passed by, the crowd cheered enthusiastically for the next part of the parade, which was everyone's favorite: the fruits of conquest. A long procession of heavy wagons rumbled by, filled with the loot from our homeland. The crowd screamed in delight, and begged the soldiers for favors. Happy to please, the soldiers tossed out garments, brass trinkets, and even jewelry and coins, and laughed as greedy spectators fought over the spoil. After the heavy wagons came lighter wagons fitted with cages. These bore loot of a different kind: female captives. I had to look away. If they were my cousins, it would be too much to bear.

Finally, it was our turn. Dressed only in our metal collars, my brothers and I led the male captives through the gates.

Although guards kept the crowd at a distance, our reception was painful. Sneers, insults, and scornful laughter greeted us, along with rotten fruits and even stones. We learned very quickly to keep our faces down.

It was demeaning and humiliating, of course; but I did learn some important truths that day. For one thing, winning a war is far superior to defeat and capture: even dying in battle might be better. For another, life as a slave has little to recommend it.

Our winding procession through the city seemed endless. I tried to pretend it was happening, not to me, but to somebody else. That made it a little easier. It also helped to imagine I was deaf. That way, I could ignore the hate that radiated from the masses along the parade route. After a time, I almost began to enjoy the walk. The architecture was really marvelous, and the gardens of the city were exquisite, with huge, colorful flowers and carefully pruned shrubbery. Elaborate fountains and beautiful statues of animals and gods decorated the boulevard everywhere, and many lovely parks had waterfalls splashing down to foamy pools where children played.

The royal palace was a magnificent structure of pure white granite. As we circled the pavilion, the royal entourage inspected us. It was hard not to gape in return, for the king was a real giant, as father had said: he stood at least six cubits tall. His dress was simple, with a green and black cape over steel armor, and a plain gold crown to indicate his rank. He returned military salutes with a huge steel sword. A handsome older woman, whom I assumed was the queen mother, wore an elaborately jeweled crown. Standing on the king's right, she was dressed in an elegant royal gown that glittered with emeralds. Prince Malek stood next to her. He seemed to be searching the captives, and smiled as he caught my eye. He bent down to the queen mother's ear, and she followed his gaze.

After the palace, the parade wound back to the main boulevard, where further crowds awaited. Most onlookers were satisfied with the sights of the triumph, but some shouted for blood. In those moments, we were glad to have armed soldiers escorting us. We continued through extensive commercial districts, more modest residential areas, and noisy parks filled with drunken, dancing revelers. It was a glorious day for the city, perhaps; but for us, it was emotionally numbing. As nameless captives, we were constantly pulled or pushed about, and the attention we received was only for the purpose of gloating. Suddenly, however, as we passed through a wealthy residential area, I heard my own name repeated.

"Japheth! Japheth!"

Surprised, I glanced at the nearby crowd. A beautiful girl was waving at me. To my astonishment, it was Aziza! She stood in a festive group of young women, and looked healthy and happy. She had no angry tiger stripes today, but was just as I remembered. Her sheer green gown clung to her curves, emphasizing her feminine attractions. Collecting her girlfriends, she walked right up to the column, wiggling her figure as always, and shook her finger in my face.

"Japheth, Japheth! Didn't I tell you that you would be sorry? If only you had listened to me! If only you had not been so proud and stubborn! You might have been here with me, enjoying this parade! But no! You kept your integrity, and your precious religion! Now look at you! In fact, we can all look at you, can't we, girls?"

Aziza pointed to my nakedness and laughed, as her friends giggled. She walked with us only a few steps. "So long, boys. See you in the copper mines!"

My mouth dropped open in surprise, and neither Shem nor Ham had anything witty to say. We continued to march, but I looked back, feeling puzzled and hurt. She and her friends were still laughing gaily, careless of our anguish! Was this the girl I might have married? Her cruelty, I bitterly realized, was not just the result of her brother's influence. People make choices, mother said. As I thought about it, I knew I should feel deep humiliation; instead, I felt righteous indignation.

Up to that moment, I had been dwelling mostly on my own defeat and shame. Suddenly, I began to reflect on what our Creator might think about all this. Had he not made people in his own image, and designed them for noble fellowship with him? Would he not be angry, angry enough to bring awful judgment upon such a hotbed of idolatry? The thought struck me that our time in this city might be short. At the same time, I realized that our Maker must have brought us here for a reason, for there was a reason for everything. But what was it?

As I mulled these thoughts, our column passed a row of gigantic temples. One temple, I saw, was dedicated to "Human Achievement," while another honored "The Water God." Yet another temple had a very large pillar in front, and was simply labeled "Virility." This puzzled me, but Ham whispered it had something to do with breeding sheep. Finally, we came to the largest temple, whose grounds extended all the way to the mountainside, and whose gates were guarded by huge stone behemoths. This temple seemed to be the most popular one, for a wide stream of visitors continually flowed in and out. Pungent, musky smells tickled our noses, and loud bleats sounded, as well as grunts, shrieks, trumpeting, and even roars.

"The Great Zoo!" Ham whispered.

A zoo was a happy thought, and it perked me up a little, despite being very tired and thirsty. We had had little to eat that morning, and only some sips of water. My interest in the marvelous temples and buildings was fading quickly. To distract from my thirst, I began to study the people we passed.

Most wore clothing in bright red, blue, or green; but some preferred drab yellow, brown, or gray. I wondered if the colors or style of their clothing signified religion, or perhaps social status. Many girls were dressed as provocatively as Aziza or the winking girl. Dressing like that, I supposed, might mean they were available for marriage. Women, even older matrons, openly pointed to our naked bodies and made vulgar remarks. What were they be thinking, I wondered?

Troupes of dancers, jugglers, and musicians were scattered throughout the parade route, as well as groups of religious interests. One group was dressed all in green, and led by a priest costumed as an oak tree. His followers danced around him, singing that animals were people, too, and that the earth was their mother. Frankly, I was puzzled. Beside us, two mischievous adolescents in the same group opened their garments, and urinated on the street, crying "No dams! Free the water!" That caught the attention of one of the soldiers. He raised his spear threateningly, and the boys ran away laughing.

We entered the manufacturing district, and passed spinning watermills and foundries billowing with dark smoke. A gang of heavily tattooed young men lined one side of the parade route, all dressed in black. While their expressions were dissolute and angry, their cheeks had dark stripes, just like the face of a tiger. By now I could recognize full-blooded Cainites, and these were particularly hateful ones. As soon as we got close, they threw rocks. Several captives were hit and cried out, while the Cainites laughed and cursed. Our guards finally noticed. A squad of soldiers lowered their spears to charge, and the gang scattered, cursing even more.

Our parade had traversed most of the city by now, and was ascending a long slope. We were all suffering thirst. The crowds were lessening, but we came to a group of bystanders modestly dressed in white. Several carried jugs or baskets. Unlike the other spectators, their expressions and actions showed pity. Whenever the parade slowed or paused, one or two ran up to the line of captives and offered water. If a guard noticed, he would warn them off, or push them roughly away.

At one such momentary halt, a young girl with a jug over her shoulder dashed up and boldly offered me a cup. When I took it, she gave another cup to Shem, and a third one to Ham. I was parched, and the cool, sweet water was both delicious and refreshing.

The girl's hair was mostly covered, but what I saw was very fair, the color of ripe oats. She was very pretty, too, with long lashes and strikingly blue eyes—like a deep mountain spring. She refilled my cup. As I drank, I gazed into her eyes. I had not been prepared to find such kindness or sympathy, and something about this girl reminded me of home. A soldier finally noticed, and roughly signaled her to leave. Before she turned away, she gave me a lovely smile. As our column moved ahead, I suddenly realized something: the girl had worn a necklace exactly like our mother's! Her sweet, compassionate face lingered in my mind. I thought of her often after that, and puzzled over her necklace.

By the time the parade reached the upper edge of the city, the crowds had completely thinned out. We passed through a large double gate into a great amphitheater, and our parade was disbanded. The steep walls of the valley had originally formed a natural bowl, but the sides had been carved into enough tiers to seat thousands of spectators. Our column of captives shuffled through an open field, beside a large stage that would be used for entertainments, and through another wide gate into an open area at the foot of the mountain.

A tall rock chimney stood above us, narrowly separated from a sharp spur in the mountain. Stairs had been cut into the sides of the rock all the way up to a flat top that provided a natural lookout over the entire valley. At several places along the stairway were heavy doors and broad barred casements. As I looked up to the highest one, I saw two arms stretched out through the bars, and heard a faint cry.

"God help me!"

A nearby soldier noticed my stare, and sneered. "This is Lookout Rock, slave, the celebrity prison of Mother Earth. Notorious condemned prisoners are kept there in public view until their sentence is carried out. That prisoner made the mistake of offending the queen mother herself. He wrongly assumed she would not punish him because he was her brother! He has rotted in that cell for many years, never knowing when the queen mother would select him for an entertainment. They say that has driven him mad. There is a lesson for you! But do not worry: you will not stay in this prison long. Foreign captives are put into the animal cages and sold the next day."

After hearing that story, I could not help but imagine their entertainments. After weeks or months on display like an animals, the condemned prisoners would be brought out to the cheering crowd, and then thrown to... I felt a nudge.

"Look at that!" Shem whispered, pointing behind me.

I turned to follow his finger. My mouth dropped as I saw the enormous construction site. The foundation completely spanned the valley, at least twelve hundred cubits in length. A single curved line of huge stone blocks had already been placed, and more blocks were assembled for placement. This must be the great power station we had glimpsed from the mountain! The base of the structure, rather than being straight across, was curved into the reservoir, possibly to increase its strength. From the chiseled rock up the sides of the mountain, they planned to make the dam at least three hundred cubits tall[3]. I had never seen anything this big. When it was filled, the volume and weight of the water in the reservoir would be vast, and would provide almost unlimited hydraulic power.

I glanced at the narrow walls of the valley, and the densely populated city behind us. When our own little dam had fallen, the destruction had been surprisingly disproportionate. If such a great dam ever collapsed, I could not even imagine the stupendous force that would be funneled directly onto the city.

"Somehow, I have a bad feeling about this," Shem said.

"Me, too," Ham added.

---

[1]*Editor's Note:* Edmund Cartwright patented the first successful powered loom only in 1789. "Textile machine" may not be an accurate translation. Nevertheless, this use of power suggests a highly advanced technology.

[2]*Editor's Note:* In the Middle Ages, horses prepared for tournaments or combat were frequently "barded" (armored), or "caparisoned," covered with a cape to deflect arrows. No one today knows when horses or battle elephants were first armored.

[3]***Editor's Note:*** The Grand Coulee Dam, the largest hydropower producer in the United States, is 550 feet high and 5223 feet wide, the equivalent of 367 cubits by 3482 cubits. At 300 cubits, though not nearly that size, this ancient structure must have been very large for its time.

Chapter Twenty-One: Willing to Serve

The next morning we were shouted awake and marched to the river. Guards forced us into the cold, rapid current, and instructed us to wash up. Afterward, we were marched back and fed a thick gruel before being subjected to yet another humiliation. The slave dealers had come, and they now descended on us like vultures. While their assistants took notes, the dealers handled our bodies as though we were horses, and examined our arms, legs, and teeth. Some asked questions to assess our intelligence, attitude, and capacity for a specialized position. I tried to be philosophical during the ordeal. After all, they simply wanted to know the quality of the merchandise.

When the dealers left, we were given rough brown loincloths and returned to our cage. There, for the first time since our capture, we were allowed to mingle with the other prisoners. We soon found our cousins, and heard the story of their capture. It grieved us to hear of relatives killed, and to learn the extent of our homeland's calamity. Unfortunately, our time together was short: a guard soon shouted for us.

"Japheth, Shem, and Ham, brothers from Enoch's Valley!"

Something about the way the guard shouted suggested we were leaving for good. As we stood to obey the summons, we grasped the hands of our cousins.

"God keep you, Cush," Ham said. "I hope we shall meet again; but be sure of this: your names will not be forgotten. I promise you that."

"Our Creator has a plan, cousins," Shem added. "He will preserve you, and bring us back together, I know it. Patience and prayer!"

As we stepped to the gate, the guard checked our names against a tablet, and delivered us to a detail of soldiers. As we left the cage, I glanced to the top of Lookout Rock. Arms were stretched out between the bars just like the previous evening, and the prisoner called out the same prayer.

"God help me!"

As I watched, a large green parrot glided down to perch on the ledge by his cell. My brothers and I were taken to the large double gate of the amphitheater. There, to our surprise, General Zabadanah greeted us.

"Lads," he began, "I have good news for you! My report mentioned that three brave young captives had saved my life, and that of another officer on our trip. The king took a particular interest in it, and this morning I had to tell the entire story to him and the queen mother. While I was gratified that they consider my life of such value, I am also glad for you, because they have decided to reward you! Most of the hostages we take during our conquests are put to safe menial labor, but you three have been charmed from the start. Now, because of your brave action in saving my life, a wonderful opportunity has been presented you, which with dedication and hard work may even lead to positions of leadership. Congratulations!"

We were dumfounded, and expressed our heartfelt appreciation.

"No," he demurred, "you deserve this opportunity. I shall ride with you to the palace, for I have something to discuss."

The general gestured for us to climb into his carriage, and dismissed his subordinates before joining us. He spoke quietly, so as not to be overheard.

"In reward for my services, the king has made me commander of the palace guard, the highest position any soldier could hope for. I mention this to you for two reasons. First, I am still in your debt, and think that perhaps in my new position I may be of help to you. Second, though it is a great promotion, it is a dangerous one. I have a wife and children, and would like to live longer than my predecessor, who died suddenly after displeasing the king in a slight matter. I need eyes in many places, and friends. I think I can count on you lads. Keep your ears open, and tell me anything I should know. But guard yourselves, and be careful whom you trust. The palace overflows with ambition and treachery."

We gave the general our assurances, and he escorted us to the palace steward. The steward was very respectful, almost fawning, toward the general. He congratulated him on his new position, and thanked him for bringing us. When the general departed, the steward turned to us, showing a more cynical side.

"It amuses me," he said, "that General Zabadanah believes you have been given this honor because you saved his life. He obviously does not know the queen mother. She has certainly favored you; but that cannot be the reason. Would you care to tell me what is?"

He waited for our answer. I looked at my brothers, thinking. We had met Prince Malek before, but I doubted that either beating up his subordinate or winning a minor athletic event would have earned us any significant favor. Moreover, our father had previously rebuked the king, something the prince had remembered. Worse yet, our father had recently sent the king a letter warning him to repent or face God's wrath. It seemed wiser not to bring these things up.

"Sir," I replied carefully, "I can think of no particular reason why we should be shown any special favorable interest."

"I see," he replied, obviously not believing me. "Then let me ask you another question. The conquest of Enoch's Valley has puzzled me, right from the start. It required unusual planning and extraordinary expenses, while any expected benefits were minimal, from my perspective. What is so special about your homeland?"

We shook our heads, not wanting to speculate on the king's motives.

"No? Well, at least the spoil was valuable, and we now have another port on the Hiddekel. But I shall not question the king, or in this case, the queen mother. Their reasons must have been excellent. So here you are. But before we go further, I must ask you each a simple question. Will you serve Mother Earth willingly? If not, you will be sent to the mines today. It baffles me, but some captives are quite bullheaded."

Since our capture, we had often considered our attitude towards our new situation. We had seen what happened to the cousin who foolishly chose to defy our captors. We had come to believe that our Maker had brought us here for a purpose; and it was simply a fact that we served the City of Mother Earth. The steward was not at that moment asking us to worship the false goddess Mokosh: he was simply offering us some sort of training. As long as we were not forced to actively worship idols or practice evil, we thought the best approach would be to serve with enthusiasm. That approach was more likely to gain favor, and it might lead to greater freedom, and possibly even a way to escape.

"We are willing to serve Mother Earth," we said.

"Very well," he replied. "In that case, I am pleased to enroll you in Mother Earth Academy, a two-year program in the arts, sciences, and philosophy of our great city. Together with the other elite hostages, you will learn to dress as we dress, eat what we eat, play as we play, and think as we think. If you have ability and work hard, then upon successful completion of this program you will each be given a responsible position in the kingdom of Mother Earth. Your slave brands will be burned into proud oak trees, and your careers will become as bright as the future of Mother Earth itself."

The steward stopped and sniffed. Wrinkling his nose, he rang a bell. "As a first step, you must learn not to offend us. You must groom as we groom, which includes bathing daily, and scrubbing your teeth[1]. If you fail me in any way, you will be beaten, and sent to the mines. I hope I make myself clear."

A young palace slave entered, and bowed low. The steward continued. "As of this moment, you are no longer common slaves. You are royal students, and will be treated as such. I am assigning Tuktub as your servant to help you navigate the waters of the Academy. Remember this: your performance reflects on the judgment of the queen mother, for she selected you. If you fail to measure up, she will take it personally. Adopt our ways quickly. Your training shall commence with hygiene. When I see them again in three days, Tuktub, I shall expect them to look and smell more presentable."

It was a relief to leave the office. Our new servant explained the layout of the palace, our responsibilities as students, and various rules. His manner of speech was rather cryptic.

"When steward trusts," he said, "more freedom. Keep rules, no escapes. Guards brutal, punish me, too."

The first place Tuktub took us was the palace spa, where we submitted ourselves to the groomers. Our heads were shaved, that being the custom for slaves, and we were given a bath with warm water and soap[2]. It was our first real bath since our capture, and it felt delightful. The palace facilities had running water, we saw, brought in from the mountains by aqueducts of baked clay. The abundant water was used for drinking, bathing, and an ingenious system for flushing waste[3]. After our bath, our teeth were scraped and polished, something we found highly refreshing, especially after weeks without normal tooth scrubbing. Our next stop was the laundry, where we were given a blue palace tunic, a leather utility harness, new sandals, and sun hats. Our tunics and hats, we saw, were emblazoned with the insignia of Mother Earth.

Over the years, I have learned that simply having a washed body and fresh clothing can significantly improve your attitude. That day we felt like new people! We were hungry, so Tuktub took us to the palace kitchen. After enjoying our first real meal since our capture, Tuktub showed us to our sleeping chamber, which was surprisingly luxurious, and more suited for a prince than a slave. Before leaving, he gave us instructions.

"Steward says, make you fit for Professor. You scrawny dogs, now. Rest, eat, get strong."

With full bellies, new hope, and peace and quiet, we had the best sleep we had had in months. After two more days of rest, nourishment, and light exercise, we felt almost restored. The palace steward was almost cordial when we saw him next, and he wished us the best of success. On our way to the Mother Earth Academy, Tuktub gave what for him was a lengthy address.

"I like you sons of Noah. You treat me, not like slave, but son of Adam. Professor very bad man: selfish, nose up, full of hate. Wants you to be like him. He is sabertooth: do not look in eye. Remember: you only slave! Do not correct; do not say anything: understand? Only ask questions. Much better."

Tuktub's words surprised me. He was warning us, in his own peculiar way, that the professor's purpose was not to educate us or expand our fund of knowledge, but to corrupt our view of the world, so that we would think and act wickedly, like him[4].

In the past, our teachers had always been loving relatives who were gifted in their field, and who earnestly wished to make us better, smarter, and stronger. We had a common worldview. That was not the case here, and Tuktub was putting us on guard. We came to appreciate his advice even more later on.

---

[1]*Editor's Note:* As a dentist, I was delighted to see that even people in the distant past understood the importance of oral hygiene, as seen in this passage. A following paragraph even mentions professional tooth scraping and polishing!

[2]*Editor's Note:* The mention of soap in this story is interesting. The origin of this vital element of hygiene is unknown, but it has been used at least since Babylon, 2800 years ago.

[3]*Editor's Note:* This plumbing system sounds remarkably modern. Perhaps, however, when living in a valley with abundant flowing water, this development was only natural.

[4]*Editor's Note:* This comment reminded me of the perplexing dilemma encountered by many college students in American universities today. Christian or Orthodox Jewish students, in particular, often find it awkward to be in the power of a professor who is implacably antagonistic towards their view of the world.

Chapter Twenty-Two: Mother Earth Academy

Mother Earth Academy was conducted in a walled courtyard along the edge of the palace gardens. As we entered, a guard checked off our names, pointed to a bench facing the podium, and said we should stand and be silent unless spoken to. The other students already stood quietly by their own benches. They looked at us with curiosity as we entered, but said nothing. After what seemed like a long time, the students suddenly stiffened.

"Good morning, Professor[1]!" one shouted.

A tall man strode in past the guards, wearing bright colors in the latest fashion. His green robe sparkled with threads of silver and gold, and was accented with a purple sash. His long gloves were bright yellow, and his tall, rakishly tipped hat was scarlet. Tinkling sounds came from his feet. His bright blue sandals had silver bells, which nearly made me laugh! When he reached the podium, he turned to the students. His face might have been handsome, except for the disdainful curl of his lip, and his general look of contempt.

"Very well. Be seated," he instructed. "We shall begin. Let me first ask, as I did last time: why are you here? Speak up, students!" After a period of silence, the professor lost patience. "Each of you is here, class, because you failed to save your kingdoms, and they were conquered. Now, repeat after me: 'I am a failure!' Shout it!"

We all stood and shouted, "I am a failure!"

"Yes, you are failures!" he continued. "Your people suffer today because of you. That brings us to the second question. What are you, now, students? Speak up! You know the answer!"

Our classmates spoke reluctantly: "I am a worthless slave."

"Shout it this time," the professor demanded. "I did not hear you!"

"I am a worthless slave!" they shouted.

"Yes; you are worthless slaves," the professor said. "You may have been princes before, but now you are slaves: property. The king owns you, just like his horse, or his chariot, or his dog. And it is your own fault, because you failed. But what is your biggest fault, your biggest sin? Let me help you with this one. Your biggest fault is that you see everything all wrong! You are blind to reality, and deceived by the very things you supposed were true. And what is the most important thing about being deceived? It is that you do not know it! Repeat after me: I have sinned, I am blind, and it is my fault! Repeat it loudly, unless you wish to be beaten!"

We all shouted out: "I have sinned, I am blind, and it is my fault."

"Correct. You have sinned, you are blind, and it is your own fault! But if you open your eyes, you will begin to think correctly, as we do. Only if you begin to think correctly will you ever be of value. That is why I am here: to open your minds to the truth. Be seated."

The professor looked around the room, his mouth slightly open. He reminded me of a snake, though his tongue did not dart out quite as far.

"Ah! New students today! I suppose I must introduce myself again. Students, I am Professor Adrammelech." He paused, slightly nodding, as if he expected us to recognize his name. When we looked blank, he frowned.

"I suppose it was too much to hope that you had ever heard of the 'Scholar of Nephil,' or the 'Philosopher of Nephil.' My works on the mysteries of human knowledge are universally acclaimed! You ought to be surprised that someone of my caliber has been recruited to teach mere slaves. It actually is beneath me, but the queen mother has great hopes for you. I expect you to learn quickly. You shall refer to me as 'Honorable Professor', or as 'My Master'. Is that clear?"

"Yes, my Master," shouted our fellow students, and we followed along.

"Our newcomers shall now stand up, and state their names and origin."

We stood, gave our names, and said we had come from Enoch's Valley. The professor's face reddened, and a small smile crept over him. We glanced at each other, puzzled. What was he so gleeful about?

"Enoch's Valley!" he said, bursting with laughter. "The hotbed of the Adamite religion? This is a treat, class! Our new students believe that we are sinful heathen, doomed to eternal hellfire and destruction. They think we need to be saved by falling down to worship their Almighty Creator. Recently, one of the preachers from Enoch's Valley sent our own king, the mighty Nezzar, a letter saying their Creator would destroy our entire city if he did not repent! That, of course, was before we conquered them!" He was convulsed with laughter, but finally calmed down, and tried to look serious.

"It will be amusing," he continued, "to see how long our new students keep their antique beliefs. Shall we review the evidence that disproves their mythical six-day creation? Shall we inform them of the recent discoveries of science? I doubt they have even heard of the fire particle released from substances that burn[2]. And they will probably try to deny the spontaneous formation of life from stagnant water[3], something anyone can see. Can they offer a sound explanation for the remarkable anatomic similarity of animals and man, if their mythical Adam was created separately? What do you think, class? Shall we have them stand to defend their religious beliefs? Well, young Adamites, do you have the courage? This is your chance to save lost souls. Speak up, if you dare!"

The professor backed away from his podium and crouched like a cat ready to pounce. Somehow, we knew this was an important moment, one that required both shrewdness and diplomacy. Ham and I looked at Shem. He was the one who had those skills. He nodded, and bowed respectfully to the professor.

"Thank you, most honorable professor. We marvel that you can know our beliefs, for you do not know us, nor have we spoken a word. But who are we to speak? As you say, we are mere slaves, and simply grateful to be alive. Esteemed master, we know nothing of the ways of Mother Earth, but feel privileged to be your humble students. We wish only to hear what you believe, and why you believe it."

Shem bowed again. The professor stood back, somewhat at a loss.

"I see," he sighed. "Perhaps we shall pursue this later. Today we have much to cover. Since you three are new, let me explain that you belong to me for the best part of each day. The rest of your time will be spent in physical training, or in culture and etiquette. If you perform well academically, you will later be given work assignments consistent with your talent and abilities. Your time with me is most important, for I will cleanse your mind from false reasoning. When you see the world as it really is, your thinking will change, and you will become a new person, serving Mother Earth from the heart. As the patriarch Cain said, "as a man thinks in his heart, so he is."

The three of us glanced at each other. Cain said that?

"If you embrace Mother Earth," he continued, "you will flourish. If you are stubborn, you will be punished. Understand? Good. Let us begin, class, by reviewing what we learned last time." He took a breath.

"First of all, there is no Almighty Creator God. There was no Garden of Eden. There is no sin, and no damnation to be saved from. No deity can save us or give us meaning: we must save ourselves. Only we can give ourselves dignity and value. There is no absolute truth, and there are no absolute rules that apply to everybody, everywhere, and at all times. In fact, absolute truth is a myth: the gibberish of doddering old fools who wish to enslave us. Everything is relative. Man makes his own rules, based on reason, and guided by those of us who are intelligent and educated. While the individual must bow before the good of society, there is otherwise no reason to suppress natural pleasures or creativity! We can and must establish an ideal society free from guilt, sin, and shame: a society where people can fulfill their true potential[4]!"

The professor removed his hat and placed it on his podium. I had marveled that he had been able to keep such a ridiculous thing on his head, and somehow felt relieved. The professor talked quickly now, pacing back and forth.

"When Nezzar became king, Mother Earth was just a dirty little town. Many of her citizens were Adamites like those in Enoch's Valley, fanatic believers in an antique religion whose moral code repressed their healthy urges and natural creativity. When our queen mother came here, she began asking questions. Suppose the patriarch Cain were right, after all? Suppose there were no all-powerful Creator? Then where did we come from? What is man's true purpose and destiny? What is wrong with the world, and what can we do about it[5]?"

As he continued, he became increasingly agitated, really seeming to believe what he said. And for someone who denied any belief in a Creator God, he certainly talked a lot about him.

"The queen mother had seen the truth," the professor declared, "because her eyes were opened by the gods: the Old Ones! One of the gods, a brother of the earth goddess Mokosh, saw her great beauty. He chose her out, and gave her a son supernaturally, without the aid of a man. Yes! Our king is an actual hero: a real giant, if you will, with superhuman size and strength! Do you see now, students, why your cities could not resist us?"

"Let me tell you something," he continued. "The main problem with the world is ignorance and superstition! The rigid religious rules of the Creator keep us from following our true desires, and finding happiness; and they also keep our world from finding true social justice. We cannot get what we deserve, because other people have it. The greedy few enjoy the labors and riches of the many, because they have robbed and extorted their fellow man! We must shake off their repressive dictatorship, and embrace the brotherhood of mankind!"

The professor's eyes were wide now. He fairly quivered with excitement, and waved his arms dramatically. I found his reasoning impossible to follow, but he was entertaining, in a crazy sort of way.

"We will create a perfect Cainite society," he went on, "unrestrained by absolute moral standards. The new man will be educated, like me, and live in harmony with the earth. Our world will become another Garden of Eden, except without its oppressive Creator. We will all share a common purse. With all the tremendous production from our advanced technology, we will be rich, yet we will share our wealth gladly, and only take if necessary. We will have perfect security, and enjoy luxury and affluence like never before!"

The professor paused, searching our faces for a kindred spirit. One or two students seemed to agree with him, but most nodded as if in agreement, but actually tapped their feet with impatience. The professor pushed on.

"But what steps must we take? There are three, my eager students. The first one is what I call the Great Flattening. We must remove the destructive influences of a supernatural Creator, and take away false ideas and moral restraints. The religious fanatics who have robbed the wealth of others must themselves be robbed. That is the purpose of our great army, and the vast industrial power supporting it. It will require shedding much blood, but we will conquer, if we stay strong. The next step is to create a New Man, an Uncreated Man, who is capable of becoming a god himself. As the Creator God religion shrivels away like anything else that is dead, we can use other religions or non-religious philosophies to release us from that enslaving belief. By the way, if you are smart, and wish to advance quickly, you will learn to worship the earth goddess Mokosh. Our glorious queen mother is the physical embodiment of the earth goddess, and has her wisdom. If you are seen at her altar, you may gain her favor."

The professor seemed to have great stamina for talking. He hardly needed to breathe, and often repeated himself. It was obvious that his purpose was to insert doubts in the Creator, and refute his absolute moral standards. While some of the professor's ideas were interesting, his manner was annoyingly self-centered. He liked to preach, but his beliefs were anything but sensible. He continued to talk until the sun was directly overhead.

"The final step," he said, "is to set up an ideal human society with true social justice. The patriarch Cain may have envisioned it, but he was so misunderstood and persecuted by religious fanatics that he never lived to see it. We will! Class, I can see that your tiny brains have overflowed. We shall break for today. Physical training is next, followed by culture and etiquette. Tomorrow we will discuss social justice, and explain how obsolete religions rob people of personal pleasure and fulfillment. You may stand."

The professor carefully placed his hat on his head at a precarious angle, and walked out, leaving the class visibly relieved. When he was completely gone, Shem whispered a line from a favorite children's story.

"That boy does not have the sense he was born with!"

"He never did have the sense he was born with!" Ham added, turning to me.

"And he never will have the sense he was born with!" I concluded.

Our physical training proved a much better experience. After changing into athletic gear, we were taken beyond the palace walls to a large playing field. An obstacle course had been constructed next to a quiet stream, with sand pits, wooden walls, and climbing ropes. It reminded me much of our course at home. Our instructor was a large muscular man named Shimron, whose scars suggested he had seen battle. Before addressing us, he lined us up like soldiers.

"Almost every royal hostage over the past five years," he began, "has been a delicate butterfly. As a soldier, King Nezzar believes in the value of training, and he has charged me to tone up your flabby bodies. Do not fear: I will not make you into soldiers. That would require putting down your drinking cups, and leaving your feasts early. If you were smart, though, you would work at becoming one. When you return to your homes, it will be to serve Mother Earth. Your countrymen may envy you, or even hate you as a traitor. You would be wise to learn to defend yourself. Even kings do not always die in bed."

Shimron put us through a variety of exercises, including running, climbing, and swimming. My brothers and I did not find it difficult, especially after our rigors in the wilderness. The physical effort was healthy, and the cool swim at the end was refreshing. Our classmates did not seem to like it: one whined that it was beneath him to "sweat like a pig." Shimron noticed our enjoyment, and was impressed how willingly we entered into the training.

"You three are exceptional!" he remarked. "Are you the captives from Enoch's Valley that fought off the death raptors? If so, these exercises will be no challenge for you. You should ask for training in arms, instead. And by the way: if you truly are Adamites, I suggest you be on guard this evening. The thrust of a sword is not the only way to destroy a man." He winked. "A bit of advice."

We puzzled over this advice as we walked to the palace for our class in "Culture and Etiquette." The students were seated around a big table, and given a hearty meal of fruits, vegetables, and breads. Being a royal student had its benefits, I thought. All I needed next was a tasty dessert and a soothing hot drink, and I would be ready for bed. However, no dessert was offered. Instead, servants brought large bowls filled with hot, savory chunks of an unfamiliar food. Seeing our fellow students eagerly taking the morsels, Shem and I reached out for a piece, too.

"Roasted animal flesh!" Ham whispered.

Shem and I gagged, and began to push back from the table, but Ham held us.

"Don't make a big deal of it, brothers. Take another potato, instead."

None of our classmates noticed our misstep: they were too busy gorging themselves on the juicy pieces. We turned back to our food and pretended to eat, but we actually felt sick.

Despite our personal revulsion, this meal was our first opportunity to talk with the other students, and we suppressed our feelings long enough to enter into conversation. Most of our fellows, we learned, had been in the palace for weeks. Some had been captured during the violent conquest of their city, but more had been willingly delivered by their kings as their cities surrendered. The young men were pleasant enough, but they seemed to feel they were entitled to a life of luxury. None showed fear for their own persons. They were not common people, after all, but noble. They expected that their training would advance them to a place of power and privilege in the growing empire of Mother Earth.

After the meal, a party of instructors entered the room, led by a strikingly beautiful woman who instantly got our attention. Her figure was tall but voluptuously feminine, and she was tantalizingly draped in a thin emerald green garment. Her voice was low and melodious.

"I am Athaliah," she said, "the director of the Ministry of Culture." As she continued speaking, I noticed that she often made subtle gestures drawing attention to her curves. Although as attracted as everyone else, I found it irritating. This woman clearly knew her powerful effect on men, and enjoyed enticing them.

"I welcome you to the City of Mother Earth! Let me introduce my handsome associates. Jubalech is the director of music, while Naphish is the director of arts and entertainment. It is our pleasure to bring you the superior culture of Mother Earth, including her music, arts, and entertainments. Although you may not be here altogether by personal choice, trust me: when you choose to embrace it, you will find nothing more enjoyable. Students, from now on, your evenings belong to me. Together we shall explore art, music, dancing, and everything else that gives pleasure. And now, I present Mother Earth!"

We had not noticed the musicians and dancers enter; but at her signal, cymbals clashed, drums began to beat, and the music began. Scantily dressed dancers posed, leaped, and twirled with movements so sensual that my mind raced back to forbidden stories of fertility rites among the remote savages. Heads and shoulders all around us began to bob rhythmically with the music, while my brothers and I looked on with open-mouthed astonishment. Servants put drinks before us, and distracted by the loud noise and whirling activity, we unconsciously sipped them, just like the other students. The drinks were excellent, and tasted like exotic fruits, although some had a sharp edge. My head began to buzz. Perhaps I was getting tired, I thought: the sun had already set. Aromatic smoke filled the air, and the long evening of wild entertainment passed by in a blur.

In between the songs of love and vengeance, Athaliah spoke of the pleasures found in the various public entertainments and celebrations of the city. The other instructors told of Mother Earth's galleries of art, her marketplaces, her Great Zoo, and even her Temple of Virility. Our job, they suggested, was simply to enjoy it all. The dancers and singers performed with energy and rhythm, appealing to every fleshly desire. It was all like a dizzying dream. I did not even remember returning to our chamber and falling asleep.

[1]*Editor's Note:* The title translated "professor" really means "revealer of the mysteries," but professor seemed more appropriate in what seemed like a college or university setting.

[2]*Editor's Note:* This sounds like the phlogiston theory, long discredited, which postulated a fire-like element within combustible substances that was released during burning.

[3]*Editor's Note:* This may be an early rendition of spontaneous generation, another popular theory only disproven by Louis Pasteur in the mid 1800's.

[4]*Editor's Note:* This discourse was to me strikingly similar to the Humanist Manifesto (I, II, III; 1933, 1973, 1999). Perhaps humanist or progressive thinking is not new, after all.

[5]*Editor's Note:* In his excellent textbook Understanding the Times, David Noebel mentions these as questions that worldviews answer. The most important questions of life have apparently changed little in thousands of years.

Chapter Twenty-Three: Choosing to Resist

The sun was high by the time I opened my eyes. I was thirsty, and had a terrible headache. My dreams had been feverish, with Athaliah screaming: "think of me, Japheth, think of me!" I closed my eyes again.

"I feel just awful," I finally announced. "I think I was poisoned!"

Ham groaned, and sat up. "Me, too! I had horrible dreams. I was part of Sandal's gang, and everyone was laughing and eating smoked pig flesh. Athaliah kept dancing around, trying to touch me."

"She was in my nightmare, too!" Shem added. "A great behemoth was lumbering down the hill toward us, but our feet were stuck in the mud, and we could not move. Father came to rescue us, but Athaliah and the professor pushed him away. Enoch's parrot was flying around at the same time, shrieking 'judgment on all!' I tried to scream, but no sound came out!"

Tuktub came to our room a few minutes later, bringing breadfruit and three cups of a special tonic. He somehow knew we would be sick.

"Professor very bad man," he said, shaking his head in disapproval. "Strong spirits hook you. Drink this: helps."

The tonic was sharp and peppery, and burned on the way down. Its effect, however, was instant: my very next breath felt clean and icy cold. My eyes began to open, my aches started going away, and I perked up. My brothers felt better, too. Tuktub, we said, was a great fellow, and no mistake!

We barely made it to class on time. The professor's lecture started out much like the previous day, and soon became an annoying harangue. It was a model for all the lectures that followed, filled with foolish assertions and nonsensical conclusions. He constantly jumped from one wrong idea to another. Even if my headache had not returned, it would have been painful.

At first, he talked about what the state, or government, should do to create an ideal human society. The state should guarantee equal success for everyone, he asserted, so that no one feels bad. Riches are bad for the masses, because when one person becomes rich, another person has to become poor. He went on to justify Mother Earth's system of slavery, asserting that all people actually belong to each other. When leaders accumulate slaves or become rich in private property, he said, it is morally good, because they use these things for worthwhile purposes. His talk made my head worse. All of his ideas were wrong, and deliberately confusing. Unfortunately, he was just warming up.

As the morning progressed, the professor attacked absolute moral codes for suppressing natural urges and creativity. Our classmates, however, seemed to find the way he rationalized self-indulgence rather appealing. Because everything is relative, he said, what is bad for one person may be good for another. His statement sounded familiar. He went on to assert that physical pleasures of any kind are morally good, and should not be refused! Our fellow students cheered that one. And if the pleasures of traditional marriage are good, he maintained, then multiple temporary marriages are great! After all, if a little pleasure is good, a lot is a lot better! When we fully embrace the worldview of Mother Earth, he declared, it opens the door to every kind of pleasure!

"Like the Temple of Virility?" one student asked, smiling.

"Especially the Temple of Virility!" The professor laughed, nearly toppling his scarlet hat. "The queen mother wants you to enjoy every satisfaction. The Garden of Eden was only a myth that gave the patriarchs control over the weak minds of their followers. Good and bad are only relative; we must trust and follow our feelings. Power—raw power—is the greatest good. Power places us far above those who would judge us! Learn the power of Mother Earth, and experience her pleasures. If you do, you will never turn back!"

The professor eventually stopped talking and left. My headache, which had become severe, slowly began to subside. Physical training was next. It was a relief to sweat out some of the poison, and I soon began to improve. Thankfully, the culture and etiquette class that day was only a short tour of the city, for Athaliah was otherwise engaged.

Later, in the cool of the evening, my brothers and I found a quiet corner of the palace gardens.

"Brothers," I began, "If we go on like this, I think I will die!"

"Me, too," Shem said. "That wicked professor is deliberately poisoning our minds with false ideas. Athaliah, on the other hand, is purposefully tempting us with strong spirits, forbidden foods, and sensual enticements!"

"They plan to corrupt us," Ham added, "just like Tuktub said."

"The professor lied to us from the very start," Shem began. "We were not responsible for Enoch's Valley's defeat. We fought our best; but he made us say it was our fault. I wondered why he would do that, until I remembered Cousin

Asaph telling us that our lips teach our minds. If we repeat the professor's lies often enough, we will begin to believe them! One lie will lead to another. Finally we will become as corrupt and worldly as this wicked city, and just as deserving of God's awful judgment! Thankfully, they made one serious error."

"What error is that?" I asked.

"They failed to isolate us," Shem said. "We still have each other!"

"Right!" Ham said. "If we were all alone, and chose to eat animal flesh, drink strong spirits, or surrender our bodies to the Temple of Virility, who would know? And I could fall for Athaliah. She is as pretty as a python. She and the professor know how young and moldable we are, and they have carefully designed this whole experience to shape us. His stupid philosophy is intended to loosen our moral restraints, and she is deliberately plying us with spicy food, sensual images, and strong spirits. Under those conditions, it is only natural for a young man to be as stimulated as a stallion in a breeding paddock, and just as eager to indulge in those activities[1]!"

"That is very vulgar, Ham!" Shem said with disgust.

"Well, what I mean," Ham explained, "is that once we give in, they have us hooked. They will use our guilty conscience and our natural desire for more pleasure as wedges to control us!"

"I agree," Shem answered. "Athaliah designed last night as an exercise in control. She carefully selected the music, the dancing, and even the strong spirits to shape our thoughts. She made us play the game, 'what if I could?'"

"I see it, now!" I said. "When the professor rationalized immoral acts as 'creative pursuits' or 'harmless pleasures', he was really attacking our reason! And Athaliah was twisting our normal, healthy desires into harmful lusts! I think you are right about her use of music, too. Cousin Asaph has often said that music bypasses the mind to affect the soul directly."

"In other words," Ham added, "music can be used for evil purposes as well as for good!"

"Brothers," Shem declared, "Mother Earth intends to use our natural desires to seduce us into evil! If we let her, she will rob our innocence, muddy our worldview, and destroy our faith and character. And once we fall, we will never be the same again, even if we repent. Our elders warned us that sin creates weak areas in our life, and narrows our future opportunities for godly service."

"So, what can we do?" Ham asked. "If father is right, the Creator is going to destroy this city for its wickedness. Unfortunately, we don't know exactly when. It would be a shame to let ourselves be corrupted when relief might on the way!"

"Let's think about it," Shem said. "Why has our Maker brought us here? We know there is a reason for everything. Our family mission is to save people. But if our own souls are destroyed, how can we save anyone else?"

Suddenly, I thought of something. "Brothers," I said, "do you remember what father said about inserting the truth when we can?"

"I remember," Shem answered. "He said we must question foolish assertions and silly reasoning, and patiently insert the truth when we can."

"Tuktub gave us exactly the same advice," I said.

"He did!" Shem exclaimed. "Questions are the answer!"

"Questions are the answer?" Ham asked doubtfully. "The professor is a scoffing fool[2], the very worst type! He will not listen, but only get angry."

"Maybe if the students see the faults in his reasoning," Shem suggested, "one or two will wake up."

"Even if they don't," I said, "we still need to show ourselves that we have a little integrity, a little character! We must not be so easily seduced! From a tactical standpoint, I think we should act courteously with the professor, and be careful not to make assertions! If we did, we would be obligated to defend them. The professor would use all his power to trample us."

"But the students are forced to recite stupid lies!" Ham exclaimed. "If Asaph is right, and our lips teach our minds, we will still be poisoned."

"Maybe when he makes us shout, 'I am worthless, I am a slave,'" Shem suggested, "we should say something else inside, like: 'made in God's image!'"

"I think we are getting somewhere," I said. "I only wish we had less time with this professor. Every second is an aggravation!"

"Let's leave that problem in our Maker's hands," Shem suggested. "If he wishes, he can remove us from the professor, or remove the professor from us."

After our discussion, we decided to look for opportunities to ask questions, and insert small bits of truth. We were determined to resist being corrupted. Some might call it silly, but we actually raised our arms to make a vow: "We will not be corrupted by Mother Earth!"

Looking back, I am convinced that that simple resolution was an important step in transforming our miserable experience into something that became an adventure. About a week later, we had our first opportunity to ask a question.

"Today, class," the professor began, "let us root out the antique patriarchal myth of a supernatural creation. No intelligent person believes that story. For weak-minded individuals who cannot handle harsh scientific reality, however, that type of tale offers their pointless little lives some meaning and purpose. Actually, however, everything in the world developed gradually, by accidents, bloodshed, and death, over thousands and thousands of years. The creation myth of the Adamites, while false, was a useful tool for the patriarchs. It answered emotional questions, and allowed them to control their followers. Now, doesn't that make sense?"

We glanced at each other. The professor had just asked a question. Furthermore, his mood seemed accommodating. Shem raised his hand.

"I apologize, honorable professor, but I cannot help being curious about the creation story. My great-grandfather knew the patriarch Adam personally for over two hundred years, and heard the creation story many times directly from his lips. Is there any evidence or reason to believe that Adam fraudulently invented the story?"

"You simple Adamite!" the professor laughed. "There is no need for evidence! The Eden story is subjective, like everything else. People accept the story because they want to believe it for emotional reasons, not because it actually occurred."

"But, professor," Shem asked mildly, "if everything is subjective, then could your alternative story be subjective, too? Could we be rejecting Adam's account for emotional reasons rather than because of objective facts or careful reasoning?"

"Everyone knows that everything is relative," the professor continued patiently. "There is no absolute truth, no Creator God, and no objective right or wrong. There may have been a kernel of truth in the creation myth, but the story has obviously been distorted over a thousand years. Old people forget things, and no educated person believes that story today. The only way it might be true is subjectively, in someone's mind. Remember: everything is relative, and nothing is absolutely true."

"Please forgive my ignorance, honorable professor," Shem returned calmly, "but your statement that nothing is absolutely true sounds so very absolute! How can you be so sure of it? What if your statement that 'everything is relative' were only relatively true? What if the creation story were the exception, and absolutely true?"

The professor was dumfounded for a few moments; but as he thought, his face became red with anger.

"You stupid imbecile! You son of apes and dogs[4]! Do you realize how close you are to a beating? I am in a forgiving mood today, but I will not overlook your ignorance again. Next time, think more carefully before you speak!"

Shem apologized and sat down. Some classmates wondered what happened, and later a few even asked Shem to explain. Two weeks later, the professor was again in a good mood. He had spent the previous evening with Prince Malek, riding in his prized ivory chariot and visiting various pleasure-houses. His greatest pleasure seemed to be associating with those of nobility, wealth, and power.

"Yes, class," he chattered happily, "in Mother Earth, we encourage every variety of entertainment. Everything is permitted, and all personal choices are morally the same. Diversity, whether of religion or personal preference, only strengthens us and brings us together. Tolerance is a great good! Mother Earth tolerates all differences, and even celebrates them. Only a weak society would allow people to make judgments on others. Absolute standards breed hate, as everyone knows. For the good of society, those who profess absolute standards must be destroyed!"

Ham raised his arm, and the professor nodded indulgently.

"Honorable professor, I feel very dull today, but I would still like to understand. You say tolerance is a great good. But doesn't destroying people who profess absolute moral standards sound rather intolerant to you?"

The professor stopped pacing for a moment, but responded patiently.

"You ignorant provincials are so stupid! These are sophisticated concepts. By definition, those who profess absolute moral standards are intolerant, and they cannot be allowed. It is not the other way around. I hope that clears it up."

Shem and I looked at the other students. Several were smiling surreptitiously: a little truth had been inserted, even though the professor had not realized what had happened.

"Thank you, most honorable professor. I think I understand, now." Ham nodded his thanks, and sat down.

My own turn came a few days later, when the professor was droning on about the evils of "certain religions."

"Hateful religious fanatics judge the rest of us about food, strong spirits, and even inhaling the smoke of herbs. They tell us how many days to work, what gods to worship, who to marry, and for how long. They tell us to never lie, steal, or murder; and to treat others in the way we would like to be treated. In other words, they are always telling us what to do! Their arbitrary rules restrict our freedom and our creativity, and they must be expunged! Everyone knows that you should not make moral judgments on others! Anyone who judges another person is evil, and should be destroyed!"

I raised my hand.

"I am so sorry, honorable professor, but I do not understand," I said. "You say we should not make moral judgments on others. But aren't you doing it yourself, right now?"

The professor stopped, and stared blankly with his mouth open. He finally closed it, and his eyes widened in understanding. As he looked around the room, he saw students suppressing laughter.

"Aha!" he exclaimed. "Now I understand what you are doing, you stupid idiots, you mindless offspring of skunks and pigs! You three brothers are working together, aren't you? Do you think you can play this kind of prank on me? You need to learn that the power of Mother Earth must be taken seriously! Guards!" he shrieked. "Take these three out and beat them! I want to hear their screams!"

I had pushed too far. The guards came in and roughly hauled us to an area screened off by bushes. Using canes, they gave us a painful thrashing. Thankfully, the soldiers had no liking for the professor, and our punishment sounded far worse than it was. The professor was gleeful when we returned, and our classmates were sobered.

Our efforts may not have been the wisest, in retrospect; but a few classmates questioned the professor's reasoning later themselves, and received beatings of their own. Despite the harsh consequences, we somehow felt better. We had made an effort to resist having our minds corrupted, and we had inserted a little light into a very dark place.

[1]*Editor's Note:* What I translated as "indulge in those activities" was actually a much cruder expression related to livestock breeding.

[2]*Editor's Note:* This reference to fools reminded me of the five types of fool mentioned in the Hebrew Scriptures: simple, silly, sensual, scorning, and steadfast. (Institute of Basic Life Principles)

[3]*Editor's Note:* College students today might do well to heed this ancient approach, which has also been recommended in modern days by Greg Kokl, President of Stand to Reason.

[4]*Editor's Note:* Again, I have substituted a crude insult with a much less vulgar equivalent.

Chapter Twenty-Four: The School of Arms

General Zabadanah sent for us the next day. "I heard you lads were made an example," he began. "I was concerned, because valuable military officers are sometimes ruined by unjust corporal punishment. But by the look of your faces, I did not need to worry. Your bruises will heal, and you will have learned a valuable lesson: do not tease incompetents in positions of authority." He chuckled.

"Adrammelech's mission, I understand, is to transform royal hostages into reliably obedient stooges. While I consider these efforts to be both dishonest and dishonorable, it is not my place to correct the strategies of my superiors. My own position is precarious enough. However, Shimron suggested something to reduce your exposure to the man. I talked with the palace steward about it, and he agreed to excuse you from some classes to attend a school of arms. The best one in Mother Earth is that of Zuar, a renowned swordsman who is an old comrade of mine. Despite having a long waiting list of noblemen willing to pay handsomely, he was able to find three places for you."

We thanked General Zabadanah profusely, but he waved us off, saying it was a small matter, and that he was glad to be of service. We left his office happy.

"Didn't I tell you," Shem exclaimed, "that our Creator could remove us from the professor?"

We reported to the school of arms the very next day. An assistant fitted us with training armor, and showed us around the busy school, which had a large open arena with sparring rings. Master Zuar did not immediately impress me as a warrior, for his figure was more lean and active than muscular. My opinion changed, however, the moment I saw him spar with a pupil. His technical skill was astonishing. His reflexes were like lightning, and he had marvelous agility and strength. After completing a lesson, he met with us. We found him both earnest and helpful.

"General Zabadanah told me of your exploit with the death raptors," he said. "That shows admirable boldness. He explained that you three were in a school for royal hostages, but that your physical training there was unchallenging. He thinks you may have a bright future in the army, and said you were eager to develop your skill with arms. Is that so?"

"Yes, sir!" I said. "We would like to spend our time wisely, and think improving our skills would make us more valuable to the king."

"Wisely spoken, young man. I can see that you have the physical gifts a warrior needs, with strong, healthy frames, good limbs, alert eyes, and good posture. Have you had any previous training in arms?"

"Sir, our uncle has given us lessons in the sword since we were young," I replied, "as well as instruction in the bow, the javelin, the sling, and others."

"So many?" he asked with surprise. "Very well! Let us first see what you have learned with the sword. I shall test you first, Japheth, as the eldest."

Master Zuar and I put on our helmets, which were fitted with protective metal grilles, and picked out shields and blunted swords from a rack before entering the sparring floor.

"We shall begin slowly," the master said. "Remember, this is only practice. I simply wish to see what thrusts, parries, and maneuvers you command."

Beginning with the most elemental thrusts, the master led me through a series of movements. They began slowly, but gradually became quicker. The exercises had been familiar to us since childhood. Before long, the master began making positive comments.

"Very good! Well turned; good use of the shield." One minute became two and then three as we practiced. Other teachers and pupils gathered to watch. It had been many weeks since I had sparred, and I found myself taking pleasure in it. While I considered the exercise unremarkable, Shem and Ham later told me that the instructors seemed surprised that one so young should have my level of skill.

"Who is that young man?" one teacher asked.

"A protégé of General Zabadanah, I believe," another replied.

"Well, he has the poise, speed, and reflexes of a fine swordsman," a third remarked.

Master Zuar continued our sword drill for another minute or two, and then signaled to halt. Raising his helmet, he smiled broadly, but appeared puzzled.

"Well, young nobleman, you appear to be very well trained for just a lad. You make me curious. Shall we engage further? I should like to see the extent of your skills." I was delighted that I had pleased a famed master of the sword.

There was a buzz among the onlookers. Master Zuar was rarely so impressed, I learned later. Never in their experience had he personally engaged with a new student for so long. Not knowing that, I was simply happy to have the attention of such a skilled master. We replaced our helmets, and engaged again. This time, the master showed less restraint, and attacked vigorously. I retreated for a moment, but soon recommenced. Master Zuar began using a variety of attacks: first backhand, then forehand, high thrusts and low thrusts, feints and slashes.

These were all of course quite familiar to my brothers and me. Before long, we were engaged at full speed and power, and the entire school gathered to watch the master spar with this unknown youth. By either subconscious training or by luck, I was able to find a satisfactory defense for each type of attack. The master continued to give flattering feedback.

"Well done! Superb! Now it is your turn to attack," he commanded.

In recent years, we had been instructed to employ a planned sequence of thrusts that were designed to uncover our opponent. I now employed our first planned sequence. Master Zuar parried my final thrust, but exclaimed, "Ha! I have seen that one somewhere before!"

I immediately proceeded to the second sequence in which we had been instructed. The master was surprised, and barely managed to parry it. A moment later, as we continued, he cried out in relief. "At last! I have you now!"

I did not know what he meant; but I decided to try yet another sequence in which I had been instructed. It was my favorite, and one I thought would surely succeed. After a fourth planned thrust and feint, I made the backslash that was intended to disable the opponent. To my surprise, however, and at just the critical moment, my sword was twisted out of my hand and sent sailing. The match was over.

Master Zuar dropped his shield, raised his helmet, and began laughing. His entire body heaved as he laughed and laughed, and tears came to his eyes. As the spectators looked on with open mouths, the master came over, still chuckling, and put his arm around my shoulders.

"Thank you, my young friend!" he said. "I devised that response to your maneuver more than forty years ago, and I have continued to practice it, though I feared I would never have an opportunity to use it! Why did you not tell me the name of your instructor? There is only one swordsman on earth that could, or would, teach such clever sequences: my own master Krulak!"

"You know Uncle Krulak?" we exclaimed.

"Uncle Krulak, you say? And he trained all three of you? Remarkable!" He laughed some more, and clapped our shoulders. "If you other two are even half as skilled as young Japheth here, then it would seem that Mother Earth has acquired some formidable young swordsmen! We must talk this over!"

Master Zuar took us into his private chamber, and had us tell him our story of growing up in Enoch's Valley, and learning swordsmanship at the feet of Uncle Krulak. Zuar had heard some details of the capture of Enoch's Valley, and offered us hope that Krulak might yet live. We did not tell him everything, of course; we saw no need to reveal our rescue of the Tubalites, or our battle in the swamp. In return, Zuar told us of his admiration for his old master, and offered several stories about the various battles they had fought, including some when they fought on opposing sides. At the end of our visit, Zuar offered us advice.

"Boys, Mother Earth is a wicked and dangerous city. You are very wise to polish your skill in arms, for as your uncle often told me, 'your actions train your will.' In battle, the warrior's will is everything! After all, what is war other than the imposition of your will? Frequent exercise--frequent practice--keeps your will from becoming sluggish and indolent. Laziness, or lack of initiative, is death to the warrior. When called, a warrior cannot remain seated: he must arise at once. Now, lads, you must train here at least three times each week. I will teach you all I can in swordplay, but I have other instructors to train you in the bow, the spear, the axe, and other weapons."

"After today, however, we shall keep the level of your skill quiet. Some of the most powerful noblemen in the city train here, including Prince Malek and the son of Prime Minister Logar. Many are jealous. It is not wise for a mere royal hostage to appear too skilled: people disappear for less. For my old master's sake, though, I will work you hard. You may someday have an opportunity to avenge the destruction of your homeland, and you must be ready. Frankly, I would not be sorry to see Mother Earth punished. She showers me with gold today, but her wickedness is a stench in the nostrils of the gods, and it worsens by the day. Believe me: if there really were a just Creator, he would cleanse the earth of its Mother Earths. I have long been ready to retire home to Cush. I am only waiting for the signal."

After our first lesson, we attended the school of arms three times each week. It was a great relief to be excused from some of the annoying harangues. The exercise was vigorous and healthy, and because we had made another friend, we felt less isolated.

We still had to sit through many of the painfully foolish, wasteful lectures, however, and had to recite the professor's distorted worldview. Ultimately, we began to appreciate the frequent irony in his statements. For example, when plans for a city tour fell apart because of misunderstandings and competing priorities, Shem quietly recited: "diversity brings unity!" And when the professor spoke of a former student as a genius, Ham whispered: "everything is relative!"

The professor's ridiculous passion for fashion was epitomized in his treasured scarlet hat. Every day he carefully placed it on the table, and admired its beauty. One day when he removed his hat, I saw tiny fruit flies flying around it. He waved them off. The next day when he entered the classroom wearing it, it was covered with flies. Trying to wave them away, he missed, and slapped his own face. When he removed his hat, he looked at it with puzzlement and annoyance.

On the third day, his hat was swarming with little white larvae, and mature flies hovered around his head like a cloud, though he proudly affected not to notice. When he got to the front, however, he took his hat off with both hands and studied it, his face getting redder and redder. Finally, he turned to our class angrily. He was just about to speak when a swarm of wasps flew in and attacked his hat. Screaming with fright, he dropped the hat. Covering his eyes to keep out the wasps, he turned to escape, and ran right into a pillar. Shrieking in pain and embarrassment, he ran out, followed by some of the wasps. Our class broke out in laughter.

When he returned the next day, the professor appeared to be suppressing his rage. He had gotten a new hat, this one fashionably decorated with polka dots of red, pink, and yellow. He placed his hat on the table and began to lecture as though nothing had happened. An hour later, as he was droning on about justice for the working class, I suddenly heard choking from classmates trying not to laugh. A pair of hummingbirds hovered around the professor's hat, taking turns poking it[1]. The entire class finally exploded in laughter. Spinning about angrily, the professor saw the hummingbirds, and wailed in exasperation. Snatching it from the table, he rushed out, cursing loudly.

Later, we learned that he had complained to the palace steward, demanding that all his students be severely punished. The steward, however, had refused to take him seriously. In fact, he threatened to tell the queen mother that he had lost control of himself. While the fruit fly infestation was suspicious, it was evident that the hummingbirds could only be blamed on his choice of hat. The professor was humiliated, but had to stifle his fury.

Our class was delighted. Shem and I were, too, but it occurred to us that Ham had been a little too quiet. When we cornered him, he laughed.

"Our honorable professor said that the power of Mother Earth had to be taken seriously. I just did not see why he had to be!"

[1]*Editor's Note:* I can only speculate how Ham could have such powers over insects or birds in these stories, although a friend once told me it was easy to breed fruit flies in a banana mash. Hummingbirds, however, are known to be attracted to tubular flowers in bright colors such as red, pink, or orange.

Chapter Twenty-Five: The Queen Mother

Professor Adrammelech took a holiday from his students for several weeks after that. In place of his lectures, we were given tours of the city, beginning with the great system of aqueducts that conducted fresh water from the mountains. On another tour, we explored the sewer system of the city, a network of covered trenches that drained into great settling basins.

Later, we visited the waterworks, the city's power system. A series of waterwheels, driven by waterfalls or water races, rotated great gears, which in turn drove spinning shafts and moving leather belts through a maze of subterranean tunnels. Factories even a distance away could attach leather belts to the drive shafts using a clutch device[1], and power lathes, mills, and other kinds of machinery. Our guide proudly informed us that Mother Earth had the greatest industrial capacity in the world outside of Nephil; and when the Great Dam was completed, Mother Earth would have the most hydraulic power on earth.

We visited lots of temples. Overall, my favorite was the Temple of Human Achievement. Inside the temple were hundreds of displays that highlighted man's dominion over the earth. A wide span of modern technology was presented, beginning with the mining of ore, and processes to purify it into metal. Great rooms housed artifacts showing the development of sailboats and four-wheeled carts, the manufacture of glass, pottery, and fabrics, as well as the development of modern writing, accounting, architecture, and agriculture[2].

The Temple of the Water God was fun for everyone. Novice priests showed us around the many beautiful pools, fountains, and artificial waterfalls built into the massive structure, and took us to the very top of the temple, where an aqueduct gushed a great current of water. After being given grass mats, we were brought to the edge of a long spillway and instructed to lie down. When ready, we were pushed in. The rapid water quickly swept us away on an exciting ride. We swooshed left and right, and up and down around several circuits of the temple. At the end, we were plunged into a deep pool scented with flowers. As we climbed out, goldfish tickled our feet[3].

Our city guide loved to talk, and was a very good teacher. He explained that the original settlers of the valley were Adamites who set up a representative form of government. A remnant of the old republic was still seen in the senate, where wealthy noblemen still occasionally contested the arbitrary rulings of the king. Descendants of the original inhabitants typically dressed in white or gray clothing, he said, while worshippers of the goddess Mokosh generally wore green. Nephilites proudly wore blue or black, while slaves generally dressed in drab brown. Skilled foreign workers preferred bright red and yellow, depending on their origin, but orange was never worn, because of its association with Tubal.

The king had a great fear of traitors, spies, and religious fanatics, we learned, and he had set up an entire network of secret informers. Because of them, people had learned to keep their political or religious sympathies quiet. The accusation of treason often led to an open arrest, or a sudden disappearance.

Despite the king's efforts, political or religious intrigues still erupted in violence. Extreme devotees of the goddess Mokosh, our guide explained, often resorted to violence to stop workers from logging trees or harvesting crops. Some had attempted to sabotage construction of the Great Dam, because it would restrain the flow of water over the earth. The Great

Zoo had been attacked several times, as well, because it imprisoned animals. Fundamentalist Adamites, another small group of religious fanatics, although non-violent, were also considered dangerously subversive. These fanatics, our guide explained, were sometimes observed doing small kindnesses for the poor and needy, but their motivations were completely treasonous, as everyone knew.

While we were having tours of the city, Mother Earth conquered yet another land. As royal hostages, we were required to attend the triumph. Watching the naked captives struggle along the parade route sparked painful memories.

The new captives prompted our guide to explain the workings of the slave system in Mother Earth. Recent conquests, he said, had given them a glut of slaves for the army and the mines. Normally, those born into slavery were adequate for domestic needs. Native-born slaves were provided food, clothing, shelter, and other care by their owners, but were not allowed to learn reading or writing. Permanent marriage was rarely permitted among slaves, for the law provided that the offspring of a permanent marriage would go free. While male slaves were generally employed in low-skill jobs, female slaves were given menial household or factory work, unless they were particularly attractive. In that case, a period of service in the Temple of Virility provided them an opportunity to earn their freedom.

All too soon, Professor Adrammelech got over his embarrassment, and our tours came to an end. When he returned to the classroom, his lectures were more aggressive than ever, and he applied even more pressure to make us conform. We had a sympathetic ear in Tuktub, but our greatest comfort was having brothers to talk with. On quiet evenings we shared our frustrations, and attempted to purge the professor's poison from our minds.

"Guys, do you think the Creator is really going to destroy Mother Earth?" Ham asked one evening. "He seems to be blessing it, instead! Their kingdom is expanding, their idolatrous temples are flourishing, and wealth is pouring in! Sure, some people suffer horrible poverty, slavery, and injustice; but otherwise, the system seems to work. And how can we complain? We are living in the palace!"

"Ham, we have to look at things from our Creator's perspective," Shem said. "Even if we are personally in comfort, the people here are morally insane. They are in rebellion against God, they practice gross idolatry and immorality, and their thirst for power is unquenchable. They murder and enslave their neighbors, and maintain their power through a web of fear and stupid lies. The victims of their evil system cry out for justice!"

"But even if this city is not destroyed while we watch," I added, "I refuse to submit to its temptations. When Adrammelech was screaming at us today, I felt like pinning him to the wall with a javelin. At that moment, I realized I was being tested! Do you remember what Adam told our patriarch? 'Our Maker seeks virtue in His children, but without testing, there is no virtue.' Adam failed his test, but we do not want to fail ours. If we can somehow avoid falling prey to their lies and temptations, it will be counted as virtue for us, and it will bring pleasure to our Maker."

Perhaps I was trying to firm my own resolve by speaking like that. Frankly, many times I felt myself wavering. We hoped to someday complete our time with the professor, and be given meaningful work; but the months passed very slowly.

At long last, we were given a battery of tests, and interviewed for potential work assignments. That was an encouragement! About the same time, our class had the opportunity to meet two of the most important figures in Mother Earth.

The first one was Prime Minister Logar. I was curious to meet the father of the bully Rogar, although I fervently hoped he knew nothing about me. On the day of our audience, our class walked down a long corridor of polished granite, and through great bronze doors to the senate chamber. Octagonal in shape, the chamber had massive columns that supporting a magnificent dome. The prime minister's podium was made of pure ivory, and stood on a dais surrounded by rows of luxurious couches made of rare ipilwood.

Though by no means a giant, Prime Minister Logar was large and heavy, and strongly reminded me of his son. He warmly welcomed us on behalf of the queen mother, our benefactress, whom he praised as the 'very embodiment of the goddess Mokosh.' It was obvious that he loved to talk. Unfortunately, his discourse proved both rambling and bizarre.

"Did you notice the tremor this morning, students?" he began. "We know the reason for it, don't we? For years, mankind has been stripping the earth of her green foliage, and heartlessly mining her metal ore and jewels. That tremor was a sign of her anger. Unless mankind stops harming the earth, we will all die horribly! There are always consequences when forests are leveled, you see, or when animals are enslaved and eaten. In some regions, ants have begun to swarm in vast biting armies, while in other areas clouds of locusts have consumed every green plant down to the root. This week I heard that masses of small rodents near the Pishon River, upset by man's encroachment, committed mass suicide by casting themselves off a cliff! Will mankind never learn to stop offending the earth goddess? Unless we do, earthquakes, pestilences, and devastating volcanoes will only get worse, until mankind is finally destroyed from the face of the earth!"

By this time, most of us were bewildered. We understood that he was a devout Mokosh worshiper, but none of this made sense. And anyway, why was he trying to alarm us?

"My scientific advisors have informed me," he continued, "that the earth grows cooler every year. Imagine that! Soon it will cool to the point where all the water will become solid ice[4]! And why? Because certain nations—evil nations--keep harming the earth! That is why, students, the most important thing we can do is to help our king crush those evil nations! Once we are victorious, the terrible calamities will cease, and our earth mother will once again be a paradise like the fabled Garden of Eden! I would love to tell you more, but I must go. Just remember this: worship your mother, the earth goddess Mokosh!"

For a time after he left, we sat stunned. Where had he gotten all those unrelated facts, if they really were facts? Where was his logic or reason?

"How was someone like that ever chosen for such an important position?" Shem wondered.

We thought about it, and concluded that our visit had given us a valuable insight into the selection of government ministers. By birth, Logar was noble; and by report, his fortune was enormous. Those two qualifications alone may have been adequate for his selection as prime minister. They may have even been enough to overcome the significant personal hardship of having only the brain of a pigeon.

But we did not dwell on the prime minister for long. A day later we learned our work assignments. Our opinion of decision makers in Mother Earth instantly improved, for my brothers and I got exactly the assignments we had hoped for. Ham was assigned to the Great Zoo, Shem was given the Hall of Records, and I was to assist the chief engineer of the Great Dam.

Soon after that, we discovered that our class had been granted an unexpected honor: an audience with the queen mother herself. The news caused considerable flutter among our teaching staff. The day before our audience, Professor Adrammelech spent hours reviewing what he had taught. He cautioned us strongly.

"Do not forget your training!" he said, trembling. "The queen mother has power beyond anything you have encountered. If she asks, repeat the answers I have taught you! Anyone who would condemn her own brother for a trifling reason would not hesitate to slay you, and perhaps even your esteemed faculty! And whatever you do, do not look her straight in the eye!"

On the day of our audience, the palace steward led our class down the wide corridors of the palace to the queen mother's reception hall. Professor Adrammelech followed him, fashionably but carefully dressed in his most colorful robe. Cultural Minister Athaliah came next, sensuously attired in silks and feathers. Music Director Jubalech and Arts Director Naphish were behind them, also dressed in their richest clothing. The students trailed in last. We were dressed in our finest palace tunics and robes, and were lined up according to our favor with the professor. That meant that Shem, Ham, and I were the last to enter.

As we waited for the queen mother, we gawked at the magnificence of the chamber. The walls were white granite, and there were polished green stone columns, gold lampstands, and rich ornamentation. When the queen mother entered, we all bowed low. She was a mature but still beautiful woman, and about our own height. Her elegant gown was green and black, and she wore a delicate tiara crusted in emeralds, rubies, and diamonds, as well as a necklace composed of exceedingly rare green Mother Earth diamonds.

Accompanied by only a few attendants, she entered in an unrushed regal manner, and bowed her head slightly to acknowledge our obeisance. She was smiling, which was a relief, and she welcomed us in a low, cultured voice. After that, she immediately began to move down the line of students. She spoke to each one, repeating their names, and asked each a question or two. After hearing the answer, she would faintly smile, say a few more words, and move on to the next[4]. When she finally got to us, she brightened at our names, as though she were genuinely pleased to meet us. We could not help but smile in return. There was something about her that seemed familiar.

"Shem, is it?" she asked patiently. "I have a question for you. What do you know about right and wrong?"

"We have been taught that everything is relative, your Majesty," Shem replied, bowing.

She looked at Shem sharply. "Excellent. I shall not ask if you really believe that. Your behavior will reveal it as your training continues."

She looked Ham over slowly before asking her question. "Well, Ham, what do you think of pleasure?"

"The answer, I believe, your Majesty, is that if it feels good, it is good."

"I see," she said, looking at his face doubtfully. Finally, she turned to me. I kept my eyes looking straight ahead, as we had been instructed.

"Japheth," she said, shaking her head sadly, "it has not escaped my royal notice, that as the last in this line, you are the least favored." Her look might have been tender pity. "Here is my question for you. What is the greatest good?"

"According to our professor, your Majesty," I replied carefully, "the greatest good is power—raw power." These were the exact words we had been taught.

"Correct," she said, deliberately catching my eyes, something we had been told to avoid. Her eyes were vivid green, and dazzled me. Her nostrils flared a challenge. "That makes Mother Earth very good, doesn't it? Let me get right to the point, Japheth. I know something of your homeland, and I can easily imagine why your professor found you difficult. My general spoke highly of you, and said you and your brothers even saved his life from death raptors! That is admirable, and it shows impressive courage and skill. Those are qualities we need in army officers, as he suggested. My grandson has also spoken well of you. He said you defend the young and weak, even Tubalites! That shows heart, though questionable judgment. So: you three brothers are the sons of Noah, the son of Lamech, the son of Methuselah: am I right?" She smiled sweetly.

"Yes, your Majesty," I answered, smiling in return, and astonished at her knowledge and interest in our relatives.

Her serene smile vanished. "Well, your father Noah is a bold one!" she spat out her words harshly. "He actually had the temerity to rebuke my son—the king! Five years ago, when he visited this city, he threatened us with his God, and told us to repent! Our royal persons! And right before we conquered you, he sent a letter to us repeating his threats! I am familiar with your patriarchal religion. As children, you are constantly taught to fear committing some moral offense that will send you to hell; you are taught that physical pleasure is bad. You cannot even choose your own friends! Every healthy desire is repressed, and even your own brothers would betray you! What emotional scars you must bear, Japheth, and what anger! How happy, how relieved you must be to live in Mother Earth and be free of all that repression, even though you are now only a slave--mere property!"

I could only imagine what the other students thought, hearing her angry tirade. Even the confident Athaliah turned pale, I heard later. The queen mother glanced from me to the other students, and smiled before returning to me.

"But you are safe in Mother Earth, young Japheth!" she said. "The Academy is opening your eyes to see that there is no reason to fear any divine calamity. And our strength increases daily. When our Great Dam is complete, the power of our industry will be unmatched. Our army is already the world's finest, and once our secret weapon is perfected, no one will be able to stop us—not even the Creator God of Enoch's Valley!"

She turned again to peer directly into my eyes. I remembered the warning, but I had no power to turn away. It was eerie. Although akin to my experience with Great Aunt Naomi, this was not pleasant. I felt my soul skidding off its track.

"Join us, Japheth," she said softly. "Join us from the heart. Submit to us, and complete your training! Say yes! Embrace our worldview, and prosper with us. Enjoy the physical pleasures we offer, and the beauty of our art, music, and entertainment. Open yourself to the gods, Japheth. Do you see it? It is like a roaring furnace of power, Japheth: intoxicating power! Do not resist. Come conquer the world with us, and enjoy peace and prosperity for a thousand years!"

The queen mother became so enraptured with her vision that she forgot about me. She glanced up, and her spell was broken. As my eyes came back into focus, I saw her smiling at Shem and Ham, and rubbing her hands in satisfaction.

"Yes, boys," she said, "we shall bring your father Noah to our Dam Festival! He shall see what his sons have become. He shall see—they shall all see--who has real power on earth. Does an imaginary Creator have it, or the very real kingdom of Mother Earth?" She paused, but then laughed gaily. "Wait! We already did show them! But no one shall doubt when we celebrate our Dam Festival!"

The queen mother stopped laughing, and her gleeful expression suddenly became a scowl. The students paled. I marveled as I watched. While I had considered Aziza skillful at manipulating my emotions, the queen mother's skills were on an entirely different level. In mere moments, she had brought our group from the lofty pleasure of her favor to the dark depth of abject fear. Oddly, something about her reminded me of Grandma Tirza. She could be commanding, too, even haughty. But the comparison ended there. Grandma Tirza loved people, and was full of grace, while this queen mother had neither one.

"Students," she commanded, "uncover your shoulders. I want to see them!"

Pulling back the fabric of our robes, we showed her our slave brands. She looked me straight in the eye, and pressed her fingernail against my scar. It hurt.

"All of you!" she said imperiously. "Remember your marks! You are slaves, though we honor you as royal hostages. You belong to me. Your service here can be light, but only if you embrace our worldview. Trust me, and obey. Work hard, and enjoy the pleasures we offer. I am watching!"

When she strode out of the room, we sighed in relief. Her hostile personal interest in our family was unnerving. She had said that our father would see what we had become. What did she mean by that? We had much to ponder.

---

[1]*Editor's Note:* This system seems similar to the cable car power system in San Francisco. Individual trolleys use a clutch to engage a cable that runs continually beneath the pavement.

[2]*Editor's Note:* The description here reminds me of the Smithsonian museums in Washington, D.C., as well as Chicago's Museum of Science and Industry. Their technological developments seem to have been remarkably advanced.

[3]*Editor's Note:* This seems much like a modern-day water park!

[4]*Editor's Note:* Such a fear was common from 1950-1970, although today, "global warming" is more popular.

[5]*Editor's Note:* I have met only a few powerful people, but the skills described here seem to be common among them.

Chapter Twenty-Six: A Religious Festival

A week or so later we reported to our work assignments. We still were required to attend some lectures, as well as Athaliah's cultural events, but being able to work was a great relief. As royal students, we kept our quarters at the palace, and we still trained with Master Zuar; but now we had freedom to walk around the city. And another benefit was earning copper and silver coins!

Tulek, the chief engineer of the Great Dam, was a tall, broad-shouldered man with blue eyes and blond hair. As the youngest son of a noble family, he had to find employment, so he had pursued engineering. A hardworking professional, Tulek radiated competence, and he had a delightfully droll sense of humor. He kept a personal distance from me, perhaps because of his experience with other royal students, whom he had found "shallow, lazy, and addicted to pleasure." Still, he took time to plumb my knowledge of pumps, waterwheels, and gears. He seemed impressed when I explained the water-powered conveyor that I had designed for our barn.

"Perhaps you could design something similar for us," he suggested. "Right now, we have elephants drag the building stones up a sand ramp to a staging area. From there, we have cranes raise them into place, one by one. If we had a conveyor to bring the stones to the top of the construction, it would speed things up. Would you like to try?"

"I would love to!" I said. "But would you trust such a major project to a student?"

"Of course," he assured me. "I will offer advice, and I have an excellent staff. Visit the dam site, make your measurements, and then design the conveyor as well as you can. If you go wrong, I will tell you; otherwise, enjoy it!"

"Yes sir!" I said. Tulek, it appeared, was someone who trusted his people. The project would be a creative challenge, but I sensed it would be appreciated. I plunged in right away. It was a lot more work than I imagined, but it was fun.

My brothers were just as pleased with their own assignments. Zimzimah, the curator of the Great Zoo, was astounded by Ham's abilities. He decided to test him by giving him the herbivorous behemoths, the largest, most stubborn animals in the zoo. Nothing could have pleased Ham more. Shem, on his part, loved the Hall of Records, with its constant flow of news from the kingdom and all around the world. While local scandals and intrigues were often suppressed for political reasons, Shem's new friends spilled out the juiciest stories, and Shem kept us informed.

"I learned about Shahoot today," Shem said one evening. "He is something of a notoriety in Mother Earth. He began his career by marrying the ex-girlfriend of the queen mother's brother; by doing so, he covered up one of his many scandals. The queen mother was appreciative, and Shahoot began to ascend Mother Earth's ladder of wealth and influence. Five years ago, he was sent to Enoch's Valley, and we know that story. Following the conquest, he was made the governor. His adopted son Sandal has recently become a member of Prince Malek's entourage."

"And Shahoot's lovely daughter?" Ham asked.

"Prince Malek himself," Shem replied, "introduced Aziza at a royal reception. Since then, she has regularly attended such functions, and she has attracted the attention of numerous rich young noblemen. However, she seems to be concentrating on the wealthiest catch of all, the son of Prime Minister Logar!"

"Rogar the bully?" I exclaimed. How disappointing! It did not surprise me that she would find someone wealthy—but would she be foolish enough to marry him? Surely not: she must only be teasing him.

"I found out something else," Shem said, barely suppressing his excitement. "The daughter of her mother's older sister is a renowned beauty!"

"I am glad to hear that," I said, "but so what?"

"Her name," Shem burst out, "is Athaliah!"

That was a revelation. It made me start to think. We had seen how Athaliah employed her physical attractions as a tool for the purpose of corrupting us. I wondered now if Aziza had similarly employed her beauty against me. Athaliah's culture and etiquette classes were so transparently wrong they had become almost funny. She promoted gambling, a vice father always condemned, and advocated smoking herbs to cause hallucinations; and she instructed us in lascivious mixed pair dancing, which I judged could only promote immorality[1]. After hearing that, every time we attended one of Athaliah's classes, I thought of Aziza.

My work on the Great Dam was very satisfying, and I soon became immersed in it. Unfortunately, I could not entirely escape from distracting or upsetting news. Every day, Shem brought us reports about wars, famines, and earthquakes abroad, and there were local stories of crime and corruption, too.

One day Ham uncovered a scandal at the zoo, himself. After coming upon a secluded enclosure, he squeezed the story out from another keeper. Wealthy noblemen paid handsomely to have valuable rare animals brought there, so that they could kill and eat them! When Ham reported this, the curator was displeased, but told Ham that if he spoke of this to anyone, he could easily "disappear". This kind of thing, he explained, was part of the price for providing "a greater good" in Mother Earth.

I even discovered some dam corruption myself. When I compared the written contracts to the work actually done, it was obvious that the contractors were engaging in fraud, and siphoning off money. When I showed my findings to Tulek, he burst out in frustration. There was far more corruption than that, he said. Dam Minister Algar, the brother of Prime Minister Logar, had previously forced him to accept poorly chiseled stones, and had refused to let him inspect the dam's foundation, which had been laid when he was out of town. He threatened Tulek, and assured him that everything was "fine". Tulek hated being morally compromised, but he had no choice in the matter: this was how Mother Earth operated.

The patriarch used to say that he could feel things in his bones. While my bones were by no means as old, I think I felt the same thing. Somehow, I just knew, down deep, that judgment was coming. The occasional tremors only reinforced my feeling. One proverb came to mind a lot: "When the wicked arise, men hide themselves[2]." I took that as advice, and tried to hide in my work.

After an intense effort, I completed the designs for two adjustable water-powered conveyors. When I was satisfied, I made scale models and tested them. Tulek was pleased, and ordered the casting of the gears and shafts, and fabrication of the belts and swivels. Between the design and construction of the conveyors, the project demanded very long days. My brothers had been working very hard, too, and we decided we all needed a holiday. Having heard that Mother Earth's annual religious festival was fun, we asked permission to attend.

It was still cool and damp when we entered the park. I was still sleepy, but the throb of drums soon woke me. I took a deep breath, and found that the air was filled with the perfume of flowers, the aromatic smoke of incense, and the spicy aromas of food. My mouth began to water. We joined a crowd moving toward the brightly decorated booths and pavilions. Everyone was eager for entertainment and for new ideas to capture their imagination.

Nearly every god or religion was represented. Jugglers and magicians performed for coins, while vendors sold drinks and pastries, and artists showed their works, religious or otherwise. Soldiers walked around in pairs, alert for trouble: not every religion interacted nicely with the others. Priests lured passers-by with good luck charms and idols, and eagerly explained the peculiar teachings of their religions. Their goal was to recruit, and they used every trick.

At the first booth we were addressed by a gaunt fakir[3] wearing a colorful loincloth. His chest was covered with silver necklaces and garlands, and his flowered hat fairly exploded with blossoms.

"Everything is an illusion!" he declared. "You only think it is real because your senses tell you so! Actually, reality is only in your mind!"

We were well rested, and felt playful, so we laughed at this. The fakir noticed our interest, and eagerly repeated: "Everything is an illusion!"

Shem responded gaily. "It sounds to me like you are hearing things!"

"All reality is subjective," the fakir asserted. "Everything is an illusion. Only if we detect a thing through our own senses, does it actually occur!"

Ham laughed loudly. "I think YOU are an illusion!"

Scowling, the fakir turned away. We strolled on to a booth, where we stopped for fruit drinks and tasty pastries. Continuing on, we found a fat little man exhorting the crowd.

"You are a god! I am a god!" he shouted. "In fact, everyone is a god! There is no Almighty Creator, no heaven or hell. You make all your own rules, and no one can tell you what to do!"

The little speaker saw us, and took Ham's elbow.

"You are a god, my friend," he said earnestly. "If it feels good, it IS good! And as a god, whatever you think is right—is right!"

Ham could not resist. "I think the right thing is to knock you down! What do you think about that?"

The speaker hastily dropped his elbow. "Disrespectful adolescents!"

Laughing again, we wandered arm in arm through the park, and were amused to see how many religions were represented. Some of the featured gods included snakes, monkeys, trees, and even a death behemoth, which was portrayed by a huge painted statue. We listened to the religious slogans, many of which we had heard from Professor Adrammelech.

The people of Mother Earth seemed pretty desperate to find meaning and purpose in life, we thought, even to the point of bowing down before crudely made images. At the same time, they contrived all kinds of intellectual contortions to get around the tested truths preserved by the patriarchs. Still, their slogans were imaginative and attractive:

"Whatever your mind believes, you can achieve!"

"Follow our master's teachings, and your next incarnation will be better!"

"Worship the earth goddess Mokosh--your real mother[4]!"

"That is so disrespectful to real mothers!" Ham sighed. "But I suppose we should visit the pavilion. Many of my coworkers will be there."

The pavilion of the Earth Goddess Mokosh was by far the largest and most popular one. Inside, we found continuous shows featuring trained animals performing acrobatic stunts, talking birds, and balancing elephants. The booths around the pavilion sold potted flowers, as well as live mice, lizards, and fish—all for the purpose of worship. Ham introduced us to some friends from the zoo, and they entertained us with hilarious stories of animal tricks gone awry. As we looked around, we tried not to be disrespectful, but the sight of people bowing down to worship smelly animals or disgusting bugs was something we could hardly keep from ridiculing.

When we left, we came to a large pavilion dedicated to the God of Virility. It was decorated in red and blue stripes, and was very well attended. Loud music blared inside, and we heard coarse laughter from some type of crude comedy show. The thick smoke of the pavilion irritated our eyes, and we began to walk away, but three or four girls who were posted outside ran after us. They touched and boldly began to caress us, while at the same time pulling us toward the smoky entrance. One girl even threw herself at Ham, and tried to kiss him. Shem and I thanked the girls, but firmly marched Ham away. They yelled at us, "You'll be back!"

In our haste, we almost overlooked a pavilion labeled "The Creator God of the Patriarchs." Small groups of older people were entering the pavilion, while a pair of pretty young girls outside passed out tablets with information. Their attire revealed a surprising amount of skin for a patriarchal meeting, but we figured this was Mother Earth, after all.

As we entered, we heard the familiar strains of an old hymn, and eagerly joined in. After so many months in a hostile land, singing the hymn together with other believers was enough to bring tears to my eyes. When it ended, an old man in an embroidered garment hurried over to us. He wore a tall hat, and his hair curled out like a silver halo.

"You must be from the palace!" he exclaimed. "Your blue tunics give you away. I am delighted to see young people interested in the Creator God, especially when they are members of the elite! How long have you been in Mother Earth?"

"For some months," I answered. "When our homeland was conquered, we were brought here as hostages, and now we are in training at the Mother Earth Academy. But how can you worship the Creator so openly? We thought believers were considered dangerous fanatics!"

"Dangerous? Oh, no, my sons!" he exclaimed. "But let me introduce myself. I am Patriarch Demas, leader of the patriarchal congregation of Mother Earth. Please have some tea, and try these sweet potato biscuits—very tasty, are they not? I love them!" As we munched, the patriarch tapped his fingers in thought, and then began to speak.

"This valley, boys, was originally settled by descendants of Cainan, devout believers who called on the name of the Lord. The Creator blessed them greatly, and they became rich. They built a great temple and trained priests to practice a wonderful set of ceremonies. After many centuries of worship, however, King Nezzar came into power, and he and his mother brought in enticing new ideas about the earth goddess Mokosh. Our attendance began to drop. Then, when the Temple of Virility was built, how could we compete with that? The king threatened to drive us out; but as we know, God helps those who help themselves. I gathered my wisdom together, of which I have a great deal, and I was able to convince him we were no threat to his rule. Today, we get along with everyone—except Cainites, of course. They are so vicious and violent! They are not here today, are they?"

"But, Patriarch," Shem asked, puzzled, "our professor's teaching is the official policy of the king, and he speaks strongly against the Creator God. In fact, most of his teaching is specifically directed to destroy any belief in a Creator! I cannot understand how he permits your open worship."

The patriarch nodded. "The faith they consider subversive, boys, broke away from us long ago. Even today, that cult retains antique ideas like a literal six-day creation and an actual person named Adam. They even say he was created, not born, 1587 years ago, just like on our calendar. According to the myth of this cult, Adam and his wife were literally expelled from a literal Garden of Eden, and their children inherited a nature that was bent toward disobedience. These 'Adamites', as many call them, look forward to a special Rescuer, a Redeemer from God who will save his faithful ones from their sinful nature. But surely you boys are too intelligent for such tales. The Adamites follow a narrow line of patriarchs through someone named Enoch, who reportedly walked with the Creator God so closely, that one day he walked with him all the way to heaven, and could not be found!"

The patriarch laughed. "Now, that is a tall story! Our own religion, on the other hand, is fully compatible with science, and with the majority of the religions of the world. Adamites are fanatics who say the rest of us are wrong, and doomed. Now, I never said we were perfect, but we are not all that bad! Why would a loving Creator destroy his own creation? That is mad! Our God is far too transcendent to be concerned with sin. He welcomes everyone! And when I explained that to the king, by the way, he was satisfied. Unfortunately, our numbers still continue to decline. I am now the only priest left."

We glanced at each other: things were not what they had seemed. "But what about the fanatic Adamites?" I asked. "Are many still left in Mother Earth?"

"There are still a few, my son, though they try to remain hidden for obvious reasons. They dress in white, as we do, but there is one thing that always betrays them: they have genuine affection for each other! I almost wish we had some of that. But let me advise you to stay clear of them! They will only bring you trouble!" The patriarch stood and gave us an elaborate benediction. We walked away silently.

"Well," Shem sighed, "this religious festival has lost its attraction for me. I think even a godless scientific exhibit would be more refreshing. Why don't we visit the Temple of Human Achievement? I barely saw the surface the first time, and we always promised ourselves another visit."

The Temple of Human Achievement was located in the industrial area just a short distance from the Great Dam. To save time, we took a shortcut through the waterworks, planning to skirt the water races that powered the waterwheels. These races were deep and turbulent, and ordinarily fenced off or covered up for safety. Recent construction, however, had left the races unprotected. Being a Sabbath day, I expected the area to be quiet and deserted.

I was wrong. As we entered the waterworks, we heard screams of terror. A group of a few dozen people, mostly women and children dressed in white, were under attack! Seven or eight black-clad thugs with clubs were driving them toward an open water race not far from a rapidly spinning waterwheel. Though two old men had canes, the women had nothing to protect themselves and their children. In answer to their terrified cries, the thugs laughed and cursed.

[1]*Editor's Note:* Some of Japheth's moral judgments may seem quaint today, such as his condemnation of mixed pair dancing as promoting immorality.

[2]*Editor's Note:* This particular proverb is also seen twice in a single chapter of the Bible (Proverbs 28). I wonder if Solomon might have adapted some of his wise sayings from far more ancient times.

[3]*Editor's Note:* I selected this word because I was reminded of similarly dressed Hindu ascetics or mendicants.

[4]*Editor's Note:* It is an amazing cultural parallel that popular bumper stickers even today proclaim "Worship your mother — Mother Earth!"

Chapter Twenty-Seven: A Rescue of Adamites

"Cainites!" Ham growled angrily. "Just like a pack of wolves!"

"Is there anyone else to help?" Shem asked. "There are so many!"

Looking around quickly, we spied two armed soldiers standing at the corner of a nearby building. They must have observed the commotion; but even as we watched, they turned and walked away.

"Mother of Earth!" I exclaimed. "I might have guessed! Let's find weapons!"

"How about those?" Ham asked, pointing to a stack of pry bars. Each had a heavy iron claw and a strong hickory handle about four cubits long. They were not balanced like sparring staffs, but we had practiced with worse.

"Perfect!" I said. "Let's go!" We each grabbed one and took off.

By the time we arrived, the victims had been driven perilously close to the water's edge. One of the Cainites had struck a young woman down, and was in the process of tearing off her clothes while she feebly resisted. I was upon him before he noticed, and swung my weapon very hard. When it struck his head, there was a crunch, and he dropped like a log. I immediately moved to the next: surprise is essential when you are so far outnumbered. The second thug was occupied striking an old woman with his club, and saw me too late. He fell like the first.

By this time, the leader of the Cainites had noticed us. He was a muscular young man with a short beard, and well practiced in the use of a club. The brown tiger stripes on his face looked shiny, as though they were only painted on, and his face looked familiar, with very dark eyes, and a distinctively cruel curl to his lip.

"Zur!" I cried.

"Noah's boys!" Zur answered, breathing heavily. "You always show up at the wrong time! We almost got you before, but this time there will be no mistake!"

Raising his club high, he brought his whole weight down upon my head. I shielded myself with the hickory tool, but the handle shattered, and I was driven to my knees. My hands felt numb. Smiling in triumph, Zur raised his club again, but this time, before he could strike, his hand was seized from behind. A young girl had jumped on his back! Cursing, Zur spun around. She still held on, tightly gripping his arm. With a mighty effort, he pried her loose, and threw her over the edge of the water race. With a small cry, she disappeared.

Zur's utter heartlessness removed any pity I might have felt. Gripping the shattered handle like a spear, I thrust its sharp edge deep into his belly. His eyes bulged with surprise, and his body slowly collapsed.

I glanced to see how Shem and Ham were doing. Like me, they had completely surprised their first opponents. Their next ones were not particularly skilled in their weapons, and my brothers were quickly mastering them. The remaining Cainite was flat on his stomach, pinned beneath a large woman.

Jumping up, I rushed to the water's edge to desperately search the gray, turbulent water. Finally, I spotted the girl. Bobbing up and down, she was firmly in the grip of the powerful current, and rapidly being drawn into the middle of the stream. I had no time to lose. Yelling for help, I ran along the water's edge to get ahead. Throwing off my sandals, I dove into the water, and swam underwater as strongly as I could. When I surfaced, I found myself immediately in front of her.

"Put your arms around my neck," I said, pulling her close.

Shifting her onto my back, I began using my strongest stroke, while she assisted me by kicking. Although we were still rapidly being swept toward the waterwheel, we were able to move out of the center of the stream toward the edge. Although I was rapidly tiring, we soon got close enough to grab for a rock. The first rock was covered with moss. My hand slipped, and the current dragged us away. I stroked desperately, and reached again for a rock, but it slipped, too! I heard a swooshing sound, and saw the shadow of the waterwheel just ahead. We were only moments away from disaster!

Something hard nudged me. I seized it with both hands, and our forward movement stopped with a wrench. The current whipped us back and forth, but I kept my grip on what I finally realized was a stout hickory pole. Hearing a voice above me, I looked up. Shem and Ham were holding the other end! The huge waterwheel was only cubits away, ponderously churning the water.

"Just in time!" I said.

Shem and Ham held us close to the edge until we found footing. As we crawled onto the rocks, the girl remained tightly pressed against me, with her arm around my neck. I could not see her face, but I liked her already. Not many girls would have tackled someone like Zur. This girl was fearless!

She raised her eyes. She was young and very pretty, I saw; but her vivid blue eyes made my heart stop. I knew this girl! My mind raced back to the day of our parade through the city.

She was the one who had given me water! I had never forgotten her face; and now she was right in my arms!

"It's you!" I stammered.

When I was very young, and got flustered, my mother would tell me, "Use your words, Japheth!" It was a moment like that. But this was no time for conversation: we were busy. Hands reached down for us, and the girl and I clambered up. We sat down on the edge to catch our breath, and I saw her shiver. I was cold, too, so I put my arm around her, just as I would for any female cousin. This time, when our eyes met, we lingered. The girl was very pleasant to look at, I thought, and very appealing.

I must have had a silly look on my face, because when Shem appeared over my shoulder, he smiled at me in a teasing way. Ham was there, too, and winked. Women came up to wrap dry clothing around us, and I knew it was time to get up. There was a squawk from a nearby tree: a green Enoch's parrot was eyeing me with curiosity. Those birds seemed to be everywhere!

"Thank you," I said to the girl. "You risked your life to save me!"

"No, thank you!" she replied. "You risked your life for all of us first! And you risked it again just for me!"

After getting up, I walked with my brothers back to the scene of the attack. Several of those injured were being attended. The children were crying, but most appeared unharmed. Seven Cainites lay motionless on the ground, while the eighth was pinned flat on the ground by the large woman, and guarded by the two old men. As we approached, the Cainite thug looked up painfully.

"Japheth!" he cried.

Surprised, I looked at his face. His tiger stripes were painted on like Zur's, and his face looked familiar, too.

"Ziph!" I exclaimed. "You were in Sandal's gang in Enoch's Valley! What are we going we do with you?" Having a prisoner presented a serious dilemma. How could we turn him over to the authorities? They had permitted the assault!

"I say we toss him into the water," Ham offered.

"Yes," Ziph cried passionately. "Toss me in! I would rather die than live like this anymore. Sandal bullied me my whole life, but I never wanted to murder!"

"Your whole life? And you had no choice?" Shem asked doubtfully.

"I grew up a slave in his house," Ziph said. "He always had power over me. He knows that I hate hurting people, and do as little as I dare. But this time, when he finds I have failed him again, he will kill me. But are the others all dead?"

Ham nodded grimly.

"Then give me this chance to escape! I will leave Mother Earth, even become an Adamite: I swear it! But you must be quick. The soldiers will return soon!"

An old man who seemed to be a leader turned to us. "Lads, his gang might well kill him, as he said. If he is willing to repent and give his heart to the Creator, I think we should let him escape. Otherwise, he is lost. He will never be saved unless he makes a clean break from his past."

My brothers and I shrugged.

"Young man," the old man asked Ziph, "Do you promise on the soul of your mother, or whatever you hold most dear, to turn from the devil, and walk in obedience to the Creator?"

"I do, so help me God! Now let me up!" The woman rolled off, releasing him. Ziph took a few deep breaths, and rose up painfully. Walking to Zur's body, he kicked it with satisfaction. Grabbing the limp arm, he dragged the body to the edge of the race, and rolled it in. The rapid current caught it, and swept it toward the waterwheel. Ziph looked at the other bodies.

"Help me roll them in! We cannot leave any evidence."

It took us a few minutes to drag the other bodies to the water. As we soberly watched the bodies bob toward the waterwheel, Ziph took off his black outer garment and tossed it in. It followed the bodies, and disappeared into the foam of the great paddles. Ziph turned back to face us, wearing only a light cotton tunic.

"I really am sorry, Japheth, for everything I have done. I will keep my promise. If the Creator helps me escape from this wicked city, I will walk with him from now on." He looked at us a moment, and then turned and ran away.

"Let us pray, dear friends, that he does escape," the old man declared, "even for the sake of these three young men. He knows who they are, and would tell everything under torture. Let us leave here quickly: we are in danger."

We helped the injured along as the group moved quickly out of the waterworks. Walking through deserted streets, we finally entered an alley. Satisfied we had not been observed, the old man knocked at the service door of a large residence. The door presently opened, and servants welcomed us into a spacious kitchen. They were alarmed to see many people wounded. Taking the girl, they immediately bustled away, while my brothers and I found a quiet corner. A short time later, a tall, handsomely dressed nobleman and his wife entered the kitchen. When the girl pointed to us, they came over.

"How can we even begin to thank you?" the man said. "You risked your lives to save our precious daughter and all these dear friends!" Suddenly, the man stared at me.

"Japheth!" he said, obviously astonished.

"Master Tulek!" I replied, equally surprised. I hated awkward, emotional situations. I never knew what to say.

"Sir," I said a moment later, "we were happy to be of some small service to them, but it was only our duty. We are just thankful our Maker gave us success."

"Let me assure you," Tulek answered, "that this was no small service. We are overwhelmed with gratitude, and we thank our Maker for you! I have seriously misjudged you, Japheth, and must ask your forgiveness. I have been in this wicked city too long, and have been disappointed by people too often. No one from this city would have dared to interfere with a Cainite gang. We shall always be in your debt!"

"And I shall always be in your daughter's debt," I replied. "She saved my life by jumping on the leading thug. She kept him from crushing my skull!"

"She is a plucky girl," Tulek said, smiling. "But let me present my family! You have already met our daughter Kezziah, and this is my dear wife Keturah. Now please introduce us to your two friends, to whom we owe so much."

I did, but we had little time to talk, with all the bustle of bandaging and caring for the injured. We met some of the women and children, as well as Elder Himiel, the old man who was their leader. He gave Tulek a brief but flattering version of the incident, and thanked him for providing refuge for us. Because they feared that Tulek's home was being watched, the party soon departed, after giving us tearful embraces. My brothers and I were ready to follow, but Keturah stopped us.

"You cannot return to the palace like that!" she declared. "We must clean and mend your tunics first."

"Yes, Mother," Kezziah quickly added. "And we must get to know our rescuers better. I think they are believers, as we are!"

Servants soon whisked away our palace tunics. After my brothers and I cleaned up, changing into some spare clothing, we joined Tulek's family out on the terrace.

"So you are from Enoch's Valley?" Tulek asked. "Isn't that the home of the famous patriarch Methuselah? I have a good friend there from the school of Tubal-Cain. When he left, he returned home to set up a business with his brother. Have you met him? His name is Lemuel."

"Of course!" I replied. "Uncle Lemuel and Uncle Nebach are my favorite mentors!"

Tulek was delighted to hear that, and we entered into a pleasant discussion of life in Enoch's Valley. As we related some of the adventures that led us to Mother Earth's palace, Kezziah said she wanted to ask me a question.

"Japheth, have we ever met before?"

Ham laughed. "You probably did not recognize him with his clothes on!"

Tulek and Keturah were startled, and Shem made it worse by laughing.

"Please forgive my brothers, Master Tulek," I explained. "Their sense of humor comes from the zoo. But I have met your daughter before, under rather humbling circumstances. The three of us were paraded through the city as captives, and Kezziah gave us cold water. It was a simple act of kindness, but it meant a lot."

Kezziah blushed, but Tulek and Keturah looked relieved.

"I knew there was something familiar about you," Kezziah said. "So you see, father, kindnesses to strangers are sometimes rewarded, after all!"

"Dearest, you amaze us!" Tulek declared.

"And your boldness," Keturah added, "keeps me on my knees every day!"

"My mother prays a lot," Kezziah explained. "She heard a prophet of God rebuke the king four or five years ago, and she has prayed every day since then that the people of our land would repent. Mother, do you still have hope for that?"

"No, Kezziah," she said firmly. "Mother Earth will not repent. Her judgment is coming soon. God's warriors are already in the trees."

What did she mean by that, I wondered? At that very moment, a servant entered with our freshly cleaned and mended clothing, and we prepared to leave. Because it was still early, Tulek suggested that we visit the Temple of Human Achievement as we had originally planned.

"These days," Tulek explained, "you must always have an alibi. How wicked this city has become! When I was a child, my neighbors all believed in the Creator, and we could walk anywhere without fear[1]! Now, women and children are assaulted by Cainites in the middle of the day, and the very heroes who rescue them must fear being punished for it! I agree with Keturah: judgment is coming. But in the meanwhile, believers must stick together. You must visit us again soon!"

"Yes, do," Keturah said. "I like you boys. And I find it very interesting that your mother has a necklace like Kezziah's! It has an interesting story, you know."

She again piqued my curiosity, but we had to go. After thanking them again, we quietly departed. When we came to the Temple of Human Achievement, we were happy to find other students from the palace. As we toured the exhibits, we began to relax. On our way home, my brothers even found the energy to joke.

"Kezziah is a spunky girl, Japheth," Shem teased, "and she fell right into your arms! I think our parents would approve of her."

"I found it touching," Ham added, "that you were so concerned about her warmth. Let me think about this. If you were both sheep, it would be easy. I would judge that she is healthy, with strong limbs, good stamina, and a proven family pedigree. She has excellent potential to produce sturdy offspring, and would be a suitable match for breeding. I even like the color of her wool!"

We all laughed, but we were tired: it had been an exciting day. Kezziah was certainly pretty; but she was also young and impressionable. I would not dare take advantage of her gratitude. Furthermore, her father was a nobleman and my supervisor, while I was only a branded slave. It would be risky, even foolish, to think of courting her. Still, there was no harm in becoming acquainted.

Gregory Horning

[1]*Editor's Note:* This passage reminded me of America in the 1950's and 60's, when few people even felt the need to lock their homes at night.

Chapter Twenty-Eight: A Banquet

We hoped the incident was behind us, but the next morning, we were summoned to see General Zabadanah.

"Lads, early this morning," he began, "seven mangled bodies and an empty set of black garments were found on the shore near the waterworks. This discovery has caused some excitement. The eight victims have not been identified, but they were apparently Cainites that were last seen alive yesterday afternoon, when soldiers saw them talking with a group of women and children dressed all in white. About the same time, three other young men were seen in the area, dressed in royal blue. The deaths were probably accidental, although choosing to swim in such dangerous waters would have been the height of foolishness."

"One of my officers had an alternate theory. He proposed that the Cainites, who looked like strong young thugs, might not have been simply talking with the women. Instead, he asked, what if they were attacking them with clubs, like some we found nearby? And if so, what if the three young men from the palace had defended their victims, killing all eight of them in the process? His hypothesis is most unlikely. Cainites can be tough. It would take considerable strength and skill to defeat them. Somehow, though, I thought of you three."

The general inspected us as he talked: our bruises, cuts, and scrapes must have been obvious. Smiling grimly, he continued. "Now, I have little sympathy for Cainites, who rarely talk courteously with women and children. And I am confident you lads have a very good alibi for your whereabouts yesterday. For example, did you attend the religious festival?"

"Yes sir, we did," I replied, feeling relieved. "And later we spent time at the Temple of Human Achievement with some of our classmates."

The general held up his hand to stop me. "Fine! I am glad to hear it. With the corroboration of your classmates, I find no reason to think you lads had anything to do with the affair. The Cainites undoubtedly died in a swimming accident. I just hope this is the end of it, and that the bodies are not identified as the children of nobility. It shocks me to sometimes find young men from wealthy families perversely aspiring to behave like the dregs of society, even dressing and acting like Cainites[1]. But that is not your concern. You lads just keep your story straight, and be careful whom you rescue from now on."

The tragic accidental drowning of eight Cainites captivated the city's news for a week, putting us a little on edge. We were glad when a sensational new scandal was revealed. As the Cainite story faded, so did our anxiety.

The following months passed quickly. My work on the Great Dam was both absorbing and satisfying. I had some frustrations, including failures in the casting of gears, and delays with a broken swivel mechanism, but I eventually had the pleasure of seeing both conveyors in operation. Day after day, great blocks of stone glided smoothly up the conveyors for placement, and the dam steadily grew. Tulek was highly pleased, and when Prince Malek and Dam Minister Algar came to inspect, he gave me full credit for the invention.

My brothers were happy in their jobs, too. Ham loved working with the huge behemoths, and the curator kept giving him more and more responsibilities. Shem never tired of the Hall of Records. He investigated many incidents of corruption, and found that the king was heavily in debt to Nephil. Even when the plunder of conquest was added to the heavy tax revenues, it was still not enough to cover his expenses. According to some sources, the king had recently begun coveting the wealth of the nobility: all he needed was an excuse to seize it. Finding money was becoming urgent: it was said that when the king of Nephil came to the Great Dam celebration, he would insist on having his debt repaid.

Shem frequently heard juicy details about life among the rich and noble. Prince Malek's most treasured possession, it was said, was his beautiful ivory chariot, something he devoted an entire crew of slaves to keeping pristine. Even a slight smudge on one of the delicate carvings was enough to make him fly into a rage. The prince often drove the chariot to late night revelries, accompanied by Professor Adrammelech and the prime minister's son Rogar. On occasion, he attended scandalous entertainments in the apartments of the flamboyant director of culture, Athaliah. While Prince Malek himself drank strong spirits sparingly, he did not mind associating with those with reputations for drunkenness and debauchery.

The prince was impatient to be king, some said. For some years he had been currying the favor of the working classes, and his popularity had soared. The wealthy nobility, even those opposing his father in the senate, had come to favor the prince. Should anything happen to King Nezzar, it was said that Prince Malek would be popularly acclaimed as his successor.

During this time were often invited to Tulek's home, and enjoyed getting to know the family. Kezziah had an older brother named Tiras, we learned, who was the main reason Tulek still remained in a city he had grown to hate. When Tiras had been taken into the army, he had for practical purposes become a hostage. Tulek now had little choice but to continue working for Mother Earth.

Kezziah came to her father's office several times each week, bringing meals and otherwise taking care of him, and she always made a point to speak to me. We had good conversations, and I grew to treasure her wholesome, positive attitude and mature, sensible opinions. Like her father, she was very hardworking. During the day she studied with the chief physician of Mother Earth and treated the sick, while in the evenings she sewed tapestries or clothing for the poor. On occasion, she joined her Adamite friends to distribute food to the hungry. She always was kind to the less fortunate, but at the same time had realistic expectations. People in chronic need, she had learned, were generally that way because of bad choices. Merely doing them an occasional good turn was unlikely to bring about permanent improvement. The underlying causes for bad choices or habits first had to be effectively resolved.

One day Kezziah brought her father lunch, and I could not help but overhear.

"Thank you, sweetheart," Tulek told her, winking. "Tell your mother I will see her on the boat!"

I had previously heard him say something to that effect, but I did not realize they owned a boat. The next time I saw Kezziah, I asked her about it.

"Father is just silly," she explained. "Mother came from a prominent family in a distant city on the Euphrates. They met one day on the river, and fell in love. Although mother's parents liked my father very much, her uncle was the king, and he had planned to use her for a political match. In the end, mother and father eloped and sailed away. They have been married a long time, but father still likes to tell mother, 'See you on the boat!' He is still proposing to her, you see. It is his way of saying, 'I love you! Let's run away and get married!'"

One day, I was startled to learn that Kezziah had received offers of marriage herself. She had declined them, Tulek explained, because while plenty of noblemen had riches, very few trusted in the Creator God. That was her most important requirement. The news altered how I saw her. I had never considered that Kezziah might soon marry. I had just assumed we could continue on as good friends.

As a slave, of course, I was in no position to aspire to a closer relationship. My status as a royal hostage, however, was peculiar. We lived in the king's palace with the other royal hostages; we attended lectures, learned dancing, practiced at arms, and were even known by the royal family. And from my perspective, Kezziah had never considered me a slave. In fact, she was indignant to hear about the lectures we had been subjected to, as well as Athaliah's immoral temptations.

"How long," Kezziah exclaimed one day, "will our Creator tolerate this wicked city—this hotbed of idolatry, ambition, and spiritual rebellion? Japheth, you must not let yourself be deceived and corrupted! You must either find a way to resist, or you must escape!"

Kezziah had high expectations of me. I did not wish to disappoint her, but I saw no way to escape. Our family in Enoch's Valley was still in the tight grip of Mother Earth, and the professor often reminded us of the penalties for disobedience. We had only one hope: when the dam was completed, our schooling would be finished. We would be given new responsibilities, and perhaps even new freedoms.

One day, Tulek brought news of a great banquet. Hosted by the noble brothers Logar and Algar in honor of progress on the Great Dam, the banquet was to be an immense, glittering affair, with thousands of guests. Tulek was required to attend, he said, along with his family. That displeased him, because he was very protective of his wife and daughter, and did not want them exposed to the corruptions of Mother Earth society. The next day, I learned that all the royal hostages were required to attend the banquet as well.

At Tulek's request, I accompanied his family to the event, which was held in Logar's great palace. Dressed in my finest blue tunic and robe, I joined Tulek and Keturah outside the main hall. Kezziah took my arm, and we walked together up the stairs and through the great doors. When our names were announced, we entered the crowded, lavishly decorated spectacle. Huge tables were loaded down with every kind of food and drink, and thousands of excited guests talked and laughed loudly, drowning out the lively music. Much wealth was on display, especially on the women, who were dressed in the latest fashions, and heavily jeweled. The smell of spicy food was mouthwatering. Many guests stood at the tables eating or drinking strong spirits, while others danced or simply talked in smaller groups.

I knew Kezziah was pretty, of course; but that evening, with her elegant dress, golden hair, and perfect carriage, her beauty was striking. Her mother was lovely, too; and when our party entered, every eye followed us. After escorting Tulek's family to their places of honor, I left them to find my own place among the royal hostages. Shem entered with a large party from the Hall of Records, while Ham came with the family of the zoo curator, escorting his youngest daughter.

No sooner had I found Shem than the trumpets sounded. Everyone bowed as the king entered. The queen mother and Prince Malek entered after the king, and Prime Minister Logar and Dam Minister Algar followed with their wives.

Rogar entered after his father. His purple robe made him appear like a giant grape, and his expression was just as arrogant and obnoxious as I had remembered. I resolved to keep a wide distance from him. Rogar's companion, however, was a gorgeous young woman with a breathtaking figure, and as graceful as a cat. Aziza had only grown more desirable, though I saw her differently now. In my eyes, she could not compare with the sweet, wholesome Kezziah. Both were beautiful; but while Aziza conjured up powerful fleshly desires, she was not a kindred spirit. Marriage with such a person would be a never-ending struggle.

Her famous cousin made an appearance a few moments later, dressed in a scintillating metallic green gown. She drew loud applause. Many men had longing eyes, including Professor Adrammelech, who gaped at her hungrily, with his mouth open. After Athaliah came other prominent guests, including General Zabadanah and his lovely wife, high-ranking noblemen, merchants, and socialites. It appeared that everyone important had come: all considered it a magnificent party.

Shem's friends from the Hall of Records were very personable, and I was in pleasantly conversation when the prime minister interrupted the music to welcome his guests. He and his brother Algar said a few words about the Great Dam before introducing King Nezzar, who spoke only a few words. The music and dancing resumed, and I returned to talk. Suddenly, I noticed those around me backing away. Turning around, I discovered Prince Malek.

"My grandmother wishes to speak to you," he said quietly.

The guests opened a path, and the prince chatted as we walked.

"You seem to be using your talents well on the Great Dam, Japheth. Tulek has a real knack for developing his people. He has a handsome family, too, especially his daughter. He was wrong to keep her from society, but we shall soon change that. In fact, many things will change soon, Japheth. I will not always be a prince, you know. When I reign, I will need to build a good team, just as Tulek has. You have potential to be part of it, Japheth, though some do not favor you. Sandal, for example, blames you for the death of his favorite lieutenant, though he has no evidence."

My face must have reflected concern, but the prince laughed. "Do not worry, Japheth: Sandal is just jealous. Rogar is a bigger problem for you. Like an elephant, or perhaps a gorilla, he never forgets personal slights. But I have him in hand—trust me. Ah, here we are. I shall leave you."

The prince had brought me to the foot of the royal dais. The queen mother was seated on an upholstered chair above me, surrounded by a half dozen of her favorite confidants. She turned to notice me, and I bowed low.

"Come up here, my dear," she said kindly. "Sit beside me. Yes. I hope you have considered what I said to you the last time we met. I have been keeping an eye on you. I am partly pleased, and partly impatient. You are an intelligent lad, Japheth, and work hard. My grandson was impressed with your hydraulic powered conveyor system, and feels you have great potential. I agree, even though you have violent tendencies." Noticing my surprise, she chuckled ominously.

"Do not underestimate my powers, young man. I know what you and your brothers did to those Cainites! But do not worry: blunt instruments are easily replaced. Your actions, however, indicate that you still resist our agenda! If your hopeless idealism continues, you will miss out! Instead, imagine the power and luxury that could be yours when we conquer! Forget your past. Forget your failed religion, Japheth. Live in the present!" She paused. "But time is growing short. You and your brothers must grow up. Perhaps a trip to the Temple of Virility will help you. After that, you may be more inclined to see things our way." She laughed knowingly, and then nodded her dismissal.

Standing to bow again, I backed down the steps, hoping to disappear in the vast crowd. I felt naked and confused. The queen mother seemed to know everything! What was I missing? Why would this queen mother and her grandson take such an interest in three unknown hostages? Could our father have disturbed her that much? I had to find my brothers.

Ham was easy to find: everyone was watching him dance with Athaliah! I knew, of course, that she often chose him as her dancing partner in class, but the other guests would not know that. They would naturally be surprised to see her, a famed beauty and Mother Earth's Minister of Culture, choose to dance with a mere hostage. Hearing the buzz of gossip, I decided to search for Shem instead.

I found Shem dancing with Habibi, a beautiful redhead from our dancing class. But how had she found him in such a large crowd? I had little time to reflect. At that very moment, strong arms encircled my waist, and a pair of soft, warm lips tickled my ear.

"Japheth," Aziza whispered in a sultry voice. "We meet again; but this time you wear clothes! I am disappointed!"

"Aziza!" I turned slowly to face her. Her face was very close to mine, and she chuckled intimately at her private joke. I pulled back a little, and could not help but notice how enticingly her thin blue gown clung to her curves.

"I keep hearing your name, Japheth," she said. "Tonight I saw you speak with the queen mother herself! Perhaps I was hasty to let you go. The prince thinks highly of you, and General Zabadanah tells everyone what a great hero you are!" She laughed from deep in her pretty throat.

"The prince and the general are very generous in their praise, Aziza," I replied. "But I hear you have ascended the highest levels of Mother Earth society yourself, and have even won the heart of a certain wealthy young nobleman."

Aziza looked at me sharply, but then relaxed. "I am not yet committed to him, Japheth. Rogar is useful, but he bores me, and his jealousy is annoying. I think I like you better. Athaliah and I talk, you know. She finds your brother Ham has a certain animal attraction, but she thinks you have potential, too."

That word "potential" was becoming irritating. It was used far too often in Mother Earth. And as pretty as Aziza was, there were other fish in the Hiddekel. Aziza looked at me questioningly: had she read my mind?

"Is there someone else, Japheth? Has some slave girl has caught your eye?"

"No," I answered. "But even if I were free, could we ever be happy together? We think so differently! Rogar is a much better match for you."

"Do not give up so easily, Japheth!" she said, taking my hand. "Perhaps we can find a way. Prime ministers sometimes lose their positions, you know, and even their fortunes. Where would Rogar be then? Can you imagine him winning a bride if he were poor?" Aziza chuckled. "Do not worry, sweetheart. I am a forgiving person, and I keep my options open." She put her cheek against mine, and then slipped away.

When the evening finally came to a close, I rejoined Tulek's family to escort them to their carriage. As we walked out under the stars, Kezziah told me the prince had been quite charming. He had complimented her lavishly, and had accused her father of withholding the two most beautiful women in Mother Earth from the adoration they deserved. All in all, Kezziah had thoroughly enjoyed the great banquet, with its music, celebrities, and entertainment. She had noticed Ham dancing with Athaliah, but had also observed a beautiful girl greet me in a very familiar manner.

"Tell me about this girl, Japheth—do you know her well?"

"I am not sure," I began. "Do you remember me telling you about a girl in Enoch's Valley who teased me, and whose father betrayed our homeland? That was the girl who greeted me tonight. When we entered the city as captives, Aziza taunted us, but tonight she acted as though that had never happened. I cannot trust her. She lacks honesty, loyalty, and even kindness, qualities I think are essential for any lasting friendship. Wouldn't you agree?"

"I would," Kezziah answered smoothly. "So was Aziza tempting you tonight, or just teasing?"

"I think she tried both!" I laughed. "Thankfully, so far I have been able to successfully resist every female temptation both at home and in Mother Earth; and I have no intention of succumbing in the future. Instead, my dear Kezziah, I have decided to save myself for a worthy girl, one who believes in our Creator, and who intends to walk with him."

It was dark, but I sensed Kezziah was blushing. What was I thinking? It was too late to take my words back; but I certainly had never intended to express improper sentiments to this sweet young girl, or toy with her affections, as had been done to me!

[1]***Editor's Note:*** Theodore Dalrymple has recently coined a name for this phenomenon: reverse aspiration.

Chapter Twenty-Nine: The Temple of Virility

"I was surprised that Athaliah chose me to dance with last night," Ham said the next morning. "She is a big celebrity here. She could have danced with anyone, while I am only a hostage slave! While she has always treated me like a monkey before, she acted last night as though I were someone special! I knew she was up to something. For some reason, she was trying to assure herself that I was hopelessly attracted to her! I played along, and eventually discovered her scheme."

"What was it?" Shem asked.

"The queen mother had given her a special assignment! She was to make sure we 'grew up' soon and fully embraced Mother Earth. She told Athaliah to 'see to it personally.'"

Things were starting to add up. I told Shem and Ham what the queen mother had said to me, and how she had used almost exactly the same words.

"Aziza practically threw herself at me," I said. "Either Athaliah prompted her, or the queen mother herself! Even so, I do not understand what she has to gain."

"You forget you are a handsome young stallion, Japheth," Ham offered. "She probably still finds you irresistible!" He and Shem laughed.

"And Habibi is in on the plot, too," Shem said. "She is a stunning beauty, but uses her brain very little. She has convinced herself that we are princes, or at least heirs to a great fortune. Sometimes royal hostages return to their family's riches, and she thinks we will, too. I tried to tell her we are not like that. She also has the strange idea that our religion requires us to marry the first girl that seduces us! If she succeeds, she thinks I will be her door to a life of luxury and ease."

"Ah, the plantation life!" Ham said, chuckling.

"Yes," Shem and I laughed, "a life of luxury and ease!"

"But she has a point," I said. "We are believers. If these girls seduce us, our consciences would be troubled, and we would want to make things right by marrying them. And if we didn't marry them, they would wrap our guilty consciences around our necks like a leash, and threaten to expose us as hypocrites! We would find it impossible to take a stand against evil, or call anything right or wrong. And when our father came, the queen mother would gloat over how easily we submitted to temptation. Our failure would reflect poorly on our Creator, and father would be grieved, and his hand weakened."

It was sobering to think we were the objects of a special plot, but there was little to do but carry on. The following week, we had to attend a lecture by Professor Adrammelech. He glared harshly at Ham the whole time, probably jealous.

Later in the week, we attended a culture and etiquette class, and Aziza showed up! She was very pleasant to me, which made me even more certain she was up to no good. She teased me lightheartedly as we danced and tickled me. Like Athaliah with Ham, Aziza seemed to want assurance that she still had power over me. I played along, but something inside told me to run away as fast as I could. In spite of everything, I was still attracted to her!

A few days later, the professor had an announcement. "Great news!" he said. "Your class has done so well that you have been awarded a free evening at the Temple of Virility!" When the cheers subsided, he continued.

"Everyone," he said, looking straight at my brothers and me, "no matter how innocent and shy, will attend. Your time in Mother Earth Academy is drawing to a close, and each of you must grow up, assume adult responsibilities, and adopt adult pleasures." He stopped and almost giggled. "But what am I saying? Must I say that a trip to the Temple of Virility is required? What normal, healthy young man would not be eager to go?"

The class roared with laughter. The rest of the class had already visited the temple, and had found it "fun." We, however, had not attended, because as we said, our jobs required our presence. Now, with the professor pointing at us, our classmates taunted us as effeminate or stupid, and as "crazy religious fanatics." Other things were less generous. Our faces were red when we left class that day. We were healthy young men, after all, with normal desires; and the thought of indulging in the pleasures of the temple was just as tempting for us as anyone. But we knew it was not right.

"Others may, you cannot," father often said, before hammering into us strong reasons to avoid immoral activities[1]. Fleshly indulgences, he said, destroy a young man's testimony, for one thing, and lead to dissipation, moral bondage, untreatable diseases, and lasting shame and disgrace. Other elders had been equally blunt in discussing the damage that could occur from even a few moments of pleasure in a "temple of virility."

Cousin Hippach, the chief physician of Jared's Mill, had instructed us in the major groups of diseases related to various ungodly lifestyles. Some of these, of course, were associated with drinking strong spirits or using potions; but some of the diseases were contracted in temples of virility, and were horrible.

A deadly epidemic had broken out one year when Cousin Hippach was studying in the vast metropolis of Nephil. The city, of course, supported many temples of virility. Men who attended one of the temples began coming to the College of Physicians with fever and black swellings of the skin[2]. Most died very quickly. Devotees of other temples of virility soon began to suffer the same illness. Before weeks had passed, more than a thousand had died, and the epidemic continued to spread. Finally, the chief physician pinpointed the temples as the source of infection, and convinced the king to burn them down. It was an object lesson, our cousin warned, against "ungodly excess and dissipation."

Being well aware of all the dangers, the announcement that we must attend the Temple of Virility presented a major dilemma.

"If we cannot find a way out, maybe we should just be gracious about it, and go," Ham mused. "A single visit will get them off our backs. And after all, most people do not catch a deadly disease. We are already slaves in a foreign land. How much more degraded could we be? Our classmates say it is fun, and nobody else would have to know about it."

"We would know about it, Ham," I said, "and all the believers here would know, too. They would grieve to see us so defiled. Anyway, the whole point is that the queen mother intends to use our indulgence in the temple against father!"

"Yes, but our Maker wants us holy for our own sakes!" Shem said, exasperated. "I simply cannot believe he has preserved our lives so marvelously so far, just to let us fall into such abject corruption. I pray he gives us some way to slip through their fingers and escape! And I also pray that he removes our wicked corruptors once and for all!"

"Of course, I agree with you both!" Ham said. "But we had better think of something fast. Adrammelech says we either visit the temple, or we go to the copper mines. He intends to walk with us all the way to the temple!"

The night before the impending event, my brothers and I were invited to Tulek's home for dinner. Our conversation was gloomy: Mother Earth had experienced tremors that week, more Adamite friends had disappeared, and King Nezzar had conquered yet another unprepared city. Keturah felt especially unsettled, for she had experienced a vision, in which judgment suddenly fell on Mother Earth. Still, she was convinced that the Creator would rescue His chosen believers somehow.

"Well, it would be a personal convenience if the rescue happened tonight," Shem remarked dryly. "Tomorrow night, our class goes to the Temple of Virility, and Noah's innocent boys are our instructor's main target. He says it is an important part of every student's education. This time, no excuses will be tolerated. We dread being degraded like that, but despite racking our brains, we cannot think of a way out."

Tulek and Keturah looked concerned, but Kezziah, who sat next to me, turned pale, and tears came to her eyes. Shem reddened, and apologized profusely.

I felt I should say something.

"Don't worry, Kezziah," I assured her, taking her hand. "We will not let them corrupt us! We will think of something!"

Tulek shook his head sadly as his daughter left the room. "We all know how Mother Earth operates. She will never give up until your integrity is compromised. Our Creator will not punish you for being victimized; but I really hope you do find some way out!"

"What a grief that they deliberately corrupt people like that!" Keturah added. "It is just another reason why God's patience is coming to an end!"

We walked home in silence. The stream gurgled, the night birds sang sadly, and the insects buzzed; but we heard nothing, being deep in thought. There had to be something we could do! An owl cooed, and a parrot chattered and squawked.

"Wait a minute!" I blurted. "The professor may escort us to be sure we enter the temple. But how would he know what we did inside? From what little I have heard, it is very dark in there."

"They might not know exactly, Japheth," Shem said, "but what are you thinking?"

"Well, I have an idea that may keep our integrity," I said, "though not save our reputations. We would have to know the passageways, and move quickly; and above all, we would have to stick together. The plan would hinge on finding someone very familiar with the temple, and it might require some money; but it is so simple, it just might work!"

"Do we know anyone who works there?" Ham asked. We thought furiously.

"How about someone," Shem asked suddenly, "who spends every coin he gets on his own pleasure? Someone who visits the Temple of Virility so often that his own noble family shuns him, and he is forced to beg for silver outside the palace?"

Of course! We saw his pitiable case nearly every day. His family kept him from starving, but they had finally refused to continue supporting his vices.

"Johanan!" Shem exclaimed. "He will tell us everything we need for just a few silver coins."

The next evening it was growing dark when we met our class at the Temple of Virility. The admission gate was well illuminated with torches. Dressed conspicuously in the bright blue robes that marked us as royal retainers, we hurried up to find the others already eagerly crowding around Professor Adrammelech.

"At last!" the professor exclaimed. His normally disdainful tone was mixed with relief. "The shy, innocent brothers from Enoch's Valley have arrived! I knew they would finally accept the pleasure call of nature! Now when I talk with the Prince—we shall drive together tonight in his ivory chariot—I can tell him that my success is complete. All of my young charges have finally become Mother Earth men, body and soul."

After arranging for our passes, the professor gathered us together. "Students, stick with me until we pass through the main portal. After that, just let the soft hands take you away. Do not resist! Have fun! Trust your feelings: if it feels good, it IS good! Work hard, and play hard!"

As we climbed the steps to the temple's main entrance, the professor continued his discourse. As we approached the top, however, he suddenly stopped, and began to scowl. We followed his gaze.

Three figures stood in front of the door, illuminated by the light of torches. They wore shimmering, translucent emerald gowns, and Athaliah's voluptuous curves were unmistakable. She saw Ham, and smiled at him seductively. The second shapely girl was Habibi, Shem's dancing partner, while the third was Aziza. She looked at me in triumph, and my resolve melted. We had relied on going through the portal together.

Now, our plans had crumbled: these temptresses were going to grab us on the way in! My legs felt shaky.

"I need help," I said. "We have been set up!"

"Should we run for it?" Shem whispered uncertainly.

"Just a minute, guys," Ham said with quiet resolve. His face had the half smile that often preceded his pranks. "I have an idea! Stick close to me." He moved up to the professor, who stood wavering, and spoke loudly enough for everyone to hear.

"Oh, boy, oh boy!" he exclaimed. "Athaliah has come for me! She promised to take care of me herself, and I cannot wait! Can't we walk faster? Oh, boy, oh boy!"

The professor stared at Ham angrily, and shouted, "Everyone stay back!"

He began climbing fast, nearly running. We followed him closely, panting in feigned excitement. Our classmates became infected with our eagerness, and raced up the steps with us.

Spreading his arms out to protect his charges, the outraged professor charged Athaliah, angrily shouting that she had fixed her affections on one of his young students rather than on himself! His language was violent, and for a moment, Athaliah and her girls retreated from the dark portal. As the professor pressed toward them, space opened between his back and the dim entrance.

"This is our chance!" Ham whispered firmly. "Let's go!"

As though uncontrollably eager, we pushed by the professor and leaped into the temple. Behind us, Athaliah angrily responded to Adrammelech's insults, loudly calling him a stupid fool, and adding other lewd, contemptuous descriptions. Meanwhile, Aziza and Habibi were blocked against the wall, and watched in horror as our entire class, dressed in identical blue robes, surged into the dark interior.

"Athaliah! Aziza shrieked desperately. "Do something! They are getting away!"

The girls finally pushed the cursing Adrammelech aside, and ran into the dark temple, but they were too late. It took time for their eyes to adjust to the darkness, and they were unable to identify their prey. With growing fury, they watched helplessly as the blue garments disappeared right before their eyes. Finally and reluctantly, they returned to the entrance to take out their rage on the professor.

As we plunged into the dim, smoky interior, we found the low, throbbing music hypnotizing. The fumes were powerful, too: even a whiff seemed intoxicating. The soft hands of the temple priestesses reached out for us, just as Adrammelech had promised. While my brothers and I stayed in the middle, with our hands firmly clasped, our classmates took no such precautions. One by one, they were smoothly drawn into the maze of secluded spaces, and into greater darkness. By sticking together, we were able to elude the groping hands and glide quickly to the back of the atrium. Passing beneath a low arch, we turned left and headed down a long corridor.

We quickly gained confidence in Johanan's instructions, and walked at a deliberate, but unrushed pace. Coming to a curtain of hanging beads, we stepped through it into a small room and stripped off our bright blue robes. Underneath, we had drab brown tunics, the normal attire of manual laborers. After stuffing the robes into a bag, we resumed our journey through the tortuous passages, feeling much less conspicuous. The sights and sounds around us were disturbing, but we concentrated on following the long line of oil lamps.

After another turn, we ducked beneath a low arch and came to our destination, a storage room filled with cleaning supplies. An oil lamp provided enough light to keep us from knocking things over, and we soon found the small, unguarded door to the exterior. Opening it, we descended a short flight of steps to a gravel path that led through the gardens. We had escaped from the temple!

Shem led the way, but suddenly stumbled and fell. There was a loud shriek, and we stopped, our hearts racing with fear. The shriek faded into a groan, and we saw prone figures at our feet. Shem had blindly stumbled over a sleeping couple! Though rudely awakened, the two were so overcome with strong spirits that they immediately drifted back into their stupor. We waited, but all remained quiet. Sighing in relief, we continued on the path, and soon arrived at the back of the garden. Finding a tree next to the wall, we climbed up and onto the wall, and then dropped down outside. We were free!

Now, making a successful escape from the Temple of Virility was not really an accomplishment to brag about. In fact, many would think it was both pointless and stupid, while if we had been caught, the consequences might have been severe. Nevertheless, it was a small success in the face of real temptation; and for Noah's boys, it was a rare moment of virtue.

---

[1]*Editor's Note:* Again, I have substituted a euphemism for a rather explicit barnyard expression taken from animal breeding practices.

[2]*Editor's Note:* Though it is not pleasant to talk of such things, sexually transmitted diseases are a reality in any clinical practice today, including dentistry. Clinicians must constantly remain alert to the clinical signs, and be prompt in referring for proper diagnosis and treatment.

Chapter Thirty: Ham's Best Prank Ever

"Now what?" Ham asked, as we stood outside the wall. "We cannot go back to the palace right away. It would be suspicious if we returned before midnight."

"But we cannot stay outside the temple!" Shem objected. "There is a full moon, and we could easily be seen. Questions would be asked."

"Follow me," I told them. "There are people worrying about us."

My brothers understood. Quietly darting from one shade to another, we unobtrusively returned to the main boulevard, and moved along back streets to a residence we had come to know.

Tulek was surprised to see us, but relieved to learn that we had escaped. His wife and daughter were still awake, and they insisted that we come inside and tell our story. After taking refreshments to the upper terrace, we related the entire adventure. Though our original plan was to slip right through the temple, we explained how the unexpected appearance of Athaliah and her friends had nearly upset it. Kezziah and her mother were delighted with Ham's ruse, which had used Adrammelech's jealousy to frustrate the three temptresses. We sketched our journey through the dark maze of the temple and through the garden, where we had stumbled over the sleeping couple.

"So you see," I concluded, "we did find a way to escape, though there was no particular honor in it. Our reputation for purity has been lost, but we actually slipped away pretty much intact."

"Thank God!" Kezziah said simply, looking very relieved.

"Yes, my daughter," Keturah added. "We thank our Creator for protecting them from corruption tonight. Unfortunately, boys, the people of Mother Earth are perverse enough to gloat over your loss of innocence. It is ironic that they find such satisfaction in calling believers hypocrites, when any slips of our own are rarely as bad as their normal behavior. But when do believers ever claim to be better people, anyway? No, do not worry about your reputation in Mother Earth, boys. That is not in your hands. Your reputation with the Creator is the only one that matters."

I was not sure how to respond to this. Frankly, I had always thought that believers were in fact a little better. The narrowness of our escape, however, had been humbling. I supposed she was right. But even if we were really no better than other people, I certainly hoped we were no worse!

"Well, I am very glad that you boys escaped tonight, and proud, too!" Tulek said. "You showed unusual wisdom for your age: for one thing, your realized your danger. As someone who was once a young man, and especially after seeing those girls at the banquet, I can appreciate the real temptation you faced. And you may well get away with this. Your professor is under pressure, and he will be quick to report how eagerly you entered the temple. Everyone will be convinced that you were corrupted, because they would have been, in your place! Athaliah, of course, will be angry with Adrammelech, and he may hold that against you."

"Well, I pray that the Creator removes that wicked man Adrammelech!" Keturah declared indignantly. She glanced at her daughter, who looked worn out. "But this has been an exciting evening, and everyone must be tired. Boys, why don't you get a few hours of sleep here? If you return to the palace early tomorrow morning, no one will suspect you."

We followed her advice. Some hours later, waiting for dawn, we huddled together beneath the great oak tree at the south gate of the palace. The Mokosh River Tavern, a popular place for the wealthy, was right across the street. We thought about going inside for shelter, because we were drenched from the heavy night mist, but the risk of raising questions was too great.

As we shivered in our wet robes, we heard the trip-trop of approaching horses, and the grinding noise that indicated a chariot. The sound drew closer and closer. Suddenly, the heads of two horses appeared in the mist directly above us, snorting out great puffs of steamy moisture. We drew close to the trunk of the tree, hoping we were invisible.

"Grandmother will be pleased to hear of your success," a familiar voice intoned, "although you prevented her tigress from personally catching her prey. But drowning yourself in wine does nothing to win her back: it only shows your weakness. Now Rogar, you at least are not too drunk to walk. Get us a table at the tavern—a private one. I will meet you there in a quarter hour. I have someone to meet first." There was a pause. "Drammy, if you must rest in my chariot, I expect you to safeguard it. I value it more than your life. And do not drool on it! I insist on keeping the ivory spotless." There was only a dull garble in response.

Having identified the driver and passengers of the chariot, we pressed even more tightly against the massive tree. A heavy figure stepped out and lumbered unsteadily across the street to the tavern, which had several torches burning beside the door. At the same time, the tall prince hopped out and strode in the direction of a small garden beside the palace wall. We kept very still. In a few moments we heard the sound of snoring.

"Who could the prince be meeting at this hour?" Shem whispered. "I think I should go and find out."

"Good idea," Ham whispered back. "I will follow Rogar to the tavern."

"Be careful, guys," I whispered. "I will keep an eye on 'Drammy.'"

My brothers disappeared in the gray mist. The time stretched slowly as I listened to the sounds of the horses, and snoring. I strained my eyes to watch. Finally, I heard the grass rustle, and Ham plopped down beside me. Though I could not see him clearly, I knew he was grinning. He held a gourd filled with something that smelled both pungent and disgusting.

"I found the ingredients in the trash behind the tavern," Ham whispered, chuckling, "some sour old fruit, vegetable drippings, sticky stuff, and a skin of vinegar. Let's have some fun with 'Drammy,' shall we? It's only fair!"

"Ham, I don't think we…" I began, but stopped. When Ham was prepared for a prank, he was not easily dissuaded. If he were caught, which was not often, we would have our usual choices: to run or fight. Ham had already moved around the tree to the chariot, and was out of sight. I heard faint sounds of splashing and slopping. For a moment, the snoring stopped, and I held my breath. The snoring resumed, and I exhaled quietly. The horses let out a nervous whinny, making my heart race again. Just then, someone tapped me on the shoulder. It was Shem.

"The prince met with our friend Sandal," he whispered urgently. "He was disguised as a Cainite, with dark painted stripes and black clothing. I think they are plotting something bad, maybe during the Dam Festival, but I could not hear particulars. We have to get out of here! The prince is right behind me. He could be here any moment. Where is Ham?"

"Here I am," Ham whispered. He stood above us, smiling mischievously. "Let's move fast. When the prince returns, he may become upset."

"Quick, then!" I said.

We took off at a trot, bending low in the mist, and angling away from the prince's expected direction. We had no sooner ducked under some bushes, than we heard the prince's voice from the chariot.

"What in the...?" His exclamation became a heart-rending cry of anguish, followed by cursing and sharp, violent smacks. There were shrieks of pain, followed by cries for help.

A bright light suddenly shone from the open door of the tavern. Shouting erupted, and men with torches came out from the tavern. The curses, smacking blows, and shrieks continued. An alarm bell rang at the palace gate, echoed by other bells. We heard military commands. Very shortly, soldiers marched in our direction from the palace gate. Ham had been right: the prince had become upset—very upset! And Professor Adrammelech was receiving the brunt of it!

Meanwhile, hidden in the bushes, Ham was rolling on the ground in barely muffled laughter. Seeing Ham laughing with such glee, we could not help but begin to laugh and giggle too.

"What did you do, anyway?" Shem finally asked, between tears of laughter.

"I splattered artificial vomit," Ham chortled, "all over Drammy and the prince's ivory chariot!"

We broke into laughter again.

A day or two later, we reported to the academy for our lecture. Although our class stood at attention for nearly half an hour, Professor Adrammelech never showed up. Instead, the palace steward came in scowling.

"Students," he announced, "your professor will not be lecturing this morning, nor will he again in the foreseeable future."

The faces of the class brightened.

"He seriously displeased the prince," the steward continued, "something I do not recommend. You could end up in prison, too—if you are lucky! At any rate, your classroom instruction has been sufficient. The queen mother is satisfied that you have each embraced our worldview and our way of life. While you must still attend cultural events, for the time being you may return to your work assignments. You are dismissed."

As soon as the palace steward left, the entire class erupted in cheers. What a relief! What an answer to prayer! While the consequences of Ham's prank had been a little harsh, we thought they were only just. Everything the professor had done had been dishonest, in our view, with the explicit goal of corrupting both our convictions and our character. We were thankful that he had failed, and thankful to be free of his pernicious influence. This, Shem and I had to agree, was Ham's best prank ever!

Chapter Thirty-One: An Assassination Plot

Without having to suffer through the professor's lectures, the next several months were mostly pleasant. Athaliah still made us attend cultural events, including entertainments at Mother Earth's theater[1], but she rarely came personally. While our classmates enjoyed them, we found them pointlessly drenched in sensuality and violence. Working in the real world was far better.

It was a pleasure to walk by the dam construction site every day and watch my hydraulic conveyors smoothly carrying up great blocks of stone. When the dam wall had grown to half of its planned height, the two great waterwheels were installed. At that point, my life became even busier, for Tulek had assigned me the task of improving the power conduction system. The power shafts and gears were complex, but Tulek was an excellent teacher, and I learned a lot. It was almost as good as being at the School of Tubal-Cain. Furthermore, as Tulek's assistant, I had the privilege of entering the king's scientific laboratories[2], where I discovered some fascinating developments.

Cousin Abdi and Uncle Lemuel had previously wondered how Mother Earth was using sulfur. There were at least two new uses, I learned. The first one involved adding sulfur to the sap of rubber trees. When they were boiled together it produced a strong, flexible material that was harder than tar and very resilient, always returning to its original shape[3]. The laboratory workers used it to make bouncing balls; but I had already thought of other uses, including sealing valves.

The second use of sulfur was closely guarded, but I had reason to think it was used for the secret weapon the queen mother had mentioned. When sulfur was ground together with charcoal and a third mineral, I learned, the mixture was dangerously flammable. The king had made a special laboratory to develop the mixture, from which black smoke was known to pour, sometimes together with loud noises. When I told Tulek, he advised me not to ask too many questions, because curious people sometimes disappeared.

Kezziah continued to come to her father's office a few times every week. I came to treasure her visits. She was so good hearted, and so honest and sensible, that despite my resolution to keep my proper distance, I grew increasingly fond of her. She was the sister I never had. We talked about everything, from engineering problems to parents, and even discussed theological topics like the final judgment of the wicked and God's promised Rescuer.

Speaking of girls, I learned that Aziza had become engaged to marry Rogar. While I thought it was poor judgment on her part, in a way I was relieved. I had never understood what she saw in me. Rogar's great wealth, however, might have been almost enough to make him handsome.

Ham flourished at the Great Zoo. The curator appreciated his exceptional talents, and mostly let him do what he liked. However, after losing a few trainers to the zoo's flaming behemoths, the curator finally asked Ham to take them on as a special project. The animals proved a challenge even for Ham, but his prior experience helped. After experimenting with various fruits, Ham found that watermelons attracted flamers better than durians. They became the key to his training.

Shem detested much of what he learned, but found his immersion in the culture and politics of Mother Earth exciting. He constantly brought home new stories of gross immorality, dishonesty, violence, and abuse of power. Corruption clearly prevailed at every level among the public officials[4].

"I think I am becoming calloused!" Shem said one day. "Hearing about the temporary marriages of my coworkers no longer shocks me. I no longer question it when they come in sick after a night drinking strong spirits, or when they lose a week's wages through gambling. And I was not surprised today to learn that Prime Minister Logar is completely two-faced."

"What do you mean?" I asked.

"Well," Shem replied, "do you remember how he posed as a devoted worshiper of the earth goddess Mokosh? It turns out he has no concern for the health of the earth at all! He spreads his tales of suicidal rodents, earthquakes, and global cooling simply to scare landowners. Then, using the leverage of his office, he buys their land at a reduced price. Once it is his, he clear-cuts the timber, which causes erosion, and then strip mines[5] the land for ore. That, as everyone knows, destroys the delicate underground springs that are the source of the evening mists. Without those springs, everything uphill becomes permanently barren! Logar knows all this; but his personal avarice outweighs everything!"

"Would you say that his wickedness is great?" Ham asked.

"I would say," Shem replied, "that he and the rest of the people here dwell on evil continually[6]!"

"Keturah thinks God's judgment could fall on Mother Earth any day now," I said. "Do you think so, too?"

"I don't know," Shem replied, "but I do think a political crisis is brewing. The king has a long list of enemies among the nobility, and they have lately been disappearing. The nobility has finally realized this, and they are uniting against him. Prince Malek seems to be playing a role in this, too. Last week he publicly disagreed with his father and took the side of the senate. His father was angry, I heard. The queen mother has been very active lately, too. She has always been the real power behind the throne, according to most people."

Despite our speculations, nothing happened. Everything continued normally. The Great Dam grew steadily, and finally achieved its full height. We finalized the completion date, and the Dam Festival invitations were sent out. Things became even busier. While I worked long hours to finish the power conduction shafts, Shem planned out receptions and other official functions, and Ham worked with a team of keepers to train animals and develop a new show just for the festival.

The giant king of Nephil and other heads of state began to trickle in as the Dam Festival approached. Governor Shahoot was on his way from Enoch's Valley, we learned, bringing father as part of his entourage. Although we were eager to see him, we had apprehensions.

"If father has the opportunity," Ham speculated one day, "I am afraid he will tell King Nezzar exactly what he told him before: namely, that unless he repents of his terrible sins, the Creator is going to destroy him and his entire city. That could make things unpleasant for us."

When it was three weeks before the Dam Festival, Dam Minister Algar gave Tulek the order to close the water gates. He wanted to fill the great reservoir to the top, so that he could demonstrate the full power of the waterwheels.

The order presented Tulek with a moral dilemma. Tulek had been away when the first stones were laid and when the reservoir basin was sealed with a special pitch-infused fabric. Algar had ordered the fabric covered with gravel before Tulek returned. Later, he absolutely refused to allow him to inspect either the foundation or the fabric. The fabric seal was important, because the soil in those days was far deeper and more delicately organized than it is today. Without an adequate seal, the water in the reservoir could soak into the underlying soil and potentially upset the underground system of springs.

Although Tulek had assumed the work had been done properly, on the day before Algar ordered the reservoir filled, Tulek had accidentally discovered the amount the contractor was actually paid to place the fabric. Though a great sum had been budgeted, the contractor had been given a far smaller amount. Tulek now had a strong reason to suspect that Algar, whose reputation for avarice was as bad as his brother's, had personally siphoned off a large part of the money. Because the consequences of a faulty foundation could be catastrophic, Tulek now felt compelled to learn the truth. He sent me out to inspect both the foundation stones and the basin, and to do it at an hour when I would not be seen.

Dawn had not yet broken when I got to the base of the dam and began to dig. I soon discovered the disquieting truth. The dam foundation, despite the clear requirements, only had one layer of blocks below the surface! Furthermore, the stones had not been laid on a firm, compacted foundation at all, but on loose, porous soil! I checked the reservoir basin next. When I removed enough gravel to get down to the sealing fabric, I found that the sheets had not been overlapped as specified in the contract. Instead, there were large gaps between the sheets!

My heart raced as I considered the implications. With such large gaps, the basin of the reservoir effectively had no seal at all. That meant that the underlying soil could well turn to mud. The fact that the foundation stones had only been placed on loose soil made everything far worse. If the soil beneath the reservoir basin became mud, it would seep around the stones of the dam and undermine their support. The stones could shift or even sink!

I considered how the problem would have to be fixed. The entire basin of the reservoir would have to be dug up, and new fabric properly placed. Furthermore, the stone foundation of the dam would need to be completely rebuilt, which obviously could not be done without removing the entire wall of stones supported by it. Rebuilding the dam would entail tremendous cost, and would require at least two years to complete. This news would be a calamity. The more I thought about it, the worse it became. The king would not simply be displeased to learn this: blood would flow. I had to tell Tulek right away.

I took off at a run. Unfortunately, the morning mist was still very thick, and I could safely go no faster than a jog. The mist was starting to lift by the time I got to the south gate of the palace. That was where I saw something that made me stop.

The prince's ivory chariot was parked next to the great oak tree, exactly where it had been parked the night we escaped from the Temple of Virility. The tall prince was not in sight, but I saw a man turning onto the narrow path leading to the garden. Something in his gait seemed familiar. He swaggered, but had a slight limp. Somehow I knew it was Sandal's teammate Rekem. Was he meeting Prince Malek? What for? And why at such an early hour?

I had a decision to make. Should I investigate this curious meeting, or run on to give Tulek very bad news, news that could create a firestorm for everyone? Curiosity won. Ducking into the bushes surrounding the garden, I quietly crawled towards the garden.

Rekem's voice was very clear. "At my second signal, my men will drive the animals into the courtyard. The strike will be quick and painless, my prince, and the stampede will erase any evidence of foul play. The blame can be laid at the feet of the religious fanatics."

I could not hear the prince's response, because his voice was too low.

"Of course my men can be trusted!" Rekem answered. "They know the risks, but they know they will be richly rewarded! Now, with your permission, I shall return. We have only a few hours remaining, and my men must be in position."

Footsteps crunched along the gravel walkway. As I lay silently in the damp soil, I wondered what should I do next. The dam foundation would have to wait. What I had just overheard was far more urgent. Some kind of plot was to take place in just hours. When the footsteps were gone, I crawled out of the bushes and ran to the palace gate. After being admitted by the guards, I dashed up to our room and burst in. My brothers were just preparing to go to breakfast.

"A murderous plot!" I said breathlessly, "involving the prince and our old enemy Rekem!"

When they got over their surprise, I quickly outlined having seen the prince's parked chariot, and following Rekem to the small garden where I overheard the plot.

"We must tell General Zabadanah right away," Shem said firmly. "I know the royal schedule. King Nezzar plans to bring the king of Nephil on a tour of the city today. The attack could take place anywhere along the route!"

"Wait!" Ham exclaimed. "They visit the Great Zoo first. We have been preparing for weeks! If the plot involves animals, a courtyard and a stampede, the attack can only take place there! We must stop them! There will be thousands of visitors today, and even a small stampede could result in disaster!"

My brothers and I immediately ran to the palace guard headquarters, and paced anxiously outside the general's office until he arrived. In the courtyard, a parade was being assembled, with flags, banners, and showy decorations. Musicians, acrobats, and jugglers practiced, while food vendors prepared their wares. The roasted vegetables and sweet bakery smelled delicious, and none of us had had breakfast. Walking up, General Zabadanah saw our concern, and ushered us into his private office. I immediately blurted out what I had overheard, but he found the story incredible.

"You must be mistaken!" he said. "Are you accusing the prince of being involved in a murderous plot? Japheth, go over this once again. I want every detail. If you are suggesting the prince himself may be involved with murder and treason, we must be extremely careful."

The general called for an aide to bring us food and drink. As we ate, I described everything I had seen and heard. The general asked me a few questions about Rekem, and made me repeat his exact words. I said that I had not actually seen the prince, nor heard his voice distinctly. The general put his finger on his lips, and thought aloud.

"Could someone else have driven the prince's chariot? I do not think so. Is Prince Malek the kind to conspire against his own father? Possibly. But could his target be the king of Nephil? Or both? This is Mother Earth, after all!"

The general lapsed into silence. When he looked up, he was not happy, but he had made a decision. "I suppose you lads realize that even learning of such a treasonous plot is extremely dangerous, no matter how this turns out. But we cannot ignore it. This is what we shall do. First of all, Japheth, you saw and heard nothing this morning. You came here simply to discuss your training at the School of Arms. Instead, as I came to work, I was given an anonymous tip about a possible assassination attempt. Do you understand me? Our lives depend upon this. Next, Ham. You work at the zoo, do you not?"

"Yes, General," Ham replied.

"Good," he said. "If this plot plans on a stampede for cover, the zoo must somehow prevent it."

"General, let us help, too," I said.

"We all have a score to settle with Rekem," Shem added.

"Very well," he said. "I can use all of you. Let me tell you what I am thinking."

The general quickly outlined his plan. Before sending us to the curator of the zoo, he added some advice.

"From what I saw in the wilderness, you lion cubs tend to charge in quickly. This time, stay out of sight. Let my men do the hard work." With that, he called in his aide. He had a lot to do, and very little time.

My brothers and I hurried out of the palace. We found the boulevard full of traffic, and it was very slow. Worse yet, we were soon forced off the road by six huge mastodons rumbling toward us. Filling the entire width of the road, their great heads were armored with bronze plates, and their long, silver-tipped tusks projected nearly the length of their bodies. Riding each of the mastodons was a giant soldier, each easily seven cubits tall, with broad shoulders and powerful limbs.

"The Giant Guard of Nephil!" Shem exclaimed.

The giant guard eventually passed by, but a royal chariot blocked the road next, carrying another giant warrior. This one wore a feathered helmet with a gold circlet, and he carried a scepter: obviously, this was the king of Nephil. His rearguard included a hundred warriors on great black stallions. As soon as it passed, we broke into a run. We had no time to lose.

    [1]*Editor's Note:* A theater as a place of entertainment has a long history that dates back to ancient Greece, though this manuscript suggests it could be even older. Thespis, traditionally considered the first actor, won a drama competition in Athens in 534 BC.

    [2]*Editor's Note:* Mother Earth was apparently devoted to technological improvement.

    [3]*Editor's Note:* Incredibly, this seems to suggest that vulcanized rubber was discovered long before Charles Goodyear patented it in 1844, although the secret was obviously lost.

    [4]*Editor's Note:* It would appear that political corruption has existed in every age.

    [5]*Editor's Note:* Clear cutting of forests and strip-mining may still create ecological damage today.

    [6]*Editor's Note:* This quote is strikingly similar to a Bible verse describing the same period (Genesis 6:5)

Chapter Thirty-Two: The Battle for the Zoo

As we burst into his office, the curator was rehearsing his speech to the royal party. Although at first upset at being disturbed, he became outraged when Ham told him of the urgent threat.

"Those flea-infested religious fanatics!" he exclaimed. "They claim to love animals, but they really just hate people. They are blind to the fact that nature flourishes better under man's wise dominion. What is worse, their foolish actions generally hurt the animals they claim to help!" Zimzimah stopped. "Of course, assassination is a terrible thing, too; but a stampede terrifies animals, and they suffer for a long time afterwards." He began pacing back and forth.

"Anyone who would deliberately stampede a herd deserves a sound beating! Ham, I want you to pick out a few dozen sturdy young keepers. If those tree-kissers try anything, I want them punished!"

As we left his office, Ham explained that Zimzimah hated what he called 'tree-kissers.' "Since his first day at the zoo, they have been nothing but trouble to him."

After assembling a crew of muscular young men, Ham told them a plot had been discovered. The news of a possible stampede instantly angered them, and they were eager to put a stop to it. Ham introduced Shem and me, and put together three teams, one for each of us.

"Japheth, take this behemoth prod," a young keeper offered, holding out a heavy club with a knobbed end. "If you know where to hit, you can make even a bonehead[1] jump. Mokosh fanatics should be no problem!"

"Their skulls will crack like eggs!" another keeper added, laughing. "This should be fun! Just ring your bell if you see trouble."

After putting on green keeper tunics, hats, and tool harnesses, we walked up the main promenade.

"The Great Zoo was originally a large plantation," Ham explained. "As you can see, it extends from the main entrance quite a distance up the slope of the mountain. An access road goes around the periphery of the zoo, with gates to allow keepers into the enclosures. Visitors, however, can only enter the exhibits from the main courtyard by way of the promenade. After passing the special exhibits, which include my flaming behemoths this month, the promenade divides three ways — left, right, and center, which is straight west. The center walkway goes past the two lakes, where we keep the hippopotamuses, giant turtles, and the aquatic behemoths, while the left one goes to the mammals. The right one goes to the reptiles and birds. As a rule, smaller animals are downhill, while larger ones are uphill. All three walkways join at the foot of the western slope where the largest grazing animals are kept, like bison, gazelles, rhinoceroses, ground sloths, zebras, and so on."

"Where should we take our posts?" Shem asked Ham.

"Shem, you take the south predator enclosure." Ham said. "That is where we keep the sabertooths, as well as the giant lions, dire wolves, and short-faced bears. Japheth, why don't you watch the large grazing mammals in the middle pastureland? They would probably be the main targets for a stampede, because they are in such great numbers. I will keep watch over the behemoth predators on the north side, because they are the scariest. Just keep in mind that all three walkways slope downhill from the pastureland before they merge onto the promenade. If a stampede were to begin up in the pasture, it would accelerate downhill, perhaps on all three walkways, and then enter the courtyard together, crushing anybody there. We cannot let that happen!"

We came to the keeper's barn, and Ham selected elephants for us. After climbing into their neck saddles, we urged them up the promenade to the walkway overlooking the upper pasture. Ham's keepers met us there, and we spread out to watch. From my tall perch, I could see a lot of green-clad zoo workers. Although I did not know the permanent staff, I knew that many workers were temporary.

The slopes were covered with large herds. The giant bison stayed close together, but other species tended to scatter. Big hay wagons blocked the upper access gates, but I supposed that was normal. After all the excitement of the early morning, it was very refreshing to see animals peacefully grazing in the pasture. It reminded me of happy times on our plantation. I sighed, and found myself smiling.

Trumpets sounded. I heard loud cheering from the courtyard below us: the royal procession had entered. A signal horn blew from somewhere close, and green-clad keepers began to move briskly along the enclosure fences. I assumed they were making sure everything was secure. They did their checks methodically, stopping briefly at various spots before moving on. I turned my attention to the crowd, looking for suspicious characters.

A short time later, I noticed that a nearby herd of musk oxen had circled up, with their horns pointed outward. That was not a good sign. At the same time, my elephant trumpeted anxiously. I saw movement, and looked down. That was odd, I thought: a wildebeest had wandered onto the pedestrian walkway, and was now browsing on the grass beside me. My heart froze. Browsing beside me? How had the animal gotten out?

Looking around, I felt rudely awakened. I had not noticed something very obvious: large sections of the enclosure fence had fallen down! Antelopes, bison, and wild oxen were already curiously sauntering onto the walkway. I rang my bell furiously. We needed to get the fence back up fast! The sections must have been previously cut, I thought, but temporarily kept up by a rope or cord that was easily cut. That must have been what the keepers had done as they moved along the fencing! They had not been keepers at all, but conspirators!

Several keepers raced up and attempted to raise the fence sections, but they found no way to keep them up! Something flashed in my eye from the upper slopes: the hay wagons were on fire! They were moving downhill, straight for the herds of bison! Gates of many cages had been thrown open, and imposters waved brightly colored cloths to spook the animals.

"You are free, brothers and sisters!" they laughed. "Run away! Your slavery is over!"

I rang my bell until my whole squad ran up, and then slid down from my elephant. I sent some keepers into the pasture to intercept the burning wagons, and led the others in charging the imposters, who were still opening gates.

The attack had been well planned. By the time we leaped into action, hundreds of animals already milled on the walkways: we had to push through them to get to the conspirators. Visitors to the zoo finally noticed that the animals were loose. One began screaming hysterically, and her fear spread like fire. Soon all the guests were running toward the main courtyard.

The true Mokosh fanatics, or "tree-kissers," fought poorly. They quickly surrendered and were taken to an empty monkey cage. Some of the imposters, however, proved to be hardened Cainite thugs who fought viciously with knives and clubs. It took all our strength and skill to subdue them. Teamwork paid off, however, and the monkey cage began to fill up.

While we were occupied, unfenced animals continued to spill onto the walkways. Anteaters, kangaroos, tapirs, and other medium-sized animals uncomfortably bumped shoulders with large water buffalos and zebras. As the numbers increased, the animals became more anxious. Large rhinoceroses, giraffes, and giant ground sloths lumbered along the walkways, pushing the smaller animals against the walls and frightening them.

Herbivorous behemoths began to appear. A big three-horned one came first, followed by a bonehead and a pair of plate-heads. A spiny-back wiggled by, threatening the others with its horned tail. Mammalian predators showed up next, beginning with a giant lion and a leopard. These were bad enough; but when a pair of behemoth stalkers appeared, it was too much. The sight of their great mouths filled with sharp teeth was terrifying. The animals began to circle, looking for a way out.

A signal horn sounded out from nearby. Looking for its source, I found a young man in green on top of a nearby wall. As he fastened his brass horn onto a loop on his harness, our eyes met.

"Rekem!" I shouted. He replied with a curse. Jumping down, he began running north toward the behemoth enclosures. Even with a bad leg, he was fast. I rang my bell, mounted my elephant, and was soon in pursuit. The loose animals on the walkway moved out of our way as I kept my eyes on Rekem. He climbed the wall of an empty enclosure and ran to the next one.

I stayed on the promenade, and finally came close to Ham's post. When I shouted to him that I was chasing Rekem, he hopped on his elephant and joined me. We nearly got him cornered in the anteater enclosure, but he doubled back and ran south towards the mammalian predators. The herd of animals on the west walkway had gotten dense, making it difficult to move through them. By the time Ham and I got to the central promenade, the walkways were jammed with terrified animals that surged back and forth, squealing and grunting. Ham shook his head: things had become desperate.

"You try to catch Rekem, Japheth," he shouted. "I have to get ahead of them before the real stampede begins!"

Ham roughly urged his elephant down the central walkway, forcing the smaller animals aside. The air was filled with dust, and he soon disappeared. I pressed on towards Rekem, slogging upstream through the river of animals. Despite losing him momentarily a few times, I doggedly continued. When I joined up with Shem, I learned his experience had been like mine: the gates were open before he even knew it. While his keepers had subdued most of their conspirators, too, they were now fully occupied simply trying to control the animals. As we spoke, I glimpsed Rekem on the edge of the walkway ahead of us. He was trapped between the herd and a rock wall.

"There he is!" Shem cried. "Let's get him!"

The real stampede[2] began right about that moment. The bison, wildebeests, rhinoceroses, and water buffalo already comprised a river of flesh, and it now all began to flow downhill. The din was awful. Our big elephants balked at stepping into the stampede, and for several minutes we were blocked in a depression in the wall. In the brief moments when the dust cleared, we watched our quarry and he watched us. The pace of the stampede was not steady. Sometimes it speeded up, sometimes it slowed; and sometimes it even stopped altogether. When it stopped, spaces opened up. We took advantage of one such moment to force our elephants into the current after our fugitive. Rekem took off, dangerously running between the hoofs and horns of the beasts. He may have been desperate to escape, but we were just as determined to catch him.

"He ducked into that service road!" Shem shouted.

Urging our elephants through the turbulent currents, we finally came to the other side, and turned onto the vacant narrow road. Rekem was only a short distance away. Without the stampede to slow us, our elephants began to speed up. A large wagon had overturned ahead of us, dumping a full load of manure over the road. Three richly dressed young men carrying spears were tiptoeing around the pile. Running at full speed, Rekem splashed right beside them, splattering them with ooze.

"Mother of Earth!" one screamed. "I will kill you for that!"

Immediately drawing back, he threw his spear at Rekem. It went wide, and Rekem disappeared around a corner. The elegant young nobles cursed and shook their fists at him, before bending down to see the extent of the damage. They did not notice that our big elephants were lumbering towards them.

"My clothes," one loudly whined. "They are ruined forever. We must catch that stupid oaf! Even among dogs, he is a pig!"

Elephants have a lot of momentum. We shouted warnings, but the men heard nothing until we were nearly upon them. When they finally saw us, their reflexes kicked in. They jumped out of our path and flopped headfirst into the soft, sticky pile. I looked back, relieved that we had not run them down. The three figures slowly emerged from the pile, completely covered in blackish goo.

"Sorry!" I called back. "We are pursuing a terrorist!"

The horrible reek that wafted up was enough to choke us, but we could not help laughing as we continued our wild ride.

"We tried to warn them, Japheth," Shem shouted. "But what a stench! If Ham had seen that, he would laugh for weeks!"

"They sure seem upset," I said sympathetically.

When we turned the corner, we saw Rekem. He had come to the gate leading to the main courtyard, but found it completely blocked by people in the courtyard. Rekem glanced back and saw that we were very close. Seizing two men by their shoulders, he violently pulled them back and stepped over their bodies to force his way into the crowd. We slowed our elephants to a halt, slid down the trunks, and slipped through after him.

Thousands of people were jammed into the courtyard: for some reason, the great exit portals were shut. Two royal chariots were parked beneath the archway, surrounded by soldiers. Horribly, each chariot had a giant body with a spear protruding from its back. Other normal-sized human bodies lay on the pavement.

Shem and I seemed to be the only ones looking at the bodies, because everyone else had turned to stare in horror towards the animal exhibits. As we watched, their faces brightened, and then they began to cheer! Completely baffled, Shem and I followed their gaze along the central promenade. Flames were everywhere, and the promenade was filled with squealing animals.

---

[1]*Editor's Note:* A bonehead is presumably a type of dinosaur, possibly a *Pachycephalosaurus*. The translator had to guess on the names of some of the extinct animals in the manuscript, though many descriptions suggested well-known existing animals, including lions, giraffes, and anteaters.

[2]*Editor's Note:* No one knows how frequently animal stampedes occur, though they are sometimes reported. One recent stampede of exotic animals (Zanesville, Ohio, 2011) resulted in 50 animal deaths, including tigers, leopards, and lions. Human stampedes, however, have often been recorded, including one in Mecca in 1990, when 1426 people were suffocated or crushed to death.

Chapter Thirty-Three: Heroes of Mother Earth

Ham later explained that after leaving me, he drove his elephant down the central promenade. By maneuvering in and out of the herds, he finally managed to get ahead, and then sped on to the flaming behemoth enclosure, which was located at the intersection of the three promenades.

He found the gates wide open. The three huge beasts had already left their pen, and were slowly lumbering down towards the main courtyard. As they moved, their giant tails swept the walkway, knocking over benches and trash bins. Looking ahead to the courtyard, he was surprised to find it jammed with people, and he could hear screaming. The huge portals of the main gate were closed, he saw, trapping everyone!

Stopping at the flamer pen, Ham turned around in his saddle to look uphill. The top of each walkway was dark with animals that were moving downhill, picking up speed. This had become a true stampede! His elephant sensed trouble, and trumpeted nervously, but the nearby flamers placidly continued strolling toward the courtyard: they had noticed nothing.

In the course of working with the animals, Ham had learned that when flamers were pushed from behind, they were inclined to speed up. That meant that if the stampede overtook the flamers from behind, they would become the leaders, and simply add fire to the devastation. On the other hand, when flamers were challenged to their face, they were the most stubborn, obstinate creatures in the zoo, and absolutely fearless. Nothing could make them budge. That gave him an idea. It was dangerous to attempt, but unless he did something, everyone in the courtyard would face the crushing weight of a thousand crazed beasts.

Halting his elephant outside the flamer pen, Ham slid down and grabbed two watermelons from the food bin. Cradling them in his arms, he ran back to the promenade, where the nearby flamers were leisurely rambling downhill.

"Come!" he yelled, heaving the watermelon. "Come!"

The fruit landed just a few paces behind the lumbering behemoths. It broke open, and the sweet smell of the fruit filled the air. The nostrils of the monsters flared, and they turned their heads around. Seeing the fruit now, as well as smelling it, they continued to turn, and sniffed again. They were clearly interested. In a few moments the three flamers had completely reversed their course and were plodding towards the fruit.

Glancing uphill, Ham saw the stampede rapidly approaching. In a moment, the herds from all three promenades would merge together onto the main boulevard. Their speed would then increase, and the great river of animals would flood directly into the courtyard—unless he could produce a miracle. He threw another watermelon, which burst a few paces further uphill. Licking up the pieces of the first juicy red fruit, the three beasts slowly advanced toward the second fruit, still completely unaware of the juggernaut almost upon them.

Ham had done all he could. Leaving the behemoths to face the oncoming stampede, he darted to the protection of the wall, and climbed up to watch.

The flamers did not notice the thundering onslaught until the leaders of the herd were only forty or fifty cubits away. When they did notice, they did not turn to flee. Instead, they became furious. Raising their great tube-shaped heads, they spewed out angry sheets of burning oily liquid. The flames shot along the walkway and spattered over the giant bison and elk leading the stampede. Squealing in pain and terror, the animals reared up, but were slammed forward by the animals following them. Tumbling flat, they slid into the flames.

Although desperate to escape, the leading animals had nowhere to go. The angry flamers continued to blow out sheets of flame. The thatched buildings on either side of the walkway burst into fire, and the mass of confused animals saw the flames. The momentum of the herd slowed, though for a while the hapless, squealing animals in the lead were forced even closer to the fire. After long moments of shrieking terror, the herd finally skidded to a complete halt. The suffering animals in the lead turned around to frantically ram those pressing them. While it seemed to take forever, the fire, noise, and terror did the trick: the herd gradually reversed direction. Very slowly, it began moving uphill.

Ham sighed in relief. It had been a miracle that the three flaming behemoths had stopped a great stampede of terrified animals. But now that the emergency was over, there was much to do. To begin with, he would have to calm down the flamers, and return them to their enclosure. For that, he needed more watermelons. As he turned back to the food bin, he was startled to hear cheering. Glancing up, he saw that the faces of the crowd were all staring at him!

"The gods have come to save us!" one man cried out. "Praise the young god!"

People shouted out praises, and Ham turned red from embarrassment. His plan had been risky, sure: but thanks to those stubborn flamers, it had somehow succeeded. The people in the crowd, however, were taking the matter way out of proportion, which frankly horrified him. On the other hand, he had to admit that they must have had an exciting day at the zoo. Overwhelmed by emotion, they had simply become silly.

When the other keepers arrived, Ham tried to slip away. They all had a big job ahead of them, with gates to repair, animals to secure, and much to clean up. But just as Ham turned, he felt Zimzimah's big arm around his shoulders.

"You cannot leave, Ham!" he said. "You must allow the audience to show their appreciation! This day began very poorly, you know. You saved the day! Not only did you save hundreds of lives from the stampede; you turned a bad experience into an exciting one! Your heroism, which featured our newest acquisitions, was a fiery spectacle no one will ever forget! Can you imagine how popular our Great Zoo will be after this? We can double our entrance fees! Well done, my boy! You are my hero!" He clapped Ham fondly on the shoulder.

As they walked to the courtyard, Ham asked the curator how the day had begun poorly.

"Well, after King Nezzar and the king of Nephil entered," he began, "I gave my welcoming speech. The crowd loved me. I heard a horn blast, but thought nothing of it, because I was busy talking. There was a second blast, and someone closed the main gates, locking us all in! Then someone shouted that the animals were loose! I turned around, and sure enough, they were!"

"When I turned back to my audience, both kings toppled over with a spear in his back! The assassins had hidden above the gate. They raced for the staircase, but the palace guard suddenly appeared and caught two of them. The two other assassins climbed to the top of the wall. Seeing no way to escape, they leaped out over the courtyard and their bodies struck the pavement with an awful smack."

"That was when we all saw the stampede! Yes, Ham: I would say the day began poorly. But turning those flamers around changed everything! You saved our lives, and created an unforgettable, spectacular show! And now, the crowd demands to meet their new god!"

That was Ham's side of the story. I expect he must have been walking into the courtyard with the curator at about the same time that Shem and I pushed our way in and noticed the dead giants. That sight was jarring, but we soon began searching again for Rekem. When the soldiers finally unlocked the main gates, we found him along the edge of the crowd. He made a dash for it, but slowed down as he got to the gate, no doubt intending to casually slip through.

"Stop him!" I cried, pointing. "A conspirator! Don't let him escape!"

Rekem heard me, and glanced back with a guilty expression. The palace guards took off after him, but too late. Rekem pulled the gate open, smiled at us, and disappeared. Our hearts sank.

A moment later, we heard a piercing shriek, and Rekem staggered back through the gate, an arrow protruding from his belly. As we stared in shock, a second arrow struck him full in the chest, knocking him backward to the pavement. A minute later, a horse nosed through the gate with its rider holding a quivering bow. Rekem painfully lifted his head to see.

"Sandal!" he said, before lying back still.

The horseman stopped to look at the man he had just killed. His expression was hard to read, but he looked more irritated than anything else. Soldiers now pulled the gate open completely, and four white stallions entered the courtyard, drawing a well-known ivory chariot. Prince Malek glanced at the still body of Rekem, but continued on to the royal chariots, with their horrible burdens. His entourage, riding black stallions, followed him.

"Let's move someplace less conspicuous," Shem whispered. "Our job here is done." Unfortunately, we had been seen.

"Hey, everyone!" A woman yelled loudly, grabbing us. "These are the two heroes who chased down the conspirator!"

The entire audience, including Sandal and Prince Malek, turned to look at us. Many shouted, "Well done!" or something similar. Sandal caught my eye: he was not pleased. Shem gently detached the woman, and we retreated.

The prince continued his procession to the royal chariots. General Zabadanah was kneeling beside a body, but now stood up to salute.

"The king is dead!" a nearby voice cried. "Hail King Malek!" The cry was rapidly picked up and repeated, almost as though it had been rehearsed. The prince acknowledged their cries with a wan smile and a regal wave.

"Your majesty," General Zabadanah said gravely, "this acclamation may be somewhat premature."

"What do you mean?" The prince asked. "They look pretty dead to me. See?" He nudged the body with his foot.

"What he means," a deep voice interrupted, "is that it was not the king who died."

"Father!" Dumfounded, the prince spun around. Two giants had stepped down from another chariot, and now removed their helmets to reveal their faces.

"Kneel before your king!" the general cried to the crowd. Those nearby immediately fell to their knees, and everyone followed their example. The prince bowed, too. The king allowed his subjects to remain in submission, but spoke quietly to the prince.

"Malek, my son, you gave up quickly! Are you so eager to be king?"

"No, my lord! Live forever!" the prince answered. "I am so relieved! My first thought was only of you! Only later did I remember my duty to the kingdom!"

"Of course, my son." The king nodded, and then spoke loudly. "General Zabadanah, you have done us a great service today. Your discovery of the plot and your quick thinking saved many lives. You will not find us ungrateful. The heroes that volunteered to take our places were great men, men of renown, and the gods will reward them." He paused for a moment. "We will find those responsible for this attack. And when we do, all will see the fury of Mother Earth!"

He turned to General Zabadanah. "General, take charge. I shall expect answers soon, and the capture or death of all involved. My son, you may follow me to the palace. We have much to discuss, have we not?"

When the prince climbed into his chariot, his gaze fell on three figures trudging into the courtyard. Reeking with an overpowering smell, and completely covered in animal droppings, the three were so revolting that those nearby shrank away. The leading figure looked up at the prince. His eyes were white, and his filthy face quivered with frustration, rage, and embarrassment. The prince burst out laughing.

"Rogar!" he exclaimed. "Rolling in manure again? That is becoming a bad habit for you! Still," he added, urging his horses into motion, "I think you were just the sight I needed today."

The next morning, we reported to General Zabadanah.

"Boys, I am very proud of you," he said. "You discovered the plot and led the fight against the conspirators. Ham was even able to stop the stampede! By your courage, presence of mind, and skill, you saved the lives of both kings and perhaps thousand of onlookers! You boys deserve to be honored. I regret that two giant heroes lost their lives, but I could think of no other plan, and they volunteered."

The general shook his head soberly. "The king is no fool: he saw the prince unexpectedly appear immediately after the attack, and heard the rehearsed cries of acclamation. He must suspect, but he cannot condemn his only son. No, someone else must take the blame and satisfy the vengeance of Mother Earth."

"It is unfortunate that Sandal learned it was you who chased down Rekem. He may suspect you know something of the plot and tell the prince. The prince then may have the choice of eliminating Sandal, or else silencing three slave hostages who might know too much. Or course, because I learned of the plot, I am at risk, too. That is why I sent my wife and daughters away last night."

The general began to pace the room. "Today I must tell the king what we have learned. The religious fanatics did not require torture, but blurted out everything. Silly fools! They totally trusted the Cainites, and gladly took their money to attack the zoo. The two assassins are being questioned, but they know little. It will take us time to unravel the plot. The king may consider this an opportunity to blame his enemies; but until someone is finally blamed for the conspiracy and punished, we are all in grave danger."

"General," I said, "do you think we should we try to escape?"

"I do not know," the general sighed. "With your collars and slave brands, escape would be difficult. The king may not decide his course right away. If your God is real, I suggest you pray for your protection—and for mine."

A few days later, the entire city came out for the funeral of the two fallen giants. King Nezzar gave a speech honoring their sacrifice, and vowed to bring awful vengeance to the guilty parties. He pledged that Mother Earth would stand together with Nephil to conquer and destroy all their mutual enemies. After that, he promised, they would have a thousand years of peace and prosperity.

That evening we were special guests at a magnificent ceremony at the palace. General Zabadanah was honored for discovering the plot, and for saving the lives of both kings. King Nezzar gave him a chest of gold and precious gems, as well as a jeweled steel sword inlaid with gold oak trees. The king of Nephil presented him with another chest of jewels, and a beautifully tooled steel breastplate and helmet. The men of the palace guard were given heavy purses of gold, while Zimzimah and his brave zookeepers were similarly rewarded with rich gifts for capturing the conspirators. Shem and I were especially recognized for chasing down the leader of the conspirators. King Nezzar presented us with jeweled daggers, and the queen mother gave us each a gold chain with a big emerald.

"Well done, my sons!" she said as she placed them around our necks. "Your heroism is a credit to all of us! I am pleased that you have fully embraced our culture. At the Dam Celebration, your slave collars will be removed. Once your father bows in worship to our goddess, you will be made free citizens of Mother Earth. Congratulations!" She kissed us on each cheek, and we stammered our thanks.

The highest honor was bestowed last. The king explained to the audience what it meant to be a "Hero of Mother Earth." After pausing a long moment, he announced our brother. Ham slowly walked up to the dais, his face red with embarrassment. Beautiful girls presented him with a gold behemoth filled with diamonds, rubies, and emeralds. The queen mother kissed him, and placed around his neck a large green Mother Earth diamond—one of the most rare and precious gems in the world. Finally, the king placed his royal scepter into Ham's hand and raised it, lifting Ham, too!

"This young man," the king boomed, "saved countless lives and captured the admiration of our city. Few have deserved the title of 'Hero of Mother Earth' more than he. For the next seven days, he will be your god. Any request he makes must be granted, on my authority. Of course," the king chuckled, "at the end I want my scepter back!"

Laughter and applause followed. It was a deliriously happy moment for all of us. For the rest of the evening and for days afterward the sons of Noah were among the most honored celebrities in the city. Despite how we felt about Mother Earth, our hearts still swelled with pride. Somehow, though, I knew that the feeling was too good to last.

Chapter Thirty-Four: A Duel

The next morning, Ham was whisked away by a royal deputation to begin his week as the "Hero of Mother Earth." Shem and I were allowed to return to work, and Tulek and I had time to talk.

"When you did not show up," he said, "I worried that you had been arrested. By the time I got your message, Dam Minister Algar had already closed the water gates, and water was spreading over the floor of the reservoir! Tell me, Japheth: was there only a single layer of stones below ground level?"

"I am afraid so," I replied. "And the pitch-cloths were not overlapped at all."

"That means water seepage!" Tulek said, gritting his teeth. "The underlying soil will turn to mud and destabilize the entire foundation! What a fool I was! How could I let the dam minister keep me from inspecting? I must confront him now. If it is as bad as you say, the entire dam must be rebuilt!"

Tulek began pacing the floor. "But perhaps I should not be hasty. King Nezzar would be furious. And Algar could not tell him without admitting that he was the cause--unless he could blame his chief engineer! I could run away, but that would be admitting guilt, and our son Tiras would be left to face the king's wrath!"

Tulek stopped pacing, and turned to me. "Maybe this is not an emergency after all, Japheth. In fact, how can anyone predict when mud might begin to flow? The reservoir will take three weeks to fill, and the dam may well be stable until long after the festival. There is no easy solution here! But until I figure a way out, Japheth, I want you to inspect the utility tunnels at the foot of dam every day. If you find any seepage, you must tell me immediately!"

The rest of the week was quiet. Despite the water gradually rising, and another small tremor, no leaks appeared in the utility tunnels. Tulek did speak with the dam minister. Algar refused to discuss any potential problems, and asserted that many dams made the same way had lasted for decades. After threatening Tulek, he told him not to mention the foundation to anyone.

Later in the week, Shem and I joined Tulek's family for dinner, and retired to the upper terrace for fruit, pastries, and hot herbal tea. Although the story of the assassination attempt and the zoo stampede had been widely told, they wanted to hear our side of the story. That took us some time. When I mentioned the three young men who dove into the manure, our host chuckled, yet sympathized.

"I forgot to tell you something, Japheth," Shem exclaimed. "This week I learned that Rogar was one of the three men. And he richly deserved what he got. He and his friends had been practicing evil in that restricted area of the zoo!"

There was a long period of silence.

"I heard something about Rogar, too, last week," Kezziah finally said. "He is engaged to Aziza, the girl you know from Enoch's Valley!"

Shem and I exchanged glances. "I cannot think of a better match!" Shem answered. "Perhaps now she will stop toying with Japheth!"

"I certainly hope so!" Kezziah declared.

At the end of the awards ceremony, Kezziah had seen Aziza come up and closely embrace me. After teasing me about having now "grown up," Aziza had said she would still keep me in mind, "in case Rogar does not work out."

While her attractions were hard to ignore, her spell was broken. I knew now that if I ever became free, as the queen mother had promised, I would not choose to marry someone like Aziza. Instead, I would try to win a different kind of girl, someone of good character and family. At that moment, however, I saw little point in dreaming about finding a happy marriage. If the requirement for our freedom was for father to bow down and offer gifts to Mokosh, I was not getting my hopes up. Father would not consider that simply a perfunctory, meaningless gesture like most people: he would consider it an opportunity to rebuke the foolishness of idolatry.

As the full pale moon rose over the terrace, we sipped hot drinks and chatted pleasantly. I shared a contented smile with Kezziah. After nearly two years in captivity, my brothers and I had finally found satisfying work, and had found friends we could trust. I tried not to think ahead to the Dam Festival. Everything would change, and probably drastically for the worse. I glanced again at Kezziah, and sighed. If only this evening did not have to end!

"Boys," Keturah said, reading my thoughts, "We all know there are dangers ahead. If your father does not bow down before Mokosh, there will be trouble; but we may be arrested as Adamites at any moment, and Tulek may even be blamed for sabotaging the Great Dam. But we have to live in hope! Hasn't our Maker protected us marvelously so far, and shown us such favor? You two were even rewarded for bravery, and Ham was made the Hero of Mother Earth! No; even if spies find an excuse to arrest us, we must trust that our Creator will continue to watch over us."

Tulek noticed our quizzical looks. "Perhaps I should explain. Suspicious men have been loitering around our house for weeks."

"They have to be royal spies!" Kezziah declared. "Yet at the same time, father, I have seen honest officers on patrol, and they make me feel safer. This morning, three big ones passed me on the street. They were disguised in heavy green cloaks with silver stripes, but underneath I saw polished brass harnesses with big bright swords. They were real officers, all right; and they were prepared for trouble. The biggest one smiled as though he knew me."

For some reason, my mind raced back to the Valley Vigilance officers that had cleared a path for our patriarchs. The Creator always seemed to reserve good, honest officers in every police force--even in wicked cities like Mother Earth!

A day or two later, Ham's week as the "Hero of Mother Earth" came to an end, and he joined us for breakfast. He looked rested and refreshed.

"Now I know what it means to live it up!" he declared. "I got to eat delicacies from the king's table, and slept in late every morning. I rode his horses, his camels, and even his huge mastodon. Three times I went to the Temple of the Water God to play in the water slides and scented pools. But the week was not entirely fun. Every evening I had to put on a fancy robe and attend receptions as the guest of honor. Men shook my hand so much it got sore, and women kept trying to hug and kiss me. Some got pretty fresh! After a whole week of that, I was ready to get back to work. I missed my flaming behemoths, and my brothers, too. I feel as fat as a cow, and as sluggish as—well, a slug! Guys, why don't we go to the school of arms and get some exercise?"

That sounded fine, so we went. Master Zuar was happy to see us, and told us he was proud his three pupils had fought so bravely in the battle for the zoo.

"Your Uncle Krulak taught you well," he said, "but I daresay your past two years with me has not been wasted. Between my training and your diligent practice, you three actually have become formidable young warriors." Zuar glanced at the entrance, and whistled. "What is this? Prince Malek? Excuse me."

We finished putting on our padding, and were just ready to begin sparring when we heard a familiar, sneering voice. We turned around to find Sandal.

"I saw you at the zoo," he began abruptly. "With everyone shouting that you had chased down Rekem, did you think I would ignore it? It was bad enough that Mother Earth let you live; but when she honors you, it is too much! The prince says to give you a chance to join us. Okay, but you must obey me without question! And no religious nonsense! This is the real world, and sometimes we must do harsh things. Understand?"

"No thanks, Sandal," I said firmly. "You cheated, you attacked innocent Tubalites[1], and you tried to kill us. Your father betrayed our homeland! I bet you would betray Prince Malek just as easily! No, we will not join your gang. There really is an Almighty God, Sandal. Unless you come clean, and turn your life around, you will someday be very sorry."

"Enough!" Sandal growled. He waved a negative sign to the prince. "We all make choices. I choose to serve a prince with real power on earth. You have chosen to die for the sake of your imaginary religion."

A handful of soldiers left the prince's side, no doubt to arrest us. However, before Sandal even finished speaking, he was roughly shoved aside by Rogar. His face was purple with rage.

"My turn, Sandal!" he shouted, bringing up a naked sword.

We stepped back, immediately raising our shields. Master Zuar saw the disturbance and ran over. He was closely followed by his assistants, each a skilled swordsman.

"You provincial scum!" Rogar roared. "The prince made me hold my peace; but when I see the offspring of pigs and dogs being honored by the entire city, I cannot stand it! Twice now, you have humiliated me. The king was a fool to let even one of you vermin live. I will not wait! I will have my revenge today!"

Rogar's speech was surprisingly articulate, I thought; but by the time he was finished, Master Zuar and his assistants had arrived.

"Not so fast, noble Rogar!" Zuar commanded. "I must ask you to sheathe your sword. I will have no murders here. If Japheth or his brothers are under arrest, then let the prince say so. Otherwise, you must conduct yourself decently, and exercise your weapons under my rules. If you have an accusation, go to a court of justice. Here, every student is treated with respect."

"With respect?" Rogar sneered. "These are hostage slaves, Zuar!"

Prince Malek walked over, followed by his soldiers. He was obviously displeased that Rogar was yet again making himself a public spectacle.

"Rogar," the prince said calmly, "are you challenging the noble hostage Japheth to a duel?"

"A duel?" Rogar asked with surprise. He paused. "All right; let's call it that. Zuar, I challenge this drip of slime to a duel. He deserves to die like a rat, but I will treat him like a nobleman. We will see which one he dies like—a noble, or a pig! His kinfolk in Enoch's Valley were easy to slaughter, and I think he will die like one of them—weakly whining to his imaginary Creator!"

"I am not afraid of this big ox, Master Zuar," I said. "If he is willing to try his sword against mine, I am willing."

Zuar considered it. "My lord prince, shall we allow this?"

"Master Zuar," the prince began, "We have a dilemma here. Your young pupil has shown a real talent for offending the distinguished nobles of Mother Earth, despite all the mercy and favor shown him! In this case, I am not sure who is right or wrong. Perhaps we should let the gods decide. Will the prime minister's son Rogar live, or this young hostage? It appears one of them must die."

Rogar looked at the prince with astonishment. "One of them? Do you even imagine this contest is in doubt?"

"Your arrogance and presumption are not wise, Rogar," replied the prince. "But I simply cannot have you always wallowing in manure. Master Zuar, I shall permit this duel. It seems very uneven, but we will allow the young hostage to defend himself."

"Very well, your majesty," Zuar replied. "We shall prepare the center ring. Standard swords and shields." Zuar looked at me for approval, and I nodded in assent. This conflict seemed inevitable, and I was as ready as I could be.

While the assistants prepared the ring, Ham and Shem huddled with me. Ham reminded me just how bad a character

Rogar was, and how much he needed punishment; Shem prayed for my protection, and for a clear victory. Zuar came up as well to offer brief advice.

"Rogar is a strong brute," he said, "and a better swordsman than he looks. I think you can teach him a sharp lesson, but it will take skill, strength, and a cool head, as your uncle says. Stay away from his left; he likes to use his shield like a hammer. Have confidence, my young friend. Go get him!"

We were soon ready. Zuar checked our helmets, shields, and swords, and stood back. After confirming with the prince, he nodded for the duel to begin. Although we had fought with fists before, Rogar had no knowledge of my skill with the sword. As a bully, he was impatient. Most of those watching knew only that Rogar was a head taller than me, and far more powerful.

Rogar roared with hatred, raised his sword and charged. As he did, he twisted his body slightly to the right, bringing his shield closer to his body. It was a subtle action, but after Zuar's caution, I understood. I moved further to the right. Shouting to scare me, Rogar slammed his shield outward, intending to stun me before striking a powerful downward blow with his sword. However, as he brought out his shield, he opened his belly to attack. I stepped back and quickly jabbed, not his belly, but his thigh. That brought a cheer from the spectators. Ordinarily, among civilized people, this pricking of blood would have been the conclusion of the duel; but this was Mother Earth.

Rogar was enraged enough that he scarcely felt the wound. He recommenced his attack, though a little less wildly, using bold thrusts and slashes to try to maneuver me into a corner. Remembering Zuar's word about teaching him a lesson, I decided to take a little time. Circling him nimbly in the middle of the court, I deflected his blows as skillfully as possible with my shield or sword, and allowed him to expend his energy. This was a risk, since Rogar was quite formidable, and the strongest opponent I had ever faced. On the other hand, I exercised every day, and was confident I was far more fit. Keeping cool but in constant motion, I let my heavy opponent swing one mighty downward stroke after another, while I either parried or jumped away. Minutes went by, and Rogar became increasingly frustrated. While each blow was still powerful enough to cut off a limb, he had grown tired. His arrogant sneers disappeared, along with his confidence, and his guard began to open.

"End it, Rogar!" Sandal called out angrily. "Just kill the little fanatic!"

That was my cue. I began to attack, using the combinations of strokes that I had practiced for years. Suddenly, Rogar had to work hard to protect his face and belly. He was surprised, and his blows became wild. Fear began to creep over him. Finally, after skipping around one of his wild thrusts, I spoke up.

"Will you repent, Rogar? Will you turn away from all your evil?"

"Repent?" Rogar snorted. "Repent to your Creator? I would rather be dead!"

Bellowing in fury, he lowered his head and charged, bringing his shield to the right and sweeping his sword to the left. He intended to cut me in two, but I was prepared. For the last few minutes I had steadily circled to his left. When he charged, he was assuming I was still circling to the left; but I spun to the right instead. Ducking beneath his shield, I thrust deeply into his unguarded belly. With a shriek, he fell to the floor. Putting his hands to his wound, he groaned in pain.

Master Zuar strode to the center of the ring and raised my arm. His staff and many of the soldiers cheered: Rogar was apparently not well liked. Ham and Shem ran up to congratulate me, and we briefly enjoyed the moment. Out of the corner of my eye, however, I noticed Sandal approach Rogar in a rather solemn manner.

"The prince does not tolerate failure, Rogar," Sandal said brutally. Bending down over him, he drew out a dagger. "And I don't like you fooling with my sister."

As we looked on in shock, Sandal smoothly thrust the blade into Rogar's heart. Rogar jerked once, and lay still. Sandal wiped his knife on the body. When he looked up, he saw our horrified expressions. Smiling heartlessly, he returned to the prince. A few moments later we heard a loud command.

"Arrest them. They have murdered the prime minister's son!"

---

[1] *Editor's Note:* I never learned why the Tubalites were so hated by the people of Mother Earth, but that is perhaps the story of mankind: deep, long-lasting feuds often begin over trivial offenses.

Chapter Thirty-five: Father and the Queen Mother

We did not try to resist, knowing that it would be pointless. As we were marched out, Master Zuar and his staff stood grimly by the door.

"This is my signal," Zuar said.

My brothers and I were brought back to the palace, taken down a long set of stairs, and locked in a cold, damp cell. When the soldiers' footsteps faded away, the only thing to disturb the silence was the beating of our hearts. Light streamed in from two barred windows high above us; we had a jug of drinking water, a pile of straw for bedding, and a hole in the stone floor for a toilet.

The next few days were very quiet. We were left completely alone, except for the guards that brought food and water twice a day. We kept warm by walking in circles, and we passed the time in conversation. Our prospects were not good, even if we lived to see father arrive. When our time came, we hoped we would die like men.

We had many questions to ponder. Had father arrived? What had happened to Tulek and his family? Who had taken our jobs? Ham assumed the curator had dropped the new behemoth act from the show, because no one else could manage the flamers. Shem had planned various receptions and banquets, but he was sure others could take on those responsibilities. On my part, I figured that my presentation of our new power transfer system, with its huge gears, spinning power shafts, and racing belts, must have been assigned to someone else. It was humbling to realize that I was easily replaceable.

A week went by. Late one morning, we suddenly heard fumbling at the latch, and a screeching sound. The door was pulled open, and a guard gestured for us to come out. When we filed out, we were surprised to find Tuktub, our faithful servant.

"Time to scrub up," he said in his cryptic way. "You see queen now."

The guards took us upstairs, where we were given a luxurious bath and fresh blue tunics. Tuktub said little, but after a week in grimy confinement, it felt wonderful to be clean again, and properly dressed. My mood improved enough that I almost felt ready to face our next test. There is much truth in the old proverb: "a bathed body — a fresh attitude[1]."

Tuktub left us, and the soldiers marched us down a long hallway of polished marble. We passed various guard stations, went through a series of granite archways, and finally halted outside a familiar place: the queen mother's reception hall. As we waited, we heard a confrontation occurring inside.

"You stubborn fool!" a woman shouted angrily. "Have you learned nothing in three hundred years? All you had to do was bow down to our gods. Did the patriarchs never teach you to respect authority? You should at least be humble after your abject defeat!"

The victim of this verbal assault responded in a voice too low to hear, but the shrill voice of the woman projected clearly.

"You should have thought of them before! They belong to me, now! I wish you could have seen how eagerly they embraced our worldview! They are one with us, now. They love our foods, our drinks, and our pleasures — especially the Temple of Virility! What do you say to that? And Mother Earth has honored them! They could have bright futures here, except for your wretched stubbornness — and the violent nature you gave them! Despite all our kindness, they plotted to assassinate my son, and succeeded in murdering the son of our prime minister! But in spite of all this, I could still help you! Here I am a goddess. I can offer you mercy and grace, but you must repent!"

We could not hear the man's response, but the woman responded angrily.

"You intolerant religious fanatic! Are you still trying to judge? Your rules never applied to me! My eyes were opened in Nephil. I learned of my deity! I married a god, and gave birth to a giant! Can you even imagine what that is like? No? It is power—intoxicating power! You hunger for more! Power is the only thing that matters! Can't you see that I have power over you now? You may try to hold to your antique God, but he cannot save your sons now: only I can! Just admit that you were wrong, and bow down! Show our kingdom some respect! Have you no love for them? No pity? Can you look on their faces and watch them die? Oh? Do you think so? We shall see! Guards!"

"She really wants father to bow down, doesn't she?" Shem asked wryly.

It had finally dawned on me who the parties were; but why would the queen mother be so angry? Father must have known many people over the centuries, and done many things, but what was their relationship? The doors opened.

"It was never a matter of tolerating you," father was saying. "You wanted me to endorse your sin! Even now, you brag of it! Oh, that the Creator would really open your eyes! But your time grows short. You must repent now!"

Father looked thin, but as resolute and determined as ever. He saw us enter the room, and rushed to embrace us.

"How strong and healthy you boys look!" he exclaimed. "And you have grown so tall! You have flourished here, just as she said!"

"But Father!" Shem exclaimed. "How do you know the queen mother? What is all this about?"

"Didn't she tell you, boys?" father asked, looking surprised.

"Tell us what?"

"She is my long-lost sister!"

My jaw dropped in surprise. If the queen mother was our aunt, that meant her giant son—the product of a human mother and a demon father—was our cousin! I rebelled at the thought: that sort of thing only happened to bad people, ones that lived far, far away! I stared at the queen mother in horror, now seeing a family resemblance in her nose and chin. She saw my look, and smiled faintly.

"Yes, boys," she said, not unkindly. "Do you now understand why I favored you, and protected you? In spite of all that, your father still betrays me! He betrays you, as well! If he truly loved you, he would not let you die."

Father shook his head. "Gaia[2], you were like a second mother to me. It broke our hearts when you ran away! You know I cannot bow down to false gods! Kill me if you like, but do not threaten my sons: you will lose my sympathy. I must warn you that the Creator has promised me a good heritage through these boys. When you threaten them, you tempt God. That puts you in a dangerous position."

The queen mother laughed—cackled, really. "Do you think you can tell me what to do? If your God were real, and actually intended to punish me for sin, he would have done it long ago! No, Noah, you must bow down like everyone else. I cannot be soft with you! My spirit husband has warned me against that! 'Be as hard as an emerald,' he told me, 'for you are a goddess!' Perhaps you should meet him. Shall I summon him? He can be quite convincing."

"No," father said firmly. "I do not hold conversations with demons."

"In that case," she replied coldly, "we shall return to the throne room. My son will order you to bow down. When you say no, he will condemn you all, despite being our closest blood relatives! Our subjects will see, and fear, and our power will swell! You cannot stop me, Noah! Our destiny is to conquer the world and reign for a thousand years!"

"No, it is not," father insisted. "Your only hope is to repent and turn from your sin! Unless you do, Gaia, your city shall be utterly destroyed!"

The queen mother sullenly shook her head. She nodded to her guards. They marched the four of us down a long hallway to the throne room, an impressive hall with polished stone columns, lofty marble walls, and a great dome with hundreds of screened windows. We joined a great crowd, and were taken to the foot of the royal dais. The hateful glare of thousands of eyes fell upon us.

Prime minister Logar sat near the foot of the dais. When he saw me, he jumped up, pointed and screamed. "That devil murdered my son!"

Angry threats immediately rumbled through the crowd, growing louder and louder. A gong sounded, and the crowd grew quiet. The royal orator stepped to a podium.

"The royal majesty of Mother Earth will now permit Enoch's Valley to approach," he proclaimed in a rich baritone voice. "The representatives may now bow down to worship the goddess, and present the offerings of their city."

Our guards prodded father. He walked to the foot of a large green statue and joined Shahoot and cousins Achbor and Sharezer, who all stood holding golden bowls with precious stones. A similar bowl was handed to father. When the orator nodded, the representatives of Enoch's Valley came to their knees and placed the bowls at the foot of the statue.

"We worship Mokosh, the goddess of Mother Earth!" Shahoot proclaimed.

Father remained standing, looking grimly at the queen mother.

"Bow down!" The orator repeated. "Does the representative not know the meaning of the words 'bow down'?"

Father spoke slowly and distinctly. "I will not worship your false goddess, but only the one true Creator. Your king can receive his tribute directly." Raising his bowl, he poured the jewels out, and let the bowl fall to the floor. It struck with a musical clang.

The audience roared with anger, and angrily shook their fists. After a minute of that, the orator gestured for silence. The gong sounded again, and the crowd grew quiet. King Nezzar looked to his mother for a sign, but she shook her head negatively. The king growled something low to the orator.

"This is your final warning," the orator proclaimed. "The assembly knows that as brother to the queen mother, you occupy an exalted position. Nevertheless, the king proclaims that if you do not worship the goddess, you shall die. Bow down!"

Father turned his back to the king and angrily faced the audience. "I will honor those whom the Creator has put into authority," he proclaimed, "but I will not bow to worship arrogant giants or false gods. And if you people of Mother Earth do not repent of the violence, immorality, and evil that fills your heart, your demon-infested city will be destroyed. Repent or perish! This is your final warning."

When father turned his back on him, the king was outraged, and stood up. However, as father continued speaking, the king's expression gradually changed from anger to amusement. His great chest began to heave in laughter, making a deep, resonant sound that projected to the far corners of the room. The queen began to laugh, too, and finally the entire audience joined in loud, scornful peals of laughter. When father finished speaking, the king wiped away his tears and addressed the crowd, still chuckling.

"We gladly accept the worship and gifts of Enoch's Valley, and welcome their people to our empire. As for my disrespectful Uncle Noah, he has chosen his fate! Listen carefully, all of you! Anyone—anyone—who defies us will be put to death, no matter how close or dear to us personally!"

The king nodded, and two guards hauled father to the far end of the throne room, where several cages were filled with condemned prisoners. The king sat down and nodded to the orator.

"We shall now hear from the minister of justice concerning the attempted assassination of his glorious majesty," the orator declared, standing aside as a richly robed man came to the podium.

"Your majesty," the new speaker said, "I regret to inform you that we have uncovered two persons very close to the throne who planned treason against Mother Earth and the kingdom of Nephil. Not content with using their unique positions of trust to enrich themselves, these traitors insisted on adding assassination to their long list of crimes. Although they attempted to cover their tracks by releasing a dangerous stampede, we have confirmed their guilt through the testimony of many witnesses. Shall I reveal their names, your majesty?"

The crowd instantly came to their feet to shout out bitter curses and threats against the traitors. The minister of justice stood back from the podium and smiled as the furious crowd finally took up a chant: "Name them! Name them!"

After keeping them in suspense for a full minute, the minister of justice suddenly pointed to two figures at the foot of the dais.

"The traitors," he cried, "are none other than Prime Minister Logar and his brother, Dam Minister Algar!"

The noble brothers stood in astonishment, and barely resisted as the guards seized them and dragged them across to the cages. The crowd roared its approval. King Nezzar looked at his son, whose face began to redden.

"After discovering the chief plotters, your majesty," the minister of justice continued, "it was not difficult to sniff out the rest. In fact, our treasonous prime minister's son Rogar made it easy! He was discovered at the zoo completely covered in animal droppings! Unfortunately, before he could be questioned, he was violently silenced by three others in the plot: the sons of the royal traitor Noah!"

The minister of justice pointed at us with his long arm. "Jackals breed jackals, your majesty, and these sons are just as treasonous as their father. The eldest of them even had the audacity to murder the unsuspecting young Rogar in the presence of the prince! But there is even more reason to condemn them, your majesty! These three brothers were found to be leading members of the notorious Adamite cult! That evil ring, long a curse to Mother Earth, has finally been broken, as all may see: behold their guilty faces in the second prisoner cage! May I suggest, your majesty, that these three evil sons join their father in death? Mother Earth demands justice!"

The king nodded. As the guards pulled us to the cages, the hatred of the crowd poured out like a living force. It was an odd experience. The authorities unquestionably knew we were innocent, but they pretended we were guilty. I felt like an unwilling actor in a theatrical play. Tulek had said that everyone needed a cover story in Mother Earth. Today we were providing it! But whom were they really trying to fool? Why did they even feel the need to justify themselves?

As we approached the cages, I heard a squawk above us, followed by a hysterical shriek. Instinctively turning, I saw the queen mother furiously wiping her face. A large green parrot swooped over the crowd and glided up to perch on a pillar, where it began preening its feathers. It was not difficult to guess what had happened. Someone giggled, and others began to laugh.

"Ungodly words!" the parrot suddenly squawked. "Ungodly deeds! God will judge!"

Our mouths dropped open. Enoch's parrot! Where had it come from?

"Kill that bird!" the queen mother screamed, quivering in anger. "Fifty gold pieces to whoever kills it! No, a hundred!" She pointed at father, who stood in a cage with other prisoners. "Noah! You brought him here to do that!"

By this time, several soldiers were fitting arrows to their bows. The first arrow struck the pillar only a finger's breadth from the parrot. The bird dropped off the pillar, releasing droppings on a nobleman.

"Ungodly words!" the bird repeated. "Ungodly deeds! God will judge!"

Several more arrows were shot, but each ricocheted off the walls into the audience, resulting in terrified shrieks. The parrot flapped high in the dome, and found a perch on the screen of a window.

"Ungodly words!" it repeated. "Ungodly deeds!" Squeezing through the screen, it flew away.

The audience roared. Our guards hurriedly threw us into father's cage before rushing back to help restore order. I found a bench in a corner in the back of the cage, and wearily sat down: it had been a stressful day. Ironically, at that moment the prisoner cage was the only peaceful spot in the hall.

"Japheth!" The name was whispered.

Startled, I looked up. Kezziah was seated right next to me in the neighboring cage! Only the bars of the cage separated us.

"Kezziah!"

I reached through the bars to clasp her hands. There was a lot of noise around us, but when I gazed into her eyes, that all seemed far away. Suddenly, this became a very quiet, private moment, just between the two of us.

"Well, Japheth," she said, "I guess this is goodbye. You didn't really murder Rogar, did you?" It took me a moment to answer: I had been lost in her eyes.

"Rogar forced a duel on me," I said finally. "I wounded him, but did not kill him. Sandal did that later. All the charges against us were completely made up, Kezziah: none of them were true."

"Just like ours," she answered. "But God is good, and he has a good purpose in this, even if it is simply to usher us into heaven. I am glad to have known you, Japheth. Somehow, I always felt our Maker drawing us together."

"Oh, Kezziah," I said earnestly, "I have felt exactly the same thing! May I be very honest with you, now that our stay on earth is coming to an end? I am a bumbling fool, really. Up to now I have only been interested in inventing things, and maybe in sports. But since I met you, my eyes have been opened to lots of things that are far more important. I see your devotion to your family and to other believers, and your kindness to captives; and how you help the sick and make clothing for the poor. Your example has helped me see that true love really is something you do, not just something you feel."

Mine had already been a long speech, but she was listening so attentively, with such a sweet expression, so I kept talking. "Kezziah, this wicked city teaches that physical enticements and seductive manners are the way to love; but that is so wrong and deceitful! Those things only lead to entrapment and sin. A good match between two people has to include a common worldview, a compatible temperament, and a common purpose, even more than the spark everyone looks for. I hope you will forgive me for saying this, but if our lives were not ending now, and if I were free, I would look for someone with your gracious spirit, your sense of humor, and your way of looking at things. Kezziah, you are the kind of person I could talk with all day long. You are the kind I would love to work on projects with, and raise lots of children with! In fact, I cannot think of anyone else I would rather spend my whole life with, than…someone like you." I stopped, feeling ashamed.

Kezziah laughed. "Wait a minute! Are you trying to tell me something?"

I hesitated. "I guess I am, even though this is totally hopeless." I had gone way too far, but did it really matter anymore? "I love you, Kezziah, and I think I have from the first time I met you."

"And I love you, too, Japheth," she answered confidently, smiling. "I love your selflessness, your initiative, your courage and strength—and your enthusiasm, your faithfulness—and even how you love to figure things out. I love your steadiness, and how you make me laugh! Even my parents love you. But what exactly are you getting at?"

I thought about that for a while. "Kezziah, if we ever get out of this, would you meet me on the boat?"

She laughed again. "Okay, Japheth, I will, if we ever get out of this. That sounds like a proposal to me!"

Our happiness and laughter finally attracted Shem's attention. Had we gone completely crazy? But there was no time to explain: the guards were already removing the prisoners for transport. Before we were torn away, I took Kezziah's hand once again.

"Would you really?" I asked. I knew it was futile, but I was serious. When you have come to the last days of your life, you might as well be perfectly honest.

"Yes," she agreed, smiling. "I will meet you on the boat!"

I knew she meant it, and got a big grin on my face. I have no idea what the soldiers must have thought to see such radiant happiness in the faces of condemned prisoners.

---

[1] *Editor's Note:* This old proverb reminded me a little of "clothes make the man," a common modern saying.

[2] *Editor's Note:* Although it may just be coincidence, the phonetic spelling of this name is very similar to that later used to denote the primal Greek mother goddess.

Chapter Thirty-Six: Uncle Samlah

The condemned prisoners were loaded onto horse-drawn wagons. Taking a familiar route, the wagons drove up the main boulevard of Mother Earth to the amphitheater at the foot of the Great Dam. The Adamites were unloaded and prodded into the livestock cages, while those of us considered more notorious prisoners were forced up the narrow stairs of Lookout Rock. As we climbed, we passed several occupied cells, including one with Professor Adrammelech. He scowled at us, and we kept climbing.

As we passed a barred window near the top, a hand suddenly reached out and grabbed my wrist. I tried to shake loose, but the grip was powerful. I found my arm being pulled between the bars. Looking up, I was shocked to see the insanely murderous eyes of Prime Minister Logar! Fortunately, our jailer saw my plight and sharply clubbed Logar's hand. He let go with a shriek. As we resumed our climb, however, he followed us up with bitter curses.

When we came to the topmost cell, the jailer unlocked it and pushed us in. The cell was dry, and much larger than our cell in the palace. Most of it lay in cool shadows, away from the hot afternoon sun. While it had a dusty smell, there were warm, gentle breezes and the pleasant sounds of seagulls. It was really not bad. In fact, with nice furniture, a few decorations, and the freedom to come and go, it might have been a lovely place to spend a holiday.

The view through our casement was spectacular. Below us on the right side, we could see the entire amphitheater; on the left we saw the Great Dam, the city of Mother Earth, and the entire Mokosh River valley. Because our cell was higher than the top of dam, we could see that the water was nearly to the top. The great water wheels and power stations were all finished, and my hydraulic conveyors were at that moment carrying supplies up to the top. Ours would be a wonderful vantage point to enjoy the Great Dam Festival, if we could enjoy it. We were lost in our thoughts for a good while. Suddenly, a voice from the shadows startled us.

"Noah?" The voice was thin and creaky. "Noah, could it be you?" A shriveled old figure shuffled into the light.

"Is it possible?" father said, turning slowly. "Samlah?"

The two men gazed at each other in astonishment. Finally, they embraced and wept in deep emotion. My brothers and I were baffled. Who was this old man? He looked a little like father in stature and face; but while father was strong and vigorous, this prisoner looked ancient. He was bald, with pale, wrinkled skin, and a long, untended beard. He wore a tapestried vest that was crusted with jewels, and a tunic that had once been elegant; but now all was dusty, threadbare, and torn, and hung loosely on his emaciated frame. His hands had short dirty fingernails, and his knees were as calloused as an elephant's.

"If only!" he sobbed in deep anguish.

After several minutes, Shem finally asked. "Father, who is this?"

Father stirred himself. "Boys, this is my youngest brother Samlah. For three hundred years we have thought him dead!"

Of course! If the queen mother was our father's long lost sister, then her imprisoned brother had to be our uncle! The brothers talked for a little while, but Samlah grew tired, and lapsed into silence. That gave us an opportunity to talk with father, and learn about our family, and what had happened following the capture of Enoch's Valley. All the Tubalite refugees, along with mother and our great aunts, had made it safely to Tubal. Happily, many other relatives had escaped by boat from Jared's Mill as Valley Vigilance held off the enemy.

The city had been thoroughly sacked, with anything of value being carted away. When the army departed, Shahoot was left as governor. His reign had been merciless, with property being confiscated and young men pressed into slave labor. His cruel taxes had brought hunger to the valley, and most of the recent immigrants had fled for other lands. Only one good thing had come out of their defeat: many whose faith in the Creator had been lukewarm now took it seriously. Believers now showed care for others in the faith, and worship services were well attended. It had taken six months for things to stabilize, but when things appeared safe, mother had returned from Tubal, joining father and the patriarch on the plantation.

We told father some of our own adventures, and tried to set him straight about the queen mother's lies. Our story took the rest of the day. Father was angered by the nonsense pushed on us by Mother Earth Academy, but proud of our other exploits, including our rescue of the Adamites. He was amused when Shem and Ham teased me about a certain pretty girl being among those rescued. He was relieved to learn we had not become as morally corrupt as his sister had indicated. When telling him about the zoo stampede, Ham downplayed his heroism, so Shem and I had to explain that his actions had saved at least a thousand lives.

"I am so proud of you boys!" father exclaimed. "Even in this wicked, doomed city, you are fulfilling our family mission, which is…"

"To save people!" we exclaimed.

After many years of solitude, Uncle Samlah was bewildered to have company, and found our loud speech and laughter almost frightening. The sun had gone down by the time my brothers and I finished telling our story. We were hoarse from talking, anyway, and stood for a long time gazing out of the casement, quietly enjoying the panorama revealed by the full moon. Presently, Uncle Shlemuah said he was ready to talk. We quickly assembled beds out of straw, and lay down to listen. Although he complained that his tongue was stiff from disuse, it seemed to loosen up as he talked.

"Noah," he began, "my entire life has been one of stubborn foolishness! It is painful to even tell, because my actions harmed so many people. Even so, I feel I must make my confession." He paused to wipe a tear.

"Noah, you and I were raised in a godly family, and were carefully taught important truths; but I never understood them. When Gaia and I ran off to Nephil, I was dazzled with the excitement, luxury, and entertainment, and never dreamed it could be a doorway to destruction. We deliberately cut ourselves off from our family, you know. We imagined that we were free, and I used my freedom to do every selfish thing you can imagine. I took potions, ate unhealthy foods, and gambled, womanized, and indulged in every kind of vice. Gaia always had friends and plenty of money, and she gave me enough to squander. I had no idea where her ambitions were leading, but I was having fun."

"I came to view the world just like the Nephilites did. I made money, lost money, made friends, and lost them. My standards were flexible, and I fit right in. I made myself useful as Gaia rose through Nephil's circles of power and influence. Decades went by, and finally a century. Gaia had a baby that grew into a giant, and he became a famous warrior under her careful nurturing and guidance."

"She got deeper and deeper into weird religious things, but by the time I realized something was wrong, it was too late to pull her out, and I had no standing to even try. Her giant son was king of Mother Earth, and she reigned as his queen mother. By then she styled herself the living embodiment of the goddess Mokosh. Somehow, I began to get in her way."

"One of my selfish actions finally displeased her enough that she threw me in prison. Unfortunately, I learned nothing from it, but simply nursed my grudges and anger. Then, about thirty years ago, Gaia had an odd moment of sentimental weakness, and let me go free. I immediately returned to my old habits. In less than a year I had wasted a fortune, earned a score of bitter enemies, and abandoned a beautiful young Cainite woman expecting my child. When I was thrown into prison again, I knew I deserved it; but it took me years to understand the awful depth of my true disgrace. The truth was that I had forgotten my Maker, and had chosen to believe foolish lies. After doing those two things, it was only natural that I would drift into selfishness and wickedness."

Uncle Samlah buried his face in his hands. "Oh, Noah! I have often rehearsed what I would tell you if I could: how you were right, and I was wrong. Perhaps I should be happy that my miserable life on earth will end soon, but I am scared. The patriarchs said that judgment comes after death. What will I say to my Maker? He will welcome you, Noah, for you have lived your life well; but I will be cast down to the pit, and spend all of eternity in fiery torment!"

Father put his arm around him. "Brother, have you forgotten what the patriarchs told us of our Maker's mercy and grace? We have all sinned; but God has no pleasure in condemning anyone. If you are sorry for what you have done, tell him so! He wants to forgive and cleanse us, not destroy us!"

They probably talked much longer; but the next thing I knew, I was blinking in the bright morning sun. Outside our cell, the air was filled with hammering and sawing. I looked outside and saw workmen building a steep wooden ramp that stretched from the observation deck down past our cell to a neighboring ridge, and then out over the amphitheater onto the main stage. I was puzzled about the purpose of this ramp, but I had a bad feeling about it.

When I looked down to the stage, my eye was drawn to a utility hatch beside the dam, one I had often inspected. Even at our height, I could see that mud had formed a pool over the hatch. This was no small leak: the entire utility tunnel had overflowed! A chill raced through me, for this was exactly what Tulek had feared. The pool of mud was not far from the livestock cage holding the Adamites. After thinking for a few moments, I spoke to my uncle.

"Uncle Samlah," I asked, "Have you ever thought about escape?"

He looked at me sharply. "Of course," he sighed. "I tried bribing the guards, picking the lock, and loosening the bars. Nothing worked: this cell is closely watched. Finally, I realized that my only hope was to tunnel out. Lookout Rock splits off from a spur on the mountain, and I figured that the back wall of this cell was only about a dozen cubits from the mountain itself. If I could dig a tunnel through that wall, I thought that I could climb down onto the slope on some moonless night. After that, I would simply hike up through the Doubtful Wilderness, and be free. Even if I were devoured by wild beasts, it would be better than languishing here."

"Did you ever start to dig?" I asked.

"Start? I almost finished!" he cried in a high, shaky voice. He laughed almost like a hyena, his eyes glittering in crazy excitement. "God gave me hope, but he took it away! It was my foretaste of hell!"

"What do you mean?" I asked cautiously. He was not acting very stable.

"I suppose there is no longer any need for secrecy," he said, this time speaking almost sensibly. "In another week we shall each, in turn, tumble down that long ramp outside. Then, as the crowd cheers, we shall be thrown to savage beasts! You might as well learn the horror of being almost saved!"

Seizing my wrist, Uncle Samlah practically dragged me to the straw piled along the back wall. Sweeping it away, he caught up the edge of a thick blanket, and pulled it aside to reveal a dark opening.

"There it is," he announced triumphantly, "the work of decades! I began one day after a guard exchanged a small knife for one of my jewels. After that, each evening when I stretched out my hands to pray, I threw out a handful of dust. That dust was the fruit of my labor. The rock was hard, and the work was painful—look at these hands! When the knife was worn away, I used any bit of metal I could obtain, or any piece of granite, to hammer and scrape at the rock. It was slow, but I persisted, and rejoiced in even small progress. Patience pays for itself, my son! Before long, my tunnel was a finger deep, and by a year I could put my head in it. A decade later I judged myself halfway, and kept digging. Finally, about two years ago, I estimated I was only a week away from freedom. That was when your Creator stopped me! I hit a layer of crystal so hard I could not even scratch it! I widened the tunnel, but could not get around it. The layer is thin enough to see through, but I have no tool to cut it. I will perish—we will all perish—only one finger width from freedom!"

After hearing this story, each of us crawled into the tunnel to look. The crystal layer was like murky glass. Straight ahead was a wall of rock, while the slope of the mountain was to the left, and the sky to the right. As I backed out, it occurred to me that this was a basic engineering problem, and there had to be a solution! But before I could think of anything, father said he wanted to talk to us.

"I have something to tell you boys," he said. "Our Creator has commanded me to stay here until I am given other instructions. This rock, he said, was to be our place of safety. Boys, I fear that if you do somehow manage to escape, you will be placing yourself right in the middle of God's judgment. I think we must trust our Maker, and wait patiently right here."

"But, Father," I said, a little exasperated, "my own safety is not my main concern. What about those poor Adamites in that cage down there? The dam foundation is already seeping. If our Creator intends to destroy this wicked city in that way, the Adamites will be the first to die. We need to escape to save her—I mean, them!"

Father listened intently to my words. Frowning, he walked to the casement. He looked out for a long time, lost in thought. Finally, he turned back.

"You are right, my son. I was thinking only of your safety, and my own. It is foolish to get between sinners and God's hand, but if you are to attempt a good work, you must take some risks. What is our mission, boys? I must have forgotten."

"To save people!" we declared.

"Right!" father said. "Let us therefore pray that our Creator will open a way of escape. Even if I am personally forbidden to leave, perhaps you can, for the honorable purpose of rescuing fellow believers."

"The patriarch Demas does say," Ham added, "that God helps those who help themselves[1]!"

"Hmm," father answered. "I had not heard that! However, the patriarch Jared always liked to say, 'Hearts to God, and Hands to Work[2],' and the patriarch Methuselah often advises us to "Fear God, and Do what is Right!"

Having made the decision to attempt an escape, we prayed for the means. No ideas, however, presented themselves. Prayers, I have since learned, are like planting a garden: they generally require time to produce fruit. As the day went by, we kept praying and thinking. Our breakfast had consisted of a jug of water and a bucket of vegetable stew, and our dinner was exactly the same. In between, we paced back and forth, gazed at the view, stretched our muscles, talked, and finally lapsed into reflection. If only we had a hammer to shatter the crystal! But we had no hammer, and I had no other ideas. Late in the afternoon, father examined the crystal layer again, and crawled out of the tunnel with a pensive expression.

"Our Creator," he mused, "will always provide the means to do his will. But to see those means we must look at things his way. What is in our hands? Perhaps there is something we have overlooked."

We had little to overlook. We had our sandals, our blue palace tunics, and the silver slave rings around our necks: that was about it. It was kind of discouraging.

"Wait a minute," father said, looking at me quizzically. "What is that around your neck?"

"Oh; I forgot," I said, pulling out my gold chain with its valuable gem. "It is my emerald! The soldiers took my dagger, but they overlooked this."

My stone pleased father, for we had neglected to mention the honors we had received. Father was glad to hear that our bravery had been recognized, and that Ham had even been made the "Hero of Mother Earth."

When he heard the words "Hero of Mother Earth," Uncle Samlah became strangely excited. A few moments later, Ham pulled out his big green diamond to show father. Samlah shrieked wildly, and immediately seized the jewel.

"Praise the Maker!" he shouted, falling to his knees. "God does answer prayer, after all!"

It grieved me to see that. It was apparent that the shock had been too much for our poor uncle. In a single day, he had gone from perfect solitude to constant society, and from complete ignorance of his family to this unseemly, almost insane pride in his previously unknown nephew's achievement. But before I could think further, Uncle Samlah squirmed into the tunnel with Ham's necklace. A few moments later, we heard a muffled shout.

"Praise the Maker, I knew it!"

When he backed out, he was fairly glowing. "It works! It cuts the crystal! Nothing is harder than a Mother Earth diamond! Now, if we just have enough time! We shall take turns, but I go first!"

He immediately returned to the tunnel, and we crowded our heads in to watch. Using a sharp edge of the gem, he scratched a big circle into the crystal layer, and tediously retraced it, each time making the groove deeper. After an hour, he handed it to me, and others took turns after me. When the sun went down, the moon provided enough light through the crystal to see. We kept working from that moment on, stopping only when guards came by. While one scratched away, the rest of us began braiding a long rope from our blankets.

The days passed quickly. While one feverishly cut the crystal layer, the others braided the rope, or watched the preparations being made in the amphitheater below. In addition to the ramp leading down to the stage, workmen constructed big animal cages, and tiers of benches for additional seating. It was evident that a vast crowd was expected. Several curious machines were brought to the main platform, and installed to the power shaft. To our amusement, the face of the dam was painted to represent the goddess Mokosh. Two of the great watermills represented her ears, while polished brass mirrors were her eyes, and the high-pressure outflow pipe was her mouth.

One night we had a small tremor. The next morning I saw men cleaning the mud from around the utility tunnel, but I saw nothing to suggest that anyone understood the danger the mud represented. On the following day, we saw the same men shoveling the mud again. I was starting to think that any official interest in the mud was strictly cosmetic. I pointed that out to father.

"Sin is the same way," he said, shaking his head. "Its destructive effects are obvious, but sinners cannot quite figure out that one leads to the other."

At night, we often heard voices floating up from the cells below. Logar and Algar argued a lot, and blamed each other for their predicament, while other prisoners cursed loudly, and even got into fights. However, the livestock cage occupied by the Adamites was a remarkable contrast. Familiar hymns of praise rose up in the morning and evening, and I could sometimes hear Kezziah's clear voice singing the melody. We often joined in, and it encouraged us.

The Dam Festival rapidly approached. Each morning, sightseers thronged by to watch the construction, and some took the opportunity to shout threats to the prisoners. "Death to the traitors" was the most common one, but "death to the nobles" was a close second. "Death to the assassins" and "death to the Adamites" were also very popular. Some of the most notorious prisoners had many enemies. Prime Minister Logar and his brother, for example, often got personal threats. One day I heard one that surprised me: "Death to the patriarch Demas, the drunken hypocrite who visits the Temple of Virility!" Hypocrisy, it seemed, was intolerable to the citizens of Mother Earth, even when their own sins were far worse.

The pool of mud returned larger every day, prompting curses from the morning shoveling crew. And I noticed something else. From our perspective, the pavement at the foot of the dam no longer looked perfectly flat. Instead, it appeared swollen, or domed, as though something was pushing it up. This was not a good sign.

"We have to rescue them!" I told father. "The festival begins the day after tomorrow, and we have still not cut through the crystal layer! It is taking too much time!"

"We are all are anxious, my son," father answered calmly. "But we must show confidence in our Creator, and do our duty patiently, gently, and persistently, whether we live or die. We must let it take time."

[1]*Editor's Note:* This expression seems to be exactly like one so common today.

[2] ***Editor's Note:*** Again, this ancient saying appears nearly identical to a modern one, in this case one used by the American Shakers, a 19th Century sect. I am reminded of Dr. Charles Stanley's advice: "Obey God, and leave all the consequences to Him."

Chapter Thirty-Seven: The Great Dam Festival

On the final day before the festival, the amphitheater was as busy as an anthill, with workmen swarming around to finish constructing tiers of seating, and putting up colorful banners and decorations. Troupes of musicians, singers, dancers, and acrobats took to the stage to rehearse their performances, while the watermills were put into motion to test the power shafts and gears.

The long ramp outside our cell was tested as well. We heard a loud command from the lookout deck, and seconds later a full-sized human dummy came sliding down the ramp past our cell. As it gathered speed over the rows of seating, the dummy began to tumble; when it finally hit the stage, the jolt nearly ripped off the cloth limbs. A workman picked up the dummy and threw it onto the nearby hydraulic conveyor. It smoothly glided up across the face of the dam, and finally approached the top. Something was wrong, I realized: the final stage of the conveyor was missing! Horrified, I watched the dummy ascend without pause to the missing section, where it was propelled into the air! With arms and legs spinning, the dummy fell for a long time before striking the granite landing. The stuffing burst out, and the workmen raised their arms in triumph.

"Such evil!" I shouted, feeling shocked and angry. "To take something I designed for good and turn it into an instrument of death? That is it! As far I am concerned, God can completely destroy this wicked people!" Father, standing next to me, only shook his head: his own patience had evaporated long before.

Later in the day, we heard the noise of big animals. Ham gave us a running commentary as the cave bears, sabertooth tigers, giant wolves, and big lions were herded into the large cages next to the stage. They brought behemoths, too, including stalkers, which were smaller versions of the death behemoth; rippers, which hunted in packs; and Ham's three flaming behemoths.

"I think we all know why these animals were brought," Ham said. "Except for the flamers, they are all predators. But how can Zimzimah allow it? Once these animals are introduced to human flesh, they will lose their fear of man, and be twice as hard to control!"

I suppose seeing the beasts increased our motivation to escape; but we were already doing everything possible. We had made all the rope we could, and cutting through the crystal was a one-man job. Our plans were simple. Once we were through the crystal, we would climb down, create a diversion, open the cage, and somehow rescue the Adamites. If we failed to get through the crystal layer in time, our death appeared certain, one way or the other. In fact, things looked pretty glum: it was hard not to fret. As the sun went down, our guard brought us our evening meal. He, on the other hand, seemed to be in a good mood.

"Enjoy your food," he chuckled. "It will be your last. Tomorrow you will become a meal yourself. That is the way of Mokosh, and the wheel of life. Dust returns to dust, and we receive in our next incarnation what we have earned in this one. As traitors, the sages say, you will return as jackals. I am not personally sure of that--you may come back as carrion beetles--but I do know one thing: you should not have angered the queen mother. She has a temper, that one!"

"Thank you for the food," father said. "But you are wrong, you know."

"Wrong?" The guard was curious. "Wrong about what?"

"There is no second incarnation," father said earnestly. "We have only one life on earth. After that, our Maker judges us, and we go to either heaven or hell. There are no other options, and his decision is final. Friend, I urge you: be reconciled to God! He offers you a perfect paradise in heaven, but you must trust him on earth first. This wicked city is about be punished. If you value your soul, listen to me. Be honest with God about what you have done. Ask him to forgive you. He will! Then join us in this cell, and be saved from destruction. Will you do that?"

"Sorry, old man," the guard sighed. He was less cruel than he seemed. "There are many religions, but they are all made up. You don't seem that bad, just a little crazy. I hope you don't really come back as a jackal, or as a bug." He turned away and began carefully climbing back down the narrow staircase.

As soon as he was gone, I grabbed Ham's diamond and dove into the tunnel: it was my turn. But I had only just begun when Ham called me back.

"Quick, Japheth!" he whispered. "Someone else is coming!"

I backed out hurriedly and covered the hole just as our guard clanged our bars with his club. We easily recognized the well-dressed couple behind him.

"My son!" The voice in my ear sounded brokenhearted. "My son!"

"What?" I glanced back. Uncle Samlah was speaking to Sandal!

"You were never a father to me!" Sandal scowled. "I curse you every day!"

"I never meant to hurt you!" Uncle Samlah groaned.

"Shut up, old man," Sandal snapped. "Aziza and I just wanted to see all our enemies in one cell! Tomorrow our vengeance will be complete!"

Sandal," I gasped, "you are our cousin?"

"You figured that out?" Sandal sneered. "Yes. I may be a half-breed Cainite, but I am a full cousin to the king, too. See why I hate you? I am just as good as you, but because of this old man's treachery, people have always rejected me. Can you imagine having your real father up here your whole life, ridiculed by every passing slave? My stepfather never liked me, either; but at least he taught me some principles. One principle is that when people are no longer useful, you get rid of them. Well, tomorrow we get rid of all of you!"

Sandal's bitterness made me ill. I never suspected he saw the world through such a dark lens of envy and hatred. I had assumed he was just a spoiled rich brat.

"You are wrong, Sandal!" I exclaimed. "We never thought that way. I wanted to be your friend!"

"The only thing you wanted was Aziza!" Sandal spat.

"That is not true," I said indignantly. "She picked me out, and deliberately used her charms to manipulate me."

"And you were so easy!" Aziza laughed. "So oblivious, and so ridiculously gullible! You might have been useful. As cousin to the king, I could have levered you into a high position! I laughed to see you trudge in as a naked slave, looking so dejected! But even after meeting the queen mother, you still never guessed! I almost felt sorry for you. Almost. You played at being holy; but I knew you were a hypocrite! Remember the Temple of Virility, Japheth? You and your brothers were so overcome with lust that you could not even wait for me—not that I would have let you touch me! Does your father—God's holy prophet—know how his sons pushed and shoved to get in? Your only thought was personal gratification!"

"It was not that way, Aziza," I began. Her accusations were painful.

"Oh, yes it was! I know all about you! And I know all about your scrawny Adamite girl, too! I saw your lovesick puppy face at the banquet. She is another stupid religious fanatic! The two of you would be a perfect match! But why did you have to murder Rogar? He was a pig, but he was useful, and would have brought me comfort and security! Now I will have to choose someone else. It will be hard to find another as rich. His death is an inconvenience. When you die, it will only serve you right."

"But I did not kill Rogar," I said. "Your brother did that."

Aziza frowned, and gave a long look at Sandal. "You bastard!" she said, before returning to me. "Still, I will be glad to see you die. Life moves on, and I am done with you. Let's go, Sandal."

"Wait a minute, Aziza," father said. "We listened to you; now listen to me. The Creator is about to judge Mother Earth, but you still can be saved. Admit your sins and turn away from them! Ask for mercy! God does not wish you to perish..."

"Like you are going to perish tomorrow?" Sandal interjected, laughing cynically. "Well, we reject your God, and we reject all of you religious fanatics. We would rather choose Mother Earth, soon to be the greatest power on earth! Goodnight, my one-time relatives. Your puny threats will make this Dam Festival even more enjoyable. And when you are gobbled up, we will cheer!"

"Your attitude sounds almost godless, Sandal!" Shem remarked coolly.

Sandal glared, and turned to begin climbing down. At that moment, we felt a rumble. Our cell began to shake, and Uncle Samlah was knocked to the floor. I grabbed the bars and held on, while outside, Sandal and Aziza seized the railing. For a good while, the rock swayed and shook. There had been several tremors in the previous week, but this was by far the biggest. The movement slowly subsided, and our visitors carefully began their descent.

"Watch your step," Ham called out, grinning. "It is a long way down."

Father shook his head sadly. "I wish people would listen to me."

As soon as they were gone, I crawled back into the tunnel. I wanted to work, but also to escape from the others. Aziza had spoken enough truth that it hurt. I had not seen any danger, I had presumed, and I had been so easy to manipulate! All it took was a little flash of skin, a little wiggle, a little soft touch—and I had become clay in her hands! If I ever got out of this, I thought, I would be much wiser. I would not trust women, and I would listen to the wisdom of my elders.

But we were not out of it quite yet. In fact, things were desperate. I concentrated on cutting the groove in the crystal, and the hours raced by. On my second turn of the night, I felt something soft against my cheek. I thought nothing of it; but a few circles later, a piece of dust blew into my eye, and I felt air. We had cut through! I yelled out my excitement, and returned to my work with new energy. With each circuit, the fissure grew longer, and the air began to whistle through, though the crystal layer remained solid. The sky was growing lighter when my turn ended, and I gave the diamond to Uncle Samlah.

I was startled awake by a loud trumpet, and ran to the casement. A sea of people was spread out beneath us. The crowd filled the great amphitheater and spread out along the dam. Though I was no judge of crowds, there must have been hundreds of thousands there, with thousands more flooding in. Dancers, acrobats, and jugglers were performing on the stage as battalions of soldiers marched in.

Flocks of crows, seagulls, and vultures flew overhead. The birds would fly around all day long, Uncle Samlah explained, until the festival was over, when they would fight over scraps. He had seen it before. A small flock of green Enoch's parrots flew in, too. I was happier to see them. They were not only old friends from home: they were vegetarians. The vast audience generated a low, droning noise as the people talked, ate, drank, gambled, or otherwise occupied their time. Something about it reminded me of the agitated animals milling about before the stampede. Something bad was about to happen here, too; I only wished we did not have to participate in it.

"What does our Creator think of them, I wonder?" father asked, gazing at the crowd. "He ponders the human heart, and knows its depths."

I had not thought about that. What did our Creator think about this festival, or this entire people? My brothers and I had seen their teachers suppress the truth and teach foolish lies. Their leaders were filled with vile passions. Instead of wisely exercising dominion over nature, they tirelessly worked to dominate, domineer, and enslave people instead. What did our Creator think about their rejection of him, or their hatred of those who believed in him? Even the poorest people of Mother Earth loved stealing, violence, dishonesty, and immorality. They worshiped dumb idols, coveted what belonged to others, and even stayed awake at night imagining depraved things. And today, they were thirsty for bloodshed and death.

"Out of all those thousands down there," father continued, "how many do you suppose would be willing to repent, and turn to God? A thousand? A hundred? Ten?" He paused, waiting for our answer. Finally he shook his head. "No, my sons. There is not even one. The thoughts of every heart are completely filled with evil."

The blaring of trumpets announced the royal party. As thousands of spears saluted, the king rode in on his new ivory chariot, which was even more ornate than his son's. Slowly proceeding through the cheering sea of worshipers, he nodded and waved his royal scepter to acknowledge their accolades. The royal entourage joined him on the stage. We soon identified the queen mother, Prince Malek, and the two giant princes from Nephil. Father pointed out Shahoot and cousins Achbor and Sharezer.

When the royal orator succeeded in hushing the crowd, King Nezzar gave a short speech welcoming his people and the honored guests. He invited all to share in the glory of his beautiful city, his great industries, and his mighty army. Today, he said, all would see the awesome power of his Great Dam. With the mighty power of water under his control, and a new secret weapon he modestly called Nezzar Powder, the unstoppable forces of Mother Earth would soon march over the face of the earth, and dominate it for a thousand years.

"He sure likes to talk about himself!" Shem exclaimed. "I counted him say 'I' or 'me' about forty times! He takes personal credit for everything!"

"And now," the king shouted, "I ask the queen mother, the living embodiment of the earth goddess Mokosh, to release the power of our Great Dam! Glory to Mother Earth, and death to her enemies!"

An immense roar swelled from the masses of people. The queen mother, dressed in a glittering emerald gown, proceeded to a giant lever.

"Let the power of water go forth," she shouted, pulling the lever down. Water spurted from the mouth of the Mokosh image, and the six great watermills along the face of the dam slowly began to move. As the water showered onto the spillways, the applause of the great crowd was like thunder.

Despite our situation, I was somehow pleased to see the hydraulic belts, gears, and shafts spinning properly. The design had been well done: it was something to be proud of. The stupendous power generated by the dam would be ten times the previous level, and support a tremendous expansion in industry. Although the king had given no credit to Tulek for his painstaking years of work, I hoped he could see his project in operation from his cage. His had been a remarkable achievement.

While I was pleased that it actually worked, I was angry, too. The whole dam project had been hijacked and doomed by foolish bureaucrats--people who knew nothing of dam construction or its risks. By his selfishness, embezzlement, and criminal failure to follow the design he had approved, Dam Minister Algar had thoroughly sabotaged the great project. Oh, he had been condemned to die, but not for the right reasons. And because his real crimes remained secret, a dam disaster could occur at any moment.

"But, citizens," King Nezzar shouted. "We must demonstrate our new power! Behold our mighty industrial machines! Our hydraulic saw, our hydraulic press, and our new hydraulic cannon! Who shall help us test them? Shall we ask our treasonous prime minister?"

"Logar!" A shout arose from hundreds of thousands of bloodthirsty throats. "Logar! Logar!" The chant echoed through the valley, growing louder and louder.

Moments later, the shadows of soldiers passed our casement as the sobbing prime minister was dragged up the stairs. We heard a few words from the stage, the roar of the crowd, and saw a tumbling, shrieking body swish past us. Horrified, we followed its journey all the way to the stage. The crowd laughed, cheered, and continued their horrible chant: "Logar! Logar!" Battered but still struggling, Logar was dragged to a nearby platform. Soldiers pushed him feet first into a big metal cylinder with pipes connected to high-pressure water. Only Logar's head showed as the breech of the cylinder was elevated and rotated to point to a target painted high on the dam.

"Behold, King Nezzar's hydraulic cannon[1]!" the king proclaimed.

A soldier pulled a lever, and a swooshing sound erupted from the pipes. There was a deep clang, like a hammer striking an anvil, and Logar shot out from the cylinder with water spraying in all directions. His body flew like an arrow, and struck the dam with an awful splatter, leaving a glistening red smear just above the center of the target.

"Excellent shooting!" the king declared. "Just imagine my cannon shooting great stones against a walled city! Shall we anoint the dam again?"

Stimulated by the sight of blood, the immense crowd roared its approval. I turned away with a shudder of disgust. Was this what awaited us? It certainly looked that way. Unconsciously, I raised my head to pray, but at that very moment, I heard a sharp noise from the tunnel, like shattering glass[2].

"We are through!" Uncle Samlah shouted.

---

[1]*Editor's Note:* The word "cannon" may not be best: the original word indicated a "stone-spraying machine."

[2]*Editor's Note:* I was surprised by this allusion to glass: I had thought it was a modern material. The Roman historian Pliny, however, believed glass originated earlier than 5000 BC. About 90% of all glass used today is soda-lime glass, derived from fine sand. Its chemical components are largely silica, sodium oxide, and calcium oxide.

Chapter Thirty-Eight: An Escape

Rushing to the entrance of the tunnel, we put our heads down, and felt a cool breeze. Excited, we called to Uncle Samlah, but he did not respond. Instead, he backed out of the tunnel quietly, shaking his head.

"Alas, Eden!" he groaned. "All those years wasted! We cannot climb down, boys. And our rope is far too short!"

I squirmed in to see for myself. Sure enough, the crystal window had fallen out. The opposite rock face was close enough to touch, less than two cubits away. I carefully poked out my head and looked down. The walls of rock were perfectly smooth, and widened out to form a drop of hundreds of cubits. At the bottom were jagged rocks. My heart sank: any descent was utterly impossible.

"What about climbing up, Japheth?" Shem called.

I turned my head to look up. The rock walls were very close together all the way to the top. Four or five cubits above the tunnel was a wide fissure in the opposite rock face. I considered the possibilities. By bracing our arms and legs against either side, we could probably scale it. If the fissure extended any distance into the spur of the mountain, it might provide a safe way to reach the slope. If not, then by climbing another ten or twelve cubits to the lookout, we could surprise the guards, and at least make a fight of it.

Backing out, I let Shem and Ham each take a look, and we talked it over. Ham thought the climb was very easy, and volunteered to go first. Uncle Samlah liked the idea, but doubted he could do it. Father still needed to be convinced.

"Ham climbs like a monkey, Father!" Shem implored. "Japheth and I will hold the rope tightly around his waist, and catch him if he falls."

Bloodthirsty roars from the crowd finally changed father's mind. Shaking his head, he agreed to let us go. After father prayed for our success, it took only a moment to prepare. Putting our sandals around our necks, we tied the rope around Ham's waist, and crawled to the end of the tunnel. Holding onto the lip of the crystal, Ham carefully stood up. While Shem and I held the rope, he stretched out his right hand and foot to brace them against the opposite wall. Next, he reached up with his left hand and his left foot, and simply walked right up the fissure, one step at a time. He plopped into the fissure, and called down to us.

"I think it goes in a long way, but let me check. " He disappeared into the rock. As we waited, loud cheers echoed up from the amphitheater: another victim had been sacrificed.

"We can do it!" Ham called. "Come on up!"

As Ham and I held either end of the rope, Shem clambered up without difficulty, and flopped into the fissure.

It was my turn. Ham and Shem braced themselves, firmly holding the other end of the rope. I stood up and reached out my arm and leg, just as my brothers had done. A cold breeze blew up my tunic. Unconsciously, I looked down. The sight made me shudder, and I had to force my eyes to look back up. Courage, I reminded myself, is something you do—not something you feel.

I shifted my weight and began climbing, bracing my hands and feet on the opposite sides of the rock face. The surface felt rough, but with Shem and Ham helping, the climb was not difficult. In a few moments I gained the fissure, and Shem and

Ham helped me in. I breathed a sigh of relief. The crack in the spur of the mountain was winding, but it extended quite a distance, and opened up as it descended.

After a minute or two to catch our breath, we began our journey. It was not easy. We climbed over great boulders, squeezed through tight openings, and slid down slippery rock faces as water showered over us. Some obstacles required teamwork, and all the strength we had. By the time we came to a ledge close to the ground, we were exhausted, and took a rest beside a waterfall. The pool at the base of the waterfall drained into a stream that disappeared into a dark tunnel. We craned our necks to see. The tunnel was long, but it ended in bright sunshine and green foliage.

"If we succeed in reaching the ground," Ham asked, "what kind of diversion do you have in mind, Japheth? The amphitheater has a huge crowd, not to mention the entire army of Mother Earth. They will not be easy to budge."

"I was thinking," I said, "that you might get a flamer loose."

Horrible cheers echoed again through the narrow walls. We stood and walked to the edge of the stream. Ham only meant to test the water. When he stepped in, however, he found the moss slippery. He fell onto his rump, and was immediately swept away by the current. Whooping with excitement, he bounced back and forth between the steep walls of the fissure. When he entered the tunnel, his voice became an echo. Shem and I stooped down and saw his silhouette moving in the sunshine of the end of the tunnel. It suddenly disappeared. A long moment later, we heard a splash.

"I'm okay!" Ham's voice echoed. "Come on in! It's fun!"

Shem slid into the current, and I followed a minute later. It was a careening, bruising journey. At the end, I shot over the lip of the channel, and fell a long way down to splash into a deep pool of water. When I got to the surface, I looked around. The pond was right behind the amphitheater.

As I reached the edge of the pond, a big hand helped me up from the water. When I looked up, my mouth fell open in astonishment. The hand was that of an officer of Valley Vigilance! I recognized him instantly as one of the warriors who had cleared the path for the patriarchs. He was wearing full armor, with a green, silver, and gold breastplate, a brass harness with his brightly polished sword, and a shield fastened on his back. The plume of white feathers on his helmet signified leadership. His muscled face looked grim, as though he had an unpleasant, bloody job ahead of him.

I was bewildered. How had a Valley Vigilance officer in full armor ever gotten through the gates of Mother Earth? And he was not alone. Two other Valley Vigilance officers stood beside Ham and Shem, who were eating pears under the shade of a tree. The presence of these officers was inexplicable, even flabbergasting. I fumbled to speak.

"What in the...? How in the...? Why are you here?" I asked.

"We are simply obeying orders, young Japheth," he answered. "You must, too. The time is short, and we all have duties. What is your purpose here?"

His question caught me off-guard. "We are here to save the Adamites, sir," I said. "I thought that if we escaped we could create a diversion, and rescue them from the livestock cage at the foot of the rock."

The officer nodded. "Very well. There will be a diversion. You will find a tall lamppost near the cage, next to the stands. Wait there until the guards have abandoned their post. When you release the prisoners, you must have them climb to the top of Lookout Rock. Do you understand? They cannot be saved otherwise, as your father was instructed."

"Yes, sir." I did not think this was the time to ask questions.

"Carry on, then," he said. "And remember this, Japheth: vengeance is God's. Do not waste time meting out your own."

The officers left abruptly, and I turned to join my brothers. They looked at me strangely when I explained our orders. Perhaps they were surprised, as I had been, that they were so simple; but they acted as though they had not even noticed the Valley Vigilance officers! That puzzled me, but they finally shrugged in agreement, and we made our way to the amphitheater. It was not difficult to slip through the service gate. Despite the fact that our tunics were dripping wet, nobody seemed to notice: all their attention was focused on the stage at the foot of the dam. We found the tall lamppost the officer had mentioned just a short distance from the cage, and climbed up on the lamplighter pegs.

The sight from our perch was sickening. The hydraulic machines on the stage were spattered with blood, and we saw soldiers dragging two green-clad youths along the stage to a cage of sabertooths. The announcer called out their names and crimes, and said that being returned to nature was a most fitting punishment. When the soldiers threw them in, I shut my eyes.

When the roars, shrieks, and cheers subsided, I opened my eyes again and looked at the livestock cage. Tulek was near the bars, comforting Keturah and Kezziah. The deep voice of the king sounded over the amphitheater, and the crowd grew quiet.

"We have offered many sacrifices to the water god today," he said, "for he has allowed us to harness the power of this Great Dam. Now, we come to the exciting climax. Did I tell you that I had developed a new secret weapon, one more destructive than any the world has ever seen? Behold Nezzar Powder!"

The king pointed to a large fenced-off area a short distance from the stage. A tall stake had been driven into the center of the test area, and a large black barrel placed beside it. Four or five similar barrels stood beside the fence at the far end of the test area, as well as a dozen pointed tubes.

"These barrels and these tubes," the king cried, "hold a power so great that the mere threat of their use will make nations submit to us! Shall we test one?"

The great crowd roared its approval.

King Nezzar laughed. "I told them to put in extra powder today: I want a good demonstration! But on whom shall we test Nezzar powder? Shall we test it on the religious fanatics who refuse to submit to Mother Earth — those stubborn Adamites? Yes? Then let us begin with their patriarch! Send down the old hypocrite — the patriarch Demas!"

Everyone looked up to the top of Lookout Rock and cheered as an old man was pushed down the steep ramp. He accelerated quickly, practically flew over the audience, and finally tumbled down onto the platform. Two guards picked up his limp form and carried it through the crowd to the fenced area, where they tied him to the stake. Next, they fastened a long gray cord to the middle of the barrel, and unwound it all the way to the stage.

"Behold the awesome power of Nezzar powder!" the king shouted.

Picking up a torch, he touched it to the cord. It instantly caught fire, and sputtered and fizzled its way through the crowd, into the fenced area, and finally to the barrel. The powder was certainly flammable. I could not help but think it would be interesting to see what would happen when it hit the sealed container. I did not have long to wait.

With a flash, and a clap like thunder, the barrel, the victim, and a wide swath of the surrounding audience were instantly blown into vapor. The concussion knocked us off the pole, while the blast of hot air produced a great cloud of dust. Pebbles, rocks, and debris began to shower down, forcing us to duck for cover. We had never experienced anything like this. The entire vast crowd lay stunned.

"I don't think the king quite expected that!" Shem said, coughing. His face and clothing were white with dust.

"They need to work on their calibration," I added.

When the dust began to clear, I climbed back up the pole, and Shem and Ham followed me. The wide circle of complete destruction extended to the stage. Beyond that, an entire field of people lay injured or dead. The king's giant body lay very still on the stage, his head crushed by a paving stone. Though my ears still rang, I heard water. I looked up, and saw that the face of the dam had been damaged. The nearest waterwheel had been torn off, and water showered out from cracks between the stones. Ominously, a geyser of mud spurted from the pavement at the center of the blast.

Before long, we began hearing groans from the injured, and cries for help. The shower of water from the dam awakened some of those who were only stunned. They had no intention of helping the wounded. Instead, their only thought was to escape. As I watched the mud spurt out of the pavement, I pictured in my mind the great foundation stones being undermined, and beginning to shift. It was not just my imagination, either: new cracks were opening in the face of the dam, and more streams of water began spurting over the audience. I considered the great wall above us. It still held back a stupendous weight of water, but it was essentially just a stack of rocks, one that was quickly becoming unstable. Thousands of spectators were already moving toward the exits. They instinctively saw the danger, and were ready to panic.

"By the way, Japheth," Ham remarked, "the predators have gotten loose." He pointed to a pair of rippers that were pursuing a fat nobleman. Nearby, a large lion was shaking its victim by the neck. That sight was all that the crowd needed. The exits were pushed open, and a human stampede began. The strongest men led the way, and violently pushed aside the small or slow. Those thrown underfoot screamed, but the cries went unheard, because everyone was screaming.

"Look!" Shem exclaimed. Two flaming behemoths had lumbered over to an exit, and now stubbornly blocked it. As terrified people ran towards them, the flamers responded with deadly sheets of fire.

I looked at the cage full of Adamites. Their guards had disappeared. A thick current of mud flowed around the base of the cage, and it seemed to be rising quickly. My brothers had seen everything as I had, from the impending collapse of the great dam, to the rising mud, the rampaging predators, and the panicked, stampeding crowd. I wondered if Ham was having fun.

"Mother of Earth!" he exclaimed. Apparently he was not.

That was when it struck me. "This is our diversion!"

"I'll say!" Shem added.

"Let's rescue the Adamites," Ham said, "and get out of here!"

The herds of terrified spectators were skirting around the current of mud, so we jumped right in and slopped directly over to the cage. Men inside were attempting to open the gate, but it would not budge.

"Japheth!" Kezziah cried. "How did you get here?"

"I will tell you later," I said. "We are here to get you out!" I examined the latch. It was made of iron, and firmly locked.[3]

"They took the key," Tulek said. "You will have to break it in!"

We looked around the landing. The soldiers had abandoned their swords in their hasty retreat, but we needed something big and heavy. Finally, we found a heavy post a short distance away, and worked it loose from the pavement. Carrying it to the gate, we began battering the latch. It took a dozen hits, but the latch finally bent and shattered.

Three big men pulled the gate open from the inside, and came into the gateway. They were apparently looking for the best way to escape, but they stood blocking the others. The screams from thousands of desperate people, the roars from predators, and the spray of water coming from the great dam made it hard for anyone to think. The cracks between the stones widened as we watched. Water already spurted from a hundred places, and new streams of mud were flowing from the pavement. As the men wavered, there was a crunching sound, and a new spray of water showered over us.

"Listen to me!" I shouted, trying to be heard above the noise. "You must climb to the top of the rock—the stairs are right over there. It is your only place of safety!"

"Curse you Adamites!" the big man said. "We are heading for the slope." Stepping down into the mud, he began wading through it, and was followed by the other two. The way was now open, and the Adamites began coming out onto the landing, beginning with the women and children. I repeated my instruction to climb to the top of the rock, and Shem and Ham guided them to the steps. Tulek came out with Keturah and Kezziah, and clasped my shoulder.

"We thank you, Japheth," Tulek said, "even if those foolish ingrates did not."

"Kezziah never gave up," Keturah added. "She always said you would come!"

Kezziah held me very tight. Before she released me, our eyes met for a long moment before she followed her mother to the stairs. The rest of the Adamites expressed their thanks and quickly ascended the stairway. When the last one had gone, I entered the cage to make sure it was empty. The mud was now flowing in from every side: there had been no time to spare.

As I left the cage, I heard someone shout my name. Looking around, I saw a familiar face. Sandal, my old enemy, was wading through the mud in my direction. He held a naked sword, and repeated my name angrily. Three soldiers watched his progress, but stayed on the other side of the mud.

I bent down and picked up an abandoned sword. Nothing would give me more pleasure, I thought, than to pay Sandal back for all the evil he had done. From cheating at games, he had progressed to vandalism, treason, and every kind of violence and murder. This wicked City of Mother Earth had already shed a great deal of blood today. What was a little more?

---

[1]*Editor's Note:* At first I thought this a chronological anomaly. Though the pin-and-tumbler type of lock was not patented until 1843, other types of locks and keys have been used for thousands of years.

Chapter Thirty-Nine: The Great Dam Catastrophe

Sandal struck wildly at me as he stepped onto the landing. I parried it easily, feeling a little surprised that he had been so careless. His next thrust had force behind it, but not much more skill. Using one of Uncle Krulak's most elementary tricks, I wrenched the sword from his hand and sent it flying into the mud.

Something about that shocked him. After a brief pause, he shrieked hysterically, balled his hands into fists, and flew at me. I knew it was a foolish risk, but I decided to teach him a lesson on his own terms. Dropping my own sword, I blocked his fist, and replied with a solid right to his chin. That knocked him onto his seat, but after shaking his head, he got back up. When he attacked again, he was more careful, and made a quick straight jab to my face. I sidestepped it, and responded with a series of solid punches to his midsection. He made little effort to protect himself. Instead, he threw out a flurry of blows from both right and left. If he touched me, I hardly felt it. Advancing, I gave him a hard jab to his belly that knocked out his wind, and then followed it with a solid right to his chin. That one knocked him right off the landing into the mud.

Sandal sat up and stared at me with blood oozing from his lip. I somehow felt satisfied: I had always wanted to beat the stuffing out of Sandal. He looked around and noticed that his soldiers had disappeared. He glanced at the dam, which was showering out great volumes of water, and turned back to me.

"You are full of surprises today, cousin," he said, almost smiling. "I guess I need more practice. Next time, I will be ready, I promise you!" He got up and began sloshing away through the mud.

I shrugged. From the corner of my eye, I saw movement, and glanced up. The very face of the dam was buckling! Even as I watched, one of the huge waterwheels popped off and began to roll through the crowd. It was time to go. I turned for the stairs and bolted up as fast as I could. Climbing stairs is hard work. In a minute I was panting, and my heart was pounding so loudly it drowned out the screams in the amphitheater. Though I was slowing, I kept moving. I realized I might not make it to the top. If only I had not taken time to teach Sandal a lesson!

I drove myself up one step at a time, and eventually neared the top. There was a sharp crunching sound behind me, like an iron hammer splitting a boulder. I heard screeching, snapping, and grinding sounds, and the roar of falling water. I felt a strong wind, and then water surged up all around me, lifting me off the stairs and speeding me up the side of the rock. The wave paused at the crest, and began to fall. At that very moment, strong hands grabbed me. In a single smooth movement, I was drawn out of the water and back onto my feet. I was on the stairway only three steps from the top!

"Shem, haven't we saved him before?" I heard Ham ask.

"I think we have!" Shem answered.

My brothers had rescued me! I was thankful, but too surprised to think of any witty repartee. The whole thing had been done so deftly that I could only laugh.

As we turned to climb the remaining steps, there was another big crunch: the dam catastrophe was still unfolding! Up to that moment, only part of the dam had fallen. Now, it completely collapsed, and water, rock, and debris poured out as a seething flood. The amphitheater was blown apart, and without a pause the great wave surged down the narrow valley. The entire city was swallowed. Magnificent temples, stately palaces, and grand building were all covered; for a time, all we could see was water. After engulfing the city, the torrent swept down the valley, leaving only rubble in its wake.

But it was still not over. The thick soil covering the floor of the valley floor had been washed away, just as it had been in our little valley. Not only was the vast, delicate network of subterranean springs and fountains disrupted; the earth blanketing the tall slopes was left completely unsupported. The surface of the slopes melted, and began to move. As it slid downhill, it carried away trees, farms, vineyards, and any people attempting to climb to safety. The mudslides from both sides merged on the floor of the valley to form a virtual river of mud. Remaining structures were crushed, trees and wreckage were sucked in and tumbled along, and anything left was smothered. As we watched, the great City of Mother Earth was completely scrubbed from the face of the earth.

A frigid wind suddenly swept over us. Like the strange wind in Enoch's Valley, this one also carried a rush of foreign feelings. Anger was there, and frustration, and an insatiable hunger for revenge. Thankfully, the eerie feelings disappeared as quickly as they had come. All that remained was a slight smell of sulfur.

A gentle, warm breeze followed. It left us feeling fresh and clean, and filled with gratitude. How miraculously we had been saved from such an awful death! And more than that, we were free! I took a deep breath, and exhaled slowly. For the first time in years, things felt right. I heard a squawk, and looked up. A little flock of Enoch's parrots was flying over us, heading for the mountains, and home.

As we surveyed the bleak scene around us, I thought of the rich industries, great temples, and teeming population that had been the City of Mother Earth. Only traces remained. The walls of what had been a rich valley were now barren cliffs of dirty bedrock, with small trickles of water. The floor of the valley, once verdant, was a featureless table of gray mud.

"What a sight to remember, my sons!" father said. "Here lived a people that forgot their Maker."

He was right, of course. The people of Mother Earth had been very wicked, and had richly deserved their fate. But there were still lots of other godless people in the world, and some of them were probably even worse than Mother Earth. What about them? Would our Maker bring judgment on them too? If so, we could expect more of this kind of thing, until the whole world was destroyed, just as the patriarch Enoch had foreseen.

But if more disasters lay in store for this wicked world, I did not want to go through them alone. Oh, my brothers were great; but it sure would be nice to have someone else, too — a special someone who would stick with me, and be a help to me; and someone I could comfort in turn. That would be delightful!

Suddenly, I felt a warm hand in mine. Surprised, I looked down, and saw a lovely face beaming at me with very blue eyes. My heart leaped with happiness, and the awful scene around us faded away. This was the girl my heart had always wanted: she was my perfect match! Somehow, I already knew we would share lots of exciting adventures, and have a long, happy life together. I began fumbling for words, but Kezziah just smiled, with her eyes twinkling.

"So, where is the boat?"

Laughing with relief and delight, I picked her up and spun her around in a close embrace.

Chapter Forty: A Happy Ending

When you look back over a century or two, the best things in life become pretty clear. Oh, there may be moments when nothing could be better than the simple sweet taste of a juicy mango. And some may be fortunate enough to have a glorious moment of triumph when they win a hard-fought race, or knock down a bully like Sandal, or invent something that actually works. But over the course of a lifetime, the most satisfying and wonderful thing of all is to find true love. For a long moment that day, Kezziah and I were content to simply hold each other. Finally, we opened our eyes. Our quiet little group of survivors stood all alone, perched high above a sea of mud.

The disaster we had witnessed was stunning. After a time, father broke our silence to offer thanks, and we all joined in a time of heartfelt prayer. When we finished, it was time to go. The steps were slippery, so we very carefully climbed down to the bottom. We found a stream of clear water already cutting its way through the mud, so we were able to quench our thirst before resting. That evening we had a big meeting, and in the morning we began our long journey home.

It took us weeks to hike down the Mokosh River valley. As you might imagine, it was an adventure just to find food and shelter. We encountered no enemy troops, but we did have to fight off a band or two of the human jackals that always converge on disasters.

Despite suffering some hardships, our group of survivors had a successful journey. We had much time to talk, and came together in a close fellowship. Father bonded right away with Tulek and Keturah, and he was delighted with Kezziah. Our plan to marry met with his hearty approval, and because he was certain that mother would agree with him, the matter was quickly settled. Shem and Ham had always been keen on her, and they were thrilled, too. That night around the campfire, Keturah told us the story of Kezziah's patriarchal necklace.

"This necklace," she began, "was one of four given to the four daughters of the patriarch Enosh, the third from Adam. The daughters each married husbands that took them to the distant corners of the earth, and it grieved them that they would be so far from each other. Their father, being a prophet, was able to give them comfort. Before the earth came to an end, he promised, all four necklaces would again be united, worn by wives in the same family. While this is a big world, with lots of people, it seems that half of that ancient prophecy will soon be fulfilled!"

When we finally arrived at Jared's Mill, no one at the dock greeted our small band of survivors. The mill itself had been burned, many buildings abandoned, and the marketplace looked empty. As we hiked past farms, we saw fruit rotting on the trees. There were hardly any sheep, cows, or horses, and even the dogs looked starved. When we came to our plantation, mother wept for joy: our family was together again! That evening, Grandpa Lamech described how Shahoot and his corrupt gang had systematically plundered the valley, driven off its productive citizens, and brought in slaves, criminals, and worthless drifters to work the lands. At the moment, however, it seemed there was nothing we could do.

A few days later, father called for a prayer meeting, and many of the remaining believers showed up. That meeting was the turning point. A cool, fresh breeze seemed to sweep in, filling us with new purpose, energy, and confidence. All at once we were in complete agreement. Our elders now looked upon our situation with clear eyes, and they became angry. Their anger, however, was not directed at each other, as before, but at all the evil we had been subjected to. They immediately appointed Uncle Krulak as military commander, and commissioned him to take back our land.

It was astonishing to see how quickly things happened after that. Almost overnight, Valley Vigilance reassembled as a fighting force. The occupying army was tough, but their communications with Mother Earth had been cut, and they were demoralized by reports that their homeland had mysteriously disappeared. When they found themselves facing a strong force that was both skilled and utterly determined, they began to retreat. Shahoot's acting governor was shrewd. Within an hour or two of the first battle, he had his loot loaded up, and he sailed away.

There was more fighting, but in the end we killed or drove off every one of the occupying soldiers, magistrates, and foreign parasites. The sojourners who had never adopted our patriarchal worldview saw that things had changed, and either left on their own, or were forced out. It was a hard thing, but necessary. After that, we dealt with the traitors. We arrested those we could catch, and put the worst ones to death. After all we had suffered, there were very few tears. Once all that was accomplished, Valley Vigilance restored order. We buried the dead and mourned our many losses.

Finally, after more than two years of foreign occupation, our people were able to return to their own properties. Our wounds began to heal, and our community started to repair and rebuild. It was time to do something positive, our parents said, so they invited the entire patriarchal family to our wedding.

No terrifying behemoths interrupted our celebration that day, nor were there any invasions, stampedes, or dam disasters. Instead, the day was completely peaceful, and the happiest one in the history of Enoch's Valley. I felt like dancing from the moment I awoke! The birds chirped and sang like never before; the flowers sprayed out rich new perfumes, and even the gurgling of the brook sounded like music. There was happy anticipation in the air: I wanted to run and jump!

The meetinghouse was packed. While the building had been stripped and vandalized during the occupation, recent repairs had made it habitable, and Grandma Tirza's volunteers had decorated it with enough flowers and greenery to rival the Garden of Eden. Cousin Asaph began our celebration with a bouncy thanksgiving tune, and then led the congregation in a wonderful medley of magnificent hymns. After years of heart-wrenching loss, suffering, and misery, the uplifting songs of faith were overwhelming, and there were many tears.

"Beloved," the patriarch finally announced, "it is time. I now ask Japheth and Kezziah to come to the front with their parents. Shem and Ham, you come up, too."

We all stood. I could hardly take my eyes from Kezziah. Dressed in an elegant white gown, a delicate silver tiara, and her sparkling patriarchal necklace, she was "the picture of youth and beauty," as father told me later. When we got to the front, the patriarch turned us to face the congregation, and gave a short talk about the Garden of Eden, and our Creator's good purposes in joining a man and a woman in holy matrimony.

"Is there anyone here who can testify as to the suitability of this union?" the patriarch finally asked.

"I can, Patriarch," Great Aunt Naomi said, standing up. "I have come to know both of these people well, and can vouch for their good character. I have interviewed them, checked their references, and can say with confidence that their marriage is suitable. In fact, in my opinion, this an excellent match!"

"Does anyone agree with her?" the patriarch asked with a smile, looking over the congregation.

Applause and shouts of approval filled the air, and the musicians struck up lively music. Kezziah and I smiled with relief, which brought some laughter.

"Any objections?" he asked again.

Silence was his answer, so the patriarch smoothly continued.

"In that case, let us have Japheth and Kezziah exchange their vows before our Creator, and ask him to bless their union."

Weddings are usually pretty quick. Our vows, though earnest, sincere, and heartfelt, did not take much time. In just a few moments, the patriarch gave the words I was eager to hear.

"Before all these witnesses, and in the presence of God, I now pronounce you man and wife! Japheth, you may kiss the bride."

There must have been many kisses since the Garden of Eden; but as it turned out, ours was the sweetest, purest kiss of them all. Kezziah and I took a bow, as was the custom. The entire congregation burst out in applause and our parents embraced us with happy tears. As the music played, we began to slowly make our way through the congregation. Ham told me later I grinned like a chimpanzee, which I guess is a happy type of monkey.

We took our time walking down the aisle, and exchanged smiles with everyone. Grandpa Lamech and Grandma Tirza were in the front, of course, with Great-Great Aunties Libusha and Haddassa, Great Auntie Zora, and Great Uncles Taanach and Raamach. When we passed Great Aunt Naomi, she gave me a special wink. I still remember the report she had given our parents.

"A strong, hardworking girl," she said. "Intelligent, alert, thoughtful, kindly, and well grounded in the faith. And what a beauty! With such pretty features, blonde hair, and blue eyes, I expect she will produce handsome, sturdy children; and with such good character, she will raise them well!"

Uncles Nebach, Shebach, Krulak, and Lemuel were there, too, with their wives, as well as Uncle Samlah, our cousins Asaph, Zibach, Zillai, and Jazer, with all their wives and children. While it was painful to be reminded of the many family members who had been lost, I was happily surprised to see cousins Dedan and Seba. Only two days before, they had arrived on a ship, still dressed in their slave garb. One afternoon, they explained, the guards did not show up to return them to their slave quarters. After waiting for hours, the slaves finally realized they had been abandoned. Dropping their tools, they simply climbed out of the mine and walked away to freedom. Unfortunately, Cush had been sent to another mine, but we had hope that he would show up someday too.

The Adamites saved out of Mother Earth sat together. They included Tuktub, our faithful palace servant, and Johanan, the dissipated young nobleman who had become a believer only two days before he was arrested. Sadly, the three sturdy Valley Vigilance officers never made it to the top. At the time, I shared my grief with father; but he told me not to worry.

Warriors like that, he said, were prepared for every contingency. They had undoubtedly survived somehow, and would show up again someday. I liked hearing that.

Every culture has its wedding traditions, I suppose. Ours was to have the new couple greet the guests after the ceremony, after which there would be a big feast, followed by dancing, desserts, and speeches. The older women would bustle the new bride away to reveal certain secrets passed down from Eve, and when they returned, the new couple would depart to begin their new life together. After our kiss, I was ready to dispense with all that, but traditions were traditions.

After receiving hundreds of affectionate embraces, we entered the banquet hall, which was filled with mouth-watering aromas. Mother had made potato pastries, and Grandma Tirza had cooked her renowned asparagus surprises. Many others had prepared delicious dishes, and there were jugs of cool water, fruit and vegetable juices, and a wide range of succulent fruits. Grandpa Lamech gave a short speech and asked the blessing, and then Cousin Asaph and his musicians played.

The patriarch eventually hobbled over to invite Kezziah onto the dance floor. She accepted graciously, and everyone applauded. I offered Great-Great Aunt Libusha my hand, and she proved to be just as spry a dancer as her older brother. The rest of the elders followed suit, and soon scores of people circled the floor in a joyous wedding dance. When the patriarch and his sisters grew tired, the younger ones had their turn.

We clapped, swirled, and glided through one dance after another. Kezziah had never seen the matriarchal chair dance before, but after watching our dignified Grandma Tirza being carried around, she agreed to try it. When Shem and Ham lifted her up and around the floor as the honoree, she laughed with delight. The musicians took a break during dessert, and Shem and Ham took the opportunity to give speeches. They were hilarious. When they finished, the patriarch stood up again. He looked healthier and stronger than he had in many years.

"We give thanks to our Creator," he began, "for life and new hope. At 902 years of age, having hope is a wonderful thing! We thank Noah, Emma, Tulek, and Keturah for hosting this, and we thank each of you for providing the decorations, music, and delicious food. Japheth and Kezziah are such a blessing, and we are so thankful that they have chosen to marry and to keep these happy traditions!"

This brought loud applause and table rapping, until a squawking bird put a stop to it.

"Awk! Awk!" Enoch's old parrot shrieked, "Praise the Maker! Glory!" Unfortunately, it did not stop there, but went on to its usual proclamation: "Ungodly deeds! Ungodly way! Judgment on all!"

The bird quieted afterward, and began preening on its perch, surveying the audience one eye at a time. It was a very peculiar parrot. In a way, it was a comfort. For many centuries—we had no idea how long, really—that bird had lived with our family. People had often joked about that stupid parrot watching over us, but I was now starting to believe it.

"Enoch's old parrot, my children," the patriarch said graciously, "has summed up what I wanted to say. We have every reason to be grateful to our Creator, and praise him. Only weeks ago, our lives were bleak. An evil kingdom had robbed us of hope. We had had no marriages in years, and no babies! But when God brought judgment upon Mother Earth, my grandson Noah returned safely to Enoch's Valley. He brought both his sons with him, and a wonderful new group of believers, as well as my long-lost grandson Samlah! And now we celebrate a wedding! But the parrot is right to caution us. Our Maker has only begun to reveal his righteous judgment on the stubborn, evil world system around us. We have troubles ahead."

The patriarch stopped to take a sip of pomegranate juice, and then smiled confidently.

"Beloved, these Last Days are not for the timid and fearful. But let me assure you of this. For those of us that walk with our Maker like my father Enoch did, we will end up in the same wonderful place. Each of us will someday awaken in our own bed, in our own home, with a new body. That new body will have a straight back, clear eyes, good hearing, and a tongue that can taste meals more delicious than anything we have on earth. We will have a happy ending! That happy ending, beloved, is what makes all our suffering, loss, and even death bearable; and that happy ending is what makes our life on earth an exciting adventure!"

The patriarch's eyes glittered with pleasure. Grandma Tirza gestured to him.

"Tirza tells me it is time for the women to take away the new bride," he said. "But before they go, let me tell Japheth and Kezziah two things. First, love is what you do more than what you feel; and second, there is strength in unity. Talk to each other! Congratulations! We love you, and are very proud of you!"

Applause burst out, and the women stood up.

"Kezziah!" they cried gaily. "It is time to learn Eve's secrets!"

After the women left, two of my favorite uncles came over.

"Well, Japheth," Uncle Lemuel said, "now that life in Enoch's Valley is returning to normal, Uncle Nebach and I think it is time to put your stream pump on the market. As a married man, you can use the profits, especially since you will be going to the School of Tubal-Cain after all. But tell us the process for making a strong, flexible material from the sap of a tree! Could this new material help seal your leaky valves?"

"I think it might," I replied. "The material is made by cooking the sap of the rubber tree with sulfur. Now that Mother Earth has been destroyed, we may be the only ones that know the process."

"We will keep it a secret!" Uncle Nebach exclaimed. "If the material proves as useful as I think, it may send you to school with plenty of money. But tell us also about that explosive powder. Did you learn how to make it, too? You said it contained sulfur and charcoal. What was the third ingredient?"

"I am sorry, Uncle," I said, shaking my head. "I never learned it!"

"Well," Uncle Lemuel mused, "if the secret is lost, it may be just as well. It was very dangerous. On the other hand, it might have been useful in mining."

"Mining!" I exclaimed. "That reminds me! When we hiked out of Mother Earth, we found that the mudslides had uncovered caverns in the cliffs. One of them glittered with reflected light, so Shem, Ham and I climbed up to explore. In the gravel of one cavern we found colorful crystals, and picked out a handful or two. Imagine our surprise, when at the first settlement we came to, one of the bigger ones sold for a sum great enough to pay for our entire trip home! Since then, I have been thinking of a design for a fast hydraulic drill. It may be just what we need to develop mining in Enoch's Valley!"

Uncle Nebach laughed. "Tubal-Cain, my old mentor, liked to say that everything begins with mining. He was right. The depths of the earth are filled with treasures just waiting for us. On the other hand, riches attract unscrupulous scoundrels, as we have all learned. Earning riches is easier than keeping them! Japheth, I look forward to helping develop your new hydraulic drill, but I am afraid it may lead you and your brothers into even more exciting adventures."

"I would not be surprised," I replied, suddenly distracted. The women had returned with my bride, and she looked radiant. I stood up with my heart soaring.

"Excuse me, uncles," I said, "but I have a boat to catch!"

And that, my children, is the story of our adventures in the City of Mother Earth. My lovely bride and I did catch our boat, and began our lives together with a blissfully serene trip down the Hiddekel River. And let me assure you that we have lived happily together ever after—despite having to face many disasters, calamities, and even a great cataclysm.

THE END

About the Author

Gregory Horning, D.D.S., CAPT (Ret.), USN, has practiced dentistry for forty years in many settings, including military clinics, university clinics, and private practice. A diplomate of the American Board of Periodontology, he has directed two residency programs. He has taught dentistry at every level, including dental and dental hygiene students, general practice and specialty residents. He has lectured widely, conducted considerable dental research, and published over 22 professional articles. Retired from full-time practice, he is currently associated with the Park Place Dental Clinic, a non-profit clinic that provides dental treatment for low-income adults in Norfolk, Virginia.